THE VENICE SKETCHBOOK

Center Point
Large Print

Also by Rhys Bowen and available from
Center Point Large Print:

In Farleigh Field
The Tuscan Child
The Victory Garden
Above the Bay of Angels

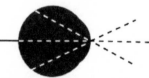

**This Large Print Book carries the
Seal of Approval of N.A.V.H.**

THE VENICE SKETCHBOOK

RHYS BOWEN

CENTER POINT LARGE PRINT
THORNDIKE, MAINE

This Center Point Large Print edition
is published in the year 2021 by arrangement with
Amazon Publishing, www.apub.com.

Originally published in the United States by
Amazon Publishing, 2021.

This is a work of fiction. Names, characters, organizations,
places, events, and incidents are either products of the
author's imagination or are used fictitiously.

The text of this Large Print edition is unabridged.
In other aspects, this book may vary
from the original edition.
Printed in the United States of America
on permanent paper.
Set in 16-point Times New Roman type.

ISBN: 978-1-64358-928-2

The Library of Congress has cataloged this record
under Library of Congress Control Number: 2021932350

*This book is dedicated to my dear friend and choir director extraordinaire, Ann Weiss.
Singing with her choir has been one of the most meaningful experiences of my life. Not only does Ann have the voice of an angel, she also has a love affair with Venice I hope she'll enjoy revisiting vicariously with this novel.*

PROLOGUE: VENICE, 1940

"I have an ulterior motive for visiting you, apart from saying goodbye. I wondered if you'd care to work for your country?"

When I looked surprised, he went on. "What I have to say from now on is all top secret, and you must sign a document to verify this." He reached into his pocket and put a sheet of paper on my table. "Are you prepared to sign?"

"Before I know what is entailed?"

"I'm afraid so. That's how it works in wartime."

I hesitated, staring at him, then walked over to the table. "I suppose there is no harm in signing. I can still say no to what you propose?"

"Oh, absolutely." Mr Sinclair sounded far too cheerful.

"Very well, then." I scanned the document, noting that betraying the trust could result in prison or death. Hardly reassuring. But I signed. He took it back and slipped it inside his jacket.

"You have a fine view here, Miss Browning," he said.

"I know. I love it."

"And I understand you own this place."

"You seem to know a lot about me," I said.

"We do. I'm afraid we had to check into your

background before making this request of you."

"And that request would be?"

In the kitchen alcove the kettle boiled, sending a loud shriek that made me rush to the stove. I poured the water into the teapot, then returned to the living room.

"You are in a prime position to watch the movement of ships. You know the Italians have navy vessels stationed here. Now they might well be allowing the German navy to use this as a base from which to attack Greece, Cyprus, Malta. I'd like you to give us a daily account of shipping activity. If ships leave the harbour here, you tell us and we'll have planes ready to intercept."

"How would I tell you? Who would be left to tell?"

"Ah." He turned a little red. "Someone will be sent to install a radio. It will be hidden so that nobody else knows about it. You can't use it when that woman of yours is here. She cannot be allowed to see it. Is that clear?"

"Of course. Although she is not the brightest. She probably wouldn't know what it was."

"Nevertheless"—he held up a warning finger—"you will broadcast as soon as possible after you witness shipping activity."

"To whom do I broadcast? And what do I say?"

"Patience, dear lady. All will be made clear," he said.

I went back into the kitchen and poured two

cups of tea, then carried them on a tray to where we'd been sitting. Mr Sinclair took a sip and gave a sigh of satisfaction.

"Ah, tea that tastes like tea. One thing I shall enjoy when I get home."

I took a drink myself and waited.

He put the cup down. "Do you know Morse code?"

"I'm afraid I don't."

"I'll get a booklet over to you. Learn it as soon as possible. Along with the radio, you will receive a codebook. You will keep that hidden apart from the radio, in a place where nobody would think of looking. Your messages will be sent in code. For example, if you see two destroyers, you might say, 'Granny is not feeling well today.'"

"And if the Germans break the code?"

"The codes will be changed frequently. You will not know in advance how you'll receive a new booklet. Maybe a package from your auntie in Rome with recipes in it." He shrugged. "Our secret service is highly resourceful. The good thing is that you will never have to make personal contact with anyone, so should you be questioned, you will not have to worry about betrayal."

"That sounds so reassuring," I said drily and saw the twitch of a smile on his lips.

He took another sip, then put down his cup once more. "One more thing," he said. "You will need a code name for communication. What do you suggest?"

I stared out across the canal. A cargo ship was moving slowly past. Was I mad to agree to this?

"My name is Juliet," I said, "so my code name could be Romeo."

"Romeo. I like it." He laughed.

CHAPTER 1

Juliet, Venice, May 20, 1928

At last Aunt Hortensia and I have arrived in Venice, after a long, sweaty, smoky and exceedingly uncomfortable train journey. Aunt Hortensia does not believe in wasting money and declared that sleeping berths on a train ride are completely useless as the cars stop, start and shake so much that sleep is impossible. So we sat up, all the way from Boulogne, on the French coast, through France, then Switzerland and into Italy. By day it was awfully hot. One could not open the windows as smoke and cinders would blow in from the engine. And during the night there was a man opposite me who snored loudly, as well as his wife, who stank of garlic and body odour. I know I shouldn't be complaining. I am fully aware of how awfully lucky I am at being taken to Italy for my eighteenth birthday. The girls in my form at school were most envious!

All that is behind us now. We are here. We came out of the Santa Lucia train station and stood at the top of a flight of steps.

"Ecco il Canal Grande!" Aunt Hortensia said in dramatic fashion, spreading out her arms as if she was on stage and had created the scene for

11

my benefit. My Italian was limited to "please," "thank you" and "good day," but I understood that this was the Grand Canal. Only it didn't look very grand. It was wide, to be sure, but the buildings on the other side were rather ordinary. And it looked dirty, too. The odour that greeted my nostrils was not particularly appetizing. It was a watery sort of smell with a hint of fish and decay. I didn't have much of a chance to study my surroundings, however, as we were immediately besieged by porters. It was a little alarming to have men fighting over us in a strange language, snatching at our bags and trying to bundle us into a gondola, whether we wanted one or not. But as Aunt Hortensia confessed, we had no alternative. We could not have managed all that luggage on one of the water buses they call "vaporetti." Of course, I was thrilled to be in a gondola, even though the gondolier was not a handsome young Italian who sang love songs, but rather a grim-faced man with a paunch.

As we came around a bend, the Grand Canal became incredibly grand. On either side of us were amazing palaces, marble coated, or in shades of rich pink with arched Moorish win-dows. They appeared to float on the water in a way that was quite surreal—I wanted to get out my sketchbook right away. It was lucky that I didn't, as the amount of traffic on the canal made the boat rock alarmingly. The gondolier muttered what must have been Italian swear words.

We were moving along quite nicely for a boat rowed with one oar, but the canal seemed awfully long.

"Ecco il Ponte di Rialto," Aunt Hortensia exclaimed, pointing at a bridge that crossed the canal ahead of us, rising up in a great arch, as if suspended by magic. It appeared to have some sort of building on it because a row of windows winked in the afternoon sunshine as we approached. I wondered if Aunt H. intended to speak in only that language from now on. If so, conversation was liable to be rather one-sided.

However, this fear was dispelled as she now produced her Baedeker and began to inform me about each building we passed: "On your left, the Palazzo Barzizza. Note the thirteenth-century facades. And that large building is the Palazzo Mocenigo, where Lord Byron once stayed . . ."

This continued until an overcrowded vaporetto pulled out from its jetty. Our boat rocked again, and she almost dropped the book into the murky depths.

Just as I began feeling a bit queasy, another bridge came into sight, this one a more flimsy iron footbridge that spanned the canal at a greater height. I expected Aunt H. to say, "Ecco Ponte something or other," but instead she said, "Ah, the Accademia Bridge. Now we are almost at our destination. That's good. I was beginning to feel rather seasick."

"You mean canal sick, don't you?" I asked, and she actually smiled.

"Over on that side is the accademia. That white marble building beside the bridge. If you were studying art in Italy, this is where you would want to go. La Accademia di Belle Arti. The Academy of Fine Arts. And it houses the finest collection of Venetian paintings, too. We shall definitely want to see it."

As she was speaking, we turned off the Grand Canal into a small side canal and pulled up at some well-worn steps. As if by magic, men came running out, hauled us up from the gondola and then grabbed our luggage. When Aunt H. went to pay the gondolier, she reacted as if she was horrified at the amount quoted.

In her stilted Italian, she asked our hotel porters if the amount was correct or if we were being taken advantage of.

"You see two defenceless Englishwomen," she said, reverting to English, "and you think you can rob them of their meagre savings. Would you behave like this to your own mother? Your own grandmother?" She repeated the gist of this in Italian.

The gondolier looked sheepish. The hotel men smiled. Then the gondolier shrugged.

"Very well," he said. "I charge you only two

hundred lire. But just this once, because you have travelled far and the young lady is exhausted."

Triumphant, Aunt H. strode into the foyer of a less-than-palatial yellow-painted building with green shutters, where a silver-haired man came forward, arms open, to greet her.

"Dear, dear Signorina Marchmont. You have returned to us. A thousand welcomes."

I could see now why Aunt Hortensia liked this place, if she was greeted in this way. Frankly, I had been disappointed that we were not staying in one of the palazzos on the Grand Canal, but Aunt Hortensia had said, more than once, "There is only one place to stay in Venice, and that is the Pensione Regina. And that is because it has a garden. When one is hot and tired from sightseeing, one can sit in the shade and drink a citron pressé."

We were taken up a flight of marble stairs into a large ornate corner room with windows on two sides, a painted wooden ceiling and furniture that looked as if it had come from a museum. At least the two beds looked normal enough, with their crisp white sheets, and there was a desk and chair in the front window, which looked out on to the garden, with a sliver of a view of the Grand Canal beyond. I went over to the window, opened it and gazed out. The scent of jasmine rose to greet me.

"Ah yes," Aunt H. said when she had inspected our bathroom. "Most satisfactory."

As I stood at the window, bells began to ring, their sound echoing out across the canals. A gondola glided past; this time the gondolier was young and handsome. I felt my spirits rise. I was in Venice, my first time in Europe. I was going to make the most of it.

May 21, 1928

I was awoken by more bells. It seems there are an awful lot of churches in this city. Nobody is allowed to sleep late! I went to the window and opened the shutters Aunt H. had insisted on keeping closed against mosquitos. The sky was a perfect pale blue, and the sound of bells echoed over the whole city. Swallows darted and swooped across the sky like tiny Maltese crosses, while seagulls screeched and below, in the courtyard, pigeons strutted.

"A city of bells and birds," I said with satisfaction. At that moment a motor barge went by, its pop-popping echoing from the narrow walls. Bells and birds and boats, I corrected.

A breakfast of warm fresh rolls, cheese and fruit, and coffee instead of tea was served to us under an umbrella in the garden, before we went out to explore the city, armed with my aunt's trusty Baedeker and map. Luckily, Aunt H. had visited several times before and knew her way, or I should have become hopelessly lost in minutes. Venice is a complete maze of alleys, canals, bridges. The first thing I noticed was that there are no real streets—at least no streets like we knew them at home—only cobbled walkways with bridges over canals. It seems the canals are actually the streets—everything is delivered by water, from goods to people to rubbish, the latter of which we watched being dropped into an open barge.

And the houses go right into the water. I thought they'd be on platforms, safely out of reach of the tides, but no—they disappear into the canals themselves, with water lapping at the downstairs windows and the lower bricks, which are all stained with seaweed. Sometimes half a door is underwater. How do they not just get washed away and crumble apart? Aunt Hortensia doesn't know either.

Anyway, it appears you can't get anywhere by walking in a straight line. Some streets end at canals with no way across. To go right, one must first go left. But Aunt H. led us unerringly to St Mark's Square. Gosh. I think for the first time in my eighteen years, my breath was taken away. I had never seen anything so magnificent as that great open space with the colonnade around it, the huge church at one end, crowned with a series of domes and statues so it looks more like a palace from an oriental fantasy. To the right of the square, the bell tower rises impossibly tall and straight, in contrast to the ornate and curvy basilica. There are outdoor cafés, and a small orchestra was playing under the colonnade, but Aunt H. declared we had too much to see to waste time with pastries.

She strode out, crossing the entire length of the square to the basilica, where she hired a guide to show us around every inch of the interior. We even went down to the crypt, which I found horribly creepy with its tombs. After this, we went for a tour of the Doge's Palace. It was full of magnificent rooms and walls hung with famous paintings.

"If you wish to be an artist, you can do no better than making careful observations here," Aunt H. said, pointing to a painting by Tintoretto that took up an entire wall. *Golly,* I thought. *How long would it take to paint something like that, even if one had the skill?* All those paintings were so large, so magnificent, I couldn't envision myself ever attempting such things. I was more entranced with the Bridge of Sighs—so called because prisoners crossed it on their way to the prison beyond and it was the last glimpse they would have of the outside world. *So sad and romantic! I must definitely return to sketch it!* I thought.

I was actually rather glad when Aunt H. said we should return to the pensione for luncheon and then a rest. It seems that everything closes at midday in Venice—shops, museums. The whole city shuts down and sleeps. I couldn't sleep, of course. I lay on my bed listening to the sounds beyond my shutters: the slap of oars, the putter of motorboats, the cooing of pigeons and the high-pitched squeaks of the swallows. And I felt ridiculously content, as if everything made sense for the first time in my life. No more Miss Masters's Academy for Young Ladies. The whole world awaited me.

At dinner that night, the menu said Fritto Misto, and in English, *Mixed Fried Fish*. What actually came on our plates were little unidentifiable bits and pieces of tentacles, whiskery shrimp and various shellfish.

"Gracious me," Aunt Hortensia said. "I think they have scraped the bottom of the lagoon for these. They don't even look edible."

Mine actually tasted quite good, although the tentacles were a little alarming to chew. We finished dinner with fruit, cheeses and coffee. Outside I could hear the city livening up. A gondolier sang as he passed beneath our window. Further away a jazz band was playing. Laughter echoed from the narrow street across the canal.

"Can we go out and explore?" I asked.

Aunt Hortensia looked as if I had asked to take my clothes off and dance naked in St Mark's Square.

"A lady does not go out unescorted after dinner," she said.

And that was that. We went to the sitting room, and Aunt Hortensia conversed with two English ladies. I excused myself, went up to my room and checked my art supplies. My lovely pristine sketchbook, a gift from Daddy. A small box of watercolours, a pen and a portable inkwell, charcoals and pencils. Everything a budding artist would need. I sighed with contentment. Tomorrow I would start sketching, and in September I would be a student at the Slade School of Fine Art in London.

I dipped my pen into the ink and wrote, *Juliet Browning. Begun May 1928.*

CHAPTER 2

Juliet, Venice, May 1928

It turns out that Aunt Hortensia was right to have been suspicious of the mixed fried fish. The next morning she reported that she had vomited in the night and felt too weak to get up. Would I please ask for a boiled egg and tea to be sent up to her, and she would stay in bed all day. I delivered her message. The proprietress was most solicitous and insisted on chamomile tea—much better for the stomach. I ate breakfast alone in the garden while the pigeons perched hopefully on unused seats. Then I went back to my aunt.

"You don't mind if I go out by myself, do you?" I asked. "I'd like to do some sketching."

She frowned. "I don't really think that would be suitable. What would your father say if I let you wander around Venice alone? What if you get lost? What if you stray to an undesirable part of the city?"

"I know the way to St Mark's Square now," I said. "I shall just go in that direction and sit and sketch. And it is broad daylight. And there are other tourists."

She considered again before saying, "Very well. I suppose I can't insist that you stay cooped up with me all day. But make sure you wear your hat, and don't sit out in the sun too much."

I tried not to show my elation as I stuffed my art supplies into my bag, put on my hat but not my gloves—who could possibly draw with gloves on?—and set off. I sat first in the square in front of Santo Stefano Church and sketched the fountain, then the children running barefoot around it. Then I moved on, pausing to sketch an interesting balcony with geraniums spilling over it, a column and even a door knocker in the shape of a lion's head. So many wonderful things. If I wasn't careful, I'd fill my whole sketchbook with Venice and have no space for Florence or Rome. I came to St Mark's Square and tried to sketch the basilica with all of its crazy domes and statues, looking like something out of *One Thousand and One Nights*. I gave up in frustration. I needed more lessons in perspective, obviously. Then the campanile. That was so tall that it went off the top of the page. Another failure. I had more success with the famous clock. And with the people who sat outside the cafés, taking their morning coffee. Perhaps I was destined to be a portrait painter!

I tried to find a good spot to sketch the Bridge of Sighs but realized that the best views were from the other side. I retraced my steps to the waterfront and stood sketching the narrow canal with its lacy marble bridge. Several tourists tried to peer over my shoulder. *Oh dear. My art skills are certainly not good enough for public scrutiny yet,* I thought. I hurriedly closed my sketchbook, and at that moment the great bells from the campanile rang out. Twelve o'clock. Golly. *I'd better return for lunch, or Aunt H. will be worried.* I made my way back to St Mark's Square and attempted to retrace my route home. I must have come out of the square by a different archway because I didn't recognize where I was. There had not been a little canal running beside the street when I came in. I pressed on, in what I hoped was the right general direction. I was just crossing the canal via a little stone bridge when I heard a sound. At first I thought it was a baby crying. It was coming from the water beneath me. Then I looked down and saw a cardboard box floating past. And from the box came the sound. Not a baby, but what sounded like the mewing of kittens. Someone had thrown a box of kittens into the canal to drown them!

I looked around. Nobody in sight. I couldn't just let the kittens float away until the box became sodden and they drowned. I went back to the side of the canal where there was a walkway, held on to a post and reached out as far as I could. The box was too far away for me to retrieve it and was moving slowly but steadily past. Soon it would pass between tall buildings where there was no footpath. There was nothing for it. I put my bag down, took off my hat, held my nose and jumped in. The water was surprisingly cold. I gasped and swallowed a mouthful, but struck out valiantly for the box. I hadn't had much opportunity for swimming in England, apart from in the sea at Torquay, where one bobbed in the waves, and I realized too late that my skirts had become awfully heavy, clinging to my legs. I tried to hold the box above me as I kicked out for the side of the canal. I managed to place it up on the walkway, then tried to climb out. That was when I realized the walkway was a good foot above the water and there were no steps in sight. I had no way out.

My sodden clothing and shoes were pulling me down now, and I was tiring fast. I tried to remember the Italian word for "help"—if I'd ever known it in the first place. What was it in Latin? If only I'd paid more attention to Miss Dear! I tried to cling to the side, but there was nothing to hang on to. Above my head, the kittens kept mewing and the box shook as if they might get out at any moment. Then suddenly I heard a noise. The put-put of an approaching motorboat. It drew level with me, and I was afraid it would run me down or go past without seeing me. I released one hand and waved.

"Help!" I cried.

A man's face appeared over the side. "*Dio mio!*" he exclaimed. "*Un momento!*" He cut the motor. Strong arms reached down, and I was unceremoniously hauled aboard. He stared at me for a moment before saying, "You are English. *Sì?*"

I nodded. "How did you know?"

"Only a British girl would be foolish enough to go swimming in a canal," he said in very proficient English. "Or did you fall in?"

"I wasn't swimming. And I didn't fall in. I jumped in, to save some kittens."

"Kittens?" Obviously the word was unknown to him.

"Baby cats."

He looked astonished. "You jump in the canal to save baby cats?"

"Someone was going to drown them. They were in a cardboard box. See. I've put them up on the path."

"And what would you do with these baby cats? Take them home with you to England?"

I hadn't thought that far ahead. "No, I don't think Aunt Hortensia would agree to that. Besides, we are heading on to Florence and Rome. I thought I'd find them good homes."

"My dear *signorina*," he said, shaking his head, "Venice is a city of cats. More cats than people. They keep the rats down, which is good, but they also have many babies. Too many."

"Oh, I see."

He studied my crestfallen face. I in turn studied him. After my shock, I had not taken in the fact that this was a sleek teak craft and that its driver

25

was young and extremely good-looking. He had a fine head of unruly dark curls and a strong, chiselled jaw. He was wearing a white shirt, open at the neck. Exactly as I had wanted my gondolier to look. When he smiled, his whole face lit up. His eyes actually sparkled.

"Don't worry," he said. "I expect we can find a place for them. One of our servants, perhaps, or we can have them taken out to our villa in the Veneto."

"Really? That would be wonderful."

He started the motor again and manoeuvred the boat to the side of the canal, lifting the kittens on board and then handing me my hat and my bag.

"Your bag is heavy. You have been shopping?"

"No. My art supplies. I've been sketching. I'm going to be an artist. I start at art school in September."

He nodded approval. "Congratulations."

"I hope they are all right," I said as the box on the seat teetered. "They may already be wet and catch cold."

I put down my bag, then opened the box of kittens cautiously. Four little black-and-white faces looked up at me. "Mew?" they said in unison.

"Look at them. Aren't they adorable?" I said, holding it open for him to see. "And they are fine. Absolutely fine." I put a hand up to my mouth as

I felt myself about to burst into tears. It wouldn't do to cry in front of a strange man. I closed the box again in case the kittens escaped.

He shook his head. "You English! In Italy, animals are either useful to us or we eat them."

"You don't have pet dogs?"

"Old ladies, maybe. We have dogs for hunting and guarding."

I had become aware that I must look an absolute fright, my dress sodden and clinging to me, my hair now plastered to my cheeks. A pool of water was collecting on the floor of the boat.

"I'm sorry. I'm making your boat wet," I said.

He grinned. "It's a boat. It is used to getting wet." Then he shook his head as he studied me. "You must remove those wet clothes, and wash off that canal water before you catch a terrible disease," he said. "The canal water is not good, signorina. My house is close by. I can take you there, and our maids can wash and press your dress. Nobody needs to know of your little adventure."

"Oh dear," I said, sorely tempted by this. "I'm afraid Aunt Hortensia would not approve of my going to the house of a strange man."

"A respectable strange man, I assure you," he said, but with a grin.

"No, I'm afraid I had better return to my hotel. My aunt will be expecting me by lunchtime."

"And what will she say about your appearance?

Or is all forgiven in England if someone jumps in a canal to rescue a cat?"

"I'm not sure about that," I said. "I shall probably never be allowed out alone again."

His eyes lit up with amusement. "You can tell her that you were trying to sketch a rooftop and had to lean out too far. She may accept that."

"Oh yes. Brilliant idea," I agreed, nodding. "Thank you."

"So, I must take you back to your hotel. Where do you stay?"

"Pensione Regina," I said. "My aunt always stays there when she comes to Venice. It has a garden."

"Ah yes. Terrible food but a garden. So typically English."

He revved up the motor and we moved forward.

"You have a lovely boat," I said, realizing as I said it how lame this sounded. Really, I would have to learn sophisticated conversation now that I was no longer a schoolgirl.

He turned to smile at me. "It belongs to my father. He lets me use it sometimes. And I agree. It is very lovely."

"How is it that you speak such good English?" I asked.

He was staring straight ahead now as the canal narrowed, passing between the walls of tall buildings. "My father wished me to be a man of the world. First I had a French tutor, then he sent me to an English boarding school. French for the language of diplomacy, then English for commerce. My family owns a shipping company, you see."

"Which boarding school did you attend?"

"Ampleforth. Do you know it? In the cold and dreary north of your country. Good Catholic priests. I hated every moment. Freezing-cold weather. Cold showers. Cross-country runs before breakfast, and the food was abysmal. They served us porridge and baked beans."

"I like baked beans on toast," I said.

"Well, you would. The English have no sense of good food," he said. "I will take you for a good meal before you leave Venice. Then you will see the difference."

"Oh, I don't think Aunt Hortensia would allow me to go for a meal with a young man," I said. "She is frightfully old-fashioned."

"Even if I met her and introduced myself?" he said. "My family goes back to the Middle Ages, you know. We have several doges in our ancestry and even a pope. Does that count?"

"Against you," I replied, smiling as I said it. "Aunt Hortensia is strongly Church of England. The pope is the enemy."

"Then I will not mention the pope." He turned to flash me a wicked grin. "But here we are talking, and I do not know your name. Aunt Hortensia would not approve."

"My name is Juliet," I said. "Juliet Alexandra Browning." I didn't add that I was only called that by my aunt, who had insisted on christening me with a Shakespearean name, and that I was usually known as the less dramatic Lettie.

His eyes opened wide. "That is amazing. Because my name is Romeo."

"Really?" I could hardly get the word out.

He looked at me, then burst out laughing. "No, not really. I am teasing you. My name is actually Leonardo. Leonardo Da Rossi. But you can call me Leo."

We emerged from the cool darkness of the side canal to the shining expanse of the Grand Canal.

"You see"—Leo gestured to the building on our left—"that is my house. It would have been simple to have had your wet clothes cleaned there."

I looked up at the magnificent palazzo, with its Moorish arched windows and extravagant decorations. *Not really,* I thought, but did not say. I suspected that Leo might not be what he claimed. But he was very handsome and had such a wonderful smile. And he was taking me home. Whether he would quietly drown the kittens or not, I wasn't so sure.

We moved up the canal, negotiating around slow-moving gondolas and large barges, until we came to where a side canal turned off to my pensione.

"You must show me your sketches before we part," he said. "May I look? I think you might make your book rather wet."

"I haven't really done much yet," I said as he lifted my sketchbook from my bag, and feeling reluctant to let anybody see my work. But he was already thumbing through pages.

"Not bad," he said, nodding. "I think you have a gift for art. The way you capture the people in the square. There is humour in it."

I suspected this was because I hadn't got the perspective quite right, but he went on, "Have you been to the Biennale yet? If you are a student of art, it is essential."

"What is it?"

He frowned. "You have not heard of our Biennale? It is a huge art exhibition in the gardens. Many countries have pavilions. Countries from all over the world exhibit the best in modern art. You would love it."

"I will tell my aunt."

"I would be happy to escort you."

I chewed on my bottom lip. "How is it you have so much free time?" I asked.

He shrugged. "I have just finished my course at the university in Padua. In the autumn I must start to learn the family business, but at this moment my time is my own. So will you let me show you the Biennale?"

"I'll certainly ask Aunt Hortensia whether we

can go," I said. "But I'm afraid she may not accept your kind offer to show us around. She feels her duty to protect me very strongly."

This made him smile. "I am hardly likely to have evil in my heart when in the presence of a formidable aunt."

I had to smile, too. "She really is formidable."

The steps leading to the pensione garden came up beside us. I touched his sleeve. "Look, could you stop a little further down the canal? I'd rather that nobody saw me getting out of your boat looking like this."

"Very well." He cut back the throttle and inched us forward to a set of steps a few yards away. "When will I see you again? Or do you not want to see me again?"

"Oh yes," I said, sounding, I'm sure, a little too eager. "But we only have two more days in Venice before we go on to Florence. I will ask Aunt H. about the Biennale. Perhaps she will say yes. Or perhaps she will still be feeling ill tomorrow, and I'll have time to myself."

"Good," he said. "Let us hope the sickness lingers for one more day. I have so much to show you of my city." He grabbed the post beside the steps and held it firmly. He assisted me out, then handed me my bag.

I looked down at the box of kittens. "You promise me you won't drown them as soon as I'm gone? Cross your heart and hope to die?"

"What?" he asked. "You wish me to die?"

"No, it's a saying. We say, 'Cross my heart and hope to die' when we promise something."

"Very well, I promise, but I do not hope to die. I plan to live long and have a good life."

I stood on the canal walkway, looking down at him. Would I ever see him again? I wondered.

"I shall be here at ten o'clock tomorrow morning," he said. "Ready to escort you and your aunt to the Biennale."

I gave him a big smile. "All right."

"Ciao, Julietta."

"Ciao, Leo."

He revved the motor and the boat sped away.

CHAPTER 3

Juliet, Venice, May 1928

Fortunately, I encountered the proprietress as I came into the front hall. She threw up her hands in horror when she saw me. "Cara signorina. What have happened?"

"I fell into a canal," I confessed.

"*Dio mio! Subito.* Taking off clothes and washing you." She bundled me into a bathroom, ran a bath and helped me out of the wet clothes, all the time making little cluck-clucking noises. She managed to make me understand that she would take care of washing my dress and undergarments. She whisked them away, then brought me a large towel and a robe. I lay back, enjoying the warm water, smiling as I thought of Leo. All my life I had dreamed of falling in love. All those years at a girls' school, with not a single boy in sight. Even the gardeners were going on eighty. And now it had really happened to me. A wonderful boy wanted to see me again. I sighed in pure happiness.

Aunt Hortensia was sitting up reading as I tried to creep into the room. She looked at me in astonishment. "You had a bath? I didn't hear the water running."

"The proprietress ran one for me downstairs," I said. "I'm afraid I had a little accident and fell into a canal."

"Juliet! I let you out of my sight alone once, and you nearly drown. What were you thinking?"

"I didn't nearly drown," I said. I took a deep breath, forming the sentence in my head before I said it. "I was trying to sketch an interesting rooftop. I'm afraid I leaned out just a little too far and lost my balance. Anyway, a very kind man came to my rescue and brought me home in his boat."

"You accepted a lift from a strange man?"

"I needed to be helped out of the water. There were no steps. And anyway, it was better than having to walk back looking like a fright and dripping water."

She sighed. "Well, I suppose no harm was done, except I presume your nice new sketchbook was lost in the water?"

"I managed to throw it up on the bank as I fell," I said, thinking quickly. "So as you say, no harm done. And the young man was educated at an English boarding school."

"Really? Which one?"

"Ampleforth."

She sniffed. "A Catholic school."

"Well, yes. Being Venetian, it is fairly likely that he's a Catholic. But he's from a good family. They own a palazzo. And he's told me all about the Biennale. Have you heard of it? The big art festival with pavilions from all over the world?"

"Modern art." She gave me a withering glance. "Miró and Picasso and all that rubbish. I hope they are not going to teach you any of that stuff at art school. Absolutely anyone could throw paint at a canvas the way they do and call it art. Even a tame chimpanzee could paint better pictures."

"But can we go and look anyway? My rescuer has offered to show us around."

"Certainly not. It is not the kind of art I wish you to see, and it would be most improper to be escorted by a strange man. Your father would think me derelict in my duty."

"He's from a very good family," I said again. "He showed me his house—or rather palazzo. It's beautiful. Right on the canal across from the Gritti Palace, and made of coloured marble."

She sighed. "I'm afraid the young man has been spinning you a tale, my dear. I think you are describing the Palazzo Rossi."

"That's right," I said. "He said his name was something Rossi."

"Humph." She gave a patronizing chuckle. "I hardly think so." She patted my arm. "My dear, you are young and inexperienced. This boy was probably running an errand in his employer's boat and enjoyed impressing a young foreign girl. But no matter. It would not be seemly for you to meet him again."

"He said he would come for me at ten tomorrow morning. May I not even meet him to tell him I can't join him? It would be rude to keep him waiting for nothing."

"If he actually shows up." She was sneering. "I think you'll find that his employer's boat is not available for him, and it will be you who is waiting for nothing."

"Can I at least try?"

"Better not," she said. "Anyway, I had planned to take us to Murano tomorrow, if I feel up to it."

I could see I was not going to win this case. But I couldn't bear the thought of Leo waiting for me and thinking I was the rude one for not showing up. Then I came to a decision: I tore a page from my sketchbook and wrote on it, *Leo, I'm so sorry. My aunt is being beastly and won't let me see you again. Thank you for saving my life. I'll never forget you. Your Juliet.*

Then I rose early the next morning, crept out and pinned the note (inside an envelope I had snitched from the hotel stationery) on the wooden pole used to tie up gondolas in front of the pensione. Aunt Hortensia seemed restored to her former health. We breakfasted and then found a boat to take us to the island of Murano. All the way across I wondered if Leo had come, and read my note, and felt a pang of regret. The glass-blowing on the island was interesting, if rather hot, and Aunt H. and I were both red-faced when we emerged from the interior of the factory with its furnace glowing.

"That is enough for one day, I think," Aunt H. said, bustling me towards the waiting motor vessel. I would like to have browsed in the shop and maybe bought myself a necklace of those exquisite glass beads, but Aunt H. declared the price to be exorbitant and told me I'd do better at the stalls beside the Rialto Bridge where one could bargain.

On the return journey we stopped at another island called San Michele.

"Ecco San Michele!" Aunt Hortensia proclaimed as we approached.

"Are we going to get off there, too?" I asked.

"Goodness no. It is the cemetery."

And as we drew close, I could see that the whole island was composed of white marble tombs, some like little houses, some topped with angels. I thought it might be a good place to be buried.

"Now you can see why I always choose this pensione," my aunt said when we finally returned from our jaunt and a glass of fresh-squeezed lemonade was brought to us. "So civilized to sit in the shade and recover."

She then went for a little rest. I slipped away to the place where I had left my note and was relieved to find it gone. At least he knew I had not stood him up. But then it struck me with full force that I would never see him again. Never see the way his eyes sparkled and his face lit up when he laughed. It was almost too much to bear.

After Aunt H. had recovered sufficiently, we crossed the Accademia Bridge, all fifty-two steps up one side and fifty down the other, and visited the accademia.

"It is a teaching academy like the one you will be attending in September. It also houses one of the finest collections of paintings," my aunt said. I looked around, hoping to get a glimpse of some students, but my aunt marched straight to the museum entrance. As in the Doge's Palace, I was overwhelmed with the size and opulence of the paintings. So many virgins, suffering saints and popes being crowned. I was secretly sure I would have loved the modern art at the Biennale better! I had to admire Aunt H.'s fortitude. She marched on, admiring and commenting on each painting.

Then we made our way to the Rialto Bridge and the market beside it. Aunt H. allowed me to do a little drawing, while she sat sipping a coffee at a café beside the Grand Canal. I loved sketching the market with its stalls of fruit and vegetables, women in long peasant skirts and dashing men with black moustaches. I wasn't so entranced with the fish market. The smell was too overwhelming to want to linger. I returned to Aunt H. and was offered a gelato. Delicious Italian ice cream in flavours I had never even heard of: pistachio and stracciatella. It came with a delicate wafer.

Aunt H. was one of those formidable Victorian ladies. She showed no sign of being tired as we made our way back to the pensione. I suggested taking a vaporetto, as I was really worn out by this time. But she insisted the water buses were too crowded, and she had no wish to be pressed up against an Italian man. "They pinch bottoms, you know," she whispered in horror. I tried not to smile.

Eventually we came back to the pensione and changed for dinner. We dined on mushroom risotto as Aunt H. wanted something that would not upset her delicate stomach. It was quite good; so was the creamy cake that followed it, and I was allowed a glass of local white wine called Pinot Grigio. We sat and chatted with other guests—or rather Aunt H. chatted and I sat, wishing I were out experiencing the sights and sounds of the city—and went to bed around ten.

Aunt H. fell asleep immediately. I lay there, listening to distant music. I had almost drifted off when I heard something rattle against the shutters. I got up. Was it the wind? But no draft came in. Then it happened again. I opened the shutter and looked around.

"Julietta. Down here," came the whisper.

And there he was in his boat, underneath my window.

"Come," he whispered, holding out his arms to me. "I will help you."

"I'm in my nightdress," I said, my heart beating rather loudly.

"I can see." He smirked. "Hurry. Dress quickly."

I couldn't believe what I was doing. I stumbled into my clothes, shooting hasty glances at my snoring aunt as I fumbled with buttons. Then I arranged the bolster in my bed to look like a sleeping person and started to climb out of the window. It was a long drop and I hesitated. Instantly his arms came up again, and he lifted me down into the boat, his hands around my waist.

"Now," he said, "we go."

"The shutters." I looked back at them, half open.

He stood up precariously on the rim of the boat and closed them. Then he pushed us off, moving the boat silently along the side of the canal until we were far enough away to start the motor. Off we went into the night.

When we pulled out into the Grand Canal, we looked at each other, and I gave a nervous laugh that I, good child until now, had dared to do something so naughty. He laughed, too.

"Where are we going?" I asked.

"You'll see." He was still smiling.

I did wonder for a moment whether I was being

kidnapped. We girls at school had heard about the white slave trade, and I was, as Aunt H. had said, horribly naive. But somehow he didn't look like my image of a white slaver.

"So tell me about my kittens," I said. "Are they safe?"

"They are very happy. It seems that we have had a problem with rats out at our estate in the Veneto, so our cook will take them out there and the caretaker will feed them until they grow into good rat catchers."

I gave a little sigh of relief, just hoping that I could believe him. I had no experience with boys or men, and certainly not with strange foreign men. I wanted to trust him. And he had offered to escort myself and my aunt around an art festival. That ought to indicate that he was trustworthy, right?

We reached the end of the Grand Canal where it opened to the lagoon. The vast shape of a church with a white dome loomed on our right. Lights sparkled on the water as we moved along the promenade. At this time of night it was still lively with pedestrians, and music and laughter floated towards us. I hoped he might be taking me to join the revellers, then immediately realized I was not dressed for an evening out. But we kept on going, past the entrance to St Mark's Square, until on our left were no more buildings, no more people, only darkness. Now I began to feel uneasy again.

"Where are we going?" I asked, a tremor in my voice now.

"I wanted to take you to the Biennale," he said. "Unfortunately it is not open at night, but I can show you where it is held. These are the *Giardini*, the city gardens. My favourite place to be." As he talked, he steered the boat to a landing stage, jumped out, tied it up efficiently, then held out a hand to me. I stepped on to land. He reached down to haul out a basket.

"What is that?" I asked.

"I wanted you to have a good meal while you were here," he said. "The aunt does not allow the restaurant, so it must be the picnic. Come. I show you my special spot."

"A picnic? In case you hadn't noticed, it's dark," I said.

"Is there a law against picnics in the dark? I do not think so." He took my hand. It felt wonderful, and instantly I knew I was safe with him. Paths wound between magnificent old trees and stands of bushes, some in full flower. Every now and then there were lamp posts, giving just enough light to see our way. Occasionally other couples strolled past, then an old lady walking her dog. Life went on late in Venice!

"You see that, behind the trees?" he pointed out. "That is the German pavilion." I spotted a white building with columns like a temple. "And that one over there is the English pavilion. So many pavilions dotted around the grounds. Too bad I can't take you inside. We will have to make do with the art of the gardens." And he paused beside the statue of a Greek god. It was weathered from years of rain and salt. A vine had grown up over its plinth, and bushes grew on either side.

"This is my favourite statue," he said, running his hand over its arm as if it were alive.

"Is he really Greek?"

"Napoleon put him here when he created the gardens," Leo said. "I don't know if he came from Greece or was made for the gardens in 1800. There are other such statues all over the place."

"He looks sad," I said, staring up at the bearded face.

"So would you if the salt from the sea was eating you away," he commented, his hand touching a hand that had now only stubs for fingers. "But do you know what else I like? This big old tree behind him. A plane tree, I think it is called. When I was a small boy, I used to make a fort in the little space between the statue and the tree. I would hide away and pretend I was on a desert island, all alone, and I could spy on people walking past."

"I used to make hiding places in our back garden," I said. "I used to pretend I was a rabbit or a squirrel."

He gave the statue a final pat. "You should

come back and sketch him," Leo said. "He would like that. To be in your book."

"I don't know if Aunt H. would approve. He has no clothes on."

"She will approve of the gardens. All the English like gardens, don't they?"

"We don't have much more time here. Just one day."

"But you will come back again, when you are a famous artist."

I had to smile at this. "When I see the art here, I am rather afraid I shall never rise to such heights."

"But that is the art of the past. You must have seen Picasso, Dalí, Miró? They break all the rules. They paint the world as they see it. What is in their hearts. That is what you must do."

"I hope so. I do love to paint and sketch, and Daddy has been nice enough to agree to pay for art school."

"What does this father of yours do?"

I made a face. "He was wounded in the Great War," I said. "Gassed, actually. His lungs were badly damaged. He tried going back to his job in the city for a while, but lately he hasn't been doing much. He inherited a little money from his family, and we live on that. Daddy invests it, and we seem to do quite well. I've been to boarding school, and my sister will start there soon."

"You have brothers?"

"Just one sister. She's much younger than me. The war came in between, you see." I paused. "Do you have brothers?"

"Unfortunately, no. I am the only boy. I have two sisters. One has gone into the convent. The other is married and producing babies on a regular basis, as good Italian wives do."

"You would have liked a brother?"

"Of course. An older brother preferably. Then he could have taken over the business, and I would have been free to do what I want with my life."

"What would that be?"

"Travel the world. Collect beautiful things. Maybe open an art gallery. Maybe write a play. I have all sorts of impractical ideas that I shall never be able to use. My father is a powerful man. We own a shipping company. We have been in commerce since Marco Polo, and my father is a good friend of Mussolini, so . . . we are favoured."

"So you really are very rich?"

"I'm afraid so."

"Isn't that a nice thing to be? I know my family used to enjoy a better life than we do now that Daddy isn't well. They used to travel to Europe, and Mummy ordered her dresses in Paris. Now it's the local dressmaker, Mrs Rush, who makes our clothes, as you can see from what I wear."

"I think you look wonderful."

I paused, blushing, unable to handle this compliment. And hardly daring to ask the next question. "Leo, you say you are rich, and you are certainly handsome. Why would you waste time with a girl like me?"

We were standing beneath a lamp, and I saw him smiling.

"There is something about you. You are not like the girls I know. They are bored with life and only want money spent on them. You—you are so keen to experience everything. You want to taste what life has to offer."

"I do. Now that I am here, I want to travel. To see the world. To be a free, independent woman." I realized as I said the words that this was exactly what I wanted. I hadn't thought much about my future beyond art school before, but now that I had experienced Venice, I knew there was a big, beautiful world I had to see. I certainly did not want my life to be confined to a prim English village.

"Not to marry?"

"Someday maybe." I blushed when I said this, glad it was dark. "But not until I know who I am and what I want."

We had been walking along the dark and silent gravel path between ghostly shapes of buildings and stands of tall trees. Now we paused again.

"Perhaps your art should be more like this?" Leo said, and I saw the shape of another statue in front of us. This one was a giant work in metal, a horse maybe, rearing up, but strangely distorted and rather alarming.

"A modern German artist," Leo said. "He shows great promise."

"I don't think I'd like to create something frightening like this," I said. "I like beauty."

"Of course you do. You are how old? Eighteen?"

I nodded.

"At eighteen, everyone likes beauty. Everyone has great visions for the future." He paused. "Ah, here we are. The spot for our picnic."

We had come to a small grassy area, surrounded by thick bushes on three sides, with the fourth side looking out on to the lagoon. Lights sparkled in the distance.

"That is the Lido over there," he said. "Our beach and lovely villas with gardens. You must go and swim."

"I didn't bring a swimming costume with me," I said. "I thought it would be all churches and art galleries. Besides," I added, "we only have one more day."

He nodded. "So, you will come back again. When you are an independent woman."

"I hope so."

He had spread a rug on the grass. "Sit," he said.

I did so. He squatted beside me, opened the basket and took out various containers, displaying them with satisfaction.

"Cheeses," he said. "Bel Paese, pecorino, Gorgonzola, mozzarella that you must eat with tomato." He pointed to them as he put them on a wooden board. "And here salamis, and prosciutto, and olives. And the bread. And the wine. And peaches from our estate. See, we will not starve."

He poured red wine into two glasses and handed me one. I took a sip. It was rich, warm and almost fruity. I had had dinner. It was the middle of the night. But I found myself tucking in as if I hadn't eaten for days. "Mmm" was all I could say.

Leo nodded, smiling, watching me eat with satisfaction as if he were a conjurer who had just pulled off a spectacular magic trick.

A cool breeze was blowing off the Adriatic Sea now, but the wine was warming through my whole body. I took a bite of peach, and juice ran down my chin.

"Oh." I dabbed at it in embarrassment. "I've never had a peach so juicy before."

Leo was laughing. "That's because they are fresh. Picked today." He reached out and wiped my chin with his fingertip. It was only the lightest of brushes against my skin, but it made me feel uneasy and excited at the same time. Reluctantly, we finished eating, but Leo filled my glass again, and I took another drink.

I lay back, looking up at the stars. I couldn't ever remember being so content.

"So tell me," Leo said, his face appearing above mine, "have you ever been kissed?"

"Never. Apart from family members." He was going to kiss me. A perfect ending to a perfect evening. My heart started beating rather fast.

"Then you are lucky that it is I who give you a first kiss," he said. "I am very good at it, so I am told."

And before I could say anything more, his lips came down to meet mine. This was no delicate brushing of a first kiss, such as I had read about in novels. I was conscious of the warmth of his mouth, the weight of his body against mine and an incredible surge of desire I had not known I possessed. I didn't want him to stop. But he sat up suddenly.

"I think I had better be a gentleman and stop right now," he said. "I should take you home."

He started packing up the remains of our picnic. I sat watching him, feeling confused. Had I somehow displeased him, disappointed him, not been good enough? I didn't want to ask.

He helped me to my feet, and we walked together in silence, this time along the edge of the lagoon rather than through the wooded paths. We reached the boat, and he helped me into it. The motor started, and we roared away, much faster than we had come, leaving a great trail of wake behind us, the wind blowing in our faces.

In no time at all, we had reached the Grand Canal. Leo slowed to a respectable pace as we negotiated among late-night gondolas.

"I have a confession to make," he said, as we neared the entrance to my pensione. "I thought I was being kind to a young girl, a visiting tourist. Giving her her first taste of excitement. But when I kissed you—I had to stop right then, or I knew I could not have stopped. I wanted you. And I think you wanted me too, is that right?"

I felt my cheeks burning and was glad that the darkness hid my blushes. Aunt Hortensia would expect me to say that such a conversation with a man was unthinkable. But for some reason it was easy to talk to Leo. I realized, with a mixture of shame and wonder, that I hadn't wanted him to stop.

"I had no idea such feelings existed," I said. "I thought being kissed would be nice."

"And it wasn't nice?"

"It was more than nice. It was . . . overwhelming. As if nothing else mattered in the world."

"I think you will become an interesting woman one day," he said. "So many girls—they are afraid if a man touches them. They think they will have to confess to their priest. At least you have the Church of England to thank that you are spared that."

We were nearing the side wall of the pensione.

A realization was now taking over—I would most likely never see him again.

"Maybe I shall find the boat is free tomorrow night," he said. "We could go dancing if you put on the right sort of dress."

"I don't think I own the right sort of dress," I said. "Not for the kind of places you would go."

"I will come anyway. I wish to see you again. This is not goodbye, is it?"

"I hope not."

He had cut the motor and eased the boat along the wall until it was below the window. Then he stood up, opening the shutters. He helped me to stand on the side of the boat, then I climbed, in a rather undignified fashion, into the room.

Aunt Hortensia was still asleep, snoring unattractively with her mouth open. I looked out and gave a thumbs up sign. He grinned, waved and steered the boat away. I kept watching until he had disappeared out into the Grand Canal. Then I undressed and got into bed, staring at the ceiling with a huge sigh of happiness.

CHAPTER 4

Juliet, Venice, May 1928

When I awoke in the morning, I wondered if I had dreamed the whole thing. Surely my friends at home wouldn't believe me when I told them. I wished I had taken a snapshot of Leo to prove how absolutely stunning he was. If I saw him again tonight, I'd give him my address in England and ask him to send me a picture of himself. I realized I had already become bold and daring!

Aunt Hortensia came out of the bathroom.

"So where are we going today?" I asked.

"The Museo Correr, I think," she said. "Maybe St George's Church, and since it is our last day, we might spend some time looking in the little shops on the Rialto Bridge. You wanted to buy a piece of Venetian glass, I remember."

I nodded in agreement. I showered, dressed and started to brush my hair, noticing with alarm that there were some pieces of dry grass at the back of my head. Thank heavens Aunt H. hadn't spotted them. I brushed hastily, and we went down to breakfast. As we had filled our plates with rolls, ham and cheese and were about to take our places under an umbrella, the proprietress appeared, calling Aunt H.'s name and beckoning to her. I sat down and started to tuck in, having no premonition of anything wrong. Aunt H. appeared a few minutes later with a face like thunder.

"Leave that and come with me, Juliet," she said.

I stood up and followed her into an empty salon, where she turned to face me.

"You wicked girl," she said, "you have brought shame and disgrace on me and your entire family!"

I opened my mouth, but she went on. "You were seen last night. Seen climbing in through our window from a boat with a young man at the helm. I presume it was the same fellow who rescued you from the canal. What were you thinking? Are you mad?"

"It was quite harmless," I said, realizing as I uttered the words that it wasn't exactly harmless. "Leo is a young man from a good family. He took me to show me the gardens and the pavilions where the Biennale is held, that's all."

"You disobeyed me. You betrayed my trust. Quite harmless, you say? Do you not realize that in Italy no young woman is allowed out alone, without a chaperone, until she is married? This young man clearly did not give a fig about your reputation. He obviously thought that you were easy pickings, because that is not how he would have behaved with an Italian girl of good family.

You are lucky that something terrible didn't happen to you. You have been sheltered from the wicked ways of men, I realize, but you must have known what a risk you took. Out alone with a strange young man in the dark, in the middle of the night?" She was wagging a finger in my face. "If I had my way, I'd march you straight back to England today. That is what you deserve. But I do not want to upset your dear father, in his present delicate condition. So we shall continue with our tour, but we are leaving Venice immediately."

"Immediately?" I blurted out the word. "No, please. You don't understand. It wasn't like that at all. He's really nice. Why won't you meet him, and then you'll see?"

"Immediately, Juliet." Her face was like stone. "Go up and pack your things."

I felt my eyes brimming with tears. "At least let me write him a note."

Her stare was withering. "A lady does not show her emotions in public. You have let down not only your family but your country." She paused to take a breath. "We will go to Florence one day early, and in future you will not be allowed out of my sight until I deposit you on your parents' doorstep. Is that perfectly clear?"

"Yes, Aunt Hortensia," I mumbled. There was really nothing else I could say. I did now realize what a stupid risk I had taken. If Leo had wanted to force himself upon me, I could not have stopped him. Maybe that had been his intention. Easy pickings. A naive English girl. But then he had stopped. He had treated me with respect. He had cared.

We finished breakfast in silence, then went upstairs to pack. I tried to think how I could leave a note for Leo, letting him know why I couldn't see him again, but Aunt H. gave me no chance. I was whisked into a waiting gondola, and off we went to the railway station. I felt as if my heart was breaking as we passed the palaces, one after another. I would never see anything so lovely again. Then I made a vow. I'd study hard, become a famous artist and have the means to travel. *One day,* I promised myself. *One day I will come back.*

That evening, at the new hotel overlooking the River Arno in Florence, I sat at the window and drew a sketch of Leo, before his image faded from my memory. Somehow I managed to capture that unruly hair, his wicked smile, the way his eyes lit up, and there he was, on the page, smiling back at me.

CHAPTER 5

Caroline, England, March 2001

Two thousand and one had not been a good year for Caroline Grant. It had started off with optimism and anticipation. Josh had spotted a piece in a fashion magazine, advertising a competition for new designers in New York.

"I should enter, don't you think?" he asked, looking up, his face alight with expectation. "This might be my big chance. What we've been hoping for."

"New York?" Caroline said, her sensible side coming to the fore. "Won't that be awfully expensive? You'd have to stay there for a while."

"It will be worth it, Cara. Just think, if I win, we've got it made. And even if I don't win, I'll be noticed. I might get offers, start my own line."

He put his hands on her shoulders, squeezing hard. "I can't go on like this any longer. Working for someone else, designing white shirts, for God's sake. I'm dying inside. Shrivelling up. You must see that."

"And what about me?" she wanted to ask. "Do you think that my job is what I dreamed of when we were in art school? I had as much talent as you, and yet you were the one who got the job with a fashion house . . . and I was the one who got pregnant."

She had met Josh on their first day in the fashion design programme at St Martin's. He was daring, with long dark hair, a cape and flashing eyes. Quite different from the solid boys she had met at school dances. She had been blown away when he sat beside her in class, whispered something irreverent in her ear and then suggested they get a cup of coffee together. They had been inseparable ever since. He was fiercely talented, she realized. But his talent was uncontrolled, and a bit over the top. Caroline also had talent, the teachers said. A flair for line and colour, a bright future ahead. But by graduation day, she had discovered she was pregnant.

Josh had professed his love for her and said that he wanted to do this "as a team." And they had married right away. He had taken a job with a commercial fashion house, designing for mass market, high street. She had stayed home after Teddy was born, until financial need forced her to find a job—as an editorial assistant at a women's magazine. It was below her qualifications, but it helped pay the bills.

"Look at us," Josh went on. "We can just afford to rent a place in London. No chance to save for a house of our own, to pay for a good school for Teddy. You're not going to inherit anything from your family; neither am I. It's all up to me, Cara.

I've got to do it, even if it means borrowing from the bank."

She knew in her heart that he was right. They were only surviving, and Josh was becoming increasingly discontent with domestic life. And then he was gone. His phone calls from New York had been ecstatic. The contest judges loved his designs. He was a finalist! But then . . . he came in second place. Caroline expected a moment of disappointment and to console him when he returned home. The next day another phone call turned things in a completely different direction.

"You'll never guess what has happened, Cara. Never in a million years. It's a miracle—"

"For God's sake, tell me," she interrupted.

"You know the singer Desiree?"

"The pop star with the wild fashion sense and wilder hair?"

"She's really quite magnetic and generous in person," he said. "Anyway, she saw the fashion show, and she wants me to design the wardrobe for her upcoming tour. Can you believe it? She wants me to stay in New York for a while so she can collaborate on the designs with me." When Caroline said nothing, he continued, "Are you still there? Go on, say something. Aren't you happy for me?"

"Of course I'm happy," she said, but she didn't mean it. What about their son? Josh hadn't even mentioned Teddy. What about her? "It's just . . . I'll miss you, of course."

"And I'll miss you too, you idiot. But this is just the start of good things; I know it."

Caroline tried to be excited and happy, but worries crept in. What if Josh wanted them to move to New York? How would she feel about that? And what about school for Teddy? He was only six, but soon he'd need a good education.

Josh phoned almost daily—Desiree's penthouse was amazing. He was working with the best team ever. She should see the incredible things he was designing. She'd be so proud of him.

Then the phone calls became much less frequent.

"So haven't you finished the tour wardrobe yet?" she asked when she telephoned him for once. "Isn't it about time you came home?"

"Ah, here's the thing." He coughed, something he always did when nervous. "You see, Desiree wants me on the tour with her. In case something isn't working or needs changing. It's only another month, but it's really worth it."

Caroline knew, even before she saw the picture in the tabloids, that something had gone really wrong. Desiree Duncan with her new "main squeeze," fashion designer Josh Grant, enjoying a Miami nightclub. Then the inevitable phone call.

"I'm sorry, Cara, but I'm not coming back.

I have come to realize that I was trapped in a marriage I never really wanted in the first place. I have always cared about you, but you never made me feel . . . the way she does. I feel alive for the first time in years. Alive and hopeful and doing what I want to do. Don't worry. I'll do my share, make sure Teddy is paid for and goes to a good school. I'll be a good dad. I love him."

After that came the letter from an American lawyer. Divorce conditions. Joint custody of Teddy. Alimony and child support. Josh was being reasonable and fair, the lawyer said. He understood that Teddy's schooling should not be disturbed, so he'd confine visits to America to the school holidays. He'd have Teddy for the summer, and for Christmas and Easter.

Caroline was furious. She got all the hard work, the day-to-day slog, and Josh would be there when Teddy opened his presents, went to the beach, hunted Easter eggs. But then, she had to agree that his schooling was important and should not be interrupted. At least he'd get a good private school education now. She'd make sure Josh paid for that.

She went about her daily life mechanically, trying not to feel anything, being strong for her son's sake. On weekends, she took Teddy and fled to her place of refuge, the house shared by her grandmother and great-aunt. It had been Caroline's only real home since her own parents divorced when she was ten. Her archaeologist mother had always been off somewhere exotic, flitting in and out of Caroline's life like a butterfly, bringing her presents from distant lands before disappearing again. Her father had promptly remarried, and the new wife had, in quick succession, produced the sons he had always dreamed of. So Caroline had spent her holidays from boarding school with Granny and Great-Aunt Lettie, whose real name, never used by the family, was Juliet. There she had always found peace, love and acceptance. She found it now.

"I never thought much of that husband of yours," Great-Aunt Lettie said in a tight, disapproving voice. "I always thought he was a bit of a bounder. Flighty. Remember how he copied that design of yours once for his project in art school? And the teacher had the nerve to suggest that you had copied him?"

Caroline nodded. The memory hurt, but also created more doubts in her mind. Had Josh used any of her designs in the New York competition? How many times had he betrayed her?

She looked at Aunt Lettie, sitting serene and still in her chair by the window. It was where she could always be found, the light streaming on to her face, her beloved radio in front of her. She had lost her sight years earlier. The doctors had diagnosed glaucoma, but she had refused any treatment or surgery, allowing the light to gradually fade from her life. Caroline knew she had previously been an efficient private secretary in banking until her failing sight made her retire to live with her widowed sister. And this was how Caroline had always known her. Sitting by her window, feeling the warmth of the sun or hearing the pattering of the rain, listening to the news, plays, music on the radio, just like the old days.

"So what will you do?" Aunt Lettie asked. "Will you contest the divorce?"

"What's the point?" Caroline sagged. "He won't be coming back, whatever I do. He's found exactly what he always wanted: fame, fortune, no domestic responsibilities."

Aunt Lettie stretched out her thin white hand and found Caroline's knee. "You will get through this, I promise you. We humans have the capacity to survive almost anything. Not only to survive but to come through triumphant. Another door will open. You'll see. A better one. A safer one. A brighter future."

Caroline took the old hand and squeezed it. "Thank you, dear Auntie. I'm so lucky I have you and Granny. You two are my rocks."

Great-Aunt Lettie smiled a sad sort of smile.

"You could give up your place in London and move down here with us," Granny said at dinner that night. "There are good schools nearby for Teddy."

"What about my job?"

"The commute is not impossible."

"But long, and expensive," Caroline countered.

"Do you enjoy your job?"

"Not particularly," Caroline admitted. "It's mainly office work, routine stuff. Occasionally I'm allowed to arrange a fashion page, choose garments, but on the whole it's quite dreary."

"Then use this as a new beginning for you as well," Granny said. "Show that no-good husband of yours that you can succeed without him."

"You're very kind, Granny. I'll think about it. I must decide what's best for Teddy."

Caroline kept up her old routine until Teddy's summer holidays, when Josh telephoned to say that Desiree had rented a place in Beverly Hills for a few months. A mansion with a pool. Teddy would love it. And there was already a nanny in place for Desiree's daughter, Autumn—just a year younger than Teddy. Josh would fly over and get Teddy as soon as school was over.

Caroline didn't have the nerve to ask what had happened to the former Mr Desiree. Husbands and traditional relationships didn't seem to matter in the world of a pop star, if you could believe the newspapers. Teddy was over the moon that he was going to see his daddy and fly on a plane to a house with a swimming pool. Josh arrived. They exchanged polite pleasantries, and off Teddy went. Caroline watched him bounding with excitement into the taxi, then waving through the window, a big smile on his face. And she tried not to feel betrayed and resentful.

Teddy telephoned her almost every day. He was really good at swimming now. He could dive off the side and pick up a ring from the bottom of the pool. Daddy and Desiree had taken them to Disneyland, and he had been on the Matterhorn and it went really fast and Autumn was scared of the haunted house, but he wasn't. Caroline had to admit he was having a wonderful adventure, but worried he'd find his old life a disappointment when he came home.

During the summer, Caroline had given more thought to Granny's suggestion. She had checked out schools near Granny's house in Surrey. She could easily commute up to London until she decided what she wanted to do with her life. And she wouldn't be paying rent on a flat she didn't really love. She'd wait and see how she fared with expenses after child support until she made the final decision, she decided. When Josh came back with Teddy at the beginning of September, she'd know.

She wondered how much Teddy had grown during the summer and looked forward to buying his uniform. Would he sound like a little American now? She counted off the days, but on September 1, Josh called and said that they'd arrived back in New York, but that Teddy had a bad ear infection. The doctor said he shouldn't fly for a week or two. He was sorry that Teddy might miss the first few days of school, but, since he was only six, it didn't matter that much.

It did cross Caroline's mind to wonder if what Josh said was true. Was he stalling? Did he never intend to return her son to her? She tried to quell the alarm bells. *Be patient,* she told herself.

And then, on September 11, the Twin Towers in New York City fell.

CHAPTER 6

Caroline, England, September 2001

The first Caroline knew of it was a strange hysterical sobbing that came from the conference room. Just coming back from grabbing lunch, she followed the sound and found people already crowded inside the door, staring at the television screen that sat on a shelf at the far end of the room. One young secretary had her hands to her mouth and was producing great heaving sobs while an older editor had an arm around her. The others were strangely silent. Caroline stared at the screen, unable to realize immediately what she was seeing. She looked to a colleague.

"What is it?"

"The World Trade Center in New York. Apparently, a plane flew into one of the skyscrapers. A big passenger jet. The upper floors are on fire."

"How terrible. How sad. All those poor people."

Suddenly the girl at the front screamed and pointed. "There's another one. Look!"

And they watched in horror as a second passenger jet flew in a direct line at the second tower, striking it in a fireball.

"It can't be an accident," someone said.

"It must be a terrorist attack."

"The news said it is most likely that idiot Osama bin Laden," said a man's voice from the back of the room.

"Oh God. How many more of them might there be?"

Caroline couldn't speak. She was finding it hard to breathe. *My son is in New York,* she thought. She hadn't ever checked where exactly Desiree's penthouse was in the city. Surely not in the financial district where the towers were. Surely somewhere suitably safe and far away . . .

She pushed her way past more people who now blocked the doorway, rushed to her desk and fumbled in her purse for her telephone book. Her hand was trembling so much that she found it hard to dial the number.

"I'm sorry. All circuits are busy," said a mechanical voice. "Please try again later."

Caroline sat beside the phone all afternoon, fighting back tears of frustration as the "all circuits are busy" message was repeated over and over.

"Of course, your son is there, isn't he?" a co-worker said, putting an arm around her. "No wonder you're worried out of your mind. I would be, too. But I'm sure he's okay."

Caroline wanted to tell her to go away, to leave her alone, but she knew the woman was just trying to be kind. She continued at home every fifteen minutes, all night, until at about three in the morning the call went through.

"Hello?" said a sleepy woman's voice. "What is it?"

"It's Caroline Grant." She gasped out the words. "Is Josh there? And Teddy? You're all safe?"

"Oh yes. We're fine. We're up in the nineties. Miles away. Josh tried to call you yesterday, after it happened, but nobody could make phone calls. Unbelievable, isn't it? Surreal, watching those towers fall."

"Awful," Caroline agreed. "Can I speak to Josh, please?"

"He's still asleep. Hold on a minute. I'll wake him for you."

Caroline heard her saying, "Your wife is on the phone, from London. You'd better wake up."

Then a long pause and Josh's voice. "Hey, Cara. We're fine. I tried to call you. Everything's okay here. The kids were quite upset when they saw it, but they'll be all right."

"Can I speak to Teddy?"

"He's still asleep. Let him be, Cara. We're trying to downplay it as much as possible. No TV. Let life go on as normal. Talk to you later, okay?"

And he hung up. Caroline stood staring at the phone, fighting back anger. She put down the receiver and heaved a shuddering big sigh of relief. They were fine. Her son was fine. She swallowed back tears. News programmes on TV had been broadcasting almost incessant updates. The Pentagon hit. Another plane crashing in a field in Pennsylvania. All flights cancelled. All transportation stalled. Saudi nationals responsible . . . and it was Osama bin Laden.

In England, once the sensation was over, interest in the Twin Towers waned. In a country used to terrorist bombings over the years and having been through the Second World War, this was only one in a long line of tragedies, soon supplanted by something new. After a few days, nobody even mentioned it at work. Caroline couldn't put it out of her mind. Teddy in the same city where planes had crashed into buildings. How was she to know that the same thing wouldn't happen again? She tried calling daily, getting through only every now and then.

Josh seemed reluctant to let her speak to Teddy. "He'll hear how upset you are, Cara. He's doing okay. Let him process this in his own good time."

She had to wait patiently to see when flights would resume. They'd all be overbooked, of course. All those people trapped in New York, waiting to get out. Finally she made contact again with Josh. "When do you think you can fly? Teddy's missing school."

"I was going to call you," Josh said. He sounded a little hesitant. "Teddy's been having nightmares. We took him to Desiree's shrink. He says the child has a real terror of planes right now and shouldn't fly for a while. So we'll find a school for him here."

"No!" Caroline surprised herself with the force of her word. "No. If he's having nightmares and he's terrified, he needs to be with his mother. No wonder he's upset, being amongst strange people after a tragedy like that. I want him home with me, Josh. I'll come and get him if necessary."

"Didn't you hear what I said, Caroline?" His voice was surprisingly calm. "The doctor says he should not fly for a while. It could do him severe psychological damage. And we're not strange people. We are his new family. He already thinks of Autumn as his sister. They share a room. They are very close. And he's got me. I'm his dad. I'm going to do what's best for him, and that means staying here at the moment."

At that moment, Caroline felt her stomach drop. She realized Josh was going to keep stalling. Perhaps he was never going to return Teddy. If she wanted her son, she was going to have to fight for him. She was going to have to get a lawyer.

She went through the motions of work, eat and sleep. Someone at work recommended a family solicitor. She met with him, and he told her it was reasonable that the child shouldn't fly at the moment. If her husband decided to apply for sole custody, that would be the time to do something legally. Since he hadn't made any such threat, all she could do was wait and see. She came out a hundred pounds poorer for the consultation and very angry. As she lay alone in her bed at night, staring at water stains on the ceiling, she fantasized about flying to New York, grabbing Teddy and rushing home with him. But then she'd be the bad one, the irresponsible one, and Josh would have a perfect reason to demand sole custody of his son.

September turned into October, and then Caroline received a telephone call from her grandmother. "I'm afraid I have sad news, darling. Aunt Lettie has had a stroke."

"A bad one? Is she in hospital?" Caroline asked.

"No, she's at home. The doctor came to the house."

"She should be in hospital. If you catch a stroke early enough . . ." Anger exploded from Caroline.

"Sweetheart, she didn't want extraordinary measures. She must have foreseen this, because she said to me, only a couple of days ago, 'If anything happens to me, no hospitals, no tubes. I've lived long enough. I don't need to be kept alive like a vegetable.' "

"So it's bad?" Caroline asked.

"The doctor says she doesn't have long, and she seems quite comfortable," Granny said. "She was quite lucid when it happened. She asked for you. Several times."

"I'll come right down," Caroline said.

She put down the phone and found that she was crying. Everything else that had happened—Josh leaving, Teddy going, the Twin Towers falling— had made her angry but not made her cry. This last straw brought her to her knees. She sat on her bed and wept. Aunt Lettie was over ninety, she knew. She should be glad her great-aunt was dying naturally and in her own bed. But when Caroline was growing up, it was Great-Aunt Lettie who listened when she complained of her absent mother, bullying girls at school or unfair teachers, and gave calm, measured advice and reassurance. "People only bully because they feel inadequate, Caroline. You should pity them. And that teacher—how old is she? An old spinster like me. Probably she resents seeing you bright young people with your lives full of hope."

"Why are you always so nice?" Caroline remembered asking her. "So kind. So forgiving?"

"I wasn't always," her great-aunt replied. "Experience makes one come to terms with life, to be at one with the mind and the heart. And most people are suffering in some way."

"Oh, Aunt Lettie," Caroline whispered. "What will I do without you?"

On the train down from London, it came to her that her grandmother would be hurting, too.

The two old women had lived together for years. Granny would now be all alone, too, if Caroline didn't move in with her. Caroline had asked for a few days' compassionate leave. She'd take it from there.

The weather matched her mood as she changed from a train to a bus in the town of Godalming, and then walked to her grandmother's house in the village of Witley. The sky was leaden with the promise of rain. A cold wind swirled up piles of leaves, and the first drops spattered on to her. Her grandmother lived in a pleasant but unpretentious bungalow at the edge of the village. It had a large garden dotted with fruit trees and a view of the twelfth-century grey stone church. Granny was passionate about her garden. Even though she was now in her eighties, she could often be found kneeling at a flower bed, weeding or deadheading. Of course, these days she had a man who came in once a week to mow, prune and dig, but she supervised him like a hawk.

The garden looked rather bleak and bare as Caroline pushed open the front gate and walked up the path between rose beds that were now just stumps of twig, having been pruned back for the winter. She took a deep breath before she knocked. She didn't want to cry in front of Granny. When her grandmother opened the door, she looked as if she might have been crying, too.

"Oh, my darling," she said in a hushed voice. "It's good of you to have come so quickly."

"Is she still alive?" Caroline's voice had dropped to a whisper.

"Oh yes. Hanging on until you got here, I think. She asked for you again."

Caroline took off her coat in Granny's warm front hall, and the two women hugged silently. The thought crossed Caroline's mind that Granny was the only person who had ever hugged her, apart from her husband and son. She couldn't recall her mother ever doing so. Her mother was never touchy-feely. And Great-Aunt Lettie had not been the sort of person you hugged. She had been kind, caring, but she kept her distance, as if she were a remnant of a bygone age of propriety.

Caroline went forward and opened her aunt's bedroom door cautiously, with a glance back at her grandmother. Great-Aunt Lettie lay amid white sheets, her eyes closed, her face peaceful, seemingly asleep. Caroline wondered if she was already dead, but she noticed a slight rise and fall of the sheet. She bent over and kissed her cheek. It was cold.

"Aunt Lettie," she whispered. "It's Caroline. I came as quickly as I could."

The sightless eyes fluttered open. "Cara . . . ?" The word came out with difficulty. A worried look crossed her face. "Need to tell you," she forced out the words, her mouth drooping on one side. "For you. Need it now."

"Need what, darling?" Caroline perched on the bed beside her and took her cold hand.

Her great-aunt's old face was crinkled into a frown. Then she muttered, "Sketches. Still there."

"Still where?" Caroline looked around the room, wondering if she had heard right and where there might be sketches.

Great-Aunt Lettie gripped Caroline's hand with surprising ferocity. "Up there. Show you."

"Up where?"

She hoped her aunt's blind gaze might direct her, but her aunt was just shaking her head angrily.

"That thing!" she said, fluttering a hand as she sought a word that wouldn't come. "You know." Then, with great difficulty, she stammered out the word "box."

"You want me to find a box?" Caroline asked, sensing her great-aunt's agitation.

Aunt Lettie took a big breath. "You go."

Now Caroline was confused. Did her great-aunt want her to go now, so that she could be alone? She attempted to stand up, but the grip on her hand was still vice-like.

She looked down at the old woman, and her eyes were now closed again, but her face was strained, worried.

"Auntie, do you want me to do something for you?" she asked. "Something with sketches?"

The mouth barely moved. "Mi—angelo."

It sounded like "Michelangelo." Caroline

couldn't recall a copy of a Michelangelo painting in the house, nor of her great-aunt showing any interest in old masters.

Then her great-aunt's eyes opened again, her stare urgent. "Still there," she said with surprising force. "You find . . ."

"Find what?" Caroline asked.

The word was barely audible against the tick of the grandfather clock in the front hall. "Venice."

She gave a little sigh. Caroline waited for her to say more. Minutes passed. Her grandmother came over to stand behind her. "I think she's gone, darling," she said.

Great-Aunt Lettie's cold hand was still gripping Caroline's. She opened the bony fingers and stood up, staring down at the body. She looked peaceful now. Caroline looked up at her grandmother. "Come and have a cup of tea. There's nothing more we can do here."

Caroline allowed herself to be led from the room.

"I suppose it shouldn't have been a shock," Granny said, her voice cracking with emotion. "She's lived a good long life, hasn't she? But it's hard to imagine the world without her."

In the doorway, Caroline paused to look back at her great-aunt. She didn't recall ever being in Great-Aunt Lettie's bedroom before, after all the years she had spent in the house. Her great-aunt was always up and dressed early in the morning, at her regular spot in the sitting room. It struck Caroline that she had been an intensely private person who only wanted to show an image of propriety to the world.

As she looked now, she saw a neat and orderly room, clothes put away, slippers beside the bed, but no personal touches. No photographs. On the wall was one small painting of a cherub, done in the Renaissance style. It struck Caroline as incongruous and not like her practical and unsentimental aunt. Michelangelo? No. Certainly not his style or expertise. Maybe it was something she had picked up as a young woman—or, conversely, something she had noticed when her sight began to fail and she could no longer appreciate less vibrant colours.

"There are no photographs," Caroline commented as she followed her grandmother into the big warm kitchen. "I have no idea what she looked like as a young woman."

"She was quite striking, actually." Granny looked up from putting the kettle on the Aga. "She had lovely rich auburn hair that I really envied, mine being more a sort of strawberry ginger. And clear blue eyes. There will be some photos in my mother's old album, but of course they are all black-and-white. We'll find them later. But right now sit down, and we'll have a cup of tea before I call the doctor. I think we both need it."

CHAPTER 7

Caroline, England, October 2001

"You'll find the house empty without her, won't you?" Caroline said as the kettle started to whistle and her grandmother lifted it from the cooking surface.

"Horribly empty," Granny said. "She has lived with me since our mother died, when your own mother was a baby. She was never intrusive, you know. Kept herself out of the way when your grandfather was still alive, as if she appreciated that this was our house and she was an interloper. But I think she really appreciated being here in those difficult years right after the war. And I certainly liked having my big sister around, especially after Jim died so suddenly and I was left with a young child."

Caroline took down two mugs from the Welsh dresser as Granny poured boiling water into the teapot.

"It was really hard for me, coming back to England, having spent the war years in India," Granny went on. "Servants to do everything. And of course your grandfather was in a Japanese prisoner-of-war camp much of that time. I was stuck miles from home, never knowing if I'd see my husband again. Poor man—he didn't know for two years that our son had died."

"I didn't even know you had a son," Caroline said.

"I don't talk about him much. It was a painful episode in my life. I was stuck in India when the war broke out. Your grandfather was called up into the army. And then our little boy got typhoid."

"Oh, Granny. How awful for you. You poor thing." Her thoughts immediately went to Teddy and the ache in her own heart. If anything happened to him, how would she bear it?

"I survived." Her grandmother gave a sad little smile. "Most of us survive the hardest things. We are quite resilient."

"I am trying to be," Caroline said. She carried the two mugs over to the table by the window. Rain was now sweeping across the expanse of lawn. They sat facing each other. "Will you be all right for money now that Aunt Lettie is gone?"

Her grandmother looked down at the tea she was stirring. "I have to admit that her pension did help with expenses."

"Then I'll definitely move in with you. I think Teddy should go to the Church of England primary school, don't you? If you want me here, of course."

"Want you here? My darling child, I can't think of anything nicer than having you and Teddy here. And don't you worry. He'll be back soon."

"God, I hope so." Caroline stirred her own tea savagely. She took a sip. It was naturally too hot, and she put it back on the table. "Granny, Aunt Lettie was trying to tell me something. Did you hear what she said? Could you understand it?"

"I couldn't really hear," Granny replied. "I heard her, but I couldn't tell you what she was talking about. Her speech was affected, wasn't it? Talking out of one side of her mouth. And she couldn't find words. I found her like that when I brought in her morning cup of tea. She said, 'Think I've had a stroke. No hospital. Caroline. Want to tell Caroline . . .' And she repeated that when the doctor left."

"Gosh," Caroline said. "I wish I knew what she had wanted. It sounded like something about sketches. I couldn't really understand. Perhaps her mind was already gone."

"Before I forget," Granny said, "Lettie left everything to you. She made a will, and you are her beneficiary."

"Really?" Caroline flushed with embarrassment. "But that's not right. Everything should go to you, Granny. You're the one who has taken care of her all these years."

Granny smiled. "To be frank, I don't think there was that much to leave. She hadn't earned any money for years, besides her pension, and our mother didn't leave anything to either of us other than this house. They lost all their money, you know, in the Great Crash of '29. Apparently my father invested in American stocks and lost everything."

"Oh dear. Our family doesn't seem to have been too lucky, does it?" Caroline said.

"I suppose my father was doing what he thought was best for us. He was wounded in the First World War, you know, and never quite well again afterward. He probably put all his hopes on making money on the stock market."

"So do you know what Aunt Lettie actually left me?" Caroline asked. "If there is any money, I'm handing it over to you."

"I do happen to know, as a matter of fact. She made me her executor. She had a savings account with about a thousand pounds in it. But apart from that, not much more than her clothes and a couple of pieces of jewellery inherited from our mother. Nothing of great value. However, there is a box in her wardrobe with your name on it. She was most insistent that you have that."

Caroline looked up. "A box. That was one of the things she tried to say. A box. Up there."

Granny nodded. "She mentioned it the other day, when she talked about no extraordinary measures—as if she knew she was going to die. 'Make sure Caroline gets it, won't you,' she said. I don't know what's in it. She never told me."

"I don't want to go in there now to get it. It seems disrespectful," Caroline said. A box with her name on it. Maybe a piece of jewellery Lettie had never told her sister about, money she'd been stashing away . . .

"Aunt Lettie won't mind," Granny replied with a smile. "She's not even there anymore, only a body she no longer needs. I expect she's looking down on us and smiling. And she was so insistent that I made sure you had the box."

Caroline hesitated. Then she got up, went to Aunt Lettie's door and tiptoed into her bedroom again, glancing across at the bed as if she still expected the old woman to open her eyes and turn to see her. She opened a wardrobe that smelled of mothballs and a hint of perfume. Je Reviens. That had been Aunt Lettie's favourite. There was a hatbox on the top shelf, but it contained several outdated hats. Then she found a simple old cardboard box in one corner and lifted it down carefully. A label was affixed to the top: *For Caroline Grant after my death. Please make sure she gets it.*

Caroline could almost swear she heard a small sigh of contentment coming from the bed as she left the room, carrying the box. She set it down on the table, across from her grandmother.

"I wonder what it could be that mattered so much to her," she said. "Should I open it now, do you think?"

"Of course. You know we're both dying of suspense." Her grandmother laughed.

Caroline eased off the lid. Inside were two leather-bound books and a jewellery case. She opened the latter, her heart beating fast. She swallowed back the "Oh," realizing how rude it would be to show disappointment. Inside the jewellery case was an old-fashioned ring with a row of small diamonds, a string of glass beads, and three keys. Two were old, almost antique-looking keys—a brass key topped by the figure of what looked like a winged lion, a large iron key so formidable that it looked as if it might unlock the door to a dungeon and then a small silver key, such as might open any kind of cabinet or box.

"What on earth?" Granny sounded as surprised as she was. "Keys? Where did she get keys?"

"You don't recognize any of them?"

"Certainly not. I've no idea what she'd want with a lot of old keys. She wasn't the type of person who collected things. I've always thought of her as a minimalist. And a realist. Unsentimental."

"And the ring and beads?" Caroline asked. "Were they her favourites?"

"I've never seen her wear them. She had a brooch from our mother she liked to wear. But apart from that, she didn't go in for much jewellery, did she?"

Caroline had already put the keys aside and was lifting out the two books. She opened the first and saw inscribed inside the cover *Juliet Browning. Begun May 1928.*

"Oh, it's a sketchbook," she said. "Sketches. So that's what Aunt Lettie was talking about. She wanted me to have the sketches. I didn't know that Aunt Lettie used to sketch."

"She was very keen on it at one time," Granny said. "She went to art school, you know. They thought she showed promise."

Caroline looked up in surprise. "Art school? She never mentioned it."

Granny shook her head. "No, she never talked about her life. Of course, she had to abandon her studies when our father lost his money and died. I remember how disappointed she was about that. She managed to get a job teaching art at a nearby girls' school. Well, someone had to provide for our mother and me. I was six years younger, still in school."

Caroline was turning pages in the book. "She was quite good, wasn't she? Oh, and look—these sketches are of Venice, aren't they? There's a gondola, and St Mark's. Venice—that's what I think she was trying to say just before she died. Something about Venice. I never knew she had travelled."

"Our aunt Hortensia took her to Italy as a present for her eighteenth birthday," Granny said. "I was always a bit resentful about that, because by the time my eighteenth birthday came around we had no money. Aunt Hortensia had let my father manage her money, too, so she lost everything, of course." She looked up and made eye contact with Caroline. "I never went to a posh boarding school like Lettie. It was a local convent for me. And no European jaunts. In fact the first time I went abroad was to India with your grandfather, right after we married."

"What year was that?" Caroline asked.

"Nineteen thirty-seven. I was twenty-one and horribly naive. India was an awful shock, I can tell you. The heat and the dust and the flies and the beggars. I would have fled straight home to my mother if I could have." She gave an embarrassed chuckle. "But I stuck it out. Jim was wonderfully patient. A good man. I'm sorry you never met him."

Caroline nodded, returning her smile, then turned back to the book. "Oh, look. She's sketched a handsome Venetian—I wonder if he was a gondolier? Oh, and she went on to Florence. See? That's the Ponte Vecchio." She closed the first book and took up the second one. "This one is also Venice," she said. "And it's dated 1938. So she did go back."

"That's right, I believe she did," Granny said. "I remember my mother writing in one of her letters that Lettie had been asked to take a party of schoolgirls on a trip abroad in the summer holidays."

Caroline was turning pages. These sketches in the second book were also of Venice, but done by a more skilled hand. The perspectives were just right. The faces of people in the market were so alive. There was a garden with trees and a fountain. More gondolas. An outdoor restaurant with lanterns . . .

"She clearly loved it," Caroline said. "Did she go often?"

"She never went back after the war," Granny said. "I think she'd seen enough of Europe by then. She was trapped there, you know."

"Trapped?"

"Yes. She got some kind of bursary to study in Europe in 1939. A stupid time to go, really, if you think about it. But it was a chance she couldn't turn down, I suppose. And then war broke out, and she couldn't get home. She managed to make her way to Switzerland and sat out the conflict. I believe she worked with refugee children."

"Oh, I see." Caroline frowned. "It's strange that she didn't go back to teaching when she came home. She obviously liked working with children."

"I don't know," Granny said. "I expect she saw some sad things during the war. I know she stayed on for a while after the German surrender, working with her refugees. She came back to England just before I did."

"How did I never know any of this?" Caroline asked.

"You never asked. The young are not interested in the lives of the old. And I expect some memories were painful for both your great-aunt and me. I know she had to work with some concentration camp survivors. That would have been very unsettling for anyone."

Caroline closed the second of the sketchbooks. "What I don't understand is that you say she has left me everything in her will. So why single out this particular box? Why was it important to her?"

"I have no idea." Granny shook her head. "She never mentioned anything except that she wanted you to have the box."

"Sketchbooks and old keys. It makes no sense. Are the keys a symbol of something? Does she want me to go back to studying art?"

"She would have mentioned that, surely," Granny said. "She was a very forthright woman, wasn't she? She would have told you in no uncertain terms if she felt that's what you should be doing."

Caroline nodded, smiling. "She wanted me to find something. Was it this box? But she told me to go. I thought she meant to leave her, but she was still gripping my hand, and then I think she said 'Venice.'"

"How strange." They were both staring at the box, then looked up at the same time, and their eyes met. Granny hesitated before she said, "I can only think . . ."

"What?"

"It sounds so ridiculous, but I'm wondering if she wanted you to go to Venice."

Caroline stared at her grandmother's serene face. "Did she ever say anything about it? Give a reason?"

Granny shrugged. "Perhaps she thought it would do you good to get away from your worries about your marriage and Teddy."

"But why Venice in particular? Why not just go abroad, travel?"

"I don't know, my dear. All I know is that she had a bee in her bonnet about the box. She wanted me to promise you would get it."

"So why not write me a note and say that she wanted me to go to Venice because she had loved it there? Or she wanted her ashes scattered there?"

Granny shook her head. "I can't tell you what she wanted."

"I went to Venice once," Caroline commented. "On my honeymoon. It was July and full of tourists and hot and smelly. Josh hated it. We only stayed a day and then left for Croatia."

"But you didn't hate it?" Granny asked.

"No. Actually, I wanted to see more." Caroline

tipped the three keys into her hand. "And these—what are they supposed to mean? Keys to Venice? Anyway, I can't go off to the Continent. I've a job and a son. And you."

"I seem to remember you telling me that you hadn't taken any vacation days this year."

"No." Caroline considered this. "Because Teddy wasn't here in the summer. I didn't want to go away without him."

"Well then." Granny smiled.

"Well what?"

"You have the time to travel. You've been told that Teddy shouldn't get on a plane for a while. And I suspect many people are still fearful of travelling after what happened, so the hotels should have good prices. Why don't you fulfil Aunt Lettie's last wish and go and enjoy a few days in Venice?"

Caroline looked out of the window. Rain was now peppering the glass. "It hardly seems the time of year to enjoy Venice. Doesn't it flood in winter?"

"It's not winter yet. It's autumn—season of mists and mellow fruitfulness. You'll probably find the Mediterranean is still warm and sunny." She reached out and covered Caroline's hand with her own. "And you could do with a break. You have been looking so tense and strained ever since Josh went away and this whole sorry business started."

"Wouldn't you look tense if your husband walked out and was trying to take your son?" Caroline said, instantly regretting her outburst.

"Of course I would. But the point is that you can't do anything about it at this moment. You have to be patient and wait it out. So I say fulfil what we think is Aunt Lettie's last wish. Take her box and go to Venice. Scatter her ashes in a place she clearly loved."

"Would you like to come with me?" Caroline asked, reaching out her hand to her grandmother.

Granny smiled and shook her head. "Oh no, my dear. My travelling days are over. Besides, if Aunt Lettie had wanted me to go, she'd have made it clear to me. She wants you to go. Not me."

CHAPTER 8

Juliet, Venice, July 1938

I never thought I'd have the chance to visit Venice again after the events of the last ten years, but here I am, back in the beloved city. It seems like a miracle. I arrived a few hours ago, together with Miss Frobisher and twelve girls from Anderley House School, where I teach. The train journey was hot and crowded, and on arrival in Venice we had to run the gamut of men trying to snatch our bags and drag them into gondolas as we emerged from the station, just as they had done ten years previously when I came here with Aunt Hortensia.

"Oh, Miss Browning, this is absolutely ghastly, isn't it?" Miss Frobisher wailed, grabbing on to my arm. "It's just too, too ghastly. Why on earth didn't we take the girls to Paris instead? The French are so much more civilized than this mob of uncouth rabble. Likely as not, we'll be murdered in our beds, if we don't die of heatstroke before we find the convent."

I tried to reassure her and was relieved when we found that the convent where we would be staying was one of the few places in Venice with no navigable canal near it. Instead we would have to walk over the Grand Canal by the Ponte degli Scalzi, a stone bridge of many steps, to the district of Santa Croce, cross another canal by a smaller, steeper bridge and then wind our way through narrow alleys. They all seemed to have different names at each corner, made even more frustrating when carrying our suitcases. It was hot and muggy, and Miss Frobisher had brought a large leather suitcase she could hardly lift. I felt sorry for her but wasn't about to offer to carry it.

"Are we nearly there, miss?" one of the girls pleaded. "My arm's about dropping off."

"When can we have a drink, miss?" another chimed in. "We're all dying of thirst."

That had been another inconvenience for us. The train we had taken had no dining car. This was all right as we had boarded in Calais in the evening and still had the sandwiches we had brought with us. But finding there was no hot drink to be had in the morning was a shock. We had to change trains in Milan and had hoped to find a drink in the station, but our train had come in late and we had to sprint between platforms, flinging ourselves on board at the last minute. My mouth felt like sandpaper, and I knew what the girls must be going through.

"This is an awful place." Miss Frobisher gasped out the words as she staggered on, her face bright, beetroot red. She was a large woman

93

and not suited to the heat. "What on earth made you suggest it, Miss Browning?"

"We are on a cultural trip, Miss Frobisher," I replied, trying to sound patient and optimistic. "Venice has such a brilliant collection of paintings and sculptures, and the buildings themselves are all works of art. The girls will find plenty to sketch and learn a lot of history." I changed my suitcase to the other hand, trying not to show that I, too, was nearing exhaustion. "I was here myself when I was eighteen, and I was entranced by the city."

"I can't say I've noticed anything historic or noteworthy yet," Miss Frobisher snapped. "A nasty, dirty train station, a mob of evil men who all smelled bad and tried to manhandle me. And did you see all those soldiers and those men in black shirts at the station? Mussolini's thugs. I've read about them. Just as bad as Hitler." She dropped her suitcase to the cobblestones, wiped off her hands on her skirt, then hefted it again. "At least we could have stayed in a proper hotel and not a heathen Roman Catholic establishment."

"Not my choice, Miss Frobisher," I said, my patience now wearing rather thin. "It was the school's board of directors'. As you know, they were a little unsure about the wisdom of this venture. Reverend Cronin felt that the parents would feel more secure knowing their daughters were safely locked up for the night in a convent."

"Will we be fed bread and water, miss?" Sheila Barber, a particularly annoying girl, demanded. "I've read about convents. They make nuns beat themselves with whips and pray twenty times a day and get up at four in the morning."

"Not this one, I can assure you, Sheila," I replied. "This order is an order of hospitality. That is what they do—host pilgrims or visitors like ourselves. I have been assured it is most welcoming."

We trudged on. In truth, I was beginning to feel as disillusioned and worried as they were. When a group of parents had approached the school, suggesting that their daughters needed exposure to the great art of the Continent before the political situation deteriorated even further, and one of them had particularly mentioned Venice, it had been more than I could resist. As art mistress, I was an obvious choice to lead such an expedition. Also I am the only teacher on the staff under fifty. The rest are spinsters who were at the right age for marriage around the time of the Great War, thus they had little chance of ever finding a husband after a whole generation of young men had been wiped out. It seemed that most of them were reluctant to travel to Europe at such an unsettled time. Finally Miss Frobisher, the history mistress, was persuaded to go with us. We were to spend the first few days in Venice and then on to Florence.

A skinny cat slunk out from a side alley.

"Mew?" it asked hopefully.

"Oh, look at that poor thing," one of the girls said. "It's so thin. Can we take it with us? It needs a saucer of milk."

I looked back at the girl and saw the hopeful eyes of myself at eighteen. "Margaret, I'm afraid you'll find that this is a city full of stray cats. People here don't value animals the way we do."

"It smells bad here, miss," the annoying Sheila complained. "Does the water come out of the canals? Do you think we'll catch some disease?"

"We shall drink only bottled water and be careful with unpeeled vegetables and fruit. Otherwise, we should be quite safe," I replied, proud of my calmness. I stopped to read a street name on a crumbling red-painted building. "Oh yes. Nearly there now. Buck up, everyone."

Have I made a mistake coming back here? I asked myself. *Am I seeing the past through rose-tinted glasses? Was it always smelly and dirty and I never noticed?*

We turned into a blind alley, so narrow that the girls had to walk in single file. There was a distinct smell of bad drains.

"It should be here." I consulted the letter. "Convent of Mater Domino? . . ."

Two small boys came out of a doorway, clutching a football. "Scusi. Dove si trova Mater Domino?" I asked them.

They stared at the girls in their school uniforms as if they were creatures from another planet and pointed silently to the end of the alley. "Il primo a destra," one of them said.

"Grazie." I turned back to Miss Frobisher. "It's just around the corner on the right."

They turned into an even narrower alleyway. We scanned the buildings one by one. Then at the far end I noticed a small plaque saying *Mater Domino* on a grey stone wall, with a cross above. And in the middle of that wall was a massive wooden door.

"This must be it," I said, a trifle dubiously. "I must say they don't make their presence well known."

"You do the talking, Miss Browning," Miss Frobisher said. "You have knowledge of the language, don't you? I only have Latin, which I am sure is no longer any use."

"I have been studying Italian at home, just for my own benefit, Miss Frobisher. I'm not sure how proficient I am."

"You made those boys just now understand you."

I had to smile. "That wasn't too hard, with all that waving and gesturing."

Beside the door was an old-fashioned bell pull. I tugged on it and heard a distant jangling.

"It looks awful," one of the girls whispered. "Why are there no windows?"

"I've heard what they do in convents," Sheila's voice came again. "They'll try to convert us, and if we don't agree, something terrible will happen to us. They brick people up in walls and toss them down wells."

"Don't be so silly, Sheila." Miss Frobisher spoke up now. I could tell she was making a supreme effort to be calm and reassuring. "You are frightening your schoolmates unnecessarily. I'm sure it looks perfectly fine inside."

At that moment a grille was slid back, and a face, framed by a severe white wimple, appeared. I heard a gasp from the girls.

"Dominus vobiscum," the woman said.

"Siamo il Gruppo dale scuola dall'Inghiterra." I had practiced phrases I thought we might need, and this one came out convincingly.

"Ah, va bene." The woman nodded. "Enter, please."

The door creaked open slowly, and we stepped into a small courtyard. High walls rose on all sides, blocking out the sunlight.

"Wait 'ere, please," the nun said in stumbling English, then disappeared into a doorway, her long skirts swishing on the ground. After a minute or so, another nun appeared. This one was younger and actually smiling.

"Welcome, dear girls," she said. "I am Sister Immaculata. I am your hostess. I show you your rooms. Please to follow."

"Actually, we are all very thirsty," I said. "There was no dining car on the train."

The nun looked puzzled.

"No drink on train. Very thirsty. Siamo assetati."

"Ah." The nun nodded. "Is too late for breakfast. All put away, I am afraid. I bring water to your rooms, sì?"

"Will it be bottled water?" Miss Frobisher demanded, putting herself between the nun and me. "It is essential that we drink bottled water only. The girls must not get sick."

"If bottled water, you must pay," the nun said.

"Very well. We will pay for bottled water, but please have some sent up to us. And at what time is luncheon? The girls are also very hungry."

"Luncheon is at one o'clock," the nun said. Then her face softened. "I send up bread and fruit to you. Va bene?"

"Sì, va bene." I returned her smile.

We were led up a steep and narrow stone staircase. The girls were in rooms with two sets of bunk beds. Miss Frobisher and I were to share a twin-bedded room. The bathroom was down the hall—simple but clean. I looked around the room, spartan in the extreme with whitewashed stone walls, two narrow iron-framed beds, on which there was a white sheet but no coverlet, and a large cross on the wall above. I noticed with amusement that the window was barred, and

I was immediately taken back to ten years before. I remembered so clearly looking down and seeing Leo's face smiling up at me from his boat, his arms stretched out to me as he urged me to come down. Was he still in Venice? Of course he would be. His family had been here since the Middle Ages. And he'd be married by now. Married and settled and happy, the way I had expected to be.

There was no canal below this window. Only a narrow street. A house with window boxes of geraniums, and behind the houses the rising roof of a church. No glimpse of the Grand Canal. And I couldn't climb out of this window anyway.

"I suppose this is adequate, Miss Browning," Miss Frobisher said. "At least it's clean. And safe. Nobody could climb in through that window."

"And we couldn't climb out—if there was a fire," I pointed out.

"That is true." She broke off when there was a tap at the door. A young girl, looking no older than our own charges, dressed in the more simple habit of a postulant, came in carrying a tray on which there was a large bottle of water, two glasses, oranges and a plate of sweet rolls.

"I think this place might be acceptable after all, don't you, Miss Browning?" Miss Frobisher poured us both a glass of water.

I turned away from the window. *I shouldn't have come,* I thought. At that moment a bell began to toll nearby, its sound resonating through the still air. Pigeons took off in alarm, flapping from nearby rooftops, and at once I was taken back.

"A city of bells and birds," I whispered to myself.

CHAPTER 9

Juliet, Venice, July 1938

The convent proved to be more pleasant than I had first thought. Luncheon was served in a long, cool dining room with whitewashed walls and rustic wooden tables and benches. It was a hearty meal of spaghetti with a tomato sauce, grated parmesan cheese and more bread and fruit. The girls tucked in with relish, and I must say that I enjoyed the meal, too. We ate alone, apparently the only guests in the convent at the moment. The nuns, it seemed, had their own dining room, or dined at a different time. We were shown a common room with armchairs and sofas that opened on to a small garden with a fountain spraying. Aunt Hortensia would have approved, I thought. Another garden in Venice.

I carried my briefcase down to the garden and sat in the shade while the girls and Miss Frobisher went up to take a nap. First I took out a new sketchbook, not as luxurious as the one my father had given me ten years ago, but then nothing was luxurious any more. Life had been a struggle for most people, and I realized that I was luckier than most—at least I hadn't had to line up for bread and soup like those poor people with no work.

I opened the sketchbook and wrote a tentative date in it. Then I stared at the blank page. Would I have time to do much sketching? Would I want to? Would I have forgotten how? For the past few years, my only art had been demonstrations for pupils—perspective, colour wheels, how to draw trees and faces. Frankly, I had lost the urge to do my own painting after I'd had to leave art school unexpectedly; besides, there had been no extra money to spend on frivolities like paints and canvases. I tucked the book back into the case and instead took out the map of Venice. I had kept Aunt Hortensia's map on my return to England in the summer of 1928, fully intending to return and paint during college holidays. It had been unfolded, pored over and folded up again many times since, and I felt that I knew my way around in my sleep. But I had not been to this part of the city before. It was not an area that tourists usually frequented, so close to the railway station and the docks. With a finger I traced out a sensible route to the Rialto Bridge. From there I could take the girls to St Mark's easily enough. There were water buses close by, but we had been told to be careful with money—no extravagances, and keep plenty for emergencies. We would take the water bus at least once up the Grand Canal—that was a necessity—and probably over to the island of

Murano, where this time I would buy myself a necklace.

Miss Frobisher was dismayed to find, when she awoke, that no tea would be served at four o'clock. "I simply can't exist without my cup of tea, Miss Browning," she said. "Is there no tearoom nearby?"

"The only tearoom I know is in St Mark's Square, called Florian, very ritzy and ornate, and I'm sure it's quite expensive. Normal people don't drink tea here. Only coffee."

"Coffee in the afternoon? Whatever next?" Miss Frobisher shook her head.

I remembered that the pensione where I had stayed with my aunt had indeed served tea in the afternoon, but then it catered to English guests, which this convent clearly didn't.

"I suspect the girls would like an ice cream instead," I suggested. "They are really awfully good here."

"That might do the trick," Miss Frobisher agreed.

The girls emerged, one by one, bleary eyed and not wanting to do much.

"We've only such a short time here that we need to do something today," I said. "How about going for an ice cream? I know a perfect gelateria near the Rialto Bridge."

That cheered everyone up. I led them, following the map, through the twists and turns of backstreets until we came out to a familiar broader area where the market was held. And when we started up the shallow steps of the Rialto Bridge and the expanse of the Grand Canal stretched in both directions, there were gasps of amazement from the girls.

"Oh, look down there. See the gondolas? And all those lovely buildings. It's like something from a film, miss. Or a fairy tale."

I found myself smiling as if I had personally created the scene for their pleasure.

"You wait until you see St Mark's Square tomorrow. And the Doge's Palace. But you've all brought your sketchbooks, haven't you? We'll buy our ice creams, and then we'll find a place to sit and sketch for a while. You can do the bridge, or the market stalls, or even an interesting rooftop or door knocker. There is never a shortage of things to draw in Venice."

They all chose different flavours of gelato. I suggested lemon and hazelnut as being refreshing, and several girls followed suit. Then we sat on the steps of an old church, licking feverishly before the ice cream melted, giving sighs of contentment. We sketched for a good hour before returning to the convent along the main thoroughfare on the other bank of the canal that led back to the station. We passed lots of interesting shops along the way—shops that sold gold and jewellery, leather goods and carnival masks—and it was clear that the girls would have to be dissuaded from shopping rather than observing art. *Just like me, all those years ago,* I thought.

Dinner was a tomato salad with mozzarella cheese, another dish of pasta, this time with tiny clams, and a cheeseboard and fruit bowl to finish. As we were leaving the table, the nun who was looking after us came in to wish us goodnight.

"Our silent hours begin at nine o'clock, so no noise after that hour. And please to remember," she said, "the convent door is locked at ten o'clock. Nobody may come in or out after that until the morning."

"You hear that, girls?" Miss Frobisher said, wagging a finger at them. "No thoughts of sneaking out, or you will be forced to sleep on the doorstep. Miss Browning and I are responsible for you, so I trust you will behave at all times."

"We can't even go out and see if there is dancing and jazz bands and things?" one of the girls asked.

I shook my head. "I'm afraid I have no experience of dance clubs or jazz bands, Mary. I was here with a strict aunt who said that ladies did not go out after dinner unaccompanied."

Even as I said it, the memory came flooding back so violently that I almost reeled from it. I had gone out at night. There had been music and the wind in my hair. A vivid image of Leo came to me, him glancing back at me and smiling as he steered his boat, and he had held my hand as we strolled through the dark gardens, and he had kissed me. Now it felt like a beautiful dream. Had he really been who he claimed to be? Did he really live in a palace, or was he a handsome imposter having a little fun with an innocent tourist? And had he thought of me after that night? I realized I'd probably never know. I had never given him my address in England, so he would have had no way of contacting me if he'd wanted to. I could hardly go to the palazzo where he claimed he lived and ask to see him— not with twelve girls and Miss Frobisher in tow. Besides, ten years had passed. I was no longer that hopeful, emotional girl. He was probably married with children by now, with no interest in seeing a naive girl he had once kissed.

We escorted the girls to their rooms for the night, then went to our own room. The air was stiflingly hot and oppressive. I stood at the window, hoping to catch a breath of night breeze. Outside the window I could hear the sounds of the city coming awake for the evening: distant laughter, music, someone singing opera. A couple walked arm in arm along the little street at the end of the alleyway. As if on cue, they paused, she lifted her face to his and he kissed her.

That will never be me, I thought with a great pang of regret.

We were awoken by bells from a nearby church at six o'clock—great reverberating sounds that made the shutters tremble. As they died away, they were echoed by a smaller, tinnier bell from within the convent.

"What on earth is that racket, Miss Browning?" Miss Frobisher asked sleepily. "It's not a fire, is it?"

"It's the bell summoning the sisters to prayer, I suspect. Six o'clock."

"Oh good heavens, we're not supposed to join them, are we?"

"Of course not." I smiled. "But it is infernally early to be woken, isn't it?"

I put on my dressing gown and went to check on the girls, some of whom had slept through the din, while others were sitting up and voiced their complaints as soon as I appeared.

"That's not fair, Miss Browning. How are we supposed to get any sleep if the blooming bells keep ringing all the time?"

"I'm afraid there's nothing we can do about bells, Daphne," I said, smiling at her grumpy face. "They are part of life here. The people are very religious, you know. Some of them go to Mass every morning. And the sisters pray several times a day."

"Golly, I'm glad I'm C of E, aren't you?" Daphne prodded her roommate.

We breakfasted on freshly baked bread, with hard-boiled eggs and jam, plus milky coffee that the girls found intriguing.

"I've never had coffee before, miss," one of them said. "My mum says it's only for grown-ups. But it's quite good, isn't it?"

"Yes, it is. So is the bread here."

After breakfast we set out, heading for the vaporetto stop outside the station. There we caught the Number One all the way up the Grand Canal. Now the girls were really impressed. They leaned out, taking snapshots, waving at gondoliers and discussing which of the palaces they'd like to own. I spotted the Palazzo Rossi, staring at the windows in the hope of seeing a face, but they remained shuttered against the heat.

We alighted at the San Marco stop and walked along the waterfront, where rows of gondolas bobbed at their moorings, until we reached the entrance to St Mark's Square. The girls reacted as I had done ten years before, marvelling in the tall bell tower, the domes of the basilica, the coffee houses with their outdoor tables, still almost empty at ten in the morning. They sat and sketched, visited St Mark's, then the Doge's Palace. Finally, as I had done ten years earlier, we went to the little bridge on the waterfront, where they got a view of the Bridge of Sighs. They all thought it so romantic.

We returned to the convent for lunch, which was a large vegetable stew this time, then a rest before we went out for gelato and sketching. The next day I took them to the Accademia. As I paid for their entry tickets, I watched a group of students going into the next-door building that housed the academy itself. They carried portfolios, and they were laughing together as if they hadn't a care in the world. *That should have been me,* I thought, then reminded myself that at least I'd had one year of instruction. Better than nothing. Better than those poor people who had no job at all, who had lost all hope.

"More paintings, miss?" Sheila complained as I led them into a room of works by old masters. "This old art is all so boring. It's all saints and things."

"Yes, miss, when can we do some shopping?" another voice chimed in.

"It is supposed to be a cultural trip, you know," I pointed out. "Tomorrow we'll go to Murano, and you can buy some glass if you like. It's very lovely."

They liked this idea, and so we visited the island the next day. I saw the same beads I had so admired when I visited with Aunt Hortensia, and this time I bought a necklace. We were waiting for the water bus to return to the city when I noticed a poster advertising the Biennale. Of course, it was an even year—the great modern art exhibition would be taking place in the gardens.

"I think you girls might enjoy seeing some more-modern art," I said as we disembarked and made our way back to the convent. "There is a famous exhibit of modern art from around the world held in some really lovely gardens. Maybe we'll go there tomorrow."

"Are you sure that modern art is suitable for the girls?" Miss Frobisher asked. "I've seen some of the things they call art these days."

"It is good for them to know what is being created, rather than just relying on the past," I replied. "They can make up their own minds whether they think modern art is equally beautiful."

And so the next morning we headed for the Giardini on the water bus. It was cool and pleasant as we approached the exhibition on the tree-lined paths. I found myself wondering exactly where Leo's tree with the statue had been, or the lawn where we had eaten a picnic and he had kissed me. The gardens were full of people, including a good sprinkling of Mussolini's black shirts, the armed squads of Italian Fascists, and local police, observing the crowd as they passed. It took away the serenity of the surroundings. What could they be looking for? Everyone here seemed so relaxed and happy to be enjoying a day in the park.

We visited the main pavilion, where Miss

Frobisher was suitably shocked at some of the painting and sculpture.

"Now how could you call that art? It's just daubs. It looks as if the canvas is spattered with blood."

"That's what the artist wanted to achieve, I suspect," I answered. "It's about the Spanish Civil War."

She approved more of the German pavilion, where the works were in keeping with Nazi propaganda, depicting happy blonde peasants in fields and impressive monuments. I realized that Jewish artists had probably fled from Germany, as would those artists whose work did not go along with party thinking.

Miss Frobisher pointed out with interest that some of the artists were Austrian. "Of course," she said. "Germany has annexed Austria, hasn't it? Nice to see them happily together now."

I kept quiet and didn't say what I was thinking. As we were about to leave, a group of German officers entered the room, talking loudly and brushing people aside with such arrogance that I had to swallow back my anger.

As they approached us, I said clearly, "Come, girls. I think we've seen enough of this, haven't we? It's all propaganda. You can't really call it art."

And I led them from the room. It was a small victory, but it felt good.

We wound through the grounds to other nations' pavilions. We had just come out of the American one when a group of what were clearly important men came towards us. Men in well-cut suits walking with that air of confidence that comes with power. A foreign delegation being shown around, I suspected. Then I saw Leo. He was in the middle of the group, saying something to the other men, who were listening attentively. I recognized him instantly. He had hardly changed at all, except that he had filled out a bit and was now wearing what was clearly an expensive business suit. Also those wild dark curls were now slicked down.

I was frozen to the spot. I wanted to call out to him, but I didn't dare. What if he had forgotten me? Walked past as if I didn't exist? But I couldn't just let him disappear without doing something. I took a tentative step forward, and at that moment he looked in my direction. I saw surprise and recognition in his eyes.

"Julietta? Is it really you?" he asked.

I could hardly make myself speak. "It really is."

"I can't believe it. You have come back. After so long."

"That's right."

He turned to the men who were accompanying him. "Un momentino, per favore." He came up to me. "I cannot talk now," he said in a low voice.

"I am showing these men around our exhibition. They are important investors, you understand. But when can we meet? Are you free for dinner tonight? You are here with your aunt again?"

I had to smile. "No, no aunt this time."

There was a sparkle of amusement in his eyes. "That is good. Then we can go to dinner without getting approval, no? Where do you stay? I will pick you up at eight."

I looked around, conscious of the pairs of eyes on me. "I must check with my associate first."

"You are here on business?"

"I'm a schoolteacher, here with a party of girls. We're staying in a convent."

I went over to Miss Frobisher. "Would it be all right if I met this gentleman for dinner tonight? He's an old friend I knew when I was staying here with my aunt, and I haven't seen him in years."

"I suppose that would be all right, if he's an old friend of the family," Miss Frobisher said doubtfully, stressing the word "family." "But remember the convent rules."

"Yes, of course." I turned back to Leonardo. "I'd love to have dinner with you, but can it be a little earlier? The convent locks its doors at ten o'clock, and unfortunately there are bars on the windows."

"Dio mio!" He shook his head. "Why do you stay in such a place?"

"The school wanted to make sure the girls were suitably chaperoned and safe."

"Which convent is this?"

"Mater Domino in Santa Croce."

He shook his head again. "I pity you. Even the Pensione Regina would have been an improvement. But no matter. I can come for you?"

"I can meet you somewhere," I said, not wanting Miss Frobisher or the girls to witness our meeting. "There is no need. It is off the beaten path."

"Which path?" He looked confused.

"I only meant that it is out of the way. Inconvenient to get to. I can take the vaporetto easily."

"Very well. It may be a little rushed for me to make my way over to Santa Croce by seven thirty. Let us eat at the Danieli, then. You know it, of course. Just to the right of San Marco on the waterfront. Easy to get to. The San Zaccaria stop?"

I nodded. "Yes. That's no problem."

"I will see you in the lobby. Seven thirty then?"

"Yes. Lovely. Thank you." I could hear myself babbling.

He held out his hand, and when he took mine he squeezed it.

"Until this evening then." And he strode back to the waiting men.

"Your face is awfully red, miss," Sheila pointed out.

"It's rather hot today, isn't it?" I said. "I expect we could all do with a cool drink."

CHAPTER 10

Juliet, Venice, July 1938

When I prepared to dress for dinner that night, I realized I had nothing suitable to wear at an important restaurant. I had not brought a long dress with me, and in truth the only long dresses I possessed were from the time when it was hoped I'd go to balls and parties and meet a young man. The time before everything in my world changed. I had brought a royal-blue tea dress that once belonged to my mother, and a fringed silk shawl. The tea dress was mid-calf and had a lowish neck, so it would have to do. The shawl was cream coloured with a gold fleck, and the beads I had bought in Murano were blue and gold—perfect.

"This man is a friend of your family, then, Miss Browning?" Miss Frobisher asked as I sat putting on my one good pair of stockings.

"I met him when I was staying in Venice with my aunt," I replied, not looking up and not exactly answering the question. "He is from a most distinguished family. In fact his family home is one of those palaces we saw from the vaporetto."

117

"My word. Quite a catch, then."

I tried not to blush again, ignoring this statement. "You don't mind being left alone with the girls for an evening?"

Miss Frobisher smiled. "I think I can say that we are quite safe within these austere walls. No, please go and enjoy yourself. The Lord knows we don't have much opportunity for excitement these days. Especially a young woman like you deserves a night out."

"Thank you." I gave her a grateful smile. I hadn't realized she had a softer side.

"And who knows?" Miss Frobisher said with a sly nod. "Something might come of it."

At seven o'clock I made my way across the Ponte degli Scalzi to the vaporetto stop at the station and managed to squeeze aboard a Number One. "Signorina." A man in workman's overalls stepped aside to let me stand in a corner, out of the wind, where I would not be crushed. I gave him an appreciative smile. The sun was setting across the lagoon, tingeing the water with a pink glow. Seagulls were whirling above. Bells rang out from a distant church. I took a deep breath, trying to take it all in—almost wanting to trap it in a bottle, to bring out on rainy days at home when I sat in the silence of my mother's drawing room.

At San Zaccaria I alighted and walked

cautiously over the cobbles, unaccustomed to high-heeled shoes, in the direction of the Danieli Hotel. When I approached the pink marble building and stood outside, I almost lost my nerve. The doormen in their smart uniforms, elegantly dressed couples going in. This was a realm where I clearly didn't belong. But I reminded myself that Leo was there, waiting for me. I could hardly believe it.

"It was meant to be," I whispered. Out of the whole of Venice, he was at the Biennale at the same moment I was. It had to be fate. I took a deep breath and went up to the doors.

"Signorina?" A doorman stepped forward to intercept me. "You stay here?"

"No, I'm meeting someone for dinner," I said. "Signor Da Rossi."

"Ah. Welcome." His gaze implied that my dress didn't measure up, but he couldn't stand in the way of someone who was meeting Leo. As I entered the foyer, I tried not to gasp at my first impression of the hotel interior. It had formerly been a palace, and it still looked like one. Marble pillars supported the ceiling on one side of the room, while on the other side the atrium was several stories high with a red carpeted staircase that wound around the walls. It was luxury such as I had never seen before, and I hesitated, feeling like a country bumpkin, horribly out of place.

But then I saw Leo. He was standing at the bar,

conversing with another man, but he spotted me instantly and came over.

"So the nuns let you escape?" He was giving me that so-well-remembered wicked smile.

"They did. And the other teacher was nice enough to agree to look after the girls."

"Is it very primitive?"

"Not too bad. The food is simple, but good."

He took my arm. "I can assure you that the food here will be a lot better. Come. We go upstairs."

I allowed myself to be steered to a lift.

"Terrazzo," he said to the lift operator, and we rode upwards in silence. I was conscious of the closeness of his presence, and as if he sensed my feelings, he gave me a little smile. We came out to the restaurant—a huge room with mirrored walls, velvet chairs, sparkling glass and silver. Leo muttered something to the maître d', and we were led through the restaurant and out to the terrace beyond. Now I really did gasp. Before us was the most spectacular view of the lagoon, the waterfront, the island of San Giorgio, all glowing in the setting sun.

"Oh, it's beautiful" was all I could say.

Leo beamed as if he had arranged it for my benefit. "I thought you'd like it. My favourite view of the city," he said. "You don't mind to sit outside?"

"No, It's perfect." I couldn't take my eyes off the scene. A waiter pulled out a chair for me at a front table, and I sat. A menu was opened for me. I glanced up at Leo. "I'll let you choose," I said. "I'm afraid my experience of Italian cuisine is limited to spaghetti."

He nodded and spoke in rapid Italian to the waiter, who retreated with a little bow.

"We shall start with a Campari, and some olives and bread," he said. "To prepare the palate. And I believe when one is in Venice, one should eat from the sea. Is that all right with you?"

"As long as it's not the fritto misto that made my aunt ill," I replied.

He chuckled. "I can assure you that any fritto misto here would be better than the one that poisoned your aunt. But no, we shall not dine on fritto misto tonight. For our first course, I have ordered a marinated octopus, a puree of red prawns, and scallops. Also a plate of foie gras, because they do it so well here."

The Campari arrived. I tried not to react with surprise at the bitterness. Leo was smiling at me.

"You haven't changed at all," he said.

"Oh, I think I have," I replied.

"Well, maybe your eyes are a little wiser, and a little sadder, maybe?"

"Life doesn't always go in the direction we expect it to."

"But you were going to art academy. You were excited about it. Did you not go? Why are you not a famous artist, but teaching schoolgirls?"

"I did do my first year there," I said. "It was wonderful. Everything I had hoped for. But my father invested all his and my aunt's money, then lost it all in the Great Crash of '29. He had been in poor health, as I think I told you, since he was gassed in the trenches, and this was too much for him. He caught pneumonia and died soon after. I had to leave college and find a job to support my mother and little sister. I was lucky to be hired as an art mistress at a girls' school near our house. Mummy knew the headmistress from church. So I've been teaching art ever since. The pay isn't particularly good, but it's enough to keep our heads above water."

"What water is this?" He looked confused again.

I laughed. "Another silly English idiom. It means to survive, but only just. And anyway, I've been learning Italian in my spare time. Ora posso parlare un po' di italiano."

He beamed at me. "Molto bene! That means you must have meant to come back here if you took the trouble to study my language." He said the words in Italian.

"I had hoped to, one day," I replied, glad that I had understood him and could find the words.

I looked up as the dishes were put on the table. The waiter spooned a little of each on to my plate. The tastes were amazing—the octopus tentacle looked alarming, but was tender as butter, with a smoky, spicy taste. The prawns were salty, fresh, like eating sea foam. The scallops crisp, then melt-in-the-mouth. Then Leo spread some pâté on a square of Melba toast and held it up to my mouth. The gesture of feeding me was somehow so intimate that I shuddered.

"You don't like foie gras?"

"Oh, but I do," I insisted.

"You didn't write to me," he said, reverting to English now. "I was disappointed."

"I thought about it, but I didn't dare to," I replied. "I couldn't really believe you'd want to write back." I didn't add that my aunt had planted seeds of uncertainty in my head. I wasn't quite sure he was who he claimed to be. "Besides, you didn't give me your address."

"Palazzo Rossi would have found me," he replied with an almost arrogant grin. "I was expecting to see you one more time. Then we could have arranged such things."

"I didn't get a chance to write to you. The next morning, my aunt found out I had been with you and took me straight to Florence. She was very angry. She said that no respectable girl goes out without a chaperone in Italy, and therefore you were up to no good."

This made him laugh. "I have never been one to abide by the rules," he said. "And I behaved like a gentleman, did I not?"

"Almost," I said. "You did kiss me."

"Well, you deserved one little kiss." His eyes were flirting with me.

I didn't like to say that it was more than one little kiss.

A bottle of Dom Pérignon champagne was opened and poured.

Leo raised his glass to me. "A toast," he said, "to welcome you back to La Serenissima. May your days here always bring you joy."

I raised my own glass to him. The glasses clinked together. Leo was smiling at me. It was almost like a beautiful dream. I was certainly not going to pinch myself in case I woke up.

A seafood risotto followed, rich and creamy and studded with prawns, mussels, pieces of fish, mushrooms, peppers. We didn't talk much while we ate, but my head was buzzing. He was glad to see me again. He was clearly a successful man, judging by the cut of his suit and the way that the staff here treated him. For the first time in many years, a small bubble of happiness grew inside me.

The main course was a whole scorpion fish, and the waiter deboned it skilfully at our table.

"It looks terrifying," I said. "Are you sure you are not about to poison me?"

He laughed. Then he said, "So you finally came to the Biennale. What did you think?"

"I found it interesting—one could see the image each country wanted to convey of itself.

The German pavilion was particularly striking. Lots of happy peasants."

"Who are half starving and told by the Führer that it has to be guns, not butter, at home," he said. "I have to go to Germany quite often these days. Good for business, of course, but I can't wait to get home. When I cross the border into Switzerland, I give a big sigh of relief."

"Do you really think they intend to go to war?"

"When it suits them," he said. "They have been producing lots of tanks and guns, that is for sure. I think Herr Hitler wants to dominate the world. He is clearly mad, but nobody seems to notice." He glanced around before he added, "And here in Italy, we are going along the same path, I fear. My father often has dealings with Mussolini, and he says Il Duce dreams of another Roman empire, dominating the Mediterranean. He is talking just like Hitler, how we need expansion room for our growing population, how Corsica and Nice and Malta should all be Italian. And what's more, he has already been fighting a war in Abyssinia."

"I saw a lot of soldiers at the station when we arrived," I said.

"Yes, he's busy recruiting—fighting for the mother country, you know. Plenty of poor boys with no work eager to sign up. But do not worry—we are nowhere near equipped for war yet. You can breathe for a while."

"Let's not talk of sad things. I only have one

more night here, then we leave for Florence."

"Oh, that is too bad," he said. "I'm afraid I am not free tomorrow. I am still in charge of the businessmen tomorrow, and in the evening I must attend the birthday party of the father of my betrothed."

"What?" I hadn't meant to blurt out the word.

He frowned. "Did I not use the right word? My English is not so good these days. Lack of practice, you know. I meant the girl I am going to marry."

"Oh no, you used the right word," I said, trying to keep my face calm and expressionless. "So you are going to be married?"

He made a face. "In three weeks' time. At her family church of San Salvatore. A big wedding with half of Venice present."

"Congratulations." I managed to say the word.

He gave a rueful smile. "I think commiserations are more in order. I put it off for as long as possible. In Venice, men are not expected to marry until we turn thirty, and I am now thirty-two, so the pressure was mounting."

"You don't want to marry her?"

He shrugged. "I have no choice in the matter," he said. "We were promised to each other the moment she was born. She is seven years younger than I. My father owns a shipping company. Her father builds ships. And she has no brothers to inherit. Therefore a match made in heaven, from a business point of view."

"But you don't love her?"

His eyes met mine. "She is not a very loveable type of person. She has grown up as the only child of a very rich man. She has had everything she wanted, and is horribly spoiled. She has temper tantrums if she doesn't get her own way all the time." He sighed. "No, I do not think it will be an easy marriage for me."

"Then why go through with it? Is money so important?"

"Not money, necessarily, but the honour and status of my family. And the business opportunity with another powerful family, of course. The whole of Venice has known that we are to marry. If I backed out, it would mean disgrace to my family as well as financial hardship. I can't do that to my father." He picked up his glass, drained it in one gulp, then banged it down again. "So I will be the dutiful son and hope that one day she might grow up and come to love me."

He was looking at me, and I could see the longing in his eyes. "That was one reason why I was so attracted to you. Here you were—a young girl so fresh, so unspoiled, so excited by everything. And Bianca—I give her a large gold bracelet, and she barely glances at it before she tosses it into a drawer. The only thing she shows any affection for is her dog. She has a little Pekinese, and she showers it with kisses."

I had to smile. "You said that Venetians didn't go for pets."

"She is the exception. And you will be pleased to know that your kittens are now old cats with great-grandchildren of their own."

"Perhaps your fiancée will change when she has children," I said. I was proud of the way I kept my voice even.

"We shall see. But I have spoiled your dinner. I should not have mentioned her."

"No, I'm glad you did. Otherwise, I might have gone away with false hopes. Not that you ever would . . ." Now I stumbled over the words, feeling my cheeks flaming.

"In another world, you and I might have made a good couple," he said. "But you—why are you not married? You are a beautiful woman."

"I'm not beautiful," I said.

"You are striking. That red hair and those clear blue eyes and your perfectly English complexion. Men would certainly notice you."

I sighed. "I don't seem to have any way of meeting men in my life. I teach girls all day and go home to be with my mother. She is rather fragile, you know. She depends on me. I am all she has, and she still grieves for my father. My little sister, Winnie, married and went out to India with her husband last year."

"And you are the dutiful daughter who stayed?" He nodded with sympathy.

"The dutiful daughter and the dutiful son," I said.

"That's right. We make a good pair." He reached across the table and took my hand. It was all I could do not to snatch mine away. "I'm so glad we met again and had this meal together. I shall remember it."

"So shall I." I attempted a bright smile, impressed by my own acting ability.

"Will you come back next year?"

"I think that's highly unlikely," I said. "And even if I did, I couldn't see you again. You'll be a married man."

"Is a married man not allowed to take an old friend to dinner?"

"Not without his wife."

He sighed. "I do not think that Bianca would want to meet you. She seems to have a jealous streak in her nature. But I promise I would behave like a gentleman all evening."

He looked hopeful, but I shook my head. "If word got back to my school that I was cavorting with a married man, that would be the end for me. The headmistress is a very committed Christian in the worst sense of the word. And believe me, the girls would tell her and probably embellish. In fact I shall have to be careful about tonight— reaffirm that you are an old friend of the family."

The waiter appeared at the table. "Are you ready for dessert now?"

"Oh, I think that maybe we should just leave it . . . ," I began, but Leo waved my protest away.

He turned to the waiter. "We'll have the panna cotta with peaches, and coffee, limoncello." He turned back to me. "We will not talk of the future. We will enjoy this moment, sitting in this beautiful night."

I looked out across the lagoon. While we had been talking, night had fallen, and lights twinkled across the water. A moon had risen over the Giardini. *I may never see it again,* I thought. *I will never have another evening like this for as long as I live.*

Dessert and coffee were served. I ate mechanically, and while I admitted the flavours were delicious, I might have been eating sand. I glanced at my watch. "I should go," I said. "I don't know how frequently the vaporetto runs at this time of night. I can't risk being late and getting locked out."

"I have my boat at the private dock," he said. "I will whisk you there in a few minutes, so don't worry."

"Oh, but I don't want to inconvenience you, and we are not close to any canal."

"Julietta, I cannot let you ride alone on a public boat at this time of night," he said. "And do you not see that I want to make the most of this moment, just as much as you do? Come." He held out his hand to me and helped me to my feet. We rode down in silence in the lift, then out through the grand foyer to where his launch was moored at a small side canal. He cast loose, and we moved smoothly out into the black water of the lagoon. Along the *riva*—the busy waterfront, past the various palaces where lights sparkled on water. It felt like a dream that was going to fade at any moment. I watched Leo as he stood up to steer, taking in his profile, his strong jaw, the way the wind blew through his hair.

Just before the bridge and the station, he turned into a narrow side canal. "I think we can reach your convent from here," he said. "Let me see if I can find a place to tie up."

"You shouldn't come with me," I said. "Someone might see."

"What could be more suitable than a man making sure that a woman gets home safely?" He eased the boat to the side of the canal where there were some seaweed-covered steps and tied a rope to the railing before jumping out. He took my hand and helped me up. Then we walked into the darkness of a narrow alleyway. Only one street lamp shone at the far end. Leo still held firmly on to my hand.

"May I kiss you?" he asked. "I should like to say goodbye properly."

"I think saying goodbye properly would involve shaking hands." I gave a shaky laugh.

"Well then, I should like to say goodbye improperly." He laughed, too.

And without waiting, he took my chin in his fingers and drew me towards him. His kiss was incredibly gentle—the merest brushing of his lips against mine. He moved away, looking at me almost angrily, then suddenly grabbed my shoulders, pulled me close and kissed me again. This time his mouth was demanding, crushing against mine, and I didn't try to resist. I could feel his heart thudding against mine through the flimsy dress.

At last we broke apart.

"I should go. I can't be late." I found it hard to get the words out. I had a horrible suspicion that I might cry if this went on any longer, and I couldn't allow that to happen.

He nodded. "Yes, you should go. I should go, too. Goodbye, Julietta. I hope you have a beautiful life."

"And you too, Leo."

He nodded, reached out to put two fingers on to my lips, then walked away at a great pace.

"Back in good time, I see, Miss Browning," Miss Frobisher said as I entered the room.

"Yes."

"A successful evening, I hope?"

"Very pleasant. I heard the updates on his family, and the meal was delicious." I turned away and stared out of the window into the blackness of the street beyond.

CHAPTER 11

Caroline, England, October 2001

"I must need my head examined," Caroline muttered as she stared at the clothes she had laid out on her bed. She had taken holiday leave from work, moved in with her grandmother in time for Aunt Lettie's funeral, helped her to go through her great-aunt's things. In truth there was not much either of them wanted to keep. The clothes were hopelessly old-fashioned and too large for Granny. There were indeed a couple of good pieces of jewellery from Victorian times—a gold brooch studded with small diamonds and a heavy gold bracelet, neither of them Caroline's taste. "I suggest we sell these if you don't want them," Caroline said.

Granny smiled. "When do I ever have the opportunity to wear a gold brooch these days? No, let's put the money towards Teddy's education."

"I'm going to make sure Josh pays for that," Caroline said bitterly. "It's the least he can do." Then she paused, correcting herself. "No, I don't think I do want his help after all. I want to forget about him. I just want my son home with me.

That's the only thing . . ." She broke off, turning away from her grandmother to hide the tears.

"We'll get him back, don't you worry," Granny said gently.

"But how? What chance do I have against the millions of that Desiree person?"

"You may find that she is the type of person who will soon lose interest in another woman's child," Granny commented.

Caroline met her gaze and managed a little smile.

"Come on. Let's get his room ready for him," Granny said, taking Caroline's sleeve. "That will make you feel better."

It was good to be busy and positive. Teddy would love having more room to himself, to have a window that looked out on a bird feeder and a great big lawn to kick his football around. Then, at Granny's urging, Caroline had bought herself an air ticket to Venice. What did one pack for Venice in October? What if it rained all the time? And what would she do there after she'd seen the art galleries? She hadn't known that Great-Aunt Lettie had once studied art. Had she, too, dreamed of being an artist, just like Caroline? *What had I wanted?* she asked herself. She had been good at art in school but had gravitated towards fashion design, seeing it as a way to rebel against the strict rules of her boarding school—and a way of actually earning a living as an artist. After years of working on the periphery of the fashion industry, she had come to realize the whole thing was an underhanded attempt to force women to keep buying clothes. Fast fashion had taken over. Topshop, H&M, Primark. What was in would be out in a month.

Josh had loved haute couture, to be outlandish and to shock. She realized that he had been dying inside, trapped in high street fashion, designing white T-shirts, and she felt a flicker of understanding for him. But not enough to forgive him for what he had done.

"You'll see, Josh Grant," she muttered. "You'll see that I'm not sitting around waiting for you to jerk the strings and play me like a puppet. How will you feel when you know I've gone off to the Continent without you?"

She hoped this speech would give her some satisfaction, but it didn't really. She realized that she didn't care if Josh stayed with Desiree and her mansion in Beverly Hills. All she wanted was her son, safely home again with her.

She telephoned Josh to tell him she'd be going abroad for a while.

"What do you mean, 'going abroad'?" His voice sounded sharp, wary.

"Exactly what I said. I just wanted you to know that I'll be out of the country for a while, should you need to call me. Granny will have my phone number when I'm settled."

"Settled? You mean you're moving abroad?" Now he sounded quite rattled.

"No, just going on a mission," she said.

"You've become a Mormon or something?"

"There is no need to be facetious, Josh. I'm just taking some time off."

"How can you do that? Have you been laid off or something?"

"No. I took no summer holiday this year, remember? It didn't seem worth it without Teddy. So I'm taking it now. Actually, I'm going to Venice."

"You hated Venice."

"No, *you* hated Venice. I never got a chance to make up my mind. And I'm going now because I'm taking Aunt Lettie's ashes to scatter in the lagoon."

"Aunt Lettie died? You never told me."

"Well, she wasn't your aunt, was she? I didn't think you ever cared for my family. You made every excuse not to visit them."

"Of course I cared. I just didn't have much to say to a couple of old women."

"Anyway, Aunt Lettie died." There was a touch of anger in her voice. "I'm upset about it. I miss her, and I'm going to take her ashes to her favourite place."

"Venice was her favourite place? I never knew she travelled abroad."

"Neither did I until now."

"How long will you be gone?"

"I can't say." She was proud of herself. Of her efficient and distant manner, which clearly had him rattled. He wanted to think of her sitting at home, pining for him. Typical Josh.

"I'd like to speak to Teddy before I go."

"He's in the shower, I think."

"Then get him out. I said I want to speak to my son."

She heard an intake of breath, but soon a little voice came on the line. "Hi, Mummy! Guess what? I'm the only boy in the class who can already read. And I can do sums, too, and the others are just drawing baby pictures and things. The teacher said if I was staying here, she'd move me up to second grade."

"That's wonderful, darling. I always knew you were very smart. How are you?"

"I'm great. I can run faster than Autumn, and we may start soccer soon."

"I hope you'll be coming home to be with me and Granny soon," she said. "And we can look into playing football here."

"In the States football is different," he said. "They wear helmets. That looks cool, too. Am I too young for that?"

"Much too young. But you can play rugby one day. It's almost the same, isn't it?"

"I guess. I have to go. I've got a towel round me and I'm cold. See ya, Mom." And he hung up. He didn't sound like a person who was traumatized and not wanting to fly. He sounded like a normal little boy, but now already with a bit of an American accent. She wanted him home desperately.

She tried not to let the worrying thoughts overwhelm her as she packed. She folded a few random garments and put them into a carry-on bag. She wouldn't stay long. She added the keys and sketchbooks. Obviously, Great-Aunt Lettie had wanted her to do something with them, even if she had no idea what that was. She had taken to wearing her aunt's ring, which fit perfectly on her ring finger. It felt good to replace the one Josh had chosen for her. And last, she put in the small vial containing some of Aunt Lettie's ashes.

On October 8 she flew from Gatwick Airport to Marco Polo Airport in Venice. It had been a horrible day when they took off—swirling clouds, drizzling rain—and it was a joy to come out into brilliant sunshine at thirty thousand feet. But cloud had lain below them all the way across France, and they had bounced and juddered over the Alps. But then she had looked down and seen green hills below her. A long, shining lake. And the plane was making its descent.

"Please fasten your seat belts" came on the intercom. The plane dipped a wing, and there was her first view of the lagoon, although it was hardly a romantic one. Below them was some kind of fuel depot with great storage tanks and electric pylons.

They touched down, and soon she was standing in the entrance hall, trying to figure out how to get out to the island. There were water taxis, of course, if she didn't mind paying over a hundred euros. There was a bus that cost almost nothing, or there was a boat, but it took over an hour, stopping at various points around the lagoon. Now that she was so close, she had no wish to dally and opted for the bus. It passed by smallholdings of dying maize, country cottages and new developments of flats before it turned on to the causeway and crossed the lagoon. Caroline found she was holding her breath.

In the distance she could see the campanile of St Mark's rising above the rest of the buildings. But the area they passed was not known for its beauty: a giant parking garage, railway tracks, warehouses, cranes, large ships in a dock, and then they came to a halt in a small square where other buses were stationed. Caroline stepped into the warm sunshine and found herself wondering what to do next. Find a hotel, of course. She and Josh had stayed at an awful dump with a bathroom down the hall and a bed that squeaked when they moved, thus spoiling a good honeymoon night. She wanted better than that, but knew Venetian prices were high. There was an information booth in the square.

"Do you know of a Pensione Regina?" she asked. On the flight over, she had studied her aunt's sketchbooks. Aunt Lettie had done a sketch of it in 1928, and it seemed fitting to stay there.

The man behind the counter checked his list and shook his head. "Nothing by that name, signora."

"My aunt stayed there, long ago."

"How long ago?"

"That was in 1928."

This made him laugh. "Then I fear the proprietor would not still be alive."

"It had a lovely garden, by the look of it."

"Ah, then may I suggest the Pensione Accademia? It, too, has a lovely garden and is well situated."

He mentioned a price that was higher than she wanted to pay, but she told herself it was only for a week at the most. And Aunt Lettie had left a thousand pounds. The man telephoned ahead for her, and she caught a water bus at the nearby stop, having been advised by the man at the tourist kiosk to get herself a weekly pass. As they pulled away from the dock and headed up the Grand Canal, she tried to remember what she could of her last time in Venice. Josh and Caroline had stayed in a pokey little place right behind St Mark's Basilica. It had been horribly hot and muggy, with just a small fan in their room, and she and Josh had sweated as they made love. She shut off that memory rapidly, staring out of the boat. She had never travelled the length of the Grand Canal like this, watching it turning from mundane to glorious. It was late afternoon, and rosy sunlight turned the white marble to a delicate glowing pink. The Rialto Bridge appeared ahead of them, seeming to float above the water. Last time she had seen Venice, it had been crowded with tourists. Now, thanks to the time of year and the events in New York, the Grand Canal had an empty feel to it. In fact it took a while before she spotted her first gondola with two Chinese tourists taking photos. It rocked precariously as the water bus passed it, and the woman almost dropped her camera. Caroline caught snatches of the gondolier singing, slightly off-key, and found she was smiling. She was in Venice, it was lovely, and she was going to make the most of it, no matter how bad things had been lately. Then the thought crept into her head: *Teddy would love to see this. I must buy him a toy gondola. He can float it on Granny's goldfish pond.* The smile faded. "If he comes back," said the whisper in her head.

The pensione was more than perfect: a former palazzo, it had painted ceilings, there was a suit of armour in the salon, and her bedroom shutters opened on to a view of the Grand Canal. What's more, the windows looked on to the garden with statues and a fountain and great umbrellas under which breakfast would be served if it was not too cold. Caroline unpacked and lay on her bed listening to the sounds of the city: the pop-popping of diesel motors echoing back from the high walls that bordered the canal, the cooing of pigeons in the garden outside, the screech of a seagull, a shouted exchange in Italian. *Maybe Aunt Lettie wanted me to come here,* she thought, *because she wanted me to heal.*

Caroline took out her phone and tried to ring Josh—just in case something happened to Teddy and he needed to get in touch with her. But it seemed that she could not call America on her mobile. Feeling frustrated, she rang her grandmother. "All well so far," she said, giving her details of the pensione where she would be staying. "Would you mind telephoning Josh for me and letting him know I have arrived safely and he can call me at the hotel number? And give my love to Teddy, and tell him I'll see him soon . . ." Her voice trailed away, and she blinked back tears.

As darkness fell, she asked the woman at the reception desk for advice on restaurants.

"You like to eat fish?" the woman said.

Caroline nodded.

"Then you come out and follow the canal to the other side of Dorsoduro. It is called the Zattere.

Good fish restaurants on the waterfront there. Don't eat near St Mark's or Rialto. All tourist places."

Caroline thanked her and set off, following the narrow canal until it opened on to a broad waterway on which lights sparkled. There was obviously outdoor seating in summer, but on this chilly evening she went inside the first restaurant she came to. There were only two couples at other tables, and she was greeted warmly. There she ordered an antipasto of tomato and mozzarella and followed it with spaghetti with clam sauce. A split of Prosecco washed it down well, and she walked back, hearing her footsteps echoing from across the canal.

Back at the pensione, she ordered a coffee, and the proprietress sat beside her after she served it. "You come alone to Venice, on business?" she asked.

"No. A personal mission," Caroline answered. "My great-aunt just died. I am bringing her ashes to a place she loved."

"Ah." The woman smiled. "You care about *famiglia*. That is important."

"Are you from Venice?" Caroline asked.

"Of course. I was born here," she answered.

"Do you remember a pensione called Regina?"

The woman frowned. "The name sounds familiar, but no. I don't think I ever knew of such a pensione. Certainly not now."

Emboldened, Caroline went to her room and returned with the box. "My aunt also left me these. Do you have any idea what they might be?"

She tipped out the three keys and held them in her hand. The woman took them, one at a time, turning them over in her hand. "This big key could open any door in this city, I think. Every house has keys like this." She took the brass key with the winged lion on it. "This one has the symbol of our city. St Mark, yes? It could be a key for a special occasion? A festival maybe? I have not seen one like it, but you will find the lion of St Mark everywhere. On souvenirs, made in China, eh?" And she laughed.

Caroline took them back. It seemed hopeless. In her room she turned the keys over in her own hand. What did Aunt Lettie want her to do with them? Find out which door the big key would fit, when it might belong to any house in the city? Did it actually come from Venice? Why would Aunt Lettie have needed to open any door apart from the pensione where she stayed? And why was Venice so special to her?

"You are so annoying, Aunt Lettie," Caroline said out loud. "If you wanted me to do something here, why didn't you just write me a note? But if these things weren't special to you, why keep them in their own little box?"

None of it made sense. But she realized one thing: at least she had not been eaten up with worry about Teddy for a little while. Maybe that was what her great-aunt wanted.

CHAPTER 12

Caroline, Venice, October 9, 2001

The next morning dawned clear and bright, and bells awoke Caroline at first light. She opened the shutters and stood at the window, taking in the traffic on the Grand Canal, the pigeons strutting importantly across the garden. A gardener was raking the gravel into neat circles. Across the small side canal, someone was putting out bedding to air on a windowsill. Caroline gave a sigh of contentment, feeling the weeks of pent-up tension easing away. She showered and went down to breakfast.

"I should serve in the garden, signora?" the waiter asked. "It is maybe too cold?"

But Caroline chose to sit outside, enjoying a buffet of fresh fruits, cheeses, hard-boiled eggs, meats, yoghurt and freshly baked brioche. Then she put the two sketchbooks into her tote, along with the box of keys and a map of the city she had picked up at the tourist office, and set out, not exactly sure where she should be going. Clearly most of the important monuments were on the other side of the canal, and she crossed the Accademia Bridge, finding herself a little breathless by the time she negotiated all the steps up and then down. When she reached a piazza on the other side, she gave a little gasp of delight. Here was one of the first sketches, exactly as Aunt Lettie had drawn it in 1928. She continued, hoping she was making for St Mark's Square. From the map, she saw there was no direct route. She studied the front doors, then gave up, realizing that almost every house had an imposing door knocker and a lock that her key might well fit. *I can hardly go up and try all the doors I pass,* she thought, *and besides, how could Aunt Lettie have needed the key to one of these houses?*

When she spotted a used-book store, she went in and after much digging managed to find a guidebook from 1930. Yes, it listed the Pensione Regina. She bought the book and, after a bit of Italian language struggle, accompanied by much hand waving, asked the store clerk where the address might be. He sent her back to the Grand Canal, where she found that the Regina was now a private residence with a large padlock on the gate. What's more, it had been completely remodelled with sleek modern lines and big windows. None of her keys would fit that new white front door. A newspaper vendor in a nearby booth pointed at the villa. "Russians," he said with a sniff. "Rich Russians. Never here."

She came away, disappointed, then struck out for St Mark's again.

Along the way she recognized more sketches: a little side canal where gondolas were tied to poles, an interesting rooftop, a disused water pump. It made her feel warm inside to know that Aunt Lettie had come this way when she was a girl—and that so little had changed. A strange thought was growing in Caroline's head: *Maybe I should get a book and start sketching?* Was that what her great-aunt wanted from her—to become the artist that Aunt Lettie had never become? Did she not approve of fashion design? It was so hard to know.

She reached the waterfront and stood staring out across the lagoon to the island with a tall church tower on it. The beauty took her breath away as she walked past gardens towards the campanile of St Mark's. This time of year there were few tourists, and she examined the souvenir booths, wondering if any of them sold keys like the one she owned. But they didn't. The souvenirs were all cheap plastic Chinese monstrosities: snow globes, baseball caps, pens, fake daggers. The last time she had seen St Mark's Square, it was packed with tourists. Now it was almost empty, and Caroline treated herself to a coffee in one of the outdoor cafés. She sat staring at the improbable rooftop domes of the basilica, smiling as she examined eighteen-year-old Lettie's attempts and then the improvement ten years later. *She had talent,* Caroline thought.

Why did she not pursue it? Had the war drained all of her creativity? She could see the parallel in her own life, that a time of stress and tragedy takes away all but the will to survive. She finished her coffee, went to pay and was horrified to learn the price. The waiter shrugged. She was paying for the experience, not the coffee.

She decided to leave the interior of St Mark's for another time. She wasn't in the mood for anything religious. Granny was quite religious, but Aunt Lettie had never been. Caroline herself had found it impossible to pray after the recent events in her life and the horror of 9/11. So she went behind the basilica to where she could get a view of the Bridge of Sighs. After standing on the little bridge looking down the canal, she decided to head for the Rialto Bridge. Aunt Lettie had sketched that area several times. After a few wrong turns, she reached the Rialto, stopping along the way to look in the enticing little shops. There was a shop that just sold pens. And one that just sold marbled paper, or masks. How could they keep going? She wondered. Did lots of people in Venice buy marbled paper? Or puppets? *What a fascinating place,* she thought. *I'd like to get to know it better.*

That made her question just how long should she stay here. It was obvious that she'd never find the locks for her keys, if they came from Venice in the first place. So should she just concentrate on a suitable site to scatter Aunt Lettie's ashes? Was there a law against dumping ashes in a canal? Maybe she could hire a water taxi and scatter them into the lagoon. But not yet. After she realized she was hungry, she stopped to have a ham and cheese panino before resuming her quest. Aunt Lettie had sketched the market at the Rialto. Was there a place she particularly loved? It was hard to tell from the sketches. Caroline wondered about the young man in the first sketchbook. Well, no use looking for him. He wouldn't be alive now! Probably a gondolier who rowed her around. Some of them were rather good-looking!

Eventually she gave up and went back to the pensione, had a rest, then went out for an aperitif and dinner. She returned home, feeling rather mellow after more wine than she would normally have drunk. Opening her shutters, she stood at her window, staring out into the night. From the distance came the sound of laughter, a voice singing, the splash of oars. A whole city full of life that did not include her.

"What do you want of me, Aunt Lettie?" she asked into the darkness. "Why did you bring me here?" Why hadn't she written a simple little note before she died? She was always so calm, so practical. *Dear Caroline, I should like my ashes scattered in Venice, a city I once loved.* That would have been so easy. Instead she'd given an impossible quest with keys that would fit any lock in the city. "And a ring," Caroline reminded herself, glancing down at her hand. "And glass beads. And two sketchbooks."

The night wind had become cold, and Caroline closed the shutters again. Maybe tomorrow would reveal some answers.

The next morning the sparkling weather was replaced with dark clouds and the threat of rain. She ate breakfast inside as raindrops peppered the windows. There was no point in going out just to become wet and miserable. Maybe, if it cleared up, she might try her hand at sketching. She would need a book and a pen, of course. That would involve locating an art shop. When the weather cleared by mid-morning, she set off in the direction of St Mark's again, splashing through puddles, her collar turned up against the chilly wind. In spite of all the speciality shops, she didn't come across one that sold art supplies. Lunchtime was approaching, and she was feeling grumpy and hungry. Why was she wasting her time here? To prove she was as good an artist as Aunt Lettie? Would that give some meaning to being here?

When she reached St Mark's Square, she went into the Correr Museum and browsed in their shop. "Where could I find art supplies?" she asked the woman behind the counter and was directed to a street on the other side of the square.

"Under the famous clock and then turn right," the woman had told her.

It had started to rain again, and she kept to the colonnade until she found the clock. A crowd of tourists had gathered, and the bells high in the campanile rang out. *Oh, it must be noon, of course,* she thought, and paused to watch as the animated clock came to life. This put her in a better mood as she ducked through the archway to the Calle Larga San Marco behind the square. She passed a bank and realized she should probably get more money if coffees were going to be that expensive and restaurants wanted cash. As she went up to the ATM, she glanced up. It was a reputable bank, wasn't it? One couldn't be too careful. And then she froze. The sign that swung in the breeze said, "Banco San Marco," and the logo was exactly like the lion that crowned her key.

Feeling rather stupid, she forced herself to go inside. She asked who might speak English.

"Scusi," she said to a man sitting at a desk behind a glass partition, "but I have this key, and I wondered if it has anything to do with your bank?"

He took it, examined it and nodded. "Of course. It is an old key from one of our vaults. A very old key."

"I see. Thank you," she said. She couldn't think what else to say. As she turned away, the man called after her. "Do you not wish to access the vault now?" he asked.

She stared in surprise. "That key is still good? After all these years?"

"If the owner has paid the yearly sum, then the vault still works," he said. "Are you the owner?"

"It belonged to my great-aunt. She left it to me in her will."

He nodded. "Very well. Show me your identification, and we shall see. Follow me, please."

After checking that things were in order, he admitted her through a security gate and then a door and then down a flight of steps that could have led to a dungeon. Down below was cold and poorly lit. His key opened another door, and she found herself in a strongroom with a long wall of safe-deposit boxes. The man examined the number on her key and nodded. "Sì. The number is still here." He bent down, selected a small brass door amongst the many and put the key into the slot. The door slid open. Caroline's heart was beating rather fast as the man retrieved a long slim box from the vault.

"You wish time to examine?" he said. "There is a private room here."

He led her through, still carrying the box, and placed it on a table. Then he retired, shutting the door behind him. Caroline could hardly make her fingers work to open the catch on the box. It was stiff, and for a moment she thought it wouldn't move, but then it came open and she gave a little grunt of disappointment. Instead of money or jewellery, there was one piece of paper. It looked like some form of official document, signed and stamped in various colours. She closed the box and came out to find the man waiting for her.

"Thank you," she said. "There was just one thing inside. Can you please tell me what it is?"

His eyes scanned the page, then he looked up. "It seems to be the deed to a property," he said. "A lease, you say, sì?"

"To a property in Venice?"

He nodded.

"My aunt had a property in Venice?" she blurted out.

"The name of your aunt?"

"Juliet Browning."

"That is what it says on this document, yes."

She wondered if the lease was long expired. "The lease was for how long?"

He examined it again. "Ninety-nine years," he said. "The letter is dated nineteen thirty-nine."

"Gosh." Caroline blurted out the word. Rapid calculation indicated about forty more years. "And where is this, do you know?"

He examined the sheet of paper again. "It is Dorsoduro 1482." He looked up and, seeing her blank face, added, "In Venice we do not have street numbers. We have the number within the *sestiere*. Impossible for foreigners to find, I think. If you like, I can look it up for you." She followed him out of the vault and up to his desk, where he consulted a big book. "Ah, yes," he said. "Zattere al Saloni. On the other side of Dorsoduro. Do you know the Zattere? It is the waterfront."

"Yes," she said, "I ate there a couple of nights ago."

"Then you will find it. Zattere al Saloni, and it says the lease is for the apartment on the fourth floor."

Still, she hesitated. "But do you think this is still good? Still valid?"

He shrugged. "It has the stamps of the city. The deed was registered and notarized. So, unless your aunt sold it to someone else . . ."

Caroline came out into bright sunlight in a daze. Great-Aunt Lettie had a place in Venice. She had lived here. Why did Granny not know? Why did Aunt Lettie herself never talk about it, never go back to visit it? Perhaps she had taken the lease and then sold it to someone else when the war broke out. *Mustn't get too excited,* she thought. *Mustn't get my hopes up too much.*

From inside a trattoria came enticing smells— garlic and maybe frying fish. Lunchtime. She should eat something. But she was now too excited, too intrigued to eat. She had to see what this property looked like. The thought whispered inside her head that she might be the owner of a flat in Venice—a place she could come to on holiday and rent out the rest of the year. It was an enticing thought.

She stopped to consult her map. The Zattere was on the far side of Dorsoduro—a long walk away—and the sky was now darkening fast again; a great bank of grey clouds hung over distant hills. She checked the water bus routes on her map—yes, one of the routes went all the way around the island and stopped on the Zattere. It might take longer than walking, but it was also more appealing at the moment. She made her way past the campanile to the vaporetto stop, bought a ticket and was told which number to take. When it came, she was lucky enough to get a seat inside. The route took her the entire length of the Grand Canal, then past the unattractive area of the parking garage, the docks and finally around to the far side of Dorsoduro. As they went through open water, the sea became quite choppy, and she was glad to be inside, watching spray hit those standing on the deck. Finally, the boat stopped at the Zattere. She disembarked and started to walk along the waterfront. The first drops of rain were falling, and she cursed leaving her umbrella in the hotel room. At least she was wearing a mac.

The street here was called Zattere Ai Gesuati, and she passed a huge Jesuit church. She crossed a bridge over a side canal. This one was called the Ponti agli Incurabili—the incurables. Beyond it, the waterfront was bordered by what could be an institution of some sort. That was hardly reassuring. But as she went on, she noticed that the houses along the waterfront were tall, attractive buildings, even if some could do with sprucing up and a coat of fresh paint. This put a spring into her step, along with the wind that drove her from behind. She came to the section of the waterfront called the Zattere allo Spirito Santo—of the Holy Spirit—and finally, after another bridge, close to the tip of the island, there was the Al Saloni. She checked the numbers, which weren't in any kind of order, until she found herself standing outside a tall building with faded blue shutters at the windows. The pale cream stucco was peeling, showing the brickwork underneath, but there were steps leading to an impressive double front door. She double-checked the address. Yes, this was correct.

"Wow," she said. She reached into her purse and took out the big key. But as she touched the front door, it swung open. She stepped into a dark and gloomy foyer. Doors were open on either side, and there was a distinct smell of new paint. From the back of the building came the sound of hammering. The building was being renovated. A broad marble staircase curved upward. She had only gone up the first few steps when someone shouted, behind her.

"Signora? Cosa vuole? Dove sta andando?"

She turned back to see a man standing in the doorway. The collar of his overcoat had been turned up, and he had raindrops on his hair.

"I'm sorry," she said. "I'm afraid I don't speak Italian."

He came towards her, a finger raised in warning. "I ask what you do here. This is a private house. Not a place for tourists. There is nothing to see here. You must leave now."

"It's all right," she said. "I'm not a tourist. I have come to see the property I have just inherited."

"Then you are mistaken." He had reached her stair. She noticed now that he was tall, broad shouldered and quite good-looking, even if he was scowling at her. "This building belongs to the Da Rossi Corporation. As you can see, it is currently being renovated. It has been empty for many years. Let me escort you to the door."

"This is Dorsoduro 1482?"

"Yes. That is correct."

She fumbled in her purse and brought out the document. "Then it seems that I have a lease to the fourth floor."

"I don't think so." He took the paper from her and frowned again as he scrutinized it. "This cannot be. This building has always belonged to the Da Rossi family. They would not have leased to an outsider. A foreigner." He held up the paper to see it better in the poor light. "Whoever wrote this has made a mistake. There is no fourth floor. I have the plans to the building. It describes three floors and an *altana*."

"Altana?"

"Like a little shack on the roof. A shaded place to sit, yes?"

"I should like to see for myself," she said.

"Very well. If you insist. You will need strong legs." He looked amused now as he watched her walk ahead of him. The second flight wasn't quite so grand, and the third flight was a simple wooden stair going straight up. She reached the third-floor landing, trying not to let the man see she was breathing heavily. There were four doors, all shut.

He arrived beside her. "As you can see. No more staircase," he said triumphantly. He opened one door to show a room shrouded in dust sheets. Then another, to an empty space, and then a third. Finally, he opened a door to what seemed to be a large broom cupboard or anteroom. It was stacked with old bits of broken furniture, planks, a stepladder.

"I am sorry, but someone has played a joke on you, I think."

"Does the city of Venice waste its official stamps on jokes?" she asked. She insisted on walking into each of the rooms and had to admit that there was no staircase going up. Finally, she went into that big closet. It was dark inside, with a cobweb or two. She looked around, fighting off disappointment and frustration.

"I'm afraid you are right," she said at last. "But I don't understand . . ." As she examined the walls, she noticed what could have been the top of a door, behind a tabletop propped against the back wall. "Wait," she said.

He was already heading away again. He turned back.

"I think there is a door at the back of this closet." She moved a three-legged chair and then tried to shift the tabletop. "Help me move this," she said.

"Please be careful," he exclaimed. "It could be heavy, and we don't want . . ."

But she was already dragging it aside until a doorknob was visible.

"There, look," she said, pointing at it triumphantly.

He sprang forward to assist, and they moved the table aside.

"You see. There is a door." She gave him a jubilant grin.

"Yes, to more storage, I expect." He paused. "Oh no, un momento. It will probably be the way to the roof. To the altana mentioned in the plans." He tried to open it. It didn't move. "You see." He looked up with the hint of satisfaction. "I'm afraid the door no longer opens."

Caroline reached into her pocket and drew out the big key. "I wonder if this might help?" she said.

"What is this key?" he demanded. "Where did you get it?"

"My aunt left it to me." Her heart beating rapidly, she put the key into the lock and turned it. After a moment of resistance, she heard a satisfying click. The door opened slowly, with an ominous creaking sound. Ahead of her a steep, narrow staircase rose into complete darkness.

"To the roof, you see," the man said. "I don't think you should go up. These old roof terraces are dangerous."

But she had already started to climb the stairs. "Signora, it is not wise. I cannot be responsible . . . ," he called before he came after her, putting a restraining hand on her arm. Caroline shook herself free. There was a second door at the top. Caroline fumbled in the darkness but managed to find a keyhole. The key turned, the door opened, and instead of stepping out on to a roof, she was in a lovely room. Windows looked out across the island and St Mark's Basin. The furniture was covered in sheets, and a fine layer of dust lay on the window ledges.

The man had come into the room behind her. "Madonna!" he muttered.

CHAPTER 13

Juliet, Venice, July 2, 1939

I am back in Venice! I can hardly write the words, my heart is so full. Part of me feels that this is another dream come true, but again there is a nagging sliver of doubt as to whether I am doing the right thing by coming here. Of course I want to be here, and a whole year painting and learning and experiencing life? I can't imagine anything better. But to know he is here, to know he is married to someone else—I will have to learn to handle that.

I tell myself it is a big city. My chances of running into him are small. I am sure I will not move in the same circles as his family, certainly not shop in the same boutiques as his wife. And if I do meet him, I shall be polite and friendly and distant. I am a grown woman, no longer that naive and emotional girl. I have learned to shut away my feelings. I can handle this! When I think of it logically, I realize I only met the man twice. I don't really know him at all. He might be a wife beater, an alcoholic, a drug fiend, a womanizer. So to harbour feelings as if it was love between us is stupidly naive of me. Two pleasant but brief encounters, nothing more.

I still can't quite believe I'm here. As I write, I hear bells, echoing across the water. Pigeons are cooing on the rooftop opposite. Voices echo up from the narrow street below. It is as if I've never been away.

When Miss Huxtable summoned me to her study in May, I was sure I had done something wrong. Had I been too risqué in showing the girls a well-painted nude by an old master? Anyway, she asked me to sit down. Her face was relaxed and friendly. Then she told me that an anonymous benefactor had made a generous offer to the school. His granddaughters had been pupils here, apparently. He was a big admirer of Neville Chamberlain and a believer in peace at any cost. I had no idea where this could be leading or how it applied to me. Then she said, "He has proposed a bursary for one of my teachers to study abroad for a year. The hope is that the teacher will come back with a greater understanding of the world and an appreciation for other cultures, thus becoming a positive influence for world peace."

I had nodded, cautiously. "You are offering this chance to me?" I wondered why I had been selected, as the most junior member of the faculty.

She went on. She had naturally offered the chance to senior members of staff first. The French mistress, Miss Hayley, then the Latin mistress, Miss Rile, and Miss Frobisher. Even Miss Hartmann, who taught mathematics and science. All of them had turned it down. One didn't want to leave her aged mother, another thought it too dangerous at this unsettled time. Miss Frobisher had put it bluntly. She had seen quite enough of "abroad" after last summer's jaunt and had no wish to go again. Miss Hayley said she was too old a dog to learn new tricks.

And so it had come through the pecking order down to me. Not selected, but by default. The only one who hadn't refused.

"I know you have enjoyed your time in Venice," she said. "Miss Frobisher tells me you are quite taken with that city. And they do have a fine Academy of Fine Arts, so I'm told. Would you like to take this chance and study there for a year, with your expenses paid and your position here held open for you when you return?"

Only a fool would have turned that down. Of course I would take the chance. I was overwhelmed. But I reminded myself that I, too, had an aged mother. Did I dare to leave her for a year? And what about money? How would she survive if I was not earning my salary teaching?

"I'm afraid I can't go," I stammered out the words. "My mother relies on me, on my income, to survive."

"I gather the stipend will not be ungenerous. Maybe even more than the pitiful salary we can afford to pay you. So you may find you are better off than before." She paused. "And I believe your mother mentioned to me that you had an aunt who had hinted she'd like to come and live with you?"

"Yes. My aunt Hortensia. She did say her Austrian maid had left her to go home and it was impossible to find servants these days," I said hesitantly.

"Well, there you are. Perfect solution. Invite your aunt to stay while you are away."

It did seem to be a perfect solution. Aunt Hortensia still had a small private income, although not the fortune she once owned, and my mother wouldn't be alone. And Venice was not the ends of the Earth. If she needed me or fell ill, I could catch the next train home.

And so I accepted. Aunt Hortensia agreed with enthusiasm to come and stay. I wrote to the Accademia di Belle Arti—that same academy to which I had taken the girls only a year ago, where I had seen that group of students entering, laughing together without a care in the world. Would I fit in with such a crowd? I realized I was not eighteen again. I was almost thirty. I no longer had their hopeful belief that life would be full of opportunity.

I sent the academy a selection of my artwork and was accepted as a visiting overseas student. This meant I could take classes without being subject to the usual grades and exams.

To say Mummy was not too happy about the

whole thing was an understatement. She was most distressed about it.

"A whole year away? What about me?"

During the years after Daddy's death, she had come to rely on me heavily. She had never been an outgoing and confident person in the first place, and for years her life had been reduced to taking care of her husband and daughters, going to church and being part of the altar guild.

"You will have Aunt Hortensia to keep you company. And Mrs Bradley to keep the house looking nice."

"But this is so irresponsible," she said. "Why on earth would you need to study any more art? They seem to think you are competent enough to teach at the school."

"Mummy, it's a wonderful chance for me. You should be happy."

"Happy?" Her voice had risen to the point where she usually broke down in hysterics. "Out there amongst foreigners for a year? You—with no experience of the world. How will you cope? You've always lived at home. Had me to take care of you."

This was not strictly true, and I'd been taking care of her for a long time. "I'll cope."

"What will happen if Hitler decides to declare war? The whole world is in a state of chaos," she said. "That Mussolini is almost as bad. Didn't he just invade Abyssinia?"

"That's far away in Africa, Mummy. A colony. He's just colonizing, the way Britain and France have done for ages. And if war breaks out, I'll come home, of course," I said.

She clung to me then. "You're all I've got, darling," Mummy said. "I couldn't bear it if anything happened to you."

Amazingly, Aunt Hortensia was on my side. "You let her sister, Winnie, go all the way to India," she said. "Surely the girl deserves her chance at a life of her own. She has taken care of you all these years."

And grudgingly Mummy had to agree to that. I packed my meagre wardrobe, and at the beginning of July I headed for the station, laden with more than a little guilt.

And here I am. I arrived yesterday and took a room in a small hotel near the railway station, until I can find digs for the year. The room is about as spartan as that convent we stayed in last year. And not so clean, with lingering smells of smoke and sweat—also it's terribly noisy on the main thoroughfare from the train station to St Mark's. Not an encouraging arrival! The weather is hot and muggy. I lay on top of the bed last night, too uncomfortable to sleep. When I dared to open the shutters to let in any night breeze, I was immediately besieged by mosquitoes.

I was awoken at first light by a great cacophony

of church bells, reminding me forcefully that today is Sunday. So I'll not be able to accomplish anything today, even if I wanted to, except for reacquainting myself with the city. Tomorrow I'll visit the academy to find out more about where I shall be living and to plan a class schedule. Since I'm classified as a visiting student, not on the same academic schedule as Italian students, I may attend classes right away, which will be wonderful. I have brought few painting supplies with me, as I am sure the professors will have strong opinions on the only brushes/paints/canvases that are fit for painting. I seem to remember my professors at the Slade were most particular about which brushes and paints we used. The Slade. How long ago that seems now. Almost another lifetime away. This morning, I stared at myself in the speckled mirror that hung over the painted chest of drawers. Was I once that girl who gazed at the world with hopeful eyes, who had great plans for a beautiful future? I saw now the creases developing on my forehead. And Leo had commented last year that I had sad eyes.

I turned away. Leo. I must not think of him. Then I told myself there were other handsome Italians, and Leo had mentioned that men did not like to marry until after thirty. Maybe I'd meet someone here. An Italian artist. Marry. Live for the rest of my life in Venice.

So I did have a modicum of hope and fantasy left in my soul after all!

July 3, 1939

I am about to find a place to live! This morning, after a rather disappointing breakfast of bread, margarine and apricot jam, plus very watery coffee (making me appreciate the Pensione Regina and even the convent), I put on my grey dress with the broad white collar, my white hat trimmed with navy blue ribbon and white gloves and set out for the academy. The woman at the front office rattled off a string of Italian phrases so quickly at me that I couldn't understand a word.

"Could you please speak more slowly? I am just arrived from England," I said.

She sighed, as if speaking more slowly was a big inconvenience for her. "What do you want?" she asked. "The art gallery is next door. This is the school."

I explained, in carefully thought-out sentences, who I was and that I was a visiting student, wishing to enrol. Again she looked at me as if she couldn't believe that a woman of my age would be a student, but then sent me upstairs to the registrar's office. I went up the flight of broad marble steps, savouring the touch of my hand on the cool marble banister. The woman in the registrar's office was more friendly. She was assigned to help foreign students, she said. She spoke slowly and clearly and had a little English for when I didn't understand. She handed me a list of classes and told me that I could choose up to three. It was like looking at a delicious menu in a top restaurant. History of Painting. Drawing and Painting the Nude. Workshop on Colour. Painters of the Sixteenth Century. Working with Clay. Metal Sculpture.

I would like to have taken every one but decided that realistically I should not take sculpture classes since I had no experience in that medium. I therefore selected Drawing and Painting the Nude, which was something I would have done in my second year at the Slade, Beginning Oil Painting and Painting with Freedom of Expression. Maybe I'd learn to be a Picasso after all!

Then we moved on to finding a place for me to live. I was lucky, she told me. Usually Venice is packed at this time of year with visiting tourists. But this year so many people are afraid to travel, especially visitors from England, now that Italy has signed the non-aggression pact with Germany. "Let us hope there is no war," she added. "We lived through the last one, did we not? How many men died needlessly, and for what? Nothing changed except we all became poorer and lost hope."

I nodded. I wanted to say that my father was gassed, but the words were not in my vocabulary and I didn't want to admit defeat and switch to English.

She checked a ledger on her desk and wrote down several addresses. "Here are landladies who rent to students," she said. "Many do not want to risk having students in their house because they drink and destroy the furniture, but I do not think you look like the type to behave in that way."

I laughed. "I can assure you I have never been that way, even when I was a student in London years ago."

I stared down at the list she had written for me. It was hard to read handwriting that was so different from my own. I looked up again. "Can you advise me which of these might be most suitable? I'm afraid I don't know the addresses."

She checked them with me. "That is in Cannaregio. Too far to walk and not near a vaporetto stop. And besides, it's the Jewish Quarter. Not that I have anything against Jews personally, but you'd feel out of place." She waited to see agreement in my face. "And the next—oh, you do not want the ground floor."

"Why not?"

"*Acqua alta*, my dear."

I understood the words but not their meaning. High water?

"In the winter, the city sometimes floods when

171

high tides and heavy rain come at the same time. We are used to it, but you do not want to awake one morning to find your bed floating."

"Oh dear, absolutely not," I said hastily.

She ran her finger down the page. "Ah, this might be the one," she said. "It is just across the bridge from here. In the sestiere of St Mark's. Just off the piazza of Santo Stefano."

"I know where that is," I said. "I once stayed at the Pensione Regina, and I sketched in that square. It's really close."

"And relatively quiet," she said. "The rent includes breakfast and dinner, so it seems quite reasonable. Of course, not all landladies are agreeable. You would have to get a feel for yourself of whether you would be comfortable there."

"Yes," I said.

She found two others if the first didn't work. Both in Dorsoduro, the sestiere where the accademia is situated. "This is very much a quarter of working people and students," she said. "The institute of commerce and economics is nearby, you see. The Ca' Foscari. So it tends to be lively, especially around the Campo Santa Margherita. Lots of bars and cafés there. If you'd prefer a livelier scene, then maybe . . ."

"No thank you," I said. "I'd prefer quiet. I'm not used to noise. I've led a rather sheltered life teaching at a girls' school."

"I understand," she said. "And most of the students are not as . . . mature."

She had meant to say "old." Compared to the other students, I was old. I didn't even know what I was doing thinking I could go back to school again to study art. What did I hope to achieve by it, except for living for a year in the city of my fantasy? I doubted I'd ever be a good enough painter to sell my work, and these days who had money for paintings? Who even appreciated art?

I fought down the negative feelings, took the three addresses she had written out for me and went in search of my future home. I counted the fifty steps up the Accademia Bridge. At the top I paused, a little out of breath, and admired the view. In one direction the Grand Canal opened on to the lagoon, with grand palazzos on one side and the graceful dome of Santa Maria della Salute on the other. And when I crossed to the other side of the bridge and turned around, there was the curve of the canal with its white marble and pink palaces, its busy traffic of gondolas vying with vaporetti and occasional barges. I gave a great sigh. I was here. This was my new home. Whatever happened in the future, no one could take this away from me. I was going to make the most of every second!

CHAPTER 14

Juliet, Venice, July 3, 1939

I am trying the address near Santo Stefano Church first, for the reason that it is so close to the accademia. Having had to rise at crack of dawn for all these years, it would be a luxury to get up late and stroll to my nine o'clock class!

I passed a lovely white palazzo on my right and came to the long, open space that was the Campo Santo Stefano, where I remembered sitting and sketching long ago on the day that had ended with my falling into the canal. This was the real Venice, I thought. There were women pausing to talk with shopping baskets on their arm, small children running squealing around the fountain, pigeons strutting hopefully, a cat slinking out of an alleyway. I watched a woman filling a water jug from the pump, reminding me that not all homes had running water yet. But it had a good, family feel to it. It took me a while and asking several times to find the address, because, as I had discovered in Venice, one can't get there from here. The route involved going down to the church, doubling back, crossing a canal and ending up almost where I had started, not too far from the Grand Canal. The building wasn't exactly prepossessing—crumbling pink paint revealing brickwork beneath, faded blue shutters on the windows. But there were geraniums in window boxes as well as washing flapping on a line above. I saw then that there were four doorbells. It was flats, then. I rang the one with the name Martinelli beside it.

"Sì? Cosa vuoi?" came a sharp voice. "What do you want?"

In my stumbling Italian, I explained I was a student from England who'd come about the room.

"Allora. Come up," she said, and the door was buzzed open to a central stairwell. A flight of stone steps rose ahead of me, lit, it seems, by a skylight somewhere at the top of the building. Signora Martinelli was on the third floor, and it appeared there was no lift. At least it would be good for my legs! I started up, past the first floor, past the second, where a dog barked at me from inside a door, and finally to the third, where I found myself disgustingly out of breath. I paused to collect myself before I tapped timidly at the door. It was opened by a woman who looked as alarming as that nun had the year before. She was dressed entirely in black, her iron-grey hair scraped back severely into a bun. She was a large woman with meaty arms. These were now folded across an ample bosom as she eyed me up and down.

"You are not what I expected," she said. "You don't look like a student."

"No, I'm older than most," I said. "I have been a schoolteacher, but I have been given the chance to renew my art studies at the accademia for a year."

"Well, I don't expect you'll make as much mess and noise as most of the ones who show up on my doorstep," she said. "You'd better come in. I am Signora Martinelli, and you are?"

"Signorina Browning," I said.

"Not married? Never married?"

"No. Never married."

She sniffed, and I couldn't decide if being never married was a good thing or a bad one. She led me through from a square hallway to a living room. Whereas my recent experience had been of spartan surroundings, this room was the opposite: velvet drapes, swathes and swags, overstuffed chairs, knick-knacks on every shelf and table. It took me a moment to realize that the knick-knacks were all of a religious nature: statues of saints, crucifixes, a painting of Jesus with the little children, with a rosary draped over it. I noticed then that the one adornment on her person was a large silver cross.

"Sit down." She pointed to one of the armchairs. It looked so soft and full of crocheted pillows that I wondered if I'd ever be able to get out again, but I sat, obediently. Almost immediately I let out a little gasp of alarm as something brushed against the back of my neck.

"Don't mind him. That's only Bruno," she said as a large grey cat walked along the arm of the chair, rubbing against me. "He is just checking you over. If he takes to you, then I can decide that you are all right. He is a good judge of character." She was still studying me. "You like cats?"

I wasn't going to say that Aunt Hortensia had an absolutely vile cat that she had brought to live with my mother. It hid under chairs and pounced on to ankles as we went past and was making my mother's dog miserable.

"I haven't had much to do with them," I said, erring on the side of tact. "My mother has a dog who is very sweet."

"Well, he seems to like you. I'll show you to your room."

I struggled to get up again, and she led me down a dark hallway to a room at the end. It was also a little overdecorated but quite acceptable. A bed with a red velvet coverlet, a huge wardrobe and matching mahogany chest of drawers, and in the window a desk and chair. I went over to it, and my heart gave a little leap. I could actually see a sliver of the Grand Canal from here!

"Oh yes," I said. "It will suit me very well."

She nodded, then beckoned me to follow her. "The bathroom is across the hall."

It contained an enormous claw-footed tub

as well as a basin. The lavatory was next door.

"There will be only you and me," she said, "but please do not fill the bath too full. And I should instruct you on the geyser." She indicated a contraption over the bath. "The hot tap needs to be turned on very slowly at first until the flame has lit, and then you can turn it up. If you turn too fast, it explodes. Dangerous."

It certainly did sound dangerous.

I looked around. "How is the flat heated?"

"There is a boiler. With coal. It heats the radiators."

"How do you get coal up here?" I asked, blurting out the question before I realized it was probably not polite.

"We have a pulley," she says. "Rubbish goes down on the pulley. Groceries and coal come up. It works very well." And she actually smiled. "The boiler also heats the radiator in your room. It gets very cold here in winter. You are used to the cold in your country?"

"Oh yes," I said. "It can get very cold in England. And wet, too."

"Here also." She led me back to the living room, where the cat had taken over the armchair. I stood.

"I provide breakfast and an evening meal," she said. "At what hour do you require breakfast?"

"Whenever it is convenient," I said. "My first class will be at nine o'clock."

"I go to Mass at six every morning," she said. "Do you wish to accompany me? To San Maurizio, not Santo Stefano. I do not like the priest there. Too liberal. He forgives sins too easily. Three Hail Marys—what kind of penance is that?"

I had no idea what kind of penance it was. A thought suddenly occurred to her. "You are not Catholic?"

"No, I'm Church of England."

"Dio mio," she muttered. "Still, I suppose we all worship the same God, don't we?"

I nodded. In truth, I had never had too much to do with God. I attended prayers every morning at school. I went to church with my mother most Sundays, but it all seemed like a sham, a show. I felt that God hadn't actually done much for me. He had taken my father, taken my chance at a happy life.

"I must take you to Mass with me when we have a festival. Then you will see what you miss. The Festival of Redentore comes up at the end of this month. We cross the canal to the church of the Redentore, carrying candles. It is very beautiful."

"I'd like to see it," I said, and she gave an approving smile.

"So breakfast at eight, and the evening meal at eight also? Here we take our big meal in the middle of the day, so in the evening it is something simple like a soup or a salad. That is satisfactory for you?"

"Yes, perfectly satisfactory."

She named the rent she was asking for, but my mental conversion of lire wasn't yet good enough to know if it was reasonable or not. How many lire to the pound? About a hundred, correct? I thought it seemed quite reasonable, not having had to rent a room in my life before.

"And I'm sure I don't need to mention my house rules to you," she said. "No smoking, no drinking and no men in your room. But then, you are not an undisciplined young person. I expect you to know how to behave like a lady."

"Of course," I said. "I don't expect I will have much in common with the other students. I am so much older."

"I lock my door at ten, unless you tell me in advance that you will be late," she said.

And immediately my thoughts went back to the convent: they locked the door at ten, so we'd had to have dinner early, and in the darkness of the alleyway near that convent he had kissed me. I could still remember the feel of his mouth against mine, his chest thudding against mine.

"No men in my room," I muttered to myself after the signora had gone.

CHAPTER 15

Juliet, Venice, July 5, 1939

I am safely installed in my new room. I enjoy the sun shining in the morning, the pigeons cooing on the ledge outside my window and the glimpse between buildings of the Grand Canal. Bruno the cat comes to visit often, curious about all of my belongings. *So at least one person in Venice has a pet cat,* I think. *You were wrong, Leo.* And I wonder about my kittens. Leo said they were great-grandparents by now. I do hope he spoke the truth and they were not all drowned the moment my back was turned. I try not to think about him, but I do find myself glancing in the direction of the Palazzo Rossi when I pass that way.

I have been to the accademia and obtained a list of supplies for my classes. Gosh, they will be expensive, I fear, but my stipend is quite generous, and I'm not likely to spend on frivolous things like drink—although wine is cheaper here than water. Isn't that ridiculous?

And I am rediscovering Venice, free to wander and explore on my own for the first time. I think this is a city one could explore forever and still find new things. After Signora Martinelli mentioned coal and rubbish being taken up and down by a pulley, I have noticed that this is the normal delivery method for many things. A basket comes down, and a newspaper and bottle of milk go up in the early morning. Bottles of mineral water, the grocery shopping. One has to be careful not to be hit by a descending basket!

July 5, later in the day

Something really strange just happened.

I went out to buy my supplies. There is apparently a good art shop close to the Rialto Bridge. I had bought paints, brushes, a sketch-book and charcoal and was lingering on the bridge, admiring the beautiful things in the window of a jewellery store, when I heard a voice inside saying, "Grazie mille, Signora Da Rossi."

I spun around sharply and saw a stunningly beautiful and fashionable woman coming out of the shop. She was wearing a scarlet halter top with a pair of wide white linen trousers. Her dark hair was tied up with a red ribbon, and her mouth was a gash of scarlet lipstick. Could there be more than one Signora Da Rossi, or was this Leo's wife, Bianca? If so, I didn't think he had much to complain about.

I followed her with my gaze as she went down the stone steps of the bridge. At the bottom, a man stepped out of the shadows. A tall, dark man, and for a moment my heart did a little flip that it was Leo. But it wasn't. It was another man altogether. She opened the box she was carrying and displayed what was inside. He nodded approval, then took out the contents—a heavy gold necklace—and she turned her back to him as he put it around her neck. She turned again, showing off the necklace. He nodded approval again, and she stepped forward, raising her face to be kissed. He kissed her, stroked her cheek, then let his hand slide down over one bare shoulder before she walked away in one direction and he in the other.

I tried to process what I had seen. Was this really Leo's wife? And in that case, who was the man? Perhaps a relative, but the way he had looked at her made me think that he was more likely to be a lover. Did Leo know? Did he care? I felt hot and angry inside that she had been given the prize I so desired and clearly didn't care about him. If she behaved so openly in a town like Venice, surely Leo must know that she was unfaithful.

I tried to think charitably. Perhaps she wasn't actually unfaithful but just liked other men adoring her, spoiling her. Leo had said, after all, that she was a spoiled child. I walked on, but the anger wouldn't go away. Also the realization that Venice was such a small place. If I had bumped into her on one of my first days here, surely it couldn't be too long before I ran into him. How would I handle it? Would I have the strength and resolve to smile politely and keep on walking? I had to.

After that, the whole day was soured for me. I had planned to shop at the market, to buy flowers for my room, perhaps a small bouquet for my landlady, but I couldn't bring myself to buy anything that would bring joy or beauty. Instead I stopped in a small coffee shop and had a coffee and a couple of open-faced sandwiches. I realized in the future I should eat a more substantial lunch, as the evening meal chez Signora Martinelli was not going to be large. Last night it was a hard-boiled egg sliced with some tomatoes, mozzarella cheese and coarse bread. It seems that meat is an expensive luxury in Italy, but fish is plentiful and cheap. I dropped hints that I love fish, but she said it makes the place smell. I think I'll be eating my fish out at lunchtime.

I carried my supplies home and got a disapproving look from the signora. "I hope there will not be any paint used on these premises," she said.

Oh dear. She's not the warmest of people, and I find myself thinking of my comfortable room at home, the generous meals cooked by my mother. I've only been here three days—I can't possibly be homesick already. Seeing Bianca Da Rossi must have really upset me. To know that she is beautiful was bad enough. To know that she doesn't seem to care a fig for Leo is even worse. I tell myself it is none of my concern. I must get on with my life.

July 6

Today was my first day of classes. Signora Martinelli boiled me an egg for breakfast, as if she sensed this was a momentous occasion for me. She made it clear that eggs were a luxury usually reserved for Sundays. It was a clear and windy day, which was good, as the canals tend to smell bad when the air is still. I tucked my portfolio under my arm, and off I went to meet my destiny! That sounds a little dramatic, doesn't it? But that's how it felt. My chance to escape from the mundane, the routine, the boring, and to discover my true potential.

My first class was the one I'd been dreading but looking forward to the most. The one on painting with freedom of expression. I went up the marble staircase, then up a less dramatic staircase to the next level and into a room that smelled of turpentine and oil paints. It was a lovely space, as befits a former palace, with a high vaulted ceiling and tall windows that let in slanted light. I lowered my gaze to see it was already more than half full. Students had set up easels and laid out supplies. I slunk into an unoccupied corner.

Nobody seemed to notice me. I looked around. Some of them seemed incredibly young—no older than the girls I'd been teaching. Certainly nobody of my age. I took out my sketchbook, tentatively arranged pencils, charcoal, paints, brushes. I wasn't sure that we'd be painting on the first day but noticed the sink by the wall with lots of paint pots.

A clock somewhere nearby chimed nine, and the professor swept in, on the last stroke of the chime. He was a dramatic-looking middle-aged man with grey hair that curled over his collar, and he wore an open-necked red shirt.

"Good morning, ladies and gentlemen," he said. "I am Professore Corsetti. Some of you are familiar faces, and some are new to me. I look forward to getting to know you and your work."

That much I understood. He was speaking slowly and clearly.

"Today, for your first assignment, I want you to make a composition that includes a face, an orange and a church. You have thirty minutes to sketch it out. Begin."

That was that. A face, an orange and a church. What did that mean? I glanced at other students. They were already sketching—big, bold strokes of charcoal across the page. I took my charcoal and tentatively drew the outline of a church, then in the doorway a person, standing half in shadow so that just the face was visible, as was a hand, holding an orange. At least I knew a bit about perspective, I decided, peeking at the sketches ahead of me that seemed childishly simple in their depiction. Professor Corsetti walked around the room, grunting occasionally, nodding infrequently. When he came to me, he paused.

"You are new?" he asked.

"Sì, Professore. I am just arrived from England," I said.

"And in England one does everything correctly, no?" He shook his head. "So you draw me a nice correct church, a nicely proportioned figure and a nice round orange. Now I want you to forget everything you have learned and turn them all into one design. Incorporate the church into the face, put the face on an orange—whatever you like, but they should all be part of one glorious whole. *Capisce*?"

"I'll try," I ventured.

He left me to stumble through an orange with a surprised face on it, placed on the altar of a church. When the professor returned, he had to chuckle.

"Now you attempt to say something," he said. "It is progress."

At the end of class, we had to bring up our work. Some of them were so experimental that it was hard to see what they were—some shocking and disturbing. When it was my turn, the professor asked me, "What are you telling the world by putting that orange on the altar, eh?"

I had no idea. "That religion should not be separate from ordinary life?" I suggested, blurting out the first words that came into my head.

He nodded. "I think you have made a step in the right direction today."

As he dismissed the class, he called out certain names. Mine was amongst them. We came up to his desk.

"You are the visiting students from abroad," he said. "I should like to invite you, my foreign visitors, to a small soirée at my house tonight to make you feel welcome in Venice. Eight o'clock. It's the third floor, number 314, on the Fondamenta del Forner in San Polo, not far from the Frari. You know the Frari?"

I didn't. Neither did a couple of the others.

"It's the big church called Santa Maria Gloriosa—but to us it's the Frari," the professor said. "You will learn in Venice nobody calls anything by its real name. The vaporetti stop is San Toma. If you are coming from the other side of the Grand Canal, you can cross by the traghetto at San Toma. All right. Good. See you tonight. Come hungry. My wife likes to cook." He glanced at his watch. "And now I must run. Urgent appointment."

One of the Italian students had been lingering at a nearby desk, putting away his painting supplies. "What he means is that he has an urgent need for *un'ombra*," he said.

"What is that?" one of my fellow foreigners asked.

"A tradition in this city. The drink before luncheon. A coffee with a splash of something, or a grappa. You will find that most morning classes end very promptly for that reason." He gave us a grin, hoisted his bag on to his shoulder, picked up his easel and went.

After he had gone we stood there, checking each other out. There were five of us.

"Did everyone else understand what he said?" a large, chubby boy asked. He was wearing earnest horn-rimmed spectacles and was dressed in clothes that didn't really go together. And from his stumbling pronunciation, I could tell he was American. "My Italian is not too good. How did he say we can find his house?"

"Do you not know where San Polo is?" a girl standing next to me asked, giving him a withering look. She was svelte and olive-skinned, dressed in a simple black dress that looked somehow stunning on her. "It is the quarter next to Dorsoduro on this side of the canal. You can walk from the academy, if you don't get lost. Do you not have a map?"

Her Italian sounded really good, fluid and fluent. I studied her with more than a little envy.

"Yes, but it's no use," the American said in

Italian. "None of the streets go where you think they will, and they keep changing names." Actually he said, "Not help me. Street not going where I want and change names." Or something along those lines. His pronunciation was so bad that it was hard to decipher.

There were nods of agreement from the other students.

"It is a most disorganized city," a tall, fair boy said. "And dirty, too. I do not think they clean the canals very often."

"They say the tide takes things away eventually," the man beside the American said with a Gallic shrug. He was quite attractive, with unruly dark hair, not unlike Leo's, and wearing an open-necked white shirt. French, I decided, and not as young as the others. But then, not as old as I. None of them were. "I am Gaston. I am from Marseilles. And you are?" He turned to me.

"Juliet. From England," I said. I did not intend to be Lettie while I was away from home.

"Juliet—such a romantic name." He gave me a little grin. The name did sound romantic the way he pronounced it, and it reminded me that Leo had called me Julietta.

"I should watch this one," the other woman said, addressing me. "The French are notorious flirts." But I saw the look she flashed at him. Also a flirt, I thought.

"I am Imelda Gonzales, from Madrid," she

said. "My family has been living in Biarritz, in France, since the civil war. Such a terrible time. My brother was killed."

"At least it is now over, and the right side won," the blonde young man said. "General Franco has restored peace and order to his country."

"You think so?" Imelda said. "At what cost?"

"But you could not have wanted the communists to have gained control?"

"Perhaps I would," she said. "My father had to flee because he was a professor at the university and had expressed more . . . democratic views. When it is communist versus fascist, there is no place for middle ground. One has to choose." She stared hard at the blonde boy. "I suppose you must be from Germany and think that Herr Hitler is wonderful."

"I am Franz. Franz Halstadt." The blonde boy clicked his heels and gave a sharp little bow. "But I am from Austria. I am pleased to make your acquaintance."

"And are you happy that Germany has invaded your country?" Imelda challenged.

"We are all Germans. We are glad the trams now run on schedule," he said with a little smile. "I do not think that life is very different for the average Austrian."

"Only for Austrian Jews," the American said. I was surprised he had understood enough of the conversation to contribute.

"Children, let us not argue in our first meeting," Gaston said. "Let us be a small League of Nations, yes?"

"Agreed. Good idea. I'm all in favour of that." The American nodded fiercely.

"And what is your name?" Imelda asked him.

"Henry Dabney. From Boston," he said, holding out his hand to her before he turned to me. "And really glad to see there's someone else here who speaks English. My Italian is so bad. I took a crash course, but I've forgotten everything I've learned."

"You'll soon become more fluent when you have to speak the language every day," I said.

"How is it that you speak it quite well?" Gaston asked. "In my experience, the British are hopeless at languages. Have you lived here before?"

"No, only visited. But I have been studying at home in the hope of returning here." I paused, feeling them eyeing me with interest. "I had to interrupt my art studies when my father died, so I have been teaching at a girls' school and was given the chance to spend a year in Europe. So I have taken that chance, even if we do live under the threat of war."

"Oh, I don't think war will break out here for a while," the Frenchman said. "I hear that Mussolini has set his timetable for conquering the Mediterranean. He does not think he will be ready for at least a couple of years."

"He wants to conquer the Mediterranean?" Henry asked. "A new Roman empire?"

"Exactly," the Frenchman said. "He thinks the islands should belong to Italy, so he will work his way through them. First Crete, then Cyprus, then Malta. He'd really like Malta, but the British own it and they intend to keep it." He looked back at me. "But as I say, he needs to build up his supply of armaments first, and train an army that can fight against harder targets than a few Abyssinian tribesmen with no guns."

The Spanish girl shook her head. "He has been boasting so much about that victory. Have you heard him? 'Our great success is just the start of capturing the whole African continent.' He really does have big ideas. And all those poor boys called up into the army. None of them want to fight. What Italian enjoys fighting, eh? Like the French, they enjoy making love more." And her eyes challenged Gaston again.

Henry had clearly lost most of this conversation. I found it hard to keep up myself, with Italian being spoken in strange accents. Imelda was really fluent; so was Gaston. Franz had been almost silent until now, so I couldn't tell how much he was following. I looked from one to the other. My fellow students, with whom I'd be spending the next year. Would they become friends? Would I even make a friend while I was here? And I realized that since art school in England I had not had any real friends. My former school friends had married and were busy with children and entertaining. I had never really bonded closely with the girls at college, who all seemed more bohemian, more adventurous than I, living in digs in London and going to pubs and clubs. Since then . . . well, the other schoolmistresses were so much older, as were most people in our village. I had enjoyed the company of my sister, Winnie, until she met a young man, married him, and went off to India. Now I was out of the habit of confiding in anyone apart from my mother . . . and I never shared my innermost thoughts with her. She never knew about Leo. She would not have approved. She had always been rigid in her beliefs of right and wrong, having been brought up a Baptist and only switching to C of E when she married Daddy and moved up in status.

A bell rang. "We must not be late for our next class," Franz said. "A good impression on the first day, *ja*?"

"See you tonight, then," Gaston said.

"If Henry doesn't get lost." Imelda shot him an amused look.

I felt hopeful as I went towards my figure drawing class. It was exciting to be part of a group of people—people who teased and expressed opinions and had different views. I felt as if I had just emerged from a cocoon.

CHAPTER 16

Juliet, Venice, late evening, July 6, 1939

I have just returned from Professor Corsetti's soirée. I don't think I can sleep. I feel charged with energy and enthusiasm. This is exactly what I hoped for when I agreed to spend this year abroad.

Signora Martinelli wasn't too pleased when I told her that I would not be dining at home. "You could have told me earlier," she said.

"I'm sorry. My professor only extended the invitation after class today. Apparently, he invites all the foreign students to his house after the first class. I could not say no, could I?"

"I suppose not," she agreed. "You won't be late, I hope."

"Would it be possible for me to take a key?" I asked. "We are not invited until eight, and I would not like to be the one who leaves before everyone else."

She hesitated. "I suppose I can trust you with a key," she said.

"I'm sure I won't be very late. Just maybe a little after ten. And I promise to be quiet."

She sighed. She did a lot of sighing, I'd noticed. As if everything in this world was a great burden to her. In a way, she reminded me of my mother, who was not the most optimistic of souls.

She went to the hall table, pulled open a drawer and handed me a bunch of keys.

"The big one for the outside door," she said. "And the smaller one for the apartment. Make sure you don't lose them."

"I'll be careful," I said. "And I'm sorry to have inconvenienced you about dinner."

"It's no matter," she replied. "It was only going to be salami and a little salad anyway."

I went to my room and debated what to wear. Last year I had been caught out when Leo had invited me to dine at the posh Danieli Hotel. Ladies in Venice dressed well. So I had brought my few items of respectable clothing with me. I examined my pale-blue silk evening dress. Too formal for a student gathering, surely. I wanted horribly to fit in, to belong to the group, not to stand out as an old frumpy female. I could picture Imelda eyeing me with distaste, while she looked stunning in a simple black dress, probably with a silk scarf tossed carelessly around her in the way that Continental women can do, and we Englishwomen can't.

In the end I opted for a green and white polka-dot dress with a crossover white collar. It was more afternoon tea dress than evening gown, but I doubted that my fellow students would be wearing formal attire. And at least it had been made by the village dressmaker only a year ago, so the style was passably modern. Looking at myself in the mirror, I wished that I owned a simple black gown that could be dressed up for the occasion. I had shied away from black after my father died and Mummy had insisted on our wearing it for months. It really didn't suit me with my fair complexion. I brushed my hair into a sleek bob, considered adding a jewelled comb, then decided against it. Then off I went.

I debated going over the Accademia Bridge and then making my way around to the Frari church, but there didn't seem to be a direct route, and I was afraid of getting lost in the dying light. Then I remembered someone saying there was a traghetto at San Toma, and indeed, on my map, a dotted line was shown going across the Grand Canal there. I wasn't sure what a traghetto was, but it seemed to be some sort of ferry. I decided to risk cutting through the Campo Santo Stefano, finally arrived at the Grand Canal and found a line of people waiting to cross. Then I saw the ferry: it was a gondola! The people ahead of me were helped down into it and remained standing, packed close to overloading while they were rowed across. Then the gondola came back, and I was included in the next trip. I found it somewhat unnerving to be standing up in a gondola, especially when a vaporetto passed us, throwing up a wake. But we made it safely, and from there it was no problem to find the Fondamenta del Forner. I was learning for the first time that a *calle* was a street, but a *fondamenta* was a street that ran beside a canal.

I rang the bell and was admitted. This building had a lift, and I was pleased to ride up to the third-floor apartment rather than manage the three flights of stairs. The professor himself opened the door to me, then led me through to a large room with windows that looked out across the city. At this hour, the sun had just set and the tiled roofs were bathed in rosy twilight. Swallows flitted low; seagulls wheeled above. It was a perfect scene. And the room behind the view was equally attractive: white modern furniture, a long, low sofa and walls decorated with modern art—great splashes of colour. I didn't have time to examine these as Professor Corsetti introduced me to the assembled group.

"This is the young lady from England, Miss Browning."

I looked around to see that Imelda, Gaston and Franz were already there. Henry was not. A woman came forward, arms open in welcome. "How happy we are that you've come to our home," she said. "I am the professor's wife, Angelica. Let me introduce you to our guests."

I hadn't expected guests other than my fellow students and wondered instantly if I should have worn the more formal evening dress. This was confirmed instantly as I was led to an older woman, who was wearing a stunning midnight-blue gown with matching jacket. At her neck was a sapphire necklace. She had a narrow face topped by boyishly cropped white hair and dark, intelligent eyes that examined me with interest. The effect was that of a bird of prey, a hawk maybe. Rather alarming.

"Contessa, may I introduce Miss Browning from England," Signora Corsetti said. "My dear, this is our dear friend, Contessa Fiorito. She is a great patron of the arts in this city."

I wasn't quite sure whether I was supposed to curtsy, but I took the hand that was extended to me. It was an elegant hand with blue veins showing through very white skin.

"How lovely," she said in perfect English. "And how brave of you to come. We did not expect to see anyone from England this year, given the tense situation. But have no fear. This is Venice. We do not believe in war here."

"Can you keep it out if it happens?" I asked.

"Of course. We will simply blow up the causeway," she said and laughed. "But do not worry. Our beloved leader has big ideas, but trying to make Italians fight is like herding cats. I do not think we will go along with Herr Hitler's monstrous vision."

"Italian, please, Gabriella." The professor came over to us. "It is not fair that you two have your conversation that my other guests cannot join in. And how is her Italian to improve if she speaks her own tongue?"

"Scusi, Alfredo." The countess gave me a conspiratorial wink. "How is your Italian?" she asked in that language.

"Not too bad," I said. "I just need practice."

"And you will get it, although I have to warn you that the Venetian accent is terrible, and we have a language of our own. We do not say *buon giorno* like the rest of Italy. We greet each other with *bondì*. You'll soon get the hang of it."

"Stop talking for a moment, Gabriella," the professor said, "and let me finish my introductions. This is Vittorio Scarpa. He owns a gallery, and he assists the contessa with her collection." He put a hand on Signor Scarpa's shoulder. "If you learn from what I have to teach you, then you may end up exhibiting your paintings in his gallery, or even at the next Biennale."

"Professore, please. Do not put false hopes into their heads. If they want to exhibit at my gallery, they will need to become new Salvador Dalís. I am very, very choosy, as you well know. Only the best, right, dear Contessa?"

This man was much younger—thirties or early forties—good-looking in a very Latin sort of way: dark, wavy hair with a little too much grease for my liking; dark, flashing eyes and a suit that was

200

probably made from raw silk. When he shook my hand, his felt podgy and clammy. Not a pleasant feeling, but he gave me a condescending smile.

"Welcome to Venice," he said.

The third guest was a priest. Having grown up as a member of the Church of England, I had a deep distrust of anything Catholic. This one didn't look in any way frightening. He was a large, round man with rosy cheeks and eyes that flickered with amusement. He was introduced as Father Trevisan.

"A foreigner like you," the professor said.

"Really?" I asked.

The priest chuckled. "Because of my name. From the town of Treviso. Half an hour away on the mainland. So to Venetians I shall forever be an outsider. Although I have to point out that at least one of our doges was a Trevisan."

"Are you a member of an order, Father?" Gaston asked.

The priest gave an innocent little smile. "I was a little worried about the poverty, chastity and obedience," he said. "I am quite good at the chastity, but I'm not so good at obeying, as my superiors will tell you, and I do like a good meal and a good vintage occasionally."

We all laughed.

"Alfredo, too much talk," the professor's wife said. "Shall we not go through to dinner?"

"We are still waiting for the last guest, *cara*

201

mia," he replied. "Our American friend has not yet arrived."

"He is probably wandering around San Marco or Cannaregio looking for the address," Imelda said with a brittle laugh. "He didn't seem to know where San Polo was."

"Our city is very confusing, I must agree," Signora Corsetti said. "We will give him a little longer, but I do not wish the food to spoil. But you can start by pouring our guests a drink, Alfredo."

"Good idea." He nodded and went across to a sideboard on which there were bottles and glasses.

"Tonight we celebrate with our local fizz," the professor said, going over to the table. "Prosecco from the Veneto. The best." As he talked, he twisted the bottle top with skill, and it opened with a satisfying pop. He opened a second bottle and filled glasses. "A toast to our visitors from abroad. May they all learn to free their art from everything they have been taught." He raised his glass. We did the same and took a sip. It was fresh and bubbly, and I drank with appreciation.

We were just about to go through to dinner when the doorbell rang and a breathless Henry entered. "Scusi, Professore," he stammered. "Lost. Wrong way. From vaporetto, I went right. Asked for church, and they thought I meant San Polo."

"No problem, my boy. We have waited for you, but now we can go through to dinner, I think." He led us through an archway to a long dining room. French doors led on to a shaded balcony. They were open, and a pleasing breeze came in, tinged with a hint of sea salt. There were place cards on the table, and I took my seat, between the contessa and the priest. Franz sat opposite me.

"May I help you?" I asked the professor's wife, who had appeared with a tray of small plates.

"Oh no, thank you. You are our guests tonight," she said, placing a plate in front of me. It contained a single octopus tentacle set amid some salad greens. Having had one at the Danieli last year, I was not put off by the look of it, but I could tell that Henry and Franz were eyeing it with alarm.

"Our local delicacy," the professor said. "Shall we say grace, Father?"

The priest crossed himself, then muttered something in Latin. The others, except for Henry and myself, all crossed themselves. I would have to learn things like this if I wanted to fit in. I took a tentative mouthful of octopus, and it was as soft as butter, with a slight spiciness to it. Delicious, in fact. But I saw Henry trying to hide his under a lettuce leaf. I gave him an understanding grin.

Next came a pasta dish with tiny shrimp and then veal with a rich and herby tomato sauce.

Last of all was tiramisu, my favourite Italian dessert to date. I think everyone cleared their plates. I know I did. The professor's wife beamed with pleasure.

"You young people must come here when you need a good meal," she said. "Or a shoulder to cry on. Or to complain about my husband and what a harsh teacher he is."

"For their own good, Angelica," he said. "If I do not break down their stereotypes and rules, how will they find their expression?"

Throughout the dinner I had been engaged in conversation with the contessa. She told me she had been born in Poland but brought to Paris as a young child. Her parents were Jewish émigrés. As a young woman, she had modelled for various artists, including some well-known impressionists, and later expressionists.

"I knew Mary Cassatt," she said. "And I modelled for Manet, and Berthe Morisot. Later for Picasso once. But he had too much of a roving eye, and his mistress was terribly jealous." She touched my hand. "Some of them gave me sketches as a token of their appreciation."

"Incredible," I said. "You still have them, I hope?"

"Oh yes. I kept them as insurance against future poverty," she said. "Fortunately, I married a rich Italian count and have been well taken care of."

"Your husband also likes art?" I asked.

"My husband died twenty years ago, my dear. I have been a lonely widow ever since, but I surround myself with amusing people, and I still love to collect art." She waved a finger at me. "You must come to my soirées. You will meet the most stimulating people. Father Trevisan here is always my guest, but it is more for my wine cellar than my conversation that he comes, I believe. Your dear professor often attends. And of course Vittorio is my little shadow."

"I would like that very much," I said.

"Tell your new friends they are also invited," she said. "I will be hosting one this Sunday, as a matter of fact. Only a small affair in the summer, since so many people are at their properties in the hills to escape the heat. But it will give you a chance to see my villa."

"Where do you live?" I asked.

"On the Lido, my dear. Have you been there yet?"

"Yes, I once took a party of schoolgirls to the Lido so that they could swim."

"Ah, then you know how to take the vaporetto, and from the dock you walk in the direction of the beach. About halfway down that wide road, you come to my villa on your right. Behind tall wrought iron gates. Villa Fiorito. It says so beside the gate. When my husband was alive, we had a small palazzo in the city, but I gave it away. Too noisy."

"How can one have a small palazzo?" I asked, and she laughed.

"Small by palazzo standards. Only eighteen rooms. But too dark and depressing for me. I gave it to my departed husband Maurizio's nephew and his wife. Wasn't that nice of me?"

"Very nice," I said.

"I like making people happy," she said. "Until Sunday, then. You will enjoy my friends."

And so now I am sitting on my bed writing this with a smile on my face. Less than one week in Venice, and I have already been invited to the villa of a countess.

Today I learned to draw a face, a church and an orange, and I went to dinner with a priest and a countess. Not bad for a first day at the accademia. Just wait until I write to Mummy! Even Aunt Hortensia will be impressed.

CHAPTER 17

Juliet, Venice, July 9, 1939

Sunday. In England a day of rest. No shops open. Church bells ringing in the morning (but not at an ungodly hour like here, and in an orderly fashion, not complete cacophony). On a fine day maybe a picnic, a cricket match on the village green. But here it is a day of loud celebration. Bells ring all over the city at different times, summoning the faithful to Mass. And almost everyone is a worshipper, it seems. Signora Martinelli went to eight o'clock Mass this morning. She asked me politely if I'd like to go and if I'd mind if breakfast was late. I said I wouldn't mind at all about breakfast, but I declined her kind invitation to join her.

"There is an English church, you know. St George's. It is next to your accademia. Not at all far. I believe they have a service later in the morning, as I understand that Anglicans are not early risers, and of course for them they do not have to fast before communion as they are not receiving the blessed sacrament anyway." Another sniff.

I thanked her and tried to seem pleased at this

information, getting the feeling that anyone who did not go to some kind of church was probably damned to hell. Actually, I found myself keen to visit a Catholic church and suggested to my landlady that I might want to attend at San Marco. She nodded approval. "So beautiful," she said. "Maybe you will learn to accept the true faith after all."

We ate breakfast together—no fresh rolls today as the bakeries were closed, but cold cuts and peaches, sitting by the open window and listening to a distant bell. Then I walked to the basilica. I had only seen it as a visiting tourist before. Now it was full of people. A choir processed in, their singing echoing to the domes above. Light shone in through windows in the dome, illuminating first one alcove, then another. Gold sparkled everywhere. Gems flashed on the high altar. The sweet smell of incense wafted through the air. Used as I was to the simplicity of the English country church, I found this overwhelming, as if I was witnessing a spectacle, not a place to pray. I tried to follow the order of the Mass in a book that was half in Italian and half in Latin but was hopelessly lost. A bell rang. They knelt. Another bell. They stood. I was always half a beat late for everything and with no idea what was happening. Suddenly I felt alone. All of these people sitting with their families—a long line of children next to proud parents, the smallest one wriggling and being taken on to a father's knee. And I had nobody.

I came out feeling uncomfortable and unsatisfied. Maybe next week I would try St George's after all.

I had mentioned to the signora that I was invited to a soirée on the Lido—by a countess, no less. She was quite impressed and suggested that we have lunch together since I would be out for the evening meal I had paid for. So I returned from church, passing families heading for the vaporetto stops, carrying picnic supplies and towels. I thought a swim might be a good idea, but I had already accepted my landlady's luncheon invitation. I could tell Signora Martinelli had made an effort. There was a lace cloth on the dining table, not at the kitchen table where we usually ate. She served antipasto of melon with prosciutto, then a pasta dish sprinkled with cheese and finally a small pork chop, grilled with courgettes. I was now aware that the meat was probably a big sacrifice for her and glad that my rent would mean an occasional meat meal. She even opened a bottle of red wine.

I asked her about her family. Her husband had been dead for many years, but she had a son who now lived in Milan. He came to visit occasionally. His wife was not too simpatico. And they had no children. "Can you imagine? No children. Not one grandchild."

"My mother doesn't have any grandchildren yet," I said, "but I expect my sister, Winnie, will produce one soon. She hasn't been married long."

"And you? Why do you not marry? You are an attractive woman. There was never a man you wanted?"

"I live in a village and take care of my mother. I teach in a girls' school. There is really no opportunity to meet men."

"Maybe you will meet a good Italian man while you are here," she said.

I smiled. "That would be nice, but I have to return to my mother, I'm afraid."

We finished the meal with more fruit, and I helped her wash up. My head was feeling a little woozy, as I was not used to drinking in the middle of the day. Not used to drinking at all, actually. I went to my room and fell into a deep sleep, awaking to someone singing in the street below. I looked out and saw a man sitting on a front step, playing the accordion and singing. People had clustered around him, clapping to the music and singing along. A little girl got up and danced, twirling so that her long dark braids flew out behind her. Such a joyous scene, and again I was conscious of being the outsider, the observer.

At seven I dressed, this time in my evening gown and my fringed wrap for the journey across on the vaporetto. Signora Martinelli handed me the key without being asked, as if an evening with a countess was beyond doubt.

"Find out when the last vaporetto returns," she said. "They do not run as frequently on Sundays."

I set off, full of expectation, praying that my hair would stay in place during the crossing of the lagoon. We had been invited for eight, but I had been brought up to think it was rude to arrive on the dot. But I hadn't expected to wait so long for a vaporetto, and when it came it was horribly crowded with people going across to the Lido for dancing or gambling, as I gathered the nightclubs and casino were out there. We took a long time to disgorge passengers at San Zaccaria, and then at the subsequent stops. So it was late when we finally arrived, and I walked briskly from the landing stage, across the plaza and down the broad street called Granviale Santa Maria Elizabeta. I remembered how Imelda had been scathing about Henry when he was late. I wondered what she was saying about me now— if she had come, that is. I had extended the invitation to my fellow foreign students, and they hadn't seemed overwhelmingly excited.

"If nothing better comes up," Gaston had said. "Not exactly how I would choose to spend Sunday evening. Does anyone know where there is good dancing?"

So now I took a deep breath before opening those tall, gold-tipped gates and then walked up a gravel path between palm trees to a blood-red villa. The door was opened by an elderly male servant, who ushered me down a long marble hallway and out to a patio at the rear of the house. Lights had been hung between trees, and they flickered in a cool breeze off the Adriatic. Even though it was still not quite dark, the figures on the patio were bathed in shadow, and I paused for a moment, unsure of myself and not wanting to step out into that group.

Then the countess spotted me. "Ah, my little English friend," she said, coming forward with her arms open. "You have come. How wonderful. Do let me introduce you to my friends."

I was led forward feeling horribly shy. I saw then that the other students had come. Even Henry had made it before me. He gave me a little wave and raised a glass to me. He and Franz were standing with our professor and his wife. I recognized also the jolly priest from the other night, and the smooth Vittorio, chatting with a painfully thin but horribly elegant blonde woman, an older dark-haired man at her side.

"Let me introduce Bibi and Arturo from Spain," the countess said. "Another of our visitors, Miss Browning from England."

They nodded politely and went back to their conversation as I was led away. I was sure Bibi had taken one look at my dress and decided I was not worth talking to. I was moved on to another distinguished-looking couple. "And let me present you to Il Conte Da Rossi."

I found myself staring into the face of a man with military bearing, iron-grey hair and a face that was definitely an older version of Leo's. Why had he not mentioned that his father was a count?

The count must have seen my alarm because he gave me a friendly smile. "You need not look so worried," he said, "I do not bite, I assure you."

"It is good of you to grace us with your presence, Count," the contessa said. She addressed me. "The count is not normally known as a big patron of the arts."

"I resent that," Count Da Rossi said. "I have great appreciation of real art. Invite me to a showing of Caravaggio or Leonardo or even Renoir, and I'll be there in an instant. I appreciate beauty. But you cannot tell me that a woman with two heads, one eye and three breasts is a work of beauty!"

"Not all art is meant to be beautiful," Professor Corsetti said. "It is meant to evoke an emotional response, maybe to stir anger or sadness even."

"And what response would this lady with one eye and three breasts evoke?" the count demanded. "Pity? Loathing?"

"Perhaps fascination?"

The count shook his head.

"But you came anyway," the contessa said,

"even though you knew I was going to reveal a new piece of artwork."

"I could not resist your presence, dear Contessa," he said.

"Flatterer. But where is your son, and the adorable Bianca?"

"She was not willing to make the arduous trip across the lagoon," he said with a smile.

"She is not well? In the family way, perhaps?"

"Not that I know of. We can hope," Count Da Rossi said. "No, I rather think it was the company that did not excite her. Too many of us are old and boring."

"Rubbish!" the contessa exclaimed. "Speak for yourself. I may be old, but nobody could ever claim that I was boring, could they, darling?" She turned to Vittorio.

"Absolutely not, cara mia."

I studied this with interest. So the relationship was maybe more than gallery owner and patron, yet he must be at least thirty years her junior. But she was still an attractive woman, with such lively eyes.

"You do not have a drink." The countess took my hand and led me away from Leo's father. I was still a little shaken and so relieved that Leo and Bianca were not present.

"Ah, here is a friendly face," Countess Fiorito said, switching to English as she paused next to a man standing beside the drinks table. He was dressed in a very English blazer. "Mr Reginald Sinclair, His Majesty's consul here in Venice. Reggie, darling, one of your fellow countrymen, or rather countrywomen. Miss Browning."

"How do you do, my dear." He gave me a friendly smile. He was an older man with a pale moustache and jowls that gave him a rather hangdog look. "So nice to see a fellow English person. Most of them have fled for home, fearing the worst, I'm afraid."

"Do you think there will be a worst?"

"I'm rather afraid that I do," he said. "I'm waiting to see if and when I may be recalled. It all depends on Mussolini and if he decides to follow along with his idol Adolf. I don't think he has anything like the resources to start a proper war yet, but it would be bad if he invited the Germans to use Venice as a base and thus got us drawn in against our will."

"Oh gosh," I said. "I suppose Venice would make a good naval base."

"The Nazis would like to use Trieste, which used to be the big Austrian naval base before the Great War," he said. "But Venice is a safer harbour, and easier to hide ships amongst all the little islands." He shook his head. "But let us not dwell on what might be. Let us make the most of this perfect Venetian night and good company, what?"

I nodded. He picked up a glass of Prosecco

and handed it to me. "So you're visiting here?"

"I'm here for a year, studying at the accademia," I said. "I got a bursary to take leave from my teaching job."

"Jolly nice. I'd make the most of it, if I were you. Venice is still one of the few civilized cities in the world. The racial laws created last year by Il Duce were supposed to exclude Jews from education and teaching and then to strip them of property. None of that has happened here. The Venetians still live quite happily and do business in the ghetto and turn a blind eye to those of Jewish origin, like our dear contessa here."

I looked at him with surprise and then turned my gaze to Contessa Fiorito. I remembered now that she had mentioned her parents were Jewish émigrés. "But her husband was an Italian count," I said.

"Indeed he was, but that has nothing to do with her racial origin. Born of a poor Jewish family in Paris, so I understand. Of course she is well respected here and does a lot in the way of philanthropy for the city. Most people don't even know her heritage." He drew closer to me. "I have advised her to have an escape plan ready, just in case."

A servant approached with a tray of hors d'oeuvres. Mr Sinclair helped himself with relish, and I took a skewer of prawns. Henry Dabney and the priest came over to join me, so the worrying conversation was at an end. I had known that war was possibly looming on the horizon, but I don't think I'd ever examined the fact that I might actually be in danger.

CHAPTER 18

Juliet, Venice, July 9, 1939

Conversation dwindled as more food was brought round. Foie gras on slices of Melba toast, thin slivers of raw beef, bruschetta topped with tapenade. All equally delicious and exciting for me. I looked around as glasses sparkled in the lights dotted amongst the trees and on the jewels the women were wearing. It was hard to believe that a couple of weeks ago I had been Juliet Browning, schoolmistress, living in a small village and eating baked beans on toast for Sunday supper while we listened to the news on the radio. But then my gaze went to Count Da Rossi. He was still handsome in middle age. I turned back to listen to what Henry was saying.

"What do you think of the food?"

"It's gorgeous, isn't it?"

"A little too fancy for my taste. Give me a good steak or hamburger any day!"

"So I suppose you didn't come from this sort of background either?"

He laughed. "My dad is a self-made man. Started an auto dealership and has done very well for himself, in spite of the Depression. But my mom went to college, and she wanted that for her kids, so I started out majoring in business and then I discovered art. Of course my dad wasn't about to pay for me to study art, so I switched to industrial design. He thought I might be able to design a new automobile for him and we'd make a fortune—take over from Ford, you know." He gave a derisive chuckle. "And then I saw this scholarship offered to study in Europe, and I thought, *Why not?* So I applied, and here I am. The old man wasn't pleased, but then he's not funding it, is he? I figured it was my one chance to see a bit of the world before I'm stuck selling automobiles for the rest of my life."

I looked up at his round, earnest face. "Do you have to follow your father into his business?"

"I'm the only son. Who else would take over from him someday?"

I found myself considering this. Leo was in the same boat. Only son and obligated to be what was expected of him—to lead someone else's life, not his own. And then I realized I was not so different. I could have stayed on in college, worked as a waitress to pay for my room and board and become an artist one day. Instead I had been the dutiful daughter, living my mother's life, not mine.

"Now we're both free, at least for a while," I said.

"You're right. It's kinda surreal, isn't it? These surroundings and sipping champagne with aristocrats with oodles of money?"

"It is," I agreed.

Franz came over to join us. "It is a pleasant evening, is it not?" he asked.

"Are you used to this sort of thing?" I asked him, switching to Italian. "Henry and I were just saying it was like living in a fantasy."

"For me, too. My father owns a bakery. He thought I was mad to want to study art. Why did I need art to become a baker one day? I told him I would teach him to make very artistic bread."

We laughed, but as Franz moved off again, Henry touched my arm. "Be careful of that one," he whispered. "I think he's a German plant."

"A Nazi spy?" I was shocked.

Henry nodded. "I just have a feeling. They all say they are Austrian, don't they, and there is something about him that's not quite right. I can't put my finger on it, but . . ."

"So when do we see this acquisition of yours?" Bibi, the Spanish woman, demanded. "We are dying with anticipation."

"Very well," Contessa Fiorito replied. "Follow me, my darlings."

And she led us through French doors into a tasteful room with a white marble floor, pale-blue silk sofas and low gilded tables. On an easel in the middle of the room was a large painting, concealed under a sheet.

"Vittorio, my precious, would you do the honours?" she said. "Since you were clever enough to find it for me, and what's more, to get it to me."

Vittorio gave her a little bow of appreciation, then crossed the room and whipped off the cover in one fluid movement. There was a gasp from those present. The painting was starkly modern—great shafts of colour, what looked like a bloody hand piercing one of the shafts, and ethereal faces peering through in the darker spaces between, their mouths open in silent protest. It was highly disturbing but, I had to admit, rather brilliant in its form and design.

"Spectacular, Gabriella," Professor Corsetti said. "Don't you think so, Arturo?"

"I do. And this was the painting you had to smuggle out of Germany?"

"It was." The contessa was looking pleased and excited. "I heard about it through the grapevine, and Vittorio managed to meet with the artist and bring it out under a perfectly horrible pastoral scene by a Nazi-approved painter."

"So this artist is not a Nazi favourite, I suppose?" Mr Sinclair asked.

"Not only is he not a Nazi favourite, but he is Jewish," she said. "We have begged him to leave while he can, but he has aged parents and they won't go anywhere, and so he stays. I have told him I'll put them up here, but he stays and he paints. Asking for trouble, I'm afraid."

"In which city does he live?" Franz asked.

"In Stuttgart. By day he is an engineer at the Mercedes-Benz plant. He thinks he is safe because his division is making armoured cars and he is a valued member of the team. His paintings are signed under his pseudonym, and nobody knows he paints but his friends outside of Germany."

"He is running a big risk, I'm afraid," Mr Sinclair said.

"Yes. There are many like him, who keep on with their small, defiant protests, against all odds. Brave boys and girls."

Imelda touched my hand. "We should probably leave soon if we want to take the ten o'clock vaporetto. If we miss that, we have to wait until eleven thirty, and the last one is always so crowded."

"Good idea. Thank you," I said and went to round up Henry.

"So you really think this is the future of art, do you, Gabriella?" I heard Count Da Rossi say. "No more beauty? For me, I would have preferred the Nazi pastoral scene."

"But you have no soul, Massimo. I've always known that."

Franz was examining the painting carefully, and I wondered if he was looking for a signature. Was it possible that Henry was right and he was a German spy? I was glad the artist was signing his pictures with a pseudonym.

I went up to the contessa and thanked her for the lovely evening, saying we had to catch our vaporetto.

"Of course, my darling," she said. "But you are welcome at any time. To all my soirées. And come to tea one day, just you and me and a good British tea party, eh?"

"Don't tell me you have real British tea," I said, laughing. "All the tea I have had here is so pale and tasteless."

"But my dear, I import mine from Harrods," she said. "Where else?"

She reached forward and gave me a little kiss on my cheek. I'm afraid I blushed. I wasn't used to being kissed by countesses. We took our farewells and started down the boulevard and back to the dock. A sizeable crowd was there, waiting for the vaporetto.

"I hope we can all get on," Henry said. "We'll be squashed like sardines."

"I hope they do not let us all on," Imelda said. "With such a crowd on board, we are liable to end up at the bottom of the lagoon."

"I certainly do not want to wait until eleven thirty," Gaston said. "Shall we see if we can work our way through the crowd to the front?"

This did not look to be at all possible. There were families with picnic baskets, chairs, umbrellas barring our way forward, and fierce-looking grandmothers ready to fight for their spot. Besides, I could not push myself aboard in front of grandmothers and babies. Franz obviously agreed with me. "That would not be the correct thing to do, I think," he said.

Before we could act, we were joined by Count Da Rossi. "Ah, my young friends. You also escape from Gabriella's soirée? Me, I am easily bored with modern art, and I cannot pretend to appreciate it the way others do." Then he noticed the full extent of the crowd already standing on the jetty. "Dio mio," he said. "I do not think all these people will fit into one small boat. You will not get on to this one, I can assure you."

"We were just about to try and work our way to the front," Gaston said.

"Let me see if my launch has arrived," the count said. "I might be able to fit you all on board and give you a lift."

"That's very kind of you," Imelda said.

"I cannot leave fellow art lovers in the lurch." He had a charming smile, reminding me of Leo. "Come. Let us see if my boat has arrived yet. I told my man to come for me at ten. I was sure I would have had enough by then, but it is hard to say no to Gabriella." As he spoke, he was scanning the waterfront, where there were several smaller jetties. "Ah," he said, pointing at a sleek teak motorboat I recognized all too well. "Over here!"

We followed, I a little reluctantly. "I have

brought some young friends. Do you think we can find a place for all of them?"

"We can try." The man at the helm stepped up on to the dock, and my heart did a sudden flip as I saw that it was Leo himself.

The count was also surprised. "Leo, what are you doing here?" He looked back at us. "It is my son. He has come himself instead of our servant. What happened to Mario?"

"His brother had a birthday. I gave him the evening off. And I didn't mind a trip across the *laguna*. It's a lovely night." He hadn't seen me. He held out his hand to assist his father into the boat, then reached up to Imelda. Franz, always the gentleman, pushed me in front of him. Leo reached up and then froze. "Julietta! Am I dreaming? What are you doing here?"

"Hello, Leo," I said. "What a surprise. I'm studying here, at the academy of art."

I could feel his hand shaking as I stepped down into the boat. He turned mechanically to assist the boys down. "Studying? Here? For how long?"

"A year," I said.

"This young lady is a friend of yours, Leo?" the count asked.

"We met last year at the Biennale," Leo said smoothly. "When I was escorting that party of rich donors, remember?"

"Ah yes. You enjoyed the Biennale, Miss Browning?"

"I thought it was wonderful. And the setting in the gardens is magnificent."

"It's not what you English would call 'my cup of tea,'" he said. "Although my son keeps trying to drag me there. But so much rubbish is being called art these days."

"My father would like the whole Biennale to be full of old masters," Leo said.

"Of course. That was real art. You should see the painting that I'm sure Gabriella Fiorito paid a large sum for," he went on jovially. "Hideous. Great daubs of colour. Nothing soothing about it. Apparently done by some up-and-coming Jewish painter still working secretly in Germany."

"Well, that is Contessa Fiorito for you," Leo said. "She sees herself as the great benefactor— the Medici of our century. And she likes to rescue people, the way that others rescue stray cats." He glanced up from the wheel, and our eyes met.

He pulled down to full throttle, and the boat sped across the lagoon, the wind fresh and salty in our faces. My heart was beating so loudly I was sure that those squashed beside me on the back seat could hear it. How had I fooled myself into thinking that I could handle this? Being so close to him was torture. Why had I not realized how small Venice was, that I was bound to run into him whatever I did?

"Where should we drop you young people

off?" the count asked. "Are you all living close to the accademia?"

"Close enough, I think," Gaston said. "Please stop wherever it is convenient. We appreciate this kindness so much. Without you, we would have been standing on a dock for another hour and a half and we might not even have found room on the last boat."

"Pull into the dock at the accademia, then, Leo," his father said.

Leo manoeuvred the boat, jumped out smoothly and secured a rope. Then he held out his hand to help us disembark. I let Imelda disembark first, then it was my turn. Leo's hand held firmly on to mine.

"Thank you for the ride," I said.

"It was my pleasure," he replied. "I am delighted to know that you have the chance to study here. Now perhaps you will become a great painter after all."

"Hardly," I said. "But at least I shall improve."

"You live near the school?"

"Not too far," I said. "Within walking distance." He wanted my address, I could tell. But I wasn't going to give it to him. "Thank you again. I'll see everyone in the morning."

I started to walk away, but I delayed in crossing the Accademia Bridge until the motorboat had gone past. Then I walked home very fast, my footsteps echoing from the deserted cobblestones.

CHAPTER 19

Juliet, Venice, Monday, July 10, 1939

I tried not to think about him, but I lay awake for hours, listening to the distant noises of the city, and only fell asleep in the early morning. Thus I awoke groggy and grumpy, and had to rush to bathe and prepare for class. This morning it was Drawing and Painting the Nude, and amongst the foreign students, only Gaston and I had selected the class. It must have been an entry-level class for the Italian students, as most of them looked horribly young, and I sensed glances coming in my direction. One of them actually asked me if I was the teacher. When I introduced myself as a visiting student from England, he looked embarrassed and hurried off to his own seat.

The professor was a buxom woman with long dyed red hair that cascaded over her shoulders. She was dressed in a flowing garment that revealed cleavage. When she talked, she waved her hands around a lot, and I couldn't help feeling she should have been an actress, not an artist. She talked about the beauty of the human figure, the importance of the line. Once we had the line right, the details would fall into place. Some of the youngest students seemed to find this funny.

I suppose they were thinking about the details falling into place.

A dais had been placed in the middle of the room with a ladder-backed chair on it. The *professoressa*, having given her opening remarks about what we were to look for, called forward her model. It was a well-built man, which I found a little unnerving. He stepped on to the dais, dressed in a bathrobe. Then he calmly removed it, revealing himself to be stark naked. I heard small gasps and even titters from my fellow students. I have to admit to shock myself, realizing that this was the first naked man I had ever seen in my life. I had studied naked figures in my art books, but this was different. I tried not to stare.

Our first assignments were thirty-second sketches. Then one-minute sketches. Then five minutes.

"You are paying too much attention to detail," the professoressa complained, as she walked around the class. "Half close your eyes. Draw what you see." She paused behind me. "Not bad," she said.

The model moved from standing to sitting, then to standing with one foot on a rung of the chair, and we drew each position. Only then were we allowed to do a full rendition, either in charcoal, pastels or watercolour. I chose charcoal. We worked on it for the last hour of class, and the professoressa seemed quite pleased with mine.

"You have taken this class before, I can tell," she said. "You are new at the accademia?"

"I'm a visitor from England," I replied. "And I've had one year of college art, but never a figure class, which was why I chose this."

"Good. You have aptitude with the human form." She gave me an encouraging nod and went on to the next person.

"Clearly you have been hiding your light from us," Gaston muttered. He was sitting behind me. "Obviously, you have studied many men in great detail before this, like the handsome boat driver last night, eh?"

And I couldn't stop myself from blushing scarlet. "Don't be silly," I said. "I seem to be able to draw people, that's all."

"I feel that prim Miss Browning has more to offer than it would seem," he went on.

I ignored him. I could hear him chuckling. I didn't quite know what to make of him. He was a flirt, but what could he see in me, especially when he was clearly interested in Imelda? Was it perhaps a national sport in France to flirt? I knew so little of men in any country, only that the English boys I had met in my youth lacked any finesse in approaching the opposite sex. Too many years of boarding school, I suspect.

Anyway, the encounter had cheered me in a strange way. I had expected to feel annoyed, but now I realized it was nice to know I was not to be the older spinster, overlooked and unimportant. I gathered up my things and started down the stairs, wondering where I should go for lunch. There was a small sandwich shop on Calle della Toletta nearby that did wonderful *tramezzini*: little finger sandwiches containing interesting things like tuna and olives, ham and shrimp. They were very cheap, too. One could pick six of them and only pay pennies. I knew I should be having my main meal at midday, but somehow I couldn't face eating a whole plate of spaghetti in the heat. The only problem about the sandwich shop was that they spoke Venetian. By now I had come to realize that the local language was not just a dialect, a difference in pronunciation, but a language of its own. "Bondì" was a classic example. Nothing like "buon giorno," the normal greeting for "good day."

As I came down the staircase, I heard two students in front of me speaking the language. Quite incomprehensible. How lucky that my landlady had been born in Turin and was thus not a native speaker. While I was thinking this, I was joined by one of the girls from the class. She had a young, fresh face and light hair and eyes. I thought she might be another foreign student, but she greeted me in perfect Italian.

"Well, that opened the eyes, didn't it?" she said. "In more ways than one. If my grandmother saw me now, she'd demand that I come straight home again."

I smiled with her. "Where are you from? Not from Venice?" I asked.

"I'm from South Tyrol. Used to be Austrian, now part of Italy. We still speak German at home. I miss my mountains. How about you?"

"From England."

"Madonna!" she exclaimed. "Are you not afraid of the war? Everything we hear says that Hitler intends to invade Poland, and when he does, England has to declare war."

"England let them have Czechoslovakia. Perhaps they will come to terms over Poland," I said.

She shook her head. "Don't you understand? Poland is the excuse. Hitler wants to be pushed into a war. He wants to be the injured party. You know what he says: 'Here I am, reclaiming German territory around Danzig, and these brutish English are trying to stop our people from reclaiming our historic birthright.' And Russia will side with him, you know. And France will side with England, and pretty soon it will spread. Hitler wants the world. Stalin wants the world, too, and Mussolini just wants the Mediterranean. But who will stop them?"

"I suppose you are right. England will try to."

She nodded, leaning closer to me. "I think it will be bad. I have seen what they are doing in

Germany. Building so many tanks and machines of war. They have already taken Austria, which was the country of my grandparents." She paused on the landing halfway down the stairs. "What will you do if the war happens? Will you go home?"

"I expect I'll have to," I said. "Although everyone says that Venice will be quite safe. Nobody would ever bomb such a thing of beauty."

"I hope you are right," she said. "But Italy will side with Germany. You'll be called an enemy, won't you?"

"I'll face it when it happens," I said. "Right now I want to enjoy every moment. In fact I—"

Leo was standing at the foot of the stairs, looking up at me with that cheeky smile on his face.

"Bondì," he said in Venetian before switching to English as students streamed past us out into the glaring sunlight. "So I have found you! I was in the neighbourhood, and I was feeling hungry, and I thought you might want to come to lunch with me."

My new friend gave me a little nudge of encouragement and melted away. I stood there, clutching my art portfolio, my heart thumping.

"I can't come to lunch with you, Leo," I said. "You know that. You are a married man. It wouldn't be right for you to be seen with another woman."

"And you think the same applies to my wife?" he asked, frowning. Then his face softened. "Besides, it is only lunch. Not a nightclub at the Lido. Not even an intimate dinner at the Danieli as we once shared. You have to eat. I have to eat. Why not?"

I was going to be firm. I shook my head. "No. I'm sorry. This isn't fair to me. You are offering me something I can't have—like that carrot dangled in front of the donkey, just out of reach. Always, just out of reach. Don't you realize that every time I see you, it breaks my heart to know that you are married to someone else? And it's stupid, really, because we hardly know each other. We've met a couple of times, and they were wonderful and romantic for me, but they weren't real life. Just a beautiful dream. You don't really know me, and I don't know you. I might be absolutely awful."

This made him laugh, then the smile faded. "I know when two people are instantly attracted to each other," he said. "But I do understand. I would not want to damage your reputation in this city, and I'm sure the report of any little outing together would get back to my father quickly enough." He stood there, his eyes looking into mine in a way that I found so disconcerting.

"My tree?" he said. "Could we not meet occasionally by my tree? Have another little picnic one day? You remember in the Giardini?

Behind the statue? Nobody would see us there."

"They would see us coming or going," I said. "I've already come to realize that this is a very small town. Everybody knows everybody. This very conversation is now being reported back to your family, I can assure you." I took a deep breath, went to touch his arm, then thought better of it. "You have your life, Leo. You have a wife, and soon you'll have a family. And I'm not part of it. I can't ever be part of it, so please don't do this to me."

His eyes clouded. "I don't want to cause you pain ever. I just needed to see you. To prove that you were real. In the boat last night, I thought I was dreaming. Imagining things. You are truly here for a year?"

"If a war doesn't interrupt my studies."

He nodded. "It is a pity it is not an even year. I would have been delighted to escort you around a Biennale. If you are still here when it opens next May, perhaps . . ."

"You think the city will hold a festival of international art if the world is at war?"

"Of course. Venetians would never let a little thing like a war interfere with their art. We live and breathe our art. It is part of our bones." Without warning, he grabbed my portfolio. "Show me what you have been drawing."

"No!" I tried to snatch it back, but too late. He had untied the portfolio and opened it. And the first picture was the naked man, drawn in detail. Leo studied it for a second, then flicked through the quicker sketches. He closed the portfolio again and handed it back to me. As I took it, our fingers brushed, and for a moment his hand remained touching mine.

"You are good," he said. "You have a feel for the human figure. Start working on something for next year's Biennale. I can probably get it exhibited."

"I'm sure nobody wants to see my work," I said. "I'm all right at copying what I see, but I don't think I have vision to take an object and turn it into my creation like the great artists do."

"Then maybe you should just draw what you see. Ordinary people, going about ordinary lives. It is important that we also document that, for who knows what the future will bring."

"I must go and get my lunch," I said. "I have less than an hour before my next class."

"Are you sure . . . ," he began.

"Very sure. Go home to your family, please."

He nodded. "Very well. But it was so good to see you. Like a miracle, really. When I kissed you goodbye last year, I thought it would be for the last time."

"It was for the last time," I said. "I really have to go."

I could feel tears welling at the back of my eyes, and I was going to get away before a tell-tale tear trickled down my cheek. I staggered blindly out into the sunlight. The heat from the pavement rose up, along with the watery smell of the canal, tinged with the not-too-pleasant odour of rotting vegetation. I crossed the piazza in front of the accademia, over the little humpbacked bridge, and plunged into the deep shade of the narrow calle beyond. Why was he doing this to me? Didn't he care at all for my feelings? Then it struck me that he, too, was hurting. Tied to a woman he couldn't love and who clearly didn't love him. What could be worse? And then I realized there was one thing worse: to be in love with a man I could never have. To be left with nobody.

CHAPTER 20

Caroline, Venice, October 10, 2001

Caroline found she was holding her breath as she took a tentative step into the big silent room. As if on cue, the sun came out between billowing black clouds, sending a shaft of sunlight on to the water of the Giudecca Canal and the lagoon beyond. Caroline gave a small gasp of happiness. "It's wonderful," she whispered.

"Signora," the man began, stepping up. "Or is it signorina?"

"It's signora," she replied, feeling uneasy about his hand touching her but not knowing how to shake him off without seeming rude. She turned to face him. "I am in the middle of a divorce. My husband moved to New York." She felt stupid as soon as she had said it, as if she had wanted to let him know that she was available. Ridiculous.

"Signora," he went on, "I am afraid that this document is a fraud. Somebody pulled the wool over your aunt's eyes. Isn't that the English expression?" He went to take it from her. "Now, if you will permit, I will take this to the Da Rossi lawyer, and he can verify if it is authentic or not."

Caroline held on to the piece of paper. "You must think me very naive," she said. "Do you

238

think I'd let you take away the only proof that this apartment belongs to me? Something inconvenient would happen to it. It would fly out of a window, into a canal. 'Oh dear. What a shame. So sorry.' "

"Oh no, I assure you . . . ," he began, but she cut him off.

"Do not worry, signor. I will take it personally to your city hall. I am sure they can check it against their records of the time to see if it is still valid, and also check whether my aunt later sold her lease."

She put the document back into her purse and started to walk around the room, pulling a dust cover off the item of furniture in the window. It proved to be a handsome inlaid lemonwood desk. "Oh." She ran her hands over it. That Aunt Lettie had ever owned something as lovely . . . She opened a drawer and found it full of sheets of paper.

She took the top sheet out, gasped and looked up with a small, triumphant smile.

"Well," she said, holding it up to the man, "I think this proves that my aunt once owned this flat, don't you?" It was a drawing of the scene outside the window, and it was signed *JB*. "There you are. Juliet Browning. My great-aunt. She was an artist. I have some of her artwork with me, and I can tell you that this was done by her."

"Juliet Browning?" He was still frowning. "An

artist? Why would the Da Rossi family ever lease this place to a foreign artist? I don't think they were ever great patrons of the arts."

"Is there any older family member who might know?" she asked.

"Look," he said, glancing at his watch, "it is lunchtime. I should get something to eat. I have a busy afternoon ahead."

"That's all right," she replied. "I will take my document to the city hall and find the right department to verify its authenticity."

"To what?" His English had been remarkably good so far, but this stumped him.

"Whether it still belongs to my aunt and therefore to me."

"Ah," he said. "Would you not care to join me for lunch?"

This threw her off guard. "What would your employer say about taking a lady to lunch when you should be working?" she asked.

This made him smile, completely changing his face. He was younger than she had thought, and the smile had a sort of cocky confidence. "Ah, well, you see, I am Luca Da Rossi. I have just taken over the running of this company from my father."

"Congratulations," she said.

"I am not so sure about that. I fear I have inherited a big headache." He paused. "You know my name, but I do not know yours."

"Caroline," she said. "Caroline Grant."

"So, Caroline Grant, you will come to have lunch with me?"

She hesitated and wanted to say, "Are you trying to soften me up?" but instead she nodded graciously. There was no sense in having the owner of the building as an enemy. "Thank you," she said. "I was beginning to feel hungry."

Caroline locked the door behind her as they came down the stairs. She was already feeling possessive about the lovely space above. Now she could see why Aunt Lettie loved it here. They went down the three flights of stairs in silence and came out into blustery rain. Luca Da Rossi opened the umbrella he had retrieved from beside the front door.

"Come under," he said. "I know a little place around the corner. Not far."

Feeling awkward, Caroline allowed him to hold the umbrella over her. She was conscious of his shoulder touching hers. The wind was driving the rain so forcefully that the umbrella didn't protect them very well. They were both damp and windswept by the time he steered them into a small trattoria. Once inside, he helped her off with her mac and hung up his own overcoat. Having been in the fashion industry, she noticed the label. Armani. Very expensive. Apparently Luca was well known and was shown to the table in the window by a large, florid man with a moustache. A quick exchange happened in something that didn't even sound like Italian, then the man disappeared and came back with a bottle of white wine.

"Oh, I don't think I should drink at lunchtime," Caroline protested.

"But everybody drinks at lunchtime. Why else would there be a *riposo*?" He laughed. "The patron tells me that he has good fritto misto today. You like?"

"I've never tried it. But I'm happy to."

"And venison. This is the season for good venison from the hills."

"You eat a large lunch," she said as a waitress put a jar of breadsticks, a basket of rolls, a dish of olives and a bottle of olive oil in front of them.

"It is usually our big meal," he said. "More healthy. We sleep well because we do not have indigestion." He paused, then added, "And because we have a clear conscience." His eyes gave a flicker of amusement, almost flirtation.

Caroline took a sip of the wine—rich and fruity and warming—and broke a piece off one of the breadsticks, acutely aware that she was sitting opposite a strange man who would no doubt try to get his hands on the apartment that appeared to belong to her.

She took a deep breath before saying, "Signor Da Rossi, is there somebody in your family who might know anything about my aunt and how she came to lease this place?"

Luca frowned. "My father is too young. He was not born in 1939. My grandfather was killed in the war, and my great-grandfather died in 1960 something. My grandmother is still alive . . ."

"She might know."

He nodded, cautiously. "She is not always—how do you say?—clear in the head now. She is an old woman. Almost ninety. But we could try. I suggest that you attempt to prove that your piece of paper is not a fake and is still valid first, so that we don't bother her unnecessarily."

"Very well," she said. "I should first check at your city hall, is that right?"

He shrugged. "Really, our lawyer could do this quite efficiently."

"I'd prefer to hear it for myself," she replied, her eyes holding his. She was surprised to find his were dark blue, not brown as she had expected. "Where do I find the town hall or the city offices?"

"Ca' Loredan is the town hall," he said. "A former palazzo on the Grand Canal, close to Rialto. But you may find that ancient records like yours are kept somewhere else. Venetians do not like to do anything efficiently. There are no big beautiful city halls as you might find in America. Things are dotted around the city."

"You know America?" she asked, because she

243

had detected a slight American accent to his pronunciation.

"I spent a year at Columbia University," he said, "studying economics. And my mother is from there."

"Your mother is American?"

He nodded. "She is from New York. She met my father when she was a student. She came to do her junior year from Radcliffe here."

"And your parents are still alive? Still married?"

"Quite happily, it would seem. My father has just turned sixty and has decided to step back from the day-to-day running of the company. I have a sister who lives in Australia. They like to visit her and the grandchildren. They are there right now. It seems that grandchildren are a great attraction, and so far I have not managed to produce any." He gave a wry little grin. "You have children?"

"One son. Edward, or rather Teddy. He's six."

"And who looks after Teddy when you come here?"

"He's with his father in New York."

He must have noticed the spasm of pain on her face. "Madonna! But he is safe and well after the terrible tragedy?"

"Thank God yes, but now he's afraid to fly, apparently. Or at least, that's what his father says. Or his father says that's what the psychiatrist says."

He frowned. "An excuse to keep him?"

"It might seem that way."

"Ah." He nodded. "And so you escape to a beautiful place so that you don't worry too much?"

This suggestion was a little too close to the truth. She fought back the snapped answer but said primly, "I am here out of respect to my great-aunt who just died. The one whose flat I have just inherited. I have brought her ashes."

He held up a hand. "Sorry. I did not mean to pry."

"You're not prying, and of course this whole thing is very raw at the moment. My husband just left me, and now he won't return my son." She held up a hand. "I'm sorry. I shouldn't be unloading my troubles on a stranger."

He was looking at her with what seemed to be real concern. "Not at all. I understand how you feel. Grief and worry. They can eat away at a person."

"Yes," she said.

"I was married, too," he blurted out. "She was killed one month after the wedding. In a car crash."

"I'm so sorry."

"So am I." He sighed. "She had drunk too much. I should not have let her drive. Now I live with that."

"You can't be responsible for another person."

"That doesn't make it any easier."

"No."

His gaze held hers, and for a moment Caroline was conscious of the connection between them. It almost felt that this handsome stranger was reading her thoughts. Embarrassed, she looked down and toyed with her napkin, glad when the man with the moustache appeared with a plate containing some dubious and unidentifiable bits and pieces. She could see the whiskers of a prawn head poking out of batter, and the tiny tentacles of a squid. It looked quite alarming, and Caroline took a tentative bite. The flesh of the squid was light and tender inside the crispy batter.

She looked up and nodded. "It's good."

"You have never tried it before?"

"I've tried calamari, but not like this."

"Our seafood is the best," he said. "And the venison, at this time of year. You wait until you try it. In Venice, we eat well—if you know where to eat."

"Do you live in the city?" she asked.

"Me? I now have a flat on the Lido, overlooking the sea. I like it there better. More space. My family has a palazzo in the city. You know Palazzo Rossi? It is now a five-star hotel. My father gave it up years ago. Too expensive to keep up, with all the staff needed and the repairs. So now he has an apartment in one of the new buildings on the Grand Canal, and a hotel company leases the palazzo from us." He looked up with a satisfied grin. "It's quite profitable, apart from now, when nobody dares to travel." A waiter whisked their plates away, and Luca refilled their glasses.

"And you, Signora Grant, where do you live? What do you do?"

"I have been living in London. My husband and I were both in the fashion industry. He designed, and I work for a women's magazine."

"Very nice."

"It was. Until he went off to New York and met that woman." She was amazed at the anger in her voice.

"Ah. So now what will you do? Continue to live in London and work at your fashion magazine?"

"I've just moved in with my grandmother. She's all alone in the country now that my great-aunt has died. It's very peaceful."

"You need peace?"

"I think so. I need to accept what has happened."

He looked up suddenly and leaned across the table towards her. "I think you need to fight," he said. "The husband keeps your son. You want him back. Peace won't help you."

"No," she said, "you're right. But he holds all the cards right now: He's become rich. He's with a famous, powerful woman. And he claims her psychiatrist is telling him my son shouldn't fly."

"A famous woman?"

"Desiree—the singer?"

"Oh, her!" He gave a disparaging smirk. "I remember reading about this. He wins the fashion competition and then goes off with the singer, right?" He shook his head. "Don't worry. It won't last. If you want him back, he will come crawling, I promise you."

"You think so?" she asked.

He nodded. "Of course. Fame is a great seducer, but most famous people are—how do you say?— shallow. They want to be adored, no more. That gets tiring."

As he spoke, plates of venison were put in front of them, and they fell silent as they ate the tender meat in a rich red sauce surrounded by tiny potatoes and green beans. When the plates were cleared, cups of coffee and little almond cakes were brought.

"That was delicious, thank you," Caroline said.

Luca reached into his wallet. "Here is my card," he said. "Call me when you have checked with our city records. If the apartment is yours, then it's yours. I don't understand it, but I accept it. And I urge you to be careful, because there is renovation taking place in the building. Will you want to stay there, do you think?"

She hadn't thought about it. It seemed like a wonderful idea. "I might."

"So please call me, and we can arrange to visit my grandmother and see what she knows."

The man with the moustache came to help them on with their coats. They stepped out into the blustery day. Luca took her hand. "*Arrivederci*, Signora Caroline. It was an interesting meeting."

"Goodbye, Luca. Thank you for a lovely lunch." The words came out mechanically, her British manners kicking in. She walked away feeling excited but confused. Was Luca Da Rossi a charming enemy? If he was renovating the building to turn into apartments, he'd obviously like to get back that spectacular top floor. And she was a foreigner here. She would have to tread very carefully.

She walked briskly across Dorsoduro, not really noticing the dripping water from balconies above or the brisk wind that drove her. She had an overwhelming desire to have her claim proven valid. She was not going to let some stranger acquire her aunt's Venetian retreat. The fact that the first thing she had discovered had been a drawer full of her aunt's sketches had confirmed that Aunt Lettie had lived in that place for some time. Now she was dying to explore the rest of it—to find out just what her aunt had been doing there. She supposed the explanation was simple: Granny had said that Aunt Lettie was given some sort of bursary to study abroad for a while. So she had gone to Venice and rented a place while she studied. Except . . . why would she need a ninety-nine-year lease for an apartment if she was studying for a few months? And where had the money come from to buy such a lease? It was, as Luca could see, prime real estate.

She reached the Accademia Bridge just as a vaporetto was arriving. She jumped aboard and was grateful to be out of the rain and wind as the boat headed for the Rialto. After alighting there, she was directed to the city hall. But to her annoyance there was a sign on the big front door announcing that office hours were ten until one and then three until six. It was only just two, and it seemed that all the small shops around the bridge, likewise, were shuttered for the lunch hour. She crossed the bridge and walked around the market, which was in the last stages of closing up for the day. Only a solitary fish lay on a marble slab.

The stall-keeper called out to her. When she said she didn't understand, he switched to English. "You want? Last fish? Good price, huh?"

"I'm sorry. Staying at a hotel," she said and walked on. As she did so, she pictured herself at that market, learning to bargain with the stall-keepers, buying fresh fruit and veg and fish every day. It was a tempting daydream until she reminded herself that she had a life back in England, a son to raise, a grandmother to comfort.

At last a distant clock chimed the hour, and she crossed the bridge back to the palazzo. Alas, the furniture inside did not match the grandeur of the exterior, and the first two people she addressed did not speak English. Finally, a young woman was called, and Caroline explained what she wanted. As Luca had suspected, the records from long ago were stored in a separate building. This involved crossing the Rialto Bridge and heading towards the less desirable part of the city, then climbing several flights of stairs from a dingy courtyard. More translation was needed, much waving of hands, and then an elderly man suggested she leave the certificate with them.

"No, sorry," Caroline said. "This is not leaving my hands. Too important. Can you make a copy and check with that?"

He finally agreed that he could, then indicated the search might take a few days, maybe a week, maybe more. He shrugged. "Is very old document . . ."

The frustration boiled over. "Listen, please," she said. "It is very important that I know whether this place belongs to me. There is someone who would like to take it from me if I can't prove I own it. Please help me."

Of course, no Italian man can resist the words "please help me" from a lady. He gave her a tired smile. "For you, signora, I will do my very best. Come back tomorrow, eh?"

So she had to be content with leaving a photocopy with Signor Alessi and agreeing to meet late the next afternoon. The weather seemed to have set in for the day, so she gave up, went back to the pensione and fell into a long afternoon nap, no doubt encouraged by the wine she had drunk at midday. The rain had worsened by the evening, so she made for the closest restaurant: a small cramped room, seemingly populated by students from the nearby university, where she was pleasantly surprised by the quality of the seafood risotto.

That night it was hard to sleep, whether the food had been too rich or the discoveries of the day just too overwhelming. Caroline lay listening to the sounds of the city, trying to come to terms with finding herself the potential owner of a lovely apartment and dealing carefully with a man who might do anything he could to take it away from her. Why did he have to be so damned attractive? And then she considered this: it had been a long time since she had considered a man desirable. At least that was one small step forward and away from Josh.

The next morning dawned bright but blustery. Caroline breakfasted, chatting with the proprietress, telling her about her discovery.

"The Da Rossi family?" The woman was astonished. "They are one of the great families of Venice, you know. They go back to the Middle Ages and include a doge and a pope. They made

252

their money in shipping, and then more money in shipbuilding during the war for that pig Mussolini and for Hitler. Not something I'd be proud of." She gave Caroline a knowing nudge. "I believe the patriarch stepped down recently. Now it's his son who runs the business. But no more shipbuilding these days. That's all gone to Asia, hasn't it?"

After breakfast Caroline put on her mac and rode the vaporetto out past St Mark's, past an area of gardens, now mostly bare and leafless at this time of year, and out to the Lido. There she walked across the island to the beach, watching angry waves crashing on the sand, wishing she had worn a scarf to protect herself from the wind. She grabbed a bowl of minestrone soup at a small café and waited impatiently until she could visit Signor Alessi. At four thirty she climbed the steps to his office. He wasn't there. Caroline swallowed back frustration until a young woman appeared.

"Un momentino. He will come, signora. Wait."

She waited, and the old gentleman appeared, smiling.

"I have found the record of your lease," he said. "It was not too hard. The Da Rossi holdings are easy to find. And I am happy to tell you that the lease is all in order. *Va tutto bene*, heh? No problem."

Impulsively, Caroline leaned forward and gave

him a kiss on the cheek. "You are an angel," she said.

He looked absurdly pleased. She almost danced down the steps. The lease was all in order. The apartment was hers! She telephoned Luca Da Rossi's number and left a message: "The city confirms my lease is properly recorded and still valid. I will be taking possession of the apartment tomorrow. When can we meet with your grandmother?"

CHAPTER 21

Juliet, Venice, July 20, 1939

I have settled into a pleasant routine here. I get up, bathe, eat breakfast, usually with my landlady gossiping about who was at Mass and what they were wearing and what the priest said, and then I go to classes. I seem to have made some friends—or at least pleasant acquaintances. I have gone to lunch with Henry, who is like a loveable St Bernard puppy, and with Imelda, who is surprisingly nice to me and not as terrifying as I first imagined. She and her family have suffered through Franco, being driven from their life in Madrid and forced to survive in Biarritz, France. Her father, formerly a professor, is now working as a janitor. But she has grandparents who are fans of Franco and who are paying for her schooling. I have to confess that I have not reached the stage of friendship where I can share in a similar way with her. She remarked on the fact while we were having a before-lunch coffee one day. "You never tell me anything about yourself," she said.

"There is nothing to tell," I replied. "I have led the most ordinary of lives since my father died and I had to leave art school. I teach girls. I go home. I live in quiet solitude with my mother."

"But what about men?" she asked. "There must be men. You do not want a husband?"

"Of course I do," I replied. "But the only men in my village are the vicar, who is married, the butcher, who is also married, and several elderly farmworkers. And I can't leave my mother. She had become most dependent on me."

"So how did you manage to escape and come here?"

"My aunt agreed to live with my mother for the year."

"That was kind."

"Not entirely." I smiled. "She had just lost her Austrian maid, and I don't think she wanted to do her own housework."

"We all want something, don't we?" Imelda said. "But myself, I do not think I could live without men. I enjoy the physical relationship, don't you?"

I felt myself blushing. "I haven't had much chance to experience it. But the few times were very nice."

I've also made friends with the fair girl from South Tyrol. Her name is Veronika. She is less intrusive and disturbing, but funny and sweet and so young. Just the antidote I need to depression. And I have seen Leo again, in spite of all efforts to avoid him. Most days we have no classes after lunch. It seems to be a time for siesta here, as in

Spain. The shops all close until four. The city slumbers, apart from energetic tourists. But I find I am not able to rest in the afternoon. My brain is still buzzing after the morning's session, and I am itching to paint. We have studios reserved for students at the accademia where we can go to paint, but I have started doing what Leo suggested and going out with my sketchbook, trying to capture ordinary people going about their daily lives.

Two days ago, I was sketching in a narrow street just off the Campo Sant'Anzolo, which is on the other side of the big church of Santo Stefano, so it is in my neighbourhood. I liked the way the laundry was strung across the street, row after row. It created an interesting contrast of light and shadow. I thought it would make a good painting—maybe even a semi-abstract that Professor Corsetti would approve of. I was deep in thought when I sensed that someone was standing behind me. I spun around and saw Leo there.

"Can you not find something more beautiful than drying underclothes and sheets?" he asked, a smile on his face.

I fought to keep my face calm and distant. "Are you spying on me?"

"No, pure coincidence, I promise you. I have just come from Alberto Bertoni—the bookshop on the corner. Have you visited it yet? One of the oldest in the city. I can find amazing things there. Real treasures. I had to pass it on my way home from a business meeting with my father, so I was lured inside. And then I find you. Two pleasant surprises in one day."

He squatted down beside me, perching on the steps where I was sitting. "How are you enjoying our city? And your academy?"

"Both are wonderful, thank you."

"What are you doing in this neighbourhood?"

"I live nearby." I regretted the words as soon as I said them.

I saw the reaction his eyes. "Really? In which street?"

"I'm not going to tell you, or you will come and visit me, and we'll both get into trouble."

"All right. But not on this street, I take it?"

"No."

"You know what it is called, don't you?"

"I don't."

He was grinning. "It is Rio Tera dei Assassini."

" 'Rio Tera'—that means a former river that has been filled in to make a street."

"And 'assassini'?"

"It sounds like 'assassins.' "

"Exactly. You are right. The street of assassins."

"Goodness." I looked up, alarmed. "Assassins have their own street in Venice?"

"Of course. How else would you find them if you needed one?"

I checked to see if he was joking. He seemed quite serious. "Not today, surely?" I examined the quiet surroundings, the peeling shutters closed against the midday heat, the ubiquitous pigeons sitting on porches.

He gave a little shrug.

"But what about the police?"

"I'm sure they need assassins, too, from time to time."

"You are pulling my leg, Leo." I laughed.

"I am not touching your leg. Although I would like to."

"It's another—"

"I know. English expression. Your language is crazy, you know. We must only speak Italian from now on."

"I'm doing rather well in Italian these days," I said. "I have to chat with my landlady over meals and of course in all my classes."

"Does she speak pure Italian and not Venetian? I don't want you to learn bad things."

"She's originally from Turin, so she speaks Italian to me."

"Good." He got up again. "I will leave you to your sketching. I must get back to work. We have a big project. Bianca's father has an order for ships from Mussolini himself, and we have the task of ferrying supplies to the army across the Mediterranean and around to Abyssinia."

"To the war?"

He nodded. "My father and father-in-law have no hesitation in profiting from such things, so it would seem."

"But you would?"

"Let us say I would think very hard before I agreed." He was about to walk away, then turned back to me. "Will you come and watch me row on Sunday?"

"You are rowing? Where?"

"The regatta at the big festival. You don't know about it?"

I shook my head.

"One of the most important in our city. The Feast of the Redentore. It celebrates when we were saved from the plague in the 1500s. In the afternoon there are all sorts of rowing races. I shall compete in the two-man boat—not very successfully, I fear, but my cousin signed me up. He is younger and fitter than I am. Then everyone walks across the bridge to the Church of the Redentore for Mass—"

"Where is that?" I asked, now familiar with many of the churches but not that one.

"Over on Giudecca."

I frowned, trying to place this. "But there is no bridge. It's an island."

"There will be a bridge on Sunday." He looked pleased with himself, as if he was enjoying surprising me. "They build a bridge of barges all the way across from the Zattere, and people walk across to Mass, and then they picnic with their families and watch the fireworks. You must come. You'll enjoy it."

"I've no family to picnic with," I pointed out.

"Your new friends from the academy. They will enjoy it, too."

"I'll ask them," I agreed. "At least I'll come to watch the rowing. And then later for the fireworks. I love fireworks."

"Me too. I'll row extra hard, knowing you are watching me." He blew me a kiss and hurried off, leaving me hot, bothered and confused again. I so enjoyed talking to him. We talked so easily, as if we had never been apart. We laughed together. And yet it was wrong. Why oh why did I think it would be a good idea to come back to this place?

The next day I came home to be greeted by my landlady with a suspicious look on her face.

"Somebody left flowers for you," she said, indicating a bouquet wrapped in paper, tied with a white ribbon, lying on the hall table.

"Really? How nice!" I couldn't think who that would be. "Did they leave a note?"

"I believe there is one with it," she said, and I got the impression that she might have opened and read it.

I went over and picked up the bouquet. The sweet smell of red roses, mixed with other scents, came up to me. She was right. A little note was tucked in between the flowers. I opened it.

You see. It was easy to find out where you live. Everybody knows everybody in this town. I just had to ask for the woman from Turin!

It wasn't signed, for which I was grateful. I gave my landlady a little smile. "Do you have a vase? We can put them on the kitchen table and both enjoy them."

"You know who they are from? An admirer?"

"Just a friend."

She nodded. "Someone said they saw the Da Rossi boy in this street." She said it casually. From the way my face flushed, she confirmed her suspicion. "Not a good idea. You don't want to get involved with that family. And I've been hearing things about his wife, too. Her father has Mafiosi ties, so one understands. He wouldn't take kindly to anyone . . ."

She left the rest of the sentence hanging. Anyone who crossed his daughter. I understood.

"Just a friend from my childhood," I said. "Nothing more."

"Keep it that way."

"Don't worry. I intend to, signora," I said. I took the flowers through to the kitchen.

CHAPTER 22

Caroline, Venice, October 11, 2001

The next morning Caroline set out for the flat she had inherited. She decided to wait before checking out of the pensione, just in case the place was not immediately habitable. There were sounds of hammering and distant voices but no sign of Luca as she went up the stairs and unlocked the door leading to her great-aunt's hideaway. In bright sunlight the view was spectacular. She could see right across the lagoon, and she stood at the window for long minutes before she set out to investigate the rest of the rooms. To one side was a small kitchen with pots and pans, including two cups and plates on a draining board. Through a doorway was a bathroom on one side and a bedroom behind it. The bed still had sheets on it, although there were signs that mice had found it a comfy refuge.

"New bed," she said to herself. Then she opened drawers and saw they were full of clothes, rumpled together in haphazard fashion. This in itself was strange, as her aunt had always struck her as meticulously neat. In addition to this, how strange that Aunt Lettie had not taken anything with her when she left. The whole place looked as if she expected to return. Then she stopped, surprised: amongst her aunt's clothing, there were some items that appeared to belong to a child. A girl's jumper and skirt. A pair of socks. Who on earth had stayed at the flat with her great-aunt? Maybe Luca Da Rossi's grandmother would know more.

She looked up when she heard feet coming up the stairs and then a tap on her door. Luca came in, breathing heavily. "It is quite a climb," he said. "You will be very fit if you live here."

"I won't be living here," she said. "I have a life in England. But I should like to spend holidays here. Maybe I will rent it out during the summer."

"I congratulate you," he said. "I have talked with our lawyer and senior managers, and they are all as perplexed as I am that someone in the company granted a lease to part of our property. But the city has declared the deed to be valid. I can say no more." He walked over to the window. "You have one of the best views in the city."

"Yes, I know," she said. "I've just started to look around, and it's so strange. It's as if she left everything, expecting to be back. Look—the cups beside the sink. There is even a caddy with tea still in it. And all her clothes in the drawers in the bedroom. And some clothing belonging to a child."

"Your aunt had a child?"

"No!" Caroline had to laugh. "She was the ultimate spinster. Never married. Very prim and proper. And the clothing would fit a girl of maybe eleven or twelve. There was nobody in my family like that."

"And the other strange thing," Luca said. "The document was from 1939. England was already at war. Why did she not go home? Italy had signed a non-aggression pact with Germany and would join the war the next summer. She must have realized she'd be in danger if she stayed."

"Perhaps that's the explanation," Caroline said. "She had to leave in a hurry when the authorities came after her. That would be when she fled to Switzerland. My grandmother told me my great-aunt sat out the war in Switzerland and helped refugee children."

"Ah, then maybe that's another mystery answered," he replied. "This girl was a refugee child she was helping."

"I'm hoping your grandmother will remember."

"Ah yes. I came to tell you we can visit my grandmother today, but I cannot guarantee she will be clear-headed. Some days it is good, and some days she is off in another world."

"We can try," Caroline said. "If you have the time, that is."

He shrugged. "Those lazy bums downstairs are taking longer than I would like to refinish the rooms, so my day is my own. You want to go now, or do you want to explore this place more first?"

"No, I'd like to go now," she said. "I am planning to move in here, as soon as I get some new bedding. The mice seem to have enjoyed the warm bed."

He was looking around. "It's amazing there is not more damage, given the years between. How many? Sixty? Why are there not more spiderwebs? More dust? It's almost as if she went away last week—apart from your mice." And he laughed.

"Sleeping Beauty's castle," Caroline muttered.

"Your aunt—was she a great beauty?"

Caroline smiled. "I only knew her as an old woman. Like I said, always prim and proper. No fuss. No frills. But my grandmother said she was striking as a girl—lovely auburn hair."

"Auburn?"

"You know—copper. Dark red." I paused, looking at him. "Like yours."

"Ah yes. I am afraid I inherited my mother's red hair. I got teased for it at school. And I gather my father also had a little red in his before he went grey. A very attractive man, my father."

So are you, Caroline thought but didn't say. They set off down the stairs. The weather was clouding up fast. "Does your grandmother live far away?" she asked.

"She is in a nursing home, out on the Lido."

"So we'll have to catch a vaporetto?" Caroline glanced up nervously. It was threatening to rain again.

"No, not necessary." He waved a hand. "I have my launch. Much faster."

Luca led her to the quay and jumped down into a sleek teak craft with a cabin at the rear. He helped her to step in, then untied the rope. The motor roared to life, and the boat moved forward up the canal towards the open water. As soon as they were clear of the last buildings, Luca pulled back the throttle. Caroline was overcome with the sheer power, the speed. Luca glanced back, exhilaration on his face.

"Good, eh? My new toy." Then he added, "Don't be scared. I am a good driver."

"I wasn't scared," Caroline replied defensively.

Luca grinned, gave her a wink, and went back to steering. Caroline stared at the back of his head. The smile, the wink had definitely been flirtatious. *Watch out for Italian men,* she told herself. They cut around freighters entering the harbour and arrived at the Lido in no time at all.

Luca leapt out, tied up the craft and then held out a hand to help her. "You didn't get too wet, I hope?" he asked.

"No. I'm fine. I enjoyed it, actually."

He nodded appreciation and set off for a modern white building facing the waterfront. Inside, a white-coated nurse greeted Luca and led them through to a room at the back of the building. There a little old lady lay propped against pillows. Her hair was snow white, her face peaceful, but the eyes she opened were dark and anxious.

"What is this?" she demanded.

"Nonna, I have brought a friend to see you," he said.

Caroline got the gist of the Italian.

"This one you are finally going to marry?" the old woman asked. "Give us an heir?"

Luca gave an embarrassed grin and turned to translate for Caroline. "She wants me to marry you and produce an heir." He sat on the edge of his grandmother's bed. "This is a lady from England who's come to talk to you."

The old woman scrutinized Caroline's face, blinked and reacted with a start.

"England?" Her face was suddenly hostile. "Me, I do not like the English."

"She just wants to ask you a couple of questions, then we'll go," Luca said patiently. "She wants to know if you remember an English lady at the beginning of the war. She stayed in one of our buildings. A Miss Browning. Did you know her? Was she a friend of the family? Does that name ring a bell?"

"No. I do not know her. I never heard of this woman. Why would I be friends with an Englishwoman? Me, I hate the English. I wish

268

them all dead." She started waving her arms, as if swatting away flies. "Get that person out of here. I never wish to see an Englishwoman again. She has come to cause trouble. To give me grief."

Luca caught her hand and patted it. "No, Nonna. She does not wish to cause you any pain. She just wants to find out about her relative who used to live here, that's all."

But the old woman was now too upset to calm down. Caroline tapped Luca on the shoulder. "We should go," she whispered.

"I'm sorry," he said when they were outside again. "I don't know how much of that you understood. For some reason, she has a dislike of the British. Maybe something that happened long ago. The past and the present are mixed up for her. But she said she did not know of your aunt. Never met her."

"That's all right," Caroline said. "There would have been no reason for her to meet members of your family. I presume the leasing was done through your company. Maybe people had left the city with the threat of war and they wanted to have their buildings occupied rather than have squatters set up in them."

"I would believe that," he said, "except why the ninety-nine-year lease? That is what doesn't make sense to me." He sighed. "Well, I don't suppose we'll ever find out now, unless you discover some correspondence between your aunt and our company that might throw light on the situation."

"Or maybe some correspondence in your own archives," Caroline said.

"Possible. But the city does not think it is a forgery, so I must accept that. Someone in our company made an error in judgement, or acted on a whim, and now we'll probably never know who." He helped Caroline into the boat. "So enjoy your new apartment. And who knows, I may decide that I want to buy the lease from you. Property in Venice now goes for a good sum."

Caroline almost blurted out that she didn't want to sell it, but then stayed silent. She would not be sentimental. The money would pay for a lawyer if she needed one to get Teddy home again. They sped across the lagoon, the boat bouncing over the waves, then landing with a thud. Luca pulled up beside her building, then helped her out.

"I am afraid the builders might be noisy," he said. "And there is no heat in the building. But otherwise I hope you enjoy your stay. Let me know if you find anything of interest—some of the correspondence, maybe."

Then he revved up the boat, and off he went. Caroline made her way up the stairs to the flat and, once inside, sank into one of the chairs. It had been an emotionally draining morning. Clearly her visit had awoken a painful memory for the old woman. The more Caroline thought about it, the more she became sure that it was something the old woman had seen when she looked at Caroline that had triggered that memory. Was there a family resemblance? And she began to suspect that Luca's grandmother did remember Miss Browning after all.

CHAPTER 23

Juliet, late at night, Sunday, July 23, 1939

I don't know how to put any of this down on paper, but I must. One day I will want to remember it, all the details. Every little detail.

The day of the Festa del Redentore. My landlady informed me that she would not be preparing an evening meal for me because of the festival. "You know—the Redentore. I mentioned it to you before. One of the biggest days of the year in Venice. Everyone joined in. Those who had a boat would be out in it. She would be crossing the bridge to picnic, to attend Mass and to watch fireworks. It was a day for families, but as she had no family in the city any longer, she would be joining the other widows from the street, and their children and grandchildren. I would be welcome to join them over on the island of Giudecca if I so desired. The big Mass at the church was at seven o'clock in the evening, but there were all sorts of events before that: boat races and a market and games for the children."

"So you won't be going to church in the morning if there is a Mass in the evening?" I asked.

She looked horrified, as if I had suggested she

might want to walk around with no clothes on. "Not go to Mass? Of course I must go. To receive communion. Since one must fast from midnight onwards, it has to be a morning Mass. I could not survive with no food or drink until the evening."

To me, a member of the relaxed and easy-going Church of England, this was one of the rules that seemed strange. If an empty stomach was important to receive communion, then an hour would suffice, surely. From midnight on was excessive. But then there was much about the Catholic Church I did not understand—like confessing sins to a priest and having them forgiven. My wandering thoughts were interrupted as my landlady asked, "So you will come to the feast?"

"Probably not to the Mass," I said. "I might watch the boat races and then the fireworks. And some fellow students might join me for a picnic, but it's really a day for family, isn't it?"

"I won't be home to prepare your meal in the evening."

"Don't worry. Some stores will be open, won't they? I'll buy some picnic supplies for myself."

She actually patted my hand. "Don't bother. I have plenty of food here. There is always far too much. You are welcome to help yourself."

There is no chance of sleeping late on Sunday mornings in Venice. The first church bells start at six o'clock and are followed almost every half hour by the bells of various other churches. Sometimes there are four or five churches at once, so that the city echoes with the sound. I heard my landlady bustling around in the kitchen, talking, as usual to Bruno the cat. I thought I might as well get up, rather than lie in bed doing nothing. I bathed, dressed in my lightest cotton frock, as the day already felt hot and clammy, then went through to the kitchen. I realized the signora had a big day ahead, so I took the liberty of making the coffee and laying out bread, cheeses and jam. She looked absurdly pleased when she returned home to find breakfast waiting for her.

"I hope you didn't mind," I said. "I was sure you'd have a lot to do today."

"I'm grateful," she said. "I do have baking to do, and the day will be a hot one." She considered this, then added, "Fortunately, the widow Grevi has offered to make the *sarde in saor*. You know I do not like the smell of fish in my house."

I had seen this item on menus and gathered it was fresh sardines cooked with some kind of sauce, but I had yet to try it. Maybe this evening, if I located the signora and her party, I'd be offered some.

We sat and ate breakfast together, then I volunteered to do the washing up while she got out her recipe books and started work. The kitchen smelled enticingly of garlic and onions, then of baking. I left her to it, sitting in my room and polishing some of my sketches. By midday she tapped on my door.

"I'll be off then," she said. She was dressed in a flowery silk dress and what was clearly her best hat, looking more outfitted for a wedding than a picnic. "I just saw Signora Bertolini coming out of her house. So I can leave you to lock the door and take a key with you? And I've left you food for your own picnic on the kitchen table."

I watched her go from the kitchen window, saw her join the gaggle of widows, each carrying a large box or basket of food. They were not going to starve, that was clear. Then I saw that she had laid out slices of ham, salami, tomatoes, cheese and olives on a plate for me, and next to them a slice of some sort of quiche, and some plums. I packed the food and waited until I thought the events would start before I put my own hat on. It was going to be hot sitting in the sun. Not wanting to carry too much, I put the keys and a little money into the pocket of my dress and left my handbag and wallet at home. I presumed occasions like this might be a field day for pickpockets, and they weren't going to get much from me.

The streets were almost deserted as I came out to the piazza in front of Santo Stefano. I looked up and noticed for the first time that all the balconies were decorated with garlands, paper lanterns, flowers. When I crossed the Accademia Bridge, a steady stream of boats was coming up the Grand Canal, most of them decorated, too, all crammed full of people already eating, drinking and merrymaking. As I stood watching the spectacle below me, I saw that clouds were building over the mainland. This was not unusual for this time of year. The clouds gathered over the Dolomites, but rarely did the storms reach us out on the island.

I made my way across the sestiere of Dorsoduro to the waterfront known as the Zattere. It was strange, but I had never crossed to this side of Dorsoduro, even though it was quite a narrow sliver of land. The Zattere was a promenade that ran beside a wide waterway—too wide, really, to be called a canal. On the other side was the island of Giudecca, usually only accessible by ferry. Only today the canal was spanned by a makeshift bridge. Barges were lined up across the canal, and a wooden walkway had been laid over them. It looked rather precarious to me. The bridge terminated at a lovely white facade of a church, facing the waterfront. From my reading, I knew the style was referred to as Palladian— sort of neoclassical with columns. Behind it the rest of the church was that warm pinkish orange and had a large dome.

I looked around to see if I could spot any of my fellow students. When I had mentioned the boat races and suggested we might have a picnic somewhere and see the fireworks, I was not greeted with overwhelming enthusiasm. Imelda informed me that she had no intention of sitting in the sun and getting sunburned. Gaston said he didn't go in for religion. Franz said he might come, depending on how much work he had for class, and Henry said it sounded like fun. I said I'd try to be somewhere near the bridge. But the whole area was crammed with people, some waiting to make their way across the bridge and others having already claimed their spots to watch the races and picnic. I couldn't spot Henry and thought it unlikely I'd find anybody in the chaotic movement of people. Nor did I think I'd have much chance of finding a spot in the shade. It appeared that every inch along both sides of the canal had already been claimed with blankets, chairs, tables, picnic baskets and even some umbrellas.

Cheers further along the waterfront announced that the races had started. I joined the line to follow the stream across the bridge. It was a strange sensation walking on a pathway that rose and fell with the water—and no handrail either. I wondered how many people might fall in before the day was over, seeing the amount of wine that was being consumed. On reaching the island, I worked my way out towards the tip, where I might have a good view of the races.

They seemed to be starting out in the lagoon in front of St Mark's. The whole basin was full of watercraft, with a clear path down the middle for the races.

I squeezed into a corner of shade on some steps in front of a building and found I was sharing the excitement as the crowd around me started shouting and cheering. First came the two-man gondolas, moving remarkably fast. The gondolas had been painted for the occasion in bright colours, breaking the tradition of their usual black. I noticed some spectators wore neckerchiefs in the colour of the team they were supporting. They were particularly vocal. Since I was supporting no one in particular, I just watched, although it was exciting as teams drew level, then overtook and pipped another boat on the finish line. Another heat followed, then another. And a ceremony on one of the docks on the far bank for the victors, with much jubilation if the gondolier the crowd was supporting won. Then came the junior rowing races and finally the two-man boats. They were all quite far from me, but I thought I recognized Leo, even though most of the boats were manned by dark-haired, well-muscled oarsmen. Still, I waved and cheered as I had promised. His boat came third, and he and fellow oarsman were helped on to the dais, where they were surrounded and congratulated by family and friends, with much hugging and slapping on the back. Then it was confirmed to me that it had been Leo. I saw Bianca push her way through the crowd, looking stunning in a simple white linen dress. Even from here, I recognized her instantly. She came up to Leo and gave him a very public kiss. He put an arm around her, and they were swallowed into the crowd.

The races being over, the crowd settled down to the serious business of eating. I walked up and down a bit, wondering if I should try to find my landlady and join her party. Then I decided it was unlikely I'd find them, and besides, I did not want to intrude. And frankly I had no appetite after what I had just seen. I felt alone and out of place. Everybody here was surrounded by family and friends, all laughing, teasing, eating and drinking. I realized if I'd been back in England, it wouldn't have been much different—just my mother and me. No big family, no large circle of friends. No laughter. I sat on a step, opened my packet of food, stared at it, then decided to put it away again. I'd just go back to my room until the fireworks started. No sense at all in being here.

"Signorina! Here! Over here!" I looked up to see a large middle-aged man waving. He was seated at a table with his family. It took me a minute to realize he was waving at me. He said something.

A young man got up and came over. "My father

says you should not eat alone on such a day. Please join us, there is plenty for all."

I tried to refuse. No, I couldn't intrude on their family celebration. But the man insisted, taking my arm. Reluctantly I was led over. The father introduced them all in rapid succession. His wife, his daughter, her husband, her two children, his two sons, his mother. When they heard I was English, they were all fascinated and peppered me with questions. Did we have such feasts in England? How many brothers and sisters did I have? And why wasn't I married yet? I answered them all and heard their amazement that such a beautiful young woman did not have a husband.

"We must do something about this," the wife said. "Who do we know with unmarried sons?"

There were suggestions, laughter, and I began to relax amongst them. Food was offered, including the sardines in their sauce, polenta, pasta. Everything tasted wonderful. I found myself thinking how pale and dull our lives in England were compared to this. And then the thought crept in, unbidden. Did I want to go home at the end of the year? What if I just stayed and found a job and spent my life amongst these happy, loud, affectionate people?

Wine was offered and poured. Toasts were drunk, one of them to me. And then the church bells rang.

"We must go to Mass now if we want to get a seat," the wife said. "You come with us?"

I could hardly refuse. The wife and daughter linked arms with mine. I believe they were Giovanna and Sofia, but I wasn't quite sure which was which. We left the food and the table with the absolute conviction that nobody would touch it, and off we went into the church. It was filling up fast. We were squeezed into a pew. I felt horribly uncomfortable at flesh pressing against mine, the smells of sweat and everyone's just-consumed picnic around me, mingled with the scent of incense. More and more people streamed in. The aisles were packed. People stood around the walls. Then a bell rang, and a great procession of priests, acolytes, choir entered. I didn't understand much of what was going on. I stood when they stood, knelt when they knelt. When hymns were sung, the whole place echoed with sound. I could tell it was a moving experience for those around me, but the heat was intense. Many of the women had fans, including my adopted family, so I benefitted from a small wafting of air, but as the service progressed I started to feel really clammy, as if I might pass out. I was so relieved when they stood for the final blessing, followed by a closing song and a great fight for the doorway.

As we came out, it was getting dark. Usually there was a glowing twilight at this time, but the clouds from the mainland had now built over the city and a wind had sprung up.

"This isn't good," the wife said, gesturing dramatically with her hands. "What about the fireworks? They can't have fireworks in the rain. They said on the radio there might be a storm, but whoever believes the radio? We might have to pack up before everything is ruined, Luigi."

I helped them pack up the food into baskets. It seemed they lived on Giudecca and would take the supplies and furniture home. If it didn't rain, they'd be back for the fireworks. Did I want to come with them?

The first drops of rain spattered as she spoke, and a wind snatched at nearby tablecloths.

"I think perhaps I had better go home while I can," I said. "I don't want to get soaked going across two bridges."

"Come and visit us again," the father said. "The Olivetti family. Everyone knows where we live. Just around the corner there. You see? Come and visit. Any time. Come on a Sunday. You'll always find us having a big meal like today, eh, Giovanna?"

She nodded agreement, smiling at me.

I thanked them profusely. The wife pinched my cheek and said she'd be working on finding a good man for me. The others embraced me. It was strange and wonderful at the same time. I watched them walk away, still talking and laughing loudly as fat raindrops spattered. I wondered whether I should take shelter, then I thought it might be wiser to cross the pontoon before the storm got any worse. Unfortunately, many other people had the same idea. A long line was waiting to get on to the walkway. I joined it, and we moved at a snail's pace, getting increasingly wet. Around me there were wails and complaints as the rain intensified. I was somewhere just beyond the middle of the pontoon when the heavens opened. Rain came down in a solid sheet. The rain turned to hail, bouncing off the boards of the pontoon and stinging as it hit us. Lightning flashed nearby. Thunder rumbled. And a fierce wind stirred up waves. People were screaming and praying. As I fought to keep my balance, a large woman lost her footing and grabbed on to me. A wave slapped at the wooden planks and we went into the water together.

CHAPTER 24

Juliet, Venice, July 23, 1939

The water was surprisingly cold and took my breath away. The woman was still grabbing on to me, and we were pulled under. I fought my way to the surface, gulping to take a breath as rain and waves buffeted my face. I tasted salt and gagged. The woman was clinging on to me, arms wrapped around my neck.

"Help me. I can't swim," she shouted as she lashed out, then clung to me again.

She pulled us both under once more and then bobbed up, choking and crying. She was going to drown us both if she continued like this and nobody came to our rescue. All I could see around me was darkness and waves. I realized I'd have to free myself if I wanted to survive. Let someone else rescue her. I was conscious now of other people in the water, of screams and cries and the sound of motorboats coming towards us. A wave broke over us, and I was dragged under again. I clawed at her hands to free myself and kicked up to the surface, swivelling around so that she was now in front of me. She came to the surface coughing and choking, and I saw the panic in her eyes.

"Maria Vergine," she gasped. And of course I couldn't let her drown. I managed to turn her away from me, so that she couldn't pull me down, and held her head above water. How did you say "Don't struggle" in Italian? All sensible thought had gone out of my head.

"Be still," I managed to say. "Help will come." I just hoped I was right.

I tried to look around as we were borne up on a wave. The current had swept us away from the bridge, and from the odd glimpse I got between waves and rain, it seemed as if the barges might have been torn apart. In any case, there was nothing to grab on to. I wondered how long I could hold her up, whether I could swim with her to shore. I was not the strongest swimmer, having had little opportunity in the cold English seas, and my dress was now clinging to my legs, making it hard to move. I could make out lights in the distance but hopelessly far away. Should I let her go and save myself? The words echoed in my head. But I couldn't. Then a shape loomed up beside us. Hands reached down, and the woman was dragged onboard a boat. Then the hands came for me, and I was hauled up to safety.

I sat on the wooden deck where I was deposited, coughing and gasping. The woman was crying now, great heaving sobs, and gasping out, "Thanks be to God. Thanks to the Madonna."

"Must I always have to pull you out of the

water?" said a familiar voice, and I looked up to see Leo standing, looking down at me. His tone was light, but I saw the fear in his eyes.

The tension and shock, coupled with the relief, were too much for me.

"Do you have to make a joke of everything?" I replied in English. "I nearly drowned. She couldn't swim, and she was holding on to me and pulling us both under. If you hadn't come . . ." And I swallowed back a sob.

He put a hand on my shoulder. "It's all right. It's going to be all right. You are safe now. Don't cry."

I didn't want to cry in front of him. I forced back tears. "I'm not crying," I said defiantly.

Then I noticed that there were other people huddled together in the back of the boat. Judging from their bedraggled appearance, they were those he had already rescued.

"She is an angel sent from God," the woman said to them, pointing to me. "If she hadn't held me above water, I would be feeding the fishes by now."

Leo steered the boat towards the dock, where policemen and health brigade volunteers were waiting to haul us on shore. I let the older people go first, then Leo stopped me.

"I will take this young lady home," he said. "I know where she lives."

"That's not necessary," I said, but I was now shivering badly.

"It's no problem," Leo said. "You can't walk. You need to change out of those wet clothes as quickly as possible." He revved up the motor and threaded his way between boats, out to the end of the Zattere, past Santa Maria della Salute, then around into the Grand Canal. The storm had now subsided to a steady rain, but it was still a chaotic scene on the water, with boats trying to head in every direction—some making for home, some determined to head out to St Mark's Basin in the hope of fireworks to come. Leo cursed a couple of times, as we were almost hit. But the Accademia Bridge finally appeared ahead of us, and he turned the boat into a narrow canal just before it.

"This is as close as I can get," he said. "Are you able to walk?"

"I think so." It was hard to talk as my teeth were chattering. He tied up and helped me out of the boat. I started to stagger forward, but my legs didn't want to hold me.

"Wait until I have secured the boat," he said, jumping up on to the fondamenta, then helping me out. He put an arm around me to steady me as he led me through an alleyway and into my street. I didn't resist. I didn't think I could make it alone. This was when I remembered my keys. I felt for my pocket and was relieved to find them there, although my bag of food was now lost somewhere in the Giudecca Canal. I took the keys out, but my hand was shaking so much I couldn't put the key in the lock. Leo relieved me of it, unlocked the front door and helped me up the stairs.

"Thank you for bringing me home," I said, trying to keep my voice formal. "Now you should probably return to your people."

"I can't leave you," he said. "You're in shock." He went ahead of me into the kitchen. "Does your landlady have any grappa?"

"I'm not sure," I replied.

Leo was opening cupboards and peering on shelves. Then he exclaimed, "Ah, here we are."

"I shouldn't drink her spirits without permission," I said, reverting to true English fashion.

He glared. "I'll buy her a new bottle if she makes a fuss." And a glass was put into my hand. "Drink this, then get out of those wet clothes and have a hot bath," he said.

I took a sip of the liquid. It was fiery, and I started coughing.

"Drink it all. Good for you," Leo commanded. "I'll start the bath for you."

I was downing the rest of the grappa when I remembered the geyser.

"Leo, watch out," I called. "When you turn on the tap—"

The rest of my sentence was cut off by an impressive whoomph. Followed by a string of Italian swear words. I rushed to the bathroom.

"I nearly lost my eyebrows," he said.

"I'm sorry. I should have warned you. It has to be treated very carefully," I said. "I have the knack now, but—"

"Why don't people ever have things that work properly in their houses?" he demanded. "This must be older than Marco Polo."

"Let me see." I turned him towards me. His face had some soot on it. "I think your eyebrows survived," I said. I wiped off his nose with my finger. "Only you are a little sooty. You'd better wash, or you'll have explaining to do."

Our eyes met, and we both started to laugh.

"Oh my God, what next?" he demanded. "At least life with you is never boring. Now take those clothes off."

And he started to unbutton my dress. I don't quite know exactly what happened next, but one minute we were laughing and the next we were kissing passionately while his hands fumbled with my buttons and the dress fell to the floor. Then we were stumbling together towards the bedroom, our mouths still kissing hungrily, and then we had fallen to my bed together. I tasted the salt on his lips, felt his warm body against my icy-cold one, knew he was removing my undergarments and couldn't have stopped if I'd wanted to. But I didn't want to. I wanted him with all of my being. It was painful and wonderful at the same time. I know I cried out, but I can't tell whether it was from pain or pleasure.

And when we were both spent, he lay beside me, a look of such tenderness on his face that it melted my heart.

"What I'd really like to do is to lie here beside you all night and to wake up in the morning to see your sweet face and then kiss you gently like this." And he did so.

"Leo, this was madness," I said as the realization of what we had just done swept over me. "We can never let this happen again. Never, you understand."

He nodded. "I know. But I'm glad it has happened, aren't you?"

"Yes," I said. "I'm glad I know what it's like now."

"You were a virgin?"

"Of course." I paused, then added, "I will remember it for the rest of my life." Suddenly I shot upright. "The bath!" I shouted. We both rushed to the bathroom. The water was about half an inch from the top. Leo turned off the taps, and we looked at each other, enjoying a private joke for a moment.

"Now you can have that bath," he said. "I fear I ought to go back. They'll wonder what happened to me. They might worry that I, too, have drowned."

I nodded.

"And I won't see you for a while. My family

goes to the villa in the Veneto for the month of August." As he spoke, he was busy dressing again. His ran his fingers through his wet hair. "Take care of yourself, won't you?"

"You too."

He nodded. He went to say something else, half reached out to me, then turned and hurriedly walked away. I stood for a while, staring at that closed door, then I lowered myself into the hot bath. I no longer needed it. I wasn't shivering—in fact my whole body was on fire—but the water was soothing. I'd probably get into trouble with my landlady for using so much water, but for once I didn't care. I tried to think seriously about what had just happened. *It was only the heat of the moment,* I told myself. We were both shocked and exhausted. But then I wondered, what if he did come to see me again? Would I be able to resist him? Did I want to end up as a man's mistress? And didn't the bible tell us that adultery was wrong?

I lay in that bath until the water turned cold, then I got up and dressed in my nightclothes. A large explosion told me the fireworks had started. I opened my window and watched the night sky lighting up over St Mark's Basin. Oohs and aaahs and cheers greeted each new firework. They were magical, and I stopped worrying about what might happen and let myself enjoy this one moment. I was still standing at the window when I heard the front door open and Signora Martinelli appeared, out of breath after carrying her basket up the stairs.

"We decided to make for home before the crush of people," she said. She put the basket down on the table. "So much food left," she said. "We'll be eating our way through it for weeks."

She saw my nightclothes. "Oh, so you didn't go out to see the fireworks? So beautiful."

"I watched from here," I said. "You can see the sky from my window."

"So you can. But you went out earlier, surely? Did you go to Giudecca? To the church? To see the races? And did you hear there was trouble? A high wind broke the bridge apart. Several people drowned. Awful tragedy."

I nodded.

"So you stayed home," she went on. "And missed all the fun."

"Not quite," I replied.

CHAPTER 25

Juliet, Venice, July 1939

By the next morning, I was back to reality. In the cold light of day, I couldn't believe what had happened. Shame competed with the wonder and exhilaration that a powerful, handsome man had made love to me. He desired me. And clearly I desired him, from what I remembered of my response last night. I felt myself blushing at the passion I hadn't known I possessed. But of course it could never happen again. It must never happen again. Last night had been pure folly, brought upon by a near-death experience. From now on, I would be sensible, sane and get on with my life. Leo was away for a month, which was a good thing. It would give me time to decide whether I wanted to risk staying here, given the storm clouds of war looming over the Continent and the proximity of a man I loved desperately and who appeared to love me, too.

The most reasonable thing would be to go home right away, before he came back from the villa. I'd have to give up my art classes, but what was the point of them anyway? It didn't seem I'd ever be a great artist, and my skills were sufficient to teach bored little girls. And I should be with my mother if there was to be a war. "Just a week or so longer," I whispered to myself. I realized what it was: I couldn't go without saying goodbye. I had to see him again.

August seemed to drag on and on. It was horribly hot and muggy. The canal outside my window stank. Afternoons brought occasional thunderstorms from the mainland. Most Venetians followed the example of Leo's family and went up to the hills. Our classes were on a summer break, so there was no work to keep me occupied, and then Signora Martinelli announced she was going to pay a visit to her sister in Turin. I promised to look after Bruno and keep the place clean.

My fellow students had also abandoned me. Imelda and Gaston had gone home to their families. Henry had set off on a tour of Tuscany. I had no idea what Franz was doing. Presumably he had also gone home to Austria—or was it Germany?—if Henry's suspicions were correct, to report on what he found here.

So I was alone in a city that was almost deserted. Normally at this time of year there would be tourists, a shopkeeper told me. But who would risk coming if there was to be a war? And the British, who normally came in August—they stayed away because Mussolini had signed his ridiculous non-aggression pact with Hitler.

It was too hot to sit outside sketching for long. I tried to work on paintings. I visited churches and studied architecture. I got a parade of letters from my mother, begging me to come home before it was too late. I was tempted, but I couldn't leave before Signora Martinelli returned. There was Bruno to consider. Someone had to feed him. *Maybe it will all blow over,* I told myself. *Maybe England will make another pact with Hitler, and the threat of war will melt away.*

I started taking the vaporetto and going out to the Lido to swim. The beach was the only place that was crowded, as Venetians who could not afford to head for the hills took refuge in the water. But the Adriatic Sea was as warm as a bath, and one had to walk on the narrow planks because the sand burned the feet. Still it made a pleasant change, and there was a breeze on the crossing of the lagoon. As I was walking back after my swim one day, I passed the contessa's villa. She had invited me to call on her, I recalled, although she had probably gone away for the month of August like everyone else. However, I took the chance, went up to her front door and knocked.

It was opened by a young man I hadn't seen the last time I had visited. He was thin to the point of being almost gaunt. I told him who I was and that I'd like to see the contessa. He frowned as if he was having a hard time understanding me, and I wondered if he only spoke Venetian. Surely my Italian was now pretty good. I had chatted easily with the family at the festa. I repeated my request, slowly. He bowed and went away, returning to usher me into a room at the back of the house. It had a wonderfully high ceiling, tall arched windows. The blinds were drawn, giving it an aquarium-like feel so that it was hard to see the colour of the furniture or the paintings that filled the walls. But it was delightfully cool. An electric fan was running, and the contessa was lying on a chaise longue, listening to Mozart on the gramophone.

She opened her eyes, sat up and gave me a big smile. "My little English lady. You have come. How lovely. Josef, tell Umberto to bring citron pressé and cake."

He nodded, then left us. She motioned for me to take a chair, and I sat facing her. She was wearing a dark-green Japanese kimono and no makeup, so that her face had a skull-like appearance in the gloom.

"You have a new footman?" I asked. "I don't remember seeing him when I visited you a month ago."

"You wouldn't have. He is quite new," she said. She looked away from me, staring out into her beautiful garden. A palm tree was swaying in the breeze. When she turned back, she said, "You are English. Clearly of a good family. You were brought up to do the right thing."

"Yes," I replied, feeling confused and wondering where this conversation might be leading. Then she beckoned me closer, as if someone might overhear. "I'll let you in on a little secret, because I feel I can trust you. I am usually a good judge of character." There was another pause, and I wondered what could possibly be coming next. "My footman," she began. "He is not a footman at all. He is a Jewish painter from Germany. Nobody must know this. I am doing my best to smuggle out as many as I can—painters, writers, poets— those who are most at risk of being rounded up and transported God knows where. They have nowhere else to run, poor things. America is not accepting them, nor Britain, and France is too dangerous. Too close. So I bring them here, on the grounds of offering them employment. Then I work on their Italian and find them suitable jobs in Italy. Unfortunately, I can only bring one at a time, every now and then. I'd like to save them all, but I can't."

"It's a very noble thing you do," I said.

"Not noble at all," she said. "A righteous duty. They are my kinsmen, my fellow Jews. They reminded you I am Jewish, I'm sure."

"They did," I said. "Are you not worried for your own safety? Isn't there an anti-Jewish sentiment in Italy, too?"

"There is, but not like in Germany, and certainly not in Venice. We are a tolerant people. Jews have lived here since the Middle Ages. And in my own case the Venetians value art above all else. Why, we are already planning for next year's Biennale. How is that for optimism? We fully intend to hold an international art festival when half the world may be at war. As a major patron of the arts here, I am too valuable to them. Without people like me, there would be no Biennale." She reached across and patted my hand. "So you see, my dear, you do not need to worry for my safety." She paused, her hand resting on mine. "But what about you? You choose to stay and not go running home to safety?"

"I've been debating this," I said. "At this moment I am a little lost. I have no classes, nothing to do. My mother wants me home. But I am committed to looking after my landlady's cat, so I can't go anywhere until she returns. And frankly I don't want to leave. I love it here— everything about it: the colours, the sounds, the people, the food. Everything is so alive. Everybody knows they are alive. If I go home, it will be to silent evenings, sitting in the parlour and listening to the ticking of the clock until my mother turns on the nine o'clock news and we go to bed."

"Then you are right to stay," she said. "You cannot live someone else's life. Your life is what you make of it. You have to decide what you want."

"What I want is what I can't have," I wanted to say but didn't.

The young man reappeared, carrying a tray on which there was a jug of freshly squeezed lemonade and a plate of various goodies—biscuits dusted in powdered sugar, marzipan fruits and small cakes studded with candied peel. He poured glasses for us and offered me the plate. I took one of each, realizing a little too late that when I bit into the biscuit the powdered sugar would fly all over my navy dress.

"*Danke*, Josef," the contessa said, switching to German. I saw a flash of alarm on the man's face, but she gave him a reassuring gesture. "It is all right," she said, using English now. "The young lady knows about you. She is from England. All is well."

He gave me a shy smile.

"Josef is a fine painter," she went on. "He is lucky I was able to get him out."

Josef nodded. "They came for Father," he said, stumbling with the English words. "He was professor at university in Munich. Then they say no Jew may teach or attend university. Then they take him away. I don't know where. And they find my painting and Gestapo take me. Bad place. Many questions. They will come for me very soon, to concentration camp, I am sure. But

Contessa send people to bring me out. She save my life."

"You will keep painting and make me proud, Josef." She took a long drink of the lemonade.

I started to eat the items on my plate, being extra careful with the sugar-dusted biscuits.

"I've been thinking." The contessa broke the silence. "If you are bored with nothing to do at the moment, you can help me. I have some cataloguing to be done, and some preliminary work for the Biennale. Usually Vittorio does these things for me, but he is away in America, selling inferior paintings to people who have more money than taste."

I had to smile. "Does Vittorio work for you?" I asked. "They said he owns a gallery."

"He does, but I am his best client, and he knows, as they say in your English, on which side his bread is buttered. He flatters an old lady, and he likes the things I offer him. And he is articulate and amusing, and he makes me feel young and alive, so the relationship is symbiotic."

This made me wonder again if the relationship had a sexual component to it.

September 1, 1939

These were a couple of pleasant weeks, helping the contessa, sitting in one of her cool and shady rooms, taking tea under the enormous palm tree in her back garden. We examined submissions from artists around the world. I helped to catalogue and file her collection of rare drawings and prints. This included names that made my eyes open wide in astonishment.

"This drawing is an early Picasso!"

"Yes, darling. I know." She gave a wicked little smile. "His mistress was so jealous that he had to ask me to leave in a hurry, and he thrust the drawing into my hands."

She was certainly a woman of surprises. I can't tell you how much I enjoyed my visits out to the Lido—the witty conversation, her knowledge of art, the elegance, the refined living, all of which were so removed from my own dreary life in England. Our daily sessions continued until Vittorio returned and was clearly displeased to find me there.

"Why do you let this woman do the things I like to do for you?" he demanded, pacing around the room.

"You weren't here, my darling," the contessa replied, patting his hand. "And besides, I have enjoyed Juliet's company. Sometimes one just needs another woman around."

"But she is an amateur. What does she know about rare prints? She has probably put her fingers all over them."

"Don't sulk, darling," the contessa replied, a look of amusement on her face. "If you frown, you'll get wrinkles, and you know how much you value your beautiful face."

"Now you mock me."

"Not at all. Besides, Juliet's classes start again next week, so you can have me all to yourself once more. And if you are clever, you can find me another German Jewish artist of the calibre of Goldblum."

He seemed to be appeased. I was sorry my time with the contessa was coming to an end. She was such a cultured and amusing person, and frankly I learned more about art from her than I would have done in a year's art history course. The beginning of September approached, along with the renewal of my classes and the return of my friends and my landlady. She came home on September 1, red-faced and out of breath after climbing the stairs.

"Welcome home," I began. "You will find Bruno alive, well and as naughty as ever."

But she held up a hand to cut me off. "You have not heard the news! They were talking about it on the train station. The place was in an uproar. Germany has invaded Poland. It seems the world will be at war again."

CHAPTER 26

Caroline, Venice, October 11, 2001

Back in her aunt's former apartment, Caroline got to work. She stripped the bed and threw out the bedding. She was relieved to find that the mattress seemed to be intact, with no mice nests lurking inside. With much effort, she turned it, then opened the windows to let in blustery air as she swept, mopped and dusted. She was happy to see no recent signs of infestations, just some long-dead flies on the windowsills. It was hard work, but by the end of the afternoon, she felt an absurd sense of achievement. She wrote a list for the next day: *Buy bed linens. Buy a new electric heater.* The ancient electric fire looked as if it belonged in a museum and could set the building on fire in seconds. She was delighted to find the electricity was on in the building. And that the strange contraption over the bath actually produced hot water.

The list included food, tea, wine. *Just the basics,* she thought. It would be easy to take a main meal at one of the nearby trattorias. She couldn't wait to spend her first night here, but it would have to wait until she had new bedclothes and food. So she went back to the pensione and returned to the little trattoria for her evening meal. After dinner she used the computer that was set up for the guests in one of the salons and sent an email to Josh.

It seems that Aunt Lettie left me some property here, she wrote. *I am going to enjoy making it habitable again and look forward to bringing Teddy here next Easter. There is a lovely sandy beach, and he'll be fascinated by the gondolas.* She did not ask about Desiree.

As she finished, the proprietress invited her to a glass of limoncello, clearly curious to find out what Caroline had discovered.

She expressed amazed delight at everything Caroline told her. "An apartment on the Zattere! Dio mio, that is worth having these days. So many foreigners are buying here. Lots of Germans. We're not too happy about that. The older generation still remembers the way they treated us during the war."

"The German army was here?" Caroline asked. "I thought Italy was on the same side as the Germans."

"To start with. Then we changed sides. And the Germans were angry. They occupied the city. They were brutal, too. Lots of arrests and killing and people being shipped off to camps. They tried to starve us. Two long years they were here, until the Allies saved us. Your British army, you know."

It was amazing how long the shadow of the war had cast a pall over Europe, Caroline thought. But her aunt had escaped to Switzerland and not had to endure the German occupation—escaped in a hurry, judging by the things she left behind. The question was why she chose to stay on in Venice after war was declared and didn't return to her family in England.

The next morning Caroline set out with her list. She found a big supermarket, further down the Zattere, and was able to get sheets, a pillow and a duvet, as well as her food requirements, plus a bottle of wine. She only realized she had purchased with too much enthusiasm when she had to stagger back the whole length of the waterfront with so many bags. Gasping for air, she dropped everything on the floor inside the door, then made herself a cup of tea before anything else. It felt good to sit, sipping tea, in her own living room, watching the water traffic up and down the canal, including some big cruise ships and freighters. By afternoon the bed was made, and she had found a clean towel and washed the inside of the windows, letting in the rosy light of the setting sun. She poured herself a glass of wine—no refrigerator, she had noted—snacked on some bread and olives and felt remarkably at peace.

Was this what you wanted, dear Aunt Lettie? she thought. *You wanted your great-niece to have a place of her own, where she could put her worries aside?* This reminded her that she had yet to fulfil the reason she came in the first place, to scatter Aunt Lettie's ashes. Now it made sense that she might want them scattered in the canal outside her window. But Caroline wasn't quite ready to do it yet.

She telephoned her grandmother, describing the flat. "And I have found out what two of the keys were for so far. But the little silver key is still a mystery. I have looked all over the flat, and there is no lock that would fit this tiny key. So I have to assume it was for a box she took with her."

Instead of going out to dinner, she had bought a tin of minestrone soup, which she now ate with more bread and some cheese. The one item she hadn't acquired was an electric heater, and the room was becoming uncomfortably cold. She closed the big curtains, noting the moth holes. Another thing that would need replacing if she decided to keep this place. Then she discovered an old stone hot water bottle in the bathroom cupboard—the sort one saw in museums—and boiled water for it. The bed became pleasantly warm, and she turned in early, lying staring up at the ceiling and trying to take in everything that had happened: the flat, the old Da Rossi woman who had glared at her with hate in her eyes, her grandson Luca. She would try not to think about him, although he seemed to have been remarkably pleasant about her possession of the top floor. Maybe he was just deciding on the best strategy to remove her. Maybe his lawyers were already working on a way to disprove her lease. People were not always trustworthy, as she knew from Josh. Why did Luca have to be so damned charming?

That night she had a strange dream. She dreamed of a little girl playing the piano. Was that the girl whose clothes were still neatly folded in the bottom drawer? And how did Aunt Lettie know her? Maybe the morning and one of the drawers or cupboards would shed some light on the mystery.

She woke to light streaming in. Before her the whole panorama of the lagoon sparkled in early sunlight. The apartment was remarkably cold, reminding her she needed to find a new electric heater rapidly. She made tea, ate a roll with apricot jam, then started on her investigation, full of anticipation. In the hall cupboard she discovered a portfolio of drawings and paintings—ranging from nude sketches, sketches like the ones in the books, to strange abstracts and some finished portraits. Aunt Lettie had had talent, she thought, and put aside the paintings for later. Then she went through the desk. Some of the drawers were empty. She couldn't find any personal papers, just more sketches and some finished paintings. She checked under the bed and found a suitcase, containing more clothing, again crumpled and seemingly stuffed into the suitcase. Why had she left her clothes behind? She must have had to flee in a hurry, probably when Italy entered the war and she knew she had to go to Switzerland.

Having exhausted the places where her aunt could have kept papers, Caroline wrapped herself in a crocheted afghan she had found, seated herself in one of the big chairs and started to look at the paintings and drawings. She turned them over, one after the other, nodding in appreciation, until she came to a page that made her stop, staring: the page contained sketches of a baby. She put it aside, then continued, turning up more sketches of the same baby. What's more, she recognized it. It was the same baby that appeared as the cherub in the painting on Aunt Lettie's wall. Was it just a neighbour's child she had used as a model? Another thought struck her—of course. That was how she was connected to the Da Rossi family: she had been a nanny to their child! She couldn't wait to tell Luca. But then why had her memory invoked such hostility in old Signora Da Rossi? Perhaps there had been some kind of tragedy: The child had died, and the signora blamed Aunt Lettie? That might have been part of the reason she left in such a hurry.

Hearing footsteps coming up the stairs, she put down the drawings on the low table and stood.

There was a tap on the door, and Luca entered.

"Good morning," he said. "How are you enjoying your new residence?"

"Very much, although it's too cold at the moment. I need to find an electric heater."

"I will have my men locate one for you," he said. He went over to the window, then turned back to her. "You have not found any of your aunt's papers? Anything to do with the lease?"

"Nothing at all, except a lot of paintings and sketches—but I did find something interesting, a reason my aunt could have been connected to your family. See here." She sat in the chair and then held up the sheet of paper. "It's possible she worked as a nanny to your family, don't you think?"

Luca leaned over and examined the sketches. "Yes, it is possible. I can see a resemblance to the early photographs of my father. Oh, and you know what? There was a painting of him in the old nursery in the palazzo where I grew up. I don't know what has happened to it now. Maybe your aunt was commissioned to do the painting, and these were the sketches she used for it."

Caroline nodded. "The only thing that's confusing is that your grandmother had quite a reaction to my being British, and I got the feeling her animosity could have been about my great-aunt."

Luca shook his head. "I think it's more probable that Nonna had a bad experience, maybe with the British soldiers when the Allies occupied the city. Conquering troops are not always well behaved, you know."

"That's true," Caroline agreed, still seeing the anger in the old woman's eyes. She was suffering from dementia, that was clear. She might have got things mixed up, but . . . "I was wondering," she began hesitantly, "if there was a family tragedy. Perhaps a child she was caring for died and she was held responsible?"

Luca frowned. "I don't think so. I never heard any mention of a dead child. Besides, my father would have been born around that time, and he is still alive and well. And I'm pretty sure he wasn't a twin." He walked over to the window, then came to perch on the arm of her chair. Caroline was horribly aware of his presence. "If she was the nursemaid, that would be relatively simple to find out. We would have old employment records in the company headquarters." Caroline wished she was not sitting down. It put her in a vulnerable position, although there was nothing hostile in his demeanour. "The only thing I can't understand is the ninety-nine-year lease. Who gives one of the servants a lease to this prime piece of property? And if she was the artist and not the nanny, who rewards an artist with such a nice place as this?"

"Perhaps it wasn't nice in wartime. Perhaps it was in a dangerous position and vulnerable to hostile shelling?" Caroline said.

"You may have a point there. They wanted somebody to live in it—anybody. But you would have granted that for a month at a time, wouldn't you?"

"We may never find out." Caroline stared back at the smiling baby.

"So how long do you plan to stay here?" Luca asked her suddenly, getting up again.

"I have taken the three weeks' vacation time that were owed to me. I may not stay that long, especially if a small fire can't heat the place. I've been through my aunt's possessions, and there really isn't anything apart from the paintings. And I'm not even sure which of those I'd want. They are quite good, but . . ."

"Not your taste?"

"Not exactly, especially the abstracts and the nudes."

"I like a good nude myself," he said, giving her a wicked grin. Then he corrected himself. "Sorry, that was impolite of me."

"Not at all. I am particularly fond of some of Degas's nudes. I'm a big fan of the impressionists."

"Me too."

"Oh, you like art?"

"Some of it. I'm old-fashioned in my taste,

although my new apartment is all very modern—sleek white lines. Bare walls."

"You don't want to express yourself," she said, standing up because she didn't like feeling at a disadvantage. "It was like my great-aunt's room when she died. Nothing of herself in there at all. You'd never know what kind of person she was, except it was exceedingly neat and tidy."

"Ah well, you'd never be able to say that about my rooms," Luca said. He turned for the door. "I should go. I'll have a heater sent up. Of course when the renovation is finished, the whole building will be centrally heated. You will be nice and warm when you come back."

"Yes," she said, staring out of the window, where a large freighter was now sailing out of the canal. "I don't know when that will be. It all depends . . ."

"On when your son comes home," he finished for her.

Her eyes met his. "Yes," she said again.

On his way to the door, he paused. "Don't go for a few more days. My father emailed to say they are on their way home. Leaving the grandchildren with great sadness, but my mother has a medical appointment. You should meet them and see if he remembers anything of his old nanny."

"Thank you," Caroline said. "I'd like that."

"And my mother is American. She can speak

312

English with you, which will be a great treat for her. She gets tired of speaking Italian and Venetian all the time."

"Venetian is a separate language?"

"Oh yes. Quite different. The older generation here still speak it."

"There are so many fascinating things about this place. I rather wish I could stay longer."

"Why don't you?"

"Job? Income? Grandmother? Son?"

"You like your job?"

Again she hesitated. Why did this man that she hardly knew seem to have the ability to see into her soul, to read her mind? And why did he seem to care so much?

She shrugged. "It pays to feed us, but it doesn't make use of my talent or education."

"Which was what?"

"Fashion design. I went to art school."

"Ah. So art runs in your family. What would you like to do? Be another Armani?"

She hesitated, unsure of herself. "I'm not certain anymore. I used to think I could design a brilliant collection, but I was never like Josh. He always wanted to push the envelope and design outrageous things. Me, I went more for beauty and good lines."

"Yes, I can see that. Well, you can sell me the apartment and use the money to start your own fashion house."

She smiled. "It does sound tempting."

"Think about it." He gave her a smile. "See you soon."

After Luca had gone, she found that she was still staring at the door. Was he just being charming until his lawyers found a way to turf her out? Or would he try to buy the place from her at a steal? She just wished she knew whether she could trust him.

CHAPTER 27

Juliet, Venice, Sunday, September 3, 1939

On that Sunday morning, the bells mocked us with their serenity. "We are well and safe here," they were saying. "You can come to Mass as usual. All is well." Pigeons flapped unconcernedly; seagulls wheeled in a clear blue sky. The signora went off to church.

"We must all pray really hard that another catastrophe may be averted," she said. "We cannot suffer through another war like the last one." She gave me a look of pity. "You are too young. You do not remember, do you?"

"I was only four when it began, but I remember my mother weeping when my father was sent off to fight," I said. "And he returned home badly wounded, never the same. And I saw the names on the war memorial in our village. So many sons who did not return. You're right. We must pray that it doesn't happen again."

And so, for once, I went across the bridge to St George's Anglican church and sat, taking in the simplicity of white walls and dark polished wood, the tranquillity of the light, falling through stained glass on to the tiled floor, and tried to pray. But my head was full of such conflicting thoughts and worries that prayer wouldn't come. I had never found any closeness to God since my father died. It felt as if He had deserted us. So I sat like a statue, listened to a sermon full of hope and trust, mouthed the words of familiar hymns—"O God, our help in ages past, our hope for years to come" and "Fight the Good Fight"—but came out still feeling hollow and with no real sense of what I should be doing.

The church had been full. I had no idea there were so many expatriates in Venice. I suppose some of them must have been tourists, but many knew each other and were obviously residents. I saw Mr Sinclair, the consul I had met at the contessa's soirée. He greeted me with a nod as we exited the church after the service.

"You are still here, I see, Miss Browning. I take it you will be going home now?"

"I'm still making up my mind," I said. "I have been reassured that Venice will not be involved in any war. Nobody would dare to bomb Venice. And they say that Italy is not ready to go to war with anyone for some time. Mussolini wants to build up his army first."

"That's true enough," Mr Sinclair said. "But he has signed the non-aggression pact with Hitler. We may find ourselves dragged into a war, whether we like it or not. It will be a question of choosing sides, and Italy has sided with Germany."

"You are sure there will be war?" one of the women asked. "Will Mr Chamberlain not manage to broker peace again? Let Germany have Poland? After all, it is part of their ancestral homeland, isn't it?"

"If we don't stop Hitler from grabbing what he wants, he'll swallow the whole of Europe," Mr Sinclair said. "I'm rather afraid that war is inevitable. We have drawn a line in the sand. Hitler has crossed that line. And I don't know how long Italy can stay out of it."

We were a sombre group that went our separate ways. At two o'clock that afternoon, we heard on the radio that England and France had declared war on Germany.

Now it became obvious to me that I should go home, however much I longed to stay. I could not let my mother face a war alone, even if Aunt Hortensia was with her. And I couldn't risk being trapped in an alien country if the war came in our direction. I wondered if Leo had returned from the countryside. I really didn't want to leave without saying goodbye.

I went to my classes the next day and felt the tension in the air. The Italian boys were whispering about what they would do if they were called up into the army. None of them wanted to fight.

"My brother was killed in Abyssinia," one of them was saying. "Such a waste of life. Why would Italy want Abyssinia anyway? What use is it to anyone? Only to stoke Mussolini's vanity now that he has an empire."

"Hush. Careful what you say." Another boy touched his arm. "You never know who is listening, and there are those who think that Mussolini is the saviour of our country. They really believe he'll create a second Roman empire and we'll all live like kings."

This brought chuckles of disbelief from all those in the group. But he was right. You did never know who was listening. I found myself thinking about Franz. Henry might be right about Franz reporting to Germany on what was happening in Venice.

I tried to put worrying thoughts from my mind and to make the most of my last few classes. The radio was saying that the war was like two boxers getting into a ring, sizing each other up before any blow would be launched. So there was time to take a train home across France before Hitler or the Allies made any significant move. From what I had heard in church, Britain was not equipped to launch any offensive against Germany. We didn't have the weapons or the manpower to face the Nazi might.

At lunch Gaston talked about going home. "I must do my duty and join the French army, I suppose," he said. He said it with bravado, but I saw the utter despair in his eyes. "Not that we have much chance against Germany. I just pray it's not a repeat of the last war and that we don't all die in the trenches."

We sat in silence, pondering this. Then Imelda said, "I think I'll stay. My parents are talking about going up to the hills, to Basque country, just in case. What would I do there? Where could I go? At least Italy isn't going to declare war on anybody for a while."

"That's what I think," Henry said. His Italian had obviously improved to the point that he could understand the gist of conversations. "America is keeping out of this war, so I think I'll stick around and finish my year abroad."

"Just pray you can get home again when the German U-boats start patrolling the Atlantic," Imelda said drily.

He shrugged. "Then I'll go to Switzerland and wait until it's over. No one will touch Switzerland, will they? Or Australia? Australia would be good." He looked at me. "What about you?" He switched to English. "Do you want to go home and risk Germany invading?"

"I don't want to go," I said, "but I feel obliged to. My mother will worry terribly if I'm far away. She didn't want me to come in the first place, but my aunt agreed to stay with her. I suppose I must check to see if trains are still running normally across France and the ferries are still crossing the Channel."

"It's too bad, when we are finally settling into our routine here and the classes are so interesting," Henry said. "I feel I've learned more in a few weeks than I did in all the art classes I took at home."

"Me too," I said. "I really hate to go."

We finished eating and made our way back to the accademia, where the first person we saw was Professor Corsetti.

"The very people I wanted to see," he exclaimed. "I have instructions from my wife. She wants to hold a dinner party to welcome you back after the holiday, despite our dire situation. Is Sunday acceptable? And my wife is intent on serving shellfish. You can all eat it?"

"That is fine. I love all the seafood here," I said.

The others nodded.

"Your wife is a good cook," Gaston said. "I am sure anything she prepares will be delicious."

"Flatterer," Imelda muttered as we parted company with the professor.

Gaston smiled. "How else am I going to get a passing mark in his class? I don't think I am destined to be Picasso or Miró."

"I agree," I said. "It does not come naturally to me to distort reality."

"I've noticed that," Gaston replied. "Your nude drawings are very attentive to detail."

"Be quiet." I slapped him with my notebook, laughing.

At that moment it dawned on me that I had not had a chance to behave like this for years. To be free, to tease, to laugh and, as I began to realize, to love. Now I would be going back to the grim reality of a war, to danger, deprivation, maybe even a German invasion.

"My last days," I whispered to myself as we went up the stairs to our class.

Sunday, September 10, 1939

This evening we went to dinner at Professor Corsetti's. I agreed to meet Henry at the traghetti dock so that he didn't get lost this time.

"When are you leaving?" he asked.

I sighed. "I don't know. I had a letter from my mother today, telling me to come home immediately. I should probably go before the end of the month, but I tell myself I have paid my landlady for September and it's quite possible that the war will stay in Eastern Europe. I don't think Britain is prepared to do anything too dramatic yet."

We walked on in companionable silence. He was a nice boy, I thought. Too young for me, of course. But it was pleasant to have the companionship of a male. I hadn't seen Leo, although he must have returned from his villa by now. At least going home would cease the fantasy of being with him.

There was a bigger group this time at the professor's house. Gaston was not present, but Imelda and Franz were both there, along with two girls I hadn't met before. These were introduced as Lucrecia and Maria, new students from Sicily. They looked painfully shy and clung together, giving one-word answers to questions put to them.

The contessa greeted me warmly. "How I have been missing you," she said.

I noticed Vittorio, standing with a glass in his hand, watching her from across the room. He had not been missing me! He was jealous, although this was stupid. Then there was another professor and his wife—a professor of art history, we were told, and it was highly recommended that we take his course.

He nodded in agreement. "It is imperative to know the past before one can be free to paint in the present."

Prosecco was poured and served. I didn't like the taste of this one as much. It had a harsh metallic overtone. Possibly a cheaper vintage! I found the bad taste lingered in my mouth, and I was glad when we sat down to eat tomato salad. Then came a risotto alle seppie. The dish was an alarming shiny black colour, and we were informed it was made with the ink of the cuttlefish. It was a very traditional local dish. I took a tentative mouthful. It wasn't bad—salty and fresh-tasting—but suddenly I realized, to my horror, that I was about to vomit. I jumped up from the table, my napkin pressed to my mouth as I rushed for a toilet, where I deposited everything I had eaten so far.

The professor's wife was standing outside the door, looking concerned.

"I'm so sorry," I said. "There must be something in that dish that doesn't agree with me. I've never eaten it before."

"Don't worry, my dear. Maybe it was just the sight of such unfamiliar cuisine. It does look a little off-putting the first time."

"Perhaps I should just go home," I said. "Please make my apologies."

I made a hurried exit. Out in the fresh air, I felt better, but still a little queasy. Back with my landlady I drank some chamomile tea and ate crackers before going to bed. In the morning I felt right as rain. Obviously cuttlefish and I were not going to be the best of friends, I decided. I ate breakfast and went off to my morning classes.

By lunchtime I was feeling almost sick with hunger. My classmates were going to their favourite pasta place on Fondamenta Priuli, a tiny eatery beside a narrow canal, where the prices were good and the portions generous. But I couldn't seem to stomach the thought of pasta. Instead I opted for the sandwich shop that served the tramezzini and chose my favourites, including tuna with olives. I had taken only a couple of bites when I realized I was going to throw up again. I rushed outside and was sick in the gutter.

What was the matter with me? I wondered. Not a stomach flu, or I wouldn't have felt well this morning and been able to eat breakfast. Was it some kind of food poisoning? Bad water? I had let down my guard a little and now cleaned my teeth with ordinary tap water. Yes, that must be it, I reasoned.

I stopped off at one of the small markets and bought a bottle of mineral water and some Melba toast. That seemed to calm my stomach again, and I went to afternoon classes, but that evening I felt sick after eating salad and a hard-boiled egg. I went back to my room. Something was wrong with me. Should I see a doctor or simply go back to England while I could? I pictured my mother taking care of me, tucking me in bed with a cup of Bovril and some dry toast—our usual remedy for anything stomach related. It did seem appealing.

However, the next morning again I felt fine. I finished my morning classes and wondered about where to go for lunch. I couldn't risk another embarrassment. So I went to the sandwich place and bought two tramezzini, one with cheese and one with ham. Then I went to sit on a bench beside the Grand Canal, near the vaporetto stop.

I had only eaten a couple of mouthfuls when I felt queasy again. I stopped eating immediately and sipped water, willing my stomach to quieten down. It was pleasant to sit in the sun, watching people go past. Venice was always so lively, always something interesting to watch. I decided to get out my sketchbook. If I wasn't going to eat, at least I could be productive and work on my figure drawing.

I was engrossed in sketching the man at the newspaper kiosk when I heard a big shout of joy and saw two women greeting each other. They were rushing together, arms outstretched, delight on their faces.

"Bambino!" the older woman exclaimed. "Finalmente. Grazie a Dio!" And she put her hands on the extended belly of the young woman.

They went into animated conversation that I couldn't catch, but Italians always talk with their hands, and I could see how thrilled and surprised they were with this event. I watched with the sort of second-hand pleasure one gets from seeing other people happy, until a strange thought crept unbidden into my head.

Bambino. Weren't unexplained nausea and sickness amongst the first signs of . . . no, surely not. Why had it never occurred to me that a pregnancy could result from my encounter with Leo? Not just one time, surely? Not the first time? The only time? But then I remembered that I had not had my monthly visitor since—since July? I had never been the most regular, and this had not alarmed me, until now. But from what I had heard, pregnancy sickness was in the morning, wasn't it? Not at odd times of the day.

This reassured me, but I couldn't resist going over the bridge to the bookstore on the Street of Assassins and searching through manuals on pregnancy and birth. And there it was in black and white: Sometimes the sickness can present itself in the evenings. Old wives will tell us this is more usual if the woman is expecting a male child.

I came out of the bookshop and stood on the empty street. How well I could recall meeting Leo there. "Assassins have their own street?" I had asked.

And he had replied, seriously, "How else would you find them if you needed one?"

We had laughed.

CHAPTER 28

Juliet, Venice, September 12, 1939

I stood alone in the deep shadow, not knowing where to go next. Not knowing what to do. I couldn't tell Leo. But I had to tell Leo. He had a right to know, didn't he? And then the dreadful, final realization: I couldn't go home. I thought of my mother—pillar of the church, head of the ladies' altar guild, in our little village where gossip was a major sport. The shame would kill her. And what about me? What would I do? I certainly couldn't go back to teaching young ladies when a major boast of the school was a moral Christian upbringing. How would we live without my job? I knew Aunt Hortensia still had a small income, but would that be enough? I could picture Aunt Hortensia's face—that haughty, horsey, perpetually surprised expression.

"I always knew the girl would come to a bad end," she'd say. "Too much interest in the opposite sex even when she was young. And no judgement at all."

Wouldn't she be surprised to know that the one man she had warned me against was the creator of my ruin? Thoughts were whirling around in my brain, and I felt for a moment that I might faint. I put my hand against the cold stone wall of the nearest building, hoping to steady myself.

"All right," I said. "Think, Juliet."

I had stipend money until next summer. And the child would be born when? Nine months, wasn't it? How little I knew about pregnancy and birth. But I remember when one of the farm girls in our village was expecting. All the talk. All the speculation about who the father was and why he wasn't marrying her. And I remembered gossips going back nine months to try and work out who Lil had been seeing at that time. I did a rapid calculation in my head: end of April, beginning of May. I felt a glimmer of hope. Nine months. I could stay here, continue to take my classes if they'd let me. Then I'd have the baby, give it up for adoption and go home with nobody any the wiser. I'd write and tell my mother that everyone had reassured me that Venice would be perfectly safe and it made more sense for me to stay put and finish my course, rather than risk the journey home at this moment. Besides, with any luck, the war would be over by next summer. I knew she'd be angry about this, but it seemed like the only solution.

I rather surprised myself how dispassionately I was handling this. I suppose I was desperately trying to keep fear at bay—fear and despair. I was no longer that emotional girl who burst into tears easily. I had learned to shut off my emotions long ago. I hadn't cried when I was told I had to leave art college, because I saw how terrified my mother was, and my father so ill. I hadn't even cried when he died, because my mother was hysterical enough for both of us. So I thought I had forgotten how to feel—until Leo had made me feel alive again and I had experienced love. I couldn't even begin to think how I'd tell him about this. What if he denied it was his? Cut me dead? I couldn't make any decisions right now. If only I had someone I could tell, someone close I could talk to at this moment. But there was nobody.

So I went back to the accademia. I attended my classes. I found if I carried a bottle of fizzy water and some dry crackers that I could avert much of the sickness. The trick was to keep something in my stomach at all times, and then eat nothing too spicy or rich. I started having a clear vegetable soup with croutons for lunch at the local trattoria. It was based with chicken stock and quite nourishing. I also found some biscuits like little sponge cakes that seemed to agree with my stomach.

September 21

I have got through the next couple of weeks of classes and life. I am still completely undecided about whether to tell Leo. He would know eventually if he ran into me in the street. I wonder how soon it would show. I wondered if I could alter my clothes or if I could find a dressmaker to make me inexpensive voluminous ones. I wondered what people would say. Venice was a Catholic city. Sin was real and punishable here. I toyed again with going home to England but maybe living in London, getting a job until I couldn't work any longer, and not letting my mother know I was back home. But that seemed like such a horrible thing to do, for her as well as for me, even if I could find anyone who would hire a pregnant, unmarried woman. And I would be alone in a great city, a city that might well be in the midst of a war, and it seemed like the worst thing I could imagine. I put that thought aside. I'd risk the scorn of the Venetians.

Of the war we heard very little. Hitler's army had rolled into Poland. The Poles were putting up a valiant fight, but it was only a matter of time before Poland was lost. And the Allies? Britain and France and their commonwealth countries? The only encounters had been at sea. A ship from Canada to England had been sunk by a German submarine, and British aeroplanes had attacked a German naval base at Kiel. But men were being called up to fight in England, and my mother wrote that she had been instructed to build an air raid shelter in her back lawn.

How ridiculous, she wrote. *Can you see Aunt H.*

and me scrambling across the rose garden in our nightclothes and then going down into a dark, damp hole in the ground? Aunt H. says she'd rather risk being bombed, but she doesn't believe the Germans will dare attack us. Hitler has a fondness for the British, she says. We are of the same Aryan stock. She is absolutely convinced that we will have peace.

In Venice one would not know that there was a war on. There was plenty to eat, the markets were full of fresh produce from the Veneto, on the other side of the causeway, and the fishermen still came in each morning with boats full of fish. There was still music and laughter. Our classes progressed at the academy. The only change was that Gaston had gone home, bravely declaring that it was his duty to join the French army to stop Hitler from invading his country.

"Who would have thought it of him?" Imelda asked me when we were having coffee together. At least, she was having coffee. I had switched to herbal teas, as coffee no longer agreed with me. "I would have designated him as a playboy, wouldn't you? Out for pleasure and what he could get?"

"Yes, I suppose you're right," I said.

She looked at me critically. "Are you quite well?" she asked. "You don't seem to be eating much these days."

"Just some kind of stomach upset," I said.

"You should see a doctor," she said. "There are parasites in the water here, you know. You need to treat them as soon as possible so they don't take hold."

"No, really," I began. "I don't think . . ."

She was looking at me critically now. "I shouldn't ask this," she said, "but is it possible you are pregnant?"

I suppose my face must have flushed. Anyway, she understood. "You are? And what does the man say about this? The father?"

"I haven't told him."

"You must. He is equally responsible," she said firmly. "Will he do the right thing and marry you?"

"He can't. He's already married."

"Ah." She looked at me so intently that I had to lower my gaze. Then she said, "Is it perhaps the son of the count who gave us a ride in his boat that day? I saw how he looked at you." When I said nothing, she wagged a finger at me. "I'm right, aren't I?"

"You are too observant," I replied. "Please say nothing, Imelda. Nobody must know. I can't even tell Leo. His family—they are really powerful. I'm afraid of what might happen to me."

"If you really can't tell him, then go home, while you can. You'll be safe in England with your mother."

I shook my head. "I can't do that either. That's

just the problem. I can't go home, Imelda. My mother is a pillar of her church. We live in a small village. Everyone would know. The shame would be awful. It might even kill my mother. Anyway, I couldn't put her through that. I have decided to stay here until the baby is born and then give it up for adoption. Then I can go home as if nothing has happened, and nobody will ever know."

"You'll know." She was still looking at me in a way that made me uncomfortable. "Is that what you want? To go home and forget? Forget you ever had a child? That you ever loved this man?"

"What choice do I have?" I heard the bleakness in my voice.

"Then maybe you should talk to him," she said. "He is rich. A man of the world. He will surely know a doctor who can take care of this now, before it's too late."

I tried to digest what she meant by "take care of this."

She saw my confused look. "You know. Terminate. Get rid of the baby while it is still the size of a pea. I know it's against the law, but it's not really a baby yet, just a collection of tissue, so I'm told. You have a little procedure, and you walk out free and happy again."

I stared at her. For one awful moment, it seemed like a good idea. Go to a doctor. Have a little procedure and walk out free and happy again. But then I knew instantly that I couldn't do it.

Thou shalt not kill. A defenceless baby, who has done no wrong. Doesn't he have the right to live? Maybe if I told Leo, he'd be able to find a happy home for the child, the way he did the kittens. As I considered this, it did seem like an acceptable solution. Now all I had to do was to summon the courage to tell him.

I walked past the Palazzo Rossi and stared up at that imposing front entrance. I certainly wouldn't have the nerve to knock on that door and ask to speak to him. It would be a foolish thing to do. The only solution would be to write him a letter. I had just decided to do this when the front door opened and Bianca came out. Today she was wearing a white tennis dress, her black hair tied up in a white ribbon, and she carried a bag with a racket handle sticking out of it. Somebody inside the house must have said something to her, because she looked back and gave some sort of quip before she tossed her head, laughed and walked on. She had a satisfied little smile on her lips as she walked right past me as if I didn't exist.

I went home and wrote the letter. *I need to see you,* I said. *Can you meet me at noon at the accademia one day soon?*

That seemed like a harmless place to bump into a friend without causing talk. Better than at my landlady's house. Word that Leonardo Da

Rossi visited an unmarried woman there would circulate quickly. Frankly, I was dreading the encounter. I tried the words I wanted to use in Italian and just couldn't say them. I prayed that Leo would understand what "pregnant" was in English. Perhaps if we were speaking in a foreign tongue, we wouldn't readily be overheard.

I dropped the letter into the yellow postbox and waited, feeling sick and jittery about what might happen when we met.

September 22

I didn't have to wait long!

I came down the stairs at noon, and there he was, standing in the shade, just outside that impressive marble portico of the accademia building. He stepped into sunlight, giving me a delighted smile that absolutely melted my heart.

"You are still here!" he exclaimed. "I was afraid I would not see you again. I was so happy to get your note. I heard that the accademia was sending home the foreign students because of the war, and I was sure you had gone. Shall we find somewhere for lunch? What do you feel like eating?"

"No, nothing, really. I'd rather talk. There are things I want to say."

"Of course," he said. "You're telling me good-bye, aren't you? You have to go home before it's too late and it's no longer safe to travel through

335

France. I will help if you like. I can arrange to have one of our people travel with you to make sure you get safely across Europe."

I said nothing but started to walk across the little square to the edge of the canal, where a tree was providing a deep pool of shade. I perched on the low wall, and he came to sit beside me. Just below my reach, the waters of the canal slapped at the brick wall. A gondola glided past, the woman passenger reclining and holding on to a broad-brimmed straw hat. It was the perfect peaceful scene, contrasting with my inner turmoil.

"I will miss you so much," Leo said, "but I will be happy when I know you are safely at home. You live in a small town, no? So you will not be at risk of bombs. At least we have nothing to fear in Venice from such things. It will be declared a city of heritage that nobody would dare to touch. And my father and father-in-law will become very rich transporting supplies for German armies, so all will be well for both of us." The laugh he gave indicated that this wasn't what he really felt.

"Leo," I said, "this is what I have to talk to you about. I'm not going home."

"You're not? But you must, cara mia. While you can. What if Italy decides to join Germany, and you are an enemy? And your mother—she will go crazy with worry and fear if you are far away." He touched my hand. "I don't want to lose you, but I want what is best for you. Safest for you."

Oh God. The touch of his hand on mine was overwhelming. I felt tears welling up.

"Leo, I can't go home," I said. "I'm going to have a baby. My mother can never know."

He looked stunned, as if I had slapped him across the face. "A baby? Are you sure?"

I nodded. "Quite sure, I'm afraid. I'm finding it hard to believe, too. It seems so unfair. Just that once, and . . ." I turned my face away, unable to look at him.

His hand now gripped mine. "Don't worry, cara mia. I will do all I can to help you. If I could marry you, I would. You know that. But as it is . . ." He took a deep breath, shaking his head.

"I understand. There is not much that you can do. But I have decided that I will stay until the child is born, then I will arrange for an adoption and go home. Nobody will ever need to know what happened here."

"You will give your baby away? So easily? A good home, like the kittens?"

I wished he hadn't brought them up. I turned on him. "What do you want me to do, then?" I heard my voice crack with emotion. "What do you suggest? I'm sure you understand that I can't keep a child."

His hand tightened over mine. "Let me think about this," he said. "We will do what is best.

Maybe . . . ," he began, then stopped, leaving me wondering what "maybe" might have entailed. Instead he asked, "You have seen a doctor?"

"I am not going to get rid of the child, if that is what you are suggesting."

He looked horrified. "Of course. Under no circumstance. I meant a doctor to confirm your condition."

"There is no need. My condition is quite obvious to me."

"I will arrange for you to see our family doctor. Quite confidential, you understand. At least I can make sure your health is taken care of. And money. You should not have to worry about money."

"It's all right," I said. "I have enough. My stipend will keep me going through the year. The child will be born in early May, I think. Then I can recover and go home."

"You talk about it so easily," he said. "As if we were discussing a minor inconvenience."

I looked away, my fingers moving over the rough brickwork. "I've had some time to think about it, Leo. At first I was in a desperate panic, but I realize I have to be rational. To have no personal feelings for a baby I can never keep. It's better that way, isn't it?"

"But hard," he said, pausing a long time. "I want to do what I can. Of course I will help you to get home when the time is right. If Europe is in turmoil, then we will find a ship to take you to Malta or Gibraltar. A British island, yes?"

I nodded. The implications of staying were just becoming real. Not being able to cross a war-torn Europe. Being deposited on a British island. And what would I do there? Would there be a way to get me home?

"Or Switzerland," Leo said. "Switzerland will never get involved in a war. Let us just hope that Herr Hitler respects Switzerland's neutrality. It would be all too easy to invade and take it over."

"Don't." I closed my eyes. "Everything seems so hopeless, doesn't it?"

"We will get through it, I promise you," he said, and embraced me.

For a moment I shut my eyes, feeling the warmth and security of his arms around me. Then I realized that we could be seen. I pushed him away. He was looking at me with great tenderness that almost melted my soul. I realized I had been thinking only of myself.

"But what about you?" I choked back tears. "They are calling up young men into the Italian army and navy."

He gave me a swift grin. "One of the advantages of having a father-in-law who is hand in glove with Mussolini," he said. "They will not touch my family. I am an asset to help with smooth transportation of supplies. I will remain here and keep an eye on you."

At least I had to be content with that.

CHAPTER 29

Juliet, Venice, November 1, 1939

September has turned into October, into November. The fine summer weather I had come to associate with Venice had broken at the end of September. Clouds now gathered frequently over the Dolomites, bringing fierce squalls of rain. I helped Signora Martinelli haul up coal for the boiler. My room, with its radiator, is still cold and damp. Even the pigeons, sitting on the ledge across from my window, puff out their feathers and shiver. The swallows have long gone to warmer climes. So have the tourists. The city feels empty.

However, for me things have been improving. The bouts of sickness and dizziness gradually stopped, and I felt well again. In fact it was hard to believe I was pregnant. But I had been to see Leo's doctor, who had assured me that this was so.

"You are still relatively young and healthy," he said. "I foresee no complications. Make sure you eat well and get enough rest and fresh air. Plenty of good food to fatten you up." He eyed me critically. "You are too thin. Lots of good pasta, eh?"

And so I have gone about my usual daily routine: classes, walks, occasional evening invitations. The professor's wife has not invited me again, perhaps worried that her cooking might produce another bad result for me.

I had stayed away from the contessa, not wanting to have to reveal the truth to her and yet not wanting to lie to her either. I refused her September invitation and then again in October. Maybe I had not wanted to risk meeting Leo's father at one of her soirees, although he didn't strike me as a great lover of the arts. And then I was crossing St Mark's Square the other day, having made another attempt to sketch those impossible domes and statues of the basilica, when I bumped into her.

"My dear child, I was sure you had gone home when you didn't come to my soirée," she said, grabbing both my hands and then giving me a kiss on each cheek. "I am so delighted you decided to stay. You must come and have a cup of tea. I was headed to Florian's. Come with me."

I had always wanted to go to Florian's café on the square but never dared to alone as it seemed so impossibly grand with its exquisitely painted walls and ceilings, its gilt and mirrors, plush seats, marble tables. It was like a miniature palace. Aunt H. had told me it was the oldest café in the world. The contessa seemed to have no hesitation about entering such a formidable establishment. She slipped her arm through mine, and I was whisked through the impressive front entrance. The countess was welcomed with much bowing and shown to the best table in the Chinese room. Tea was ordered, and a selection of pastries. I wisely refused the one with lashings of cream and settled for an apple tartlet instead.

After she had taken a drink of tea, the contessa started talking again. "I was devastated when you didn't come to see me. I thought, *Have I done something to offend her? Does she not like my company?*"

"Oh no," I said hastily. "I assure you I love visiting your beautiful home. It's just the last two occasions were impossible for me. On one evening I was sick, and on the other I had a big assignment for my painting class."

She waved a hand. "In the future, you tell your professor that I require your presence. He will not dare to defy me." And she chuckled. "But you will have to come to my November soirée, of course. You will never guess who has agreed to be present—none other than the great Paul Klee! What a coup for me, huh? You know his work, of course. He was much harassed by the Nazis in Germany and has wisely retreated to his native Switzerland. But what a towering figure in the art world. Say you will come."

I could hardly refuse. I mumbled something about lots of work for school, but she wouldn't take no for an answer. "If you wish to become an artist of note, you must mix with the best," she said. And so I agreed to attend. At least I was no longer at risk of being taken sick in public. As we ate, I considered how strange it was that she would be hosting soirées with famous painters while the rest of Europe was already at war.

After we had taken our leave, again with kisses on both cheeks and my absolute promise that I would be there at the soirée, I walked home across the square. Clouds had gathered while we took our tea, and a hard, cold rain stung my face. I slipped into the shelter of the colonnade. The whole experience with the contessa had been surreal, and the rain was a reminder that real life was hard and it stung.

Leo had taken to coming to the small trattoria where I ate my lunch. On the doctor's advice, I had moved from vegetable soup to pasta at lunchtime. Filling and cheap.

"You are looking well," Leo commented the last time we met. "Blooming, in fact."

I gave him a half-amused look. He became serious.

"Julietta, I want to do more. Tell me what I can do."

I could hardly say, "Get rid of Bianca and marry me," could I? We were sitting together at a table in a dark corner where we couldn't be overheard, and most of our conversation was in English, but all the same I glanced around.

"When the time comes, you will help me find the right home for our child," I said.

He nodded. "But you will need help. At least I want to give you financial support so that you don't have to worry."

"You don't need to," I said, suddenly angry.

He looked hurt. "But I want to. Do you think I do not feel horribly responsible? Guilty?"

"Leo, you are no more guilty than I am," I said. "We are both equally responsible."

"Right, but you carry the burden and I walk away whistling. That does not seem fair, does it?" He reached across the small table and took my hand. "I am going to set up a small account for you at my bank—the Bank of San Marco. I will arrange for money to be put in every month, to cover your needs."

"But won't your family object? They are sure to notice."

He shook his head. "I have a private account, separate from my family, separate from my wife. I will arrange everything. Don't worry. If you need to move, you can get your own place."

"I like it where I am right now," I said. "Signora Martinelli is not the warmest, but it's convenient for my studies and it's nice to have meals prepared for me." I looked up, into those warm, brown eyes. "Is it wise to be seen with me like this? Think of your family's reputation."

He shrugged. "This part of the city is mainly students and laborers, and they don't care who sits with whom. I can assure you that my wife's friends don't even know that Dorsoduro exists. To cross the Accademia Bridge, for them, would be the same as going to Siberia."

In spite of everything, I laughed with him.

November 11

Saturday is always a free day for me. I explore the city. I find quaint and unusual shops. On fine days I ride the vaporetto out to one of the islands and watch the glass-blowing on Murano or the lacemaking on Torcello. Or even the fishermen bringing in their catch on the less attractive Vignole. I try to capture everything in my sketchbook, and during a long vaporetto ride across the lagoon, I find myself thinking whether I want to go back ever. Couldn't I find a job here in Venice? My Italian is now really fluent. I could visit my child, watch him or her growing up, be an adoring aunt. It did sound tempting, but then guilt about abandoning my mother crept in. Why had I been raised to be the good daughter, always to do what was right?

Saturday morning dawned blustery with the promise of rain later, but I decided to go out anyway.

I didn't like to stay in my small room, and I didn't feel welcome in Signora Martinelli's kitchen or sitting room unless I was invited. So I put on my raincoat, tied a scarf around my head, and off I went. As I came out into the square, there was suddenly a loud banging sound behind me. My first thought was gunfire, that the war had entered Venice. I turned to see a group of children, bearing down on me. They were wearing paper crowns, some wore capes, and they were carrying pots and pans, banging spoons on them as they walked. They called out something I didn't understand, and then a girl held out her hand.

Luckily, a woman returning with a laden shopping basket approached us. She put the basket down, reached in and handed out sweets. The children immediately broke into a song. I couldn't catch all the words but they went something like:

"San Martin ze'nda in sofita
Par trovar la so novissa
La so novissa no ghe gera
San Martin co culo par tera."

The Venetian language was still an enigma to me, but I did hear the words "San Martin."

"What is this day?" I asked the woman. "A feast day?" (There are so many feast days in Venice that almost every weekend a saint is celebrated at some church or other.)

She looked surprised, as if I was a visitor

newly landed from a distant planet. "St Martin's Day," she said. "The children go around the town singing and banging. They want treats or money to buy the San Martin biscuits. You have not seen them in all the bakeries?"

I thanked her and fished in my purse for small coins, which made the children break into song again. They went on their way, their high, shrill voices echoing from the stone walls: "San Martin co culo par tera . . ."

I found these celebrations exciting, after the subdued harvest festival that was the highlight of our church year in England, and went to the nearest bakery, where the window was full of beautiful big biscuits in the shape of a man on a horse, decorated with a sugar crown. Of course I bought one, but it looked too good to eat. The children I passed had no such qualms, biting off the horse's head before they went back to banging on their pots. Then suddenly I found myself looking at a small boy trailing at the back of the group. He had big, sorrowful eyes, and immediately my thoughts went to my child. Would he be unloved, unwanted? Would he be the one who trailed at the back of the group? And I realized I couldn't ever do that to him.

I turned into the Calle Larga XXII Marzo, the main street heading to St Mark's Square, and there was Leo, walking towards me.

"I was looking for you," he said. "I was on my

way to tell you that everything is set up with the bank. Do you know where it is? Come, I will show you."

He turned to walk with me towards St Mark's, crossing the small canal where I had fallen into the water, all those years ago, and where he had saved me. If he had not arrived in time, would I have drowned? I looked longingly at him. As if sensing my gaze, he turned to me and smiled. I thought, *He loves me, so no matter what happens, or what others think, that is important and worth cherishing.*

We came out through the colonnade and crossed the square, and then he led me through an arch on the other side. Just behind the square was the marble front to the bank. The symbol of St Mark's, the winged lion, hung above the door. The windows were decorated with iron latticework.

Leo paused. "Of course, it is not open today, but during the weekdays you can go in and ask for Signor Gilardi. He is the one who will take care of you. I have explained to him."

"Thank you," I said.

"It is the least I could do."

Suddenly there was a loud banging behind us, and another group of children appeared in the alleyway. Leo laughed and retrieved coins from his pocket. They must have been generous coins, because the children went away singing loudly with smiles on their faces. But I stood still, trying to come to terms with what had just happened. At the banging noise, I had felt a twitch in my stomach. I had slipped my hand inside my coat and there it was again—a tiny tapping against my hand. My baby was alive, and I could feel its kick. This changed everything and made it real.

"What's wrong?" Leo asked.

"Nothing," I replied, smiling. "I just felt the baby move for the first time."

"Really? Let me." He didn't seem to care that we were on a street. He slipped his hand inside my coat, and I directed it to the right spot. The baby obliged by another fluttering movement. A look of delighted amazement came over Leo. "It's real . . ." His eyes said everything.

November 12

Today I summoned all my courage and went to the contessa's soirée to meet the famous artist Paul Klee. Imelda had said she wasn't interested and didn't like Paul Klee's work. I think the truth was that she had met a handsome Italian student and seemed to be spending more time with him now that Gaston had gone home. But Henry, dear sweet Henry, had said he'd like to come. We had been spending more time together in the last weeks. I think he was also now beginning to experience homesickness and worry about the possible spectre of war overtaking us so far from home. It was a mental relief for me to have a conversation in English.

My first shock was that my long dress was now too tight for me. I would have to see if it could be altered. But I couldn't go in a tea dress! Then I decided that I could hold the gap together with safety pins and make sure I wore my fringed shawl, suitably draped. I met Henry, and we rode to the Lido together in the vaporetto. I was praying that Leo's father was not there and more especially that Leo would not come in the launch to pick him up. Both prayers were granted. Professor Corsetti and two other professors from the accademia were present, as was the British consul, Mr Sinclair, and the jolly priest, Father Trevisan. Vittorio was naturally there, hovering protectively near the contessa. Paul Klee spoke little Italian and seemed rather withdrawn, but the contessa, with her usual charm, managed to bring him out of his shell. His English was better, and I found myself speaking to him, along with Henry and the consul.

"You are fortunate here in Venice," Paul Klee said. "Here Jews are not yet persecuted. I had to flee for my life from Germany, and now I must remain in Switzerland for my safety. In Germany, Jews are set upon every time we go out. They smash our windows. They shut our businesses. We cannot hold jobs or go to school, and now they come at night and take us away. The Contessa Fiorito is a wonderful woman, is she not? She has helped several of my friends escape."

Franz had also come to the soirée. We didn't see much of him these days, but I noticed he was listening intently to what was being said in English. Was he really, as Henry had suspected, a German spy? These days made everyone wary.

After Paul Klee's speech, the consul drew me aside. "My dear, I think you should seriously consider going home while you can. We at the consulate have been notified that our days here are numbered and that we should be ready to leave at a moment's notice. As of now, Italy has not declared war on Britain, but they have a pact of friendship with Hitler. It may only be a matter of time."

"Thank you," I said. "I am considering it. At this moment, France still seems to be peaceful and trains are still running."

"But that could change overnight. Hitler is definitely poised to conquer Europe. He'll strike when the time is right, and when he strikes, he'll move with lightning speed. So I urge you not to leave it too late."

I thanked him again and was glad when Josef came up with a plate of canapés. How many people had now urged me to go home? Everyone I met. And yet if Germany invaded

Britain, wouldn't I be better off here, especially here in Venice, a city nobody would dare to bomb? I survived the evening without a mishap, keeping my shawl firmly draped over the safety pins holding my dress together, and made it home safely on the vaporetto. Henry, ever the gentleman, saw me home.

"I'd invite you up for a hot drink, but my land-lady has said no gentlemen callers," I said. This made him laugh.

"I hardly think I qualify as a gentleman caller," he said, "but I'm flattered that she might think I was a danger to your honour."

CHAPTER 30

Juliet, Venice, November 21, 1939

There was a notice on the board at school announcing that classes would be optional today because it was the Festival of the Madonna Della Salute and we'd probably all want to go to Mass. From what I heard, most of my fellow students saw it as a day off, not a day of religion. My landlady, on the other hand, was in raptures about it.

"One of the most holy days of our year," she said. "Will you be making the pilgrimage with me? I go to Mass this evening. It is beautiful when it is dark."

"Where is it?" I asked.

She looked at me as if I was completely stupid. "The church of the Salute, of course. You know it. The big church with the white dome at the tip of Dorsoduro. They build a special bridge for the day. A bridge of boats across the Canal Grande. And everyone carries a candle. It is a feast day to thank the Madonna for sparing the city from the plague."

The words "bridge of boats" had made my decision for me. I was not going to risk crossing that way again, even though this would be a narrower crossing than the expanse to Giudecca last summer. But I knew where bridges of boats could lead.

"Thank you, but I will not come to Mass with you," I said. "I will observe from the Accademia Bridge."

She sighed. "Am I never going to make a good Catholic of you? My confessor says I do not try hard enough to save your soul."

"I'm sure you set a fine example, signora," I said. "It's just that I have my own religion."

"Church of England, you call it?" She gave me a withering stare. "A renegade religion that defied the true pope."

"At least we are both Christians," I said.

She gave a derogatory sniff. "And about supper tonight—I have been invited to dine at the home of my friend, the widow Francetti across the street. I can leave you—"

"No need," I replied before she could finish. "I will find something to eat. I'm sure if it's a feast day, there will be stalls selling food."

"Plenty of those," she replied, again looking disapproving. "There are people who think of it as a carnival, not a holy day."

Since it seemed few of my fellow students were planning to attend class, I didn't want to find myself as the only one. I thought I might take a boat out to one of the islands, but the weather did not cooperate. It rained relentlessly all morning, making my landlady peer out of the window, sigh, then cross herself. "Such rain on the Feast of the Madonna. Never have I seen it like this. It is a bad sign, is it not?"

"Maybe it will pass before nightfall," I said.

"Let us just pray there is no aqua alta while we are at Mass," she said. "People will be in their best clothes. They will not want to wade home through high water."

"Wade?" I asked, not quite understanding the word in Italian.

She nodded. "Sometimes the water comes this high." She indicated the middle of her thigh. "Usually just over the feet, but one never knows. We must pray hard that God will keep the high water at bay for this special feast day."

Did God listen to prayers about floods? I wondered. Every year there were news reports of villages swept away, some of them presumably containing good Christians. I couldn't believe that God actively controlled weather, or then there would be perpetual sunshine over Vatican City and perpetual rain over Communist Russia. I had to smile at this thought.

At dusk my landlady appeared in her best hat and coat, carrying an umbrella "just in case God does not see fit to stop the rain."

"I'll walk with you and carry your umbrella," I said. "You'll want to carry your candle."

"If the candle can stay alight in such weather,"

she said, disappointment in her voice. "It could be that we don't light candles until we enter the church. But I am glad for the company, at least to the bridge."

So we walked together, joining a noisy throng. Some had candles in jars and lanterns, and these threw flickers of light on to the sombre walls of the streets. We passed the churches of San Maurizio and Santa Maria del Giglio and came on to the Calle Larga leading to St Mark's Square. Then we crossed a small waterway and turned towards the Grand Canal. Now there were hawkers selling balloons and toys, as well as various sweetmeats and even gelato, although I couldn't imagine who would want an ice cream on such a cold, bleak night. The narrow calle opened up, and there before us was the bridge of boats, and on the other side the Church of Our Lady of Health. Lights were strung across the piazza and in the trees. They danced crazily in the stiff wind from the lagoon. And the crowd was squeezed into a thin procession across the bridge, the candlelight bobbing up and down as they crossed.

My landlady saw some women she knew. I nodded to her and watched them join the line to cross. From inside the church I already heard singing—the voices echoing as from a great space. It was all rather moving, and I was tempted to join them after all, but the thought of being crammed in or of standing for an hour was not appealing. I stood in the shadows and was just about to go when I saw a servant carrying a lantern on a pole. And behind him a well-dressed party. As they passed under a street lamp, I recognized them. First came Count Da Rossi, looking like some Renaissance patriarch in a great cape, and behind him Leo, with Bianca holding a delicate red umbrella over her head with one hand while the other gripped Leo's arm.

Suddenly the scene had lost its magic. I turned, melted into the darkness and went home. I didn't even feel like finding an open trattoria. I made myself a cheese sandwich and a cup of tea. *What am I doing here?* I asked myself. *This is madness.* Better to face my mother's displeasure, the village gossip, my aunt's scorn than find myself trapped in a place where I had no family, nobody.

December 3, 1939

Winter has definitely arrived, but I'm still here despite it. We've had wind and blustery rain ever since the festival. At night I boil a kettle to fill the stone hot water bottle I have bought and cuddle up against it, hoping to get warm in bed. The first signs of Christmas are appearing: nuts and tangerines are now for sale in the Rialto market; there are hot-chestnut sellers on the street corners. I am so tempted by the smell every time

I pass, and I always buy a little bag and put it in my pocket to keep my hand warm.

My landlady said that Christmas officially starts with the Feast of the Immaculate Conception on December 8, which is a holiday here. I was rather confused about this: How could Mary conceive on the eighth and give birth three weeks later? But it turns out it is Mary's birth they are celebrating, not Jesus's. This religion is so complicated. And of course there is a saint for everything. My landlady prays to a different saint for her aching back and another for the success of her baking. She sees them as Jesus's little helpers.

"Why should we bother the Lord with such small trifles?" she said. "That is what the saints are for."

So I wonder which saint is in charge of childbirth. I might need the help of him or her. This is a reality that is only beginning to dawn on me: women die in childbirth. It is incredibly painful. And where will I have the baby? Will someone be with me? I glance across at my landlady over dinner. What will she think when she finds out? I've realized that one of the hardest things is not having someone to talk to. No relative, no friend of my own. Not that I could ever have confided in my mother, but perhaps my sister, Winnie, if she hadn't gone to India. And here, Imelda or the contessa came to mind, but I just can't see myself opening up to them, burdening them with my worries. I suppose it comes from years of loneliness.

December 8:
The Feast of the Immaculate Conception

I have discovered what my landlady thinks. Today was a holiday because of the feast day. I met up with Henry, who is becoming a real friend, and we walked around town watching people putting up Christmas decorations. There was a Christmas market being set up in the big Campo San Polo, selling tree ornaments of Murano glass, hand-carved wooden toys from Switzerland and Austria and lots of good sweets. I found myself feeling very homesick. Not that Christmas was an exciting festival at my house. We had a small tree, decorated with paper chains and glass balls. We went to midnight service at our church. We had a roast chicken for Christmas dinner, because a turkey was too big for the two of us. My mother made the Christmas pudding with silver threepenny pieces inside. We pulled crackers, put on paper hats and listened to the king's speech on the radio. So little really, but now it meant everything to me.

I could still go home. The words crept into the back of my brain.

"It's just beginning to sink in that I'll be away

for Christmas." Henry had an uncanny way of echoing my thoughts.

"I know," I agreed.

"I think you should go home, don't you?" he said. "I'm even thinking I should go home, while there are still ships crossing the Atlantic. The Germans would not dare to torpedo an American liner, because it would bring the States into the war."

"I am considering it," I said.

"Go while you can. There doesn't seem to be any real fighting in this part of Europe yet. Germany is still busy with Poland. But I bet you could still take a train across France. You're still getting mail from back home, aren't you?"

"I am." I nodded agreement. "I got a letter from home the other day."

It had been a particularly stern one from Aunt Hortensia. *There isn't a day goes by that your mother doesn't worry about you,* she wrote. *I can't understand why you are being so selfish and putting your own pleasure above the well-being of your dear mother. Venice may be a grand place to sit out a war at the moment, but what if you find yourself trapped behind enemy lines? What if you are taken prisoner? Your poor mother thinks of these things every day. It is especially hard for her with your dear sister stuck in India, expecting a baby any moment, and her husband now off somewhere with the British army. Please do be sensible and come home before it is too late.*

Your affectionate aunt, Hortensia Marchmont

I had no idea how to respond to that letter or to come up with a credible reason for wanting to stay away. Apart from bringing disgrace to my family, there was also a financial component. If I returned home, I'd have no stipend, no job and no way of providing money for my mother. I had arranged for half my stipend to be deposited in her bank every month. This way at least I could save the money that Leo was putting aside for me, resume my position at the school next September, and nobody would be any the wiser.

"I just got a stern letter from my mother, too," Henry said. "Rather a stern one. What if something awful happened to me? She couldn't bear to lose her only son."

"So will you go?" I asked.

"I'd really like to finish up the year here. If things get worse, then I expect I'll change my mind. But as long as Germany keeps its conquests to the east and England doesn't do much about it, then I guess we're relatively safe."

"Do you think Italy will stay out of it?" I asked.

"Bound to. Mussolini doesn't have the army or the weapons to take part in any meaningful way. He's happy to invade Albania, make his people think he's a great conqueror, but he wouldn't take on Britain."

"I hope you're right," I said. I glanced up at the sky. "I think we'd better head back, don't you? It's about to rain again."

"Damned rain," Henry commented. "These poor people putting up their booths—I hope it doesn't all get ruined."

"I suppose they are used to it. It seems to rain an awful lot."

He laughed. "You're from England. Doesn't it rain there all the time?"

"It rains frequently, but not deluges like this. When it rains here, it's as if the sky has opened."

As I spoke the words, the sky did open. We rushed for cover into the nearest church. Inside the foyer a Christmas crib scene was being erected, with a realistic stable and almost life-size statues. Not just Mary and Joseph, but lots of shepherds and Italian peasants with their animals, tradespeople carrying their wares. I found it quite moving.

We waited for a while, but it didn't seem as if the rain would stop in a hurry.

"There's a trattoria on the corner over there," Henry said. "Should we make a dash and get something to eat?"

"Good idea."

We managed to skirt around the side of the square without getting too wet and both ordered a bowl of minestrone soup, which warmed us up nicely. I was so glad that I could finally enjoy food again. We finished our soup, followed it with coffee and a pastry, and still the rain hadn't eased up. Then we were conscious of a loud siren, blaring out over the city.

"What's that?" I asked.

"Aqua alta!" a man at the next table said, waving his arms excitedly. He got up in a hurry, left some coins on the table and ran out, his coat over his head.

"What does that mean?" Henry asked.

"I think it means that some of the streets get flooded. We should go home while we can."

Henry nodded. He insisted on paying the bill. "Will you be able to get home all right?" he asked.

"I'll be fine. I expect the traghetto is still operating," I said. So we parted company. My raincoat and scarf were soon soaked through. The wind had come up, driving the rain in different directions, first hitting me in the face and then in the back of the neck. I reached the traghetto dock and found the gondola tied up with its cover on.

"Blast," I muttered. I was now in for a long walk up to the Accademia Bridge before I could cross the Grand Canal.

I slogged on, feeling more and more frustrated, as there is no such thing as a direct route in Venice. I had to retrace my steps to cross a canal, then constantly choose left or right instead of going forward. Finally I reached the

Accademia Bridge and had to battle both wind and rain, clinging to the railing as I made my way up the fifty steps and then down the other side. When I came down to the little piazza, it was already flooded. I waded through the icy water, feeling it lapping over my ankles. Other people trudged through it as if it was only a minor inconvenience—a woman carrying a laden shopping basket, another pushing a pram with the child suspended just above the water level.

I was now so cold I was shivering uncontrollably. Campo Santo Stefano loomed ahead of me. Not too far now. I stumbled into an unseen drain and fell forward. I would have gone flat on my face into the icy water if a passing man hadn't grabbed me and hauled me to my feet again. I passed a bar and was amazed to see men sitting on stools, drinking and smoking while water lapped below them. It seemed that nobody else cared too much about the rising waters.

"Madonna!" Signora Martinelli exclaimed when I came into the flat and stood in the hallway with water dripping from my clothing.

"I'm sorry," I said. "I am making your floor wet." I tried to unbutton my coat, but my fingers were numb with cold.

She came up to me. "You poor child," she said, and started unbuttoning my coat for me. "Let's put it over the bathtub to dry," she said. "And your shoes. So the aqua alta is already upon us, yes?"

"It is. The whole of Santo Stefano is flooded."

She removed my coat. My clothing beneath it was equally sodden. "Let us take those clothes off, too," she said and started to pull my jumper over my head. I was feeling so weak and exhausted that I let her. I didn't realize the danger until too late. Her hands went to the zipper on my skirt, and as she let it fall to the floor, she saw my petticoat, now tight and extended over my growing belly.

She stared. "Dio mio! What do I see? Am I correct? Is this what I think it is?" she asked, her voice harsh. She prodded at my belly with her finger. "There is a bambino inside?"

I nodded.

"I let you into my house because I thought you were a respectable woman." She almost spat out the words. "Not a tramp. Not a woman of the streets."

"I'm not, signora. I am a good woman, I promise you," I said. "I made one mistake with a man that I love, who can't marry me."

"To do this with a married man is adultery. Adultery is a mortal sin," she said coldly. "If you die before confession, you go straight to hell for all eternity."

I didn't know what to say. I was still standing there shivering. "I should take a hot bath," I said. "Or I will catch cold."

"You will leave this place," she said.

"You want me to go? Now?" I stared at her, horrified.

"I am a good Catholic woman," she said. "I would not turn you out in such weather. But I want you to leave as soon as you find another room. I cannot let my neighbours know that I have housed a person like you. What would they say? They would blame me for letting such a person into my house. I could not endure the pointed fingers, the whispers, the looks of condemnation."

"Very well," I said and set my chin. "I will leave, and I'm sorry to have caused you any grief. Believe me, I have plenty of grief myself. I cannot go home to my mother because I don't want to cause her shame."

I thought that might soften her a little, but it didn't. "You'd better take that bath," she said. "If you got sick, I would have to look after you."

And she stomped into the kitchen, slamming the door behind her.

I went into the bathroom and was so upset that I turned on the geyser too fast, resulting in a dreaded explosion and Signora Martinelli hammering on the door.

"Now you burn down my house!" she shouted. "I want you out of here."

I let the bath fill and lowered myself, feeling the life coming back to my frozen limbs. But I ᵛas still shivering. What would I do? One thing was absolutely clear after that encounter, and that was I couldn't go home. When she was glaring at me, accusing me, all I could see was my mother, saying exactly the same things. Bringing shame to her, who wouldn't for a moment think of what I might be going through. By the time I got out of the bath, I was calmer. I'd find another room. There were rooms aplenty in the city. The accademia would have a list. Then I thought, *Do I want to go through another landlady, who might feel exactly the same as the signora? Why not find myself a flat for rent?* Leo was putting money into an account for me. That should be enough to pay for a small place of my own. The idea seemed appealing. No more having to tiptoe in and out, sit at dinner and be polite when I didn't feel like eating, and having a cat find its way into my room at odd hours.

Then I took this decision one step further. Leo could find a place for me. He had offered to help. He wanted to help. He knew the city better than I did and might well know of a suitable flat. I wrote him a note and asked him to meet me at the accademia at our usual place. I'd post it in the morning—that is, if I could leave the building. I peered out of my window to see nothing but water below. No hint of where the canal ended and the walkway beside it began. I realized this would make venturing out precarious. How easy it would be to step off terra firma into a canal.

But by the morning, the water had receded with the tide. The streets were covered with mud and seaweed, making them slippery, but at least I could reach the postbox and then my classes. Signora Martinelli had put out a roll and a slice of cheese for me but was nowhere to be seen, so I left without having to face her, for which I was glad. I realized that Leo wouldn't get my note until the next day, so I made use of my free time by going to a clothing shop and buying a big jacket and a knitted skirt that would stretch with me. When I had my own space, I'd attempt to make some clothes as fabric was cheap in the market.

That evening the same situation: cold meats and bread put out for me and no sign of my landlady. I was so shocked that I could hardly eat. Here was a woman who had been nothing but friendly to me until now. I had been a model tenant—no noise, no visitors, no late nights, and I helped with the household chores. But in her mind I was now condemned to hell, and therefore she could have no contact with me in case my sin somehow came to roost on her. I was glad this wasn't my idea of God or religion!

CHAPTER 31

Juliet, Venice, December 11, 1939

The next day was Sunday and it was still raining. Again my landlady left food for me and disappeared to her own room. On Monday we'd had another episode of aqua alta with the high tide, and I had to pick my way across patches of standing water and stranded seaweed to get to the accademia. But I came out into the rain after morning classes to find Leo hidden under a big black umbrella.

"Ciao, bella," he said, bending forward to kiss my cheek.

"You shouldn't do that," I said. "People will see."

"We Italians kiss everybody," he said. "It means nothing. Shall we have something to eat?"

"All right. Let's go somewhere quiet where we can talk."

"Good. Come under my umbrella. There is room for two."

I joined him, conscious of his closeness, the warmth of his breath on my cold cheek.

"So you experienced your first aqua alta, did you not? I hope you didn't get caught outside. It can come up so fast."

369

"I did get caught, and drenched. The traghetto was not operating in the storm, and I had to walk all the way around to the bridge."

"You poor thing."

"More than you know," I said. "My landlady was most solicitous and helped me to take off my wet clothes—and then she saw my belly and she flew into a rage. She accused me of being a loose woman and said she wanted me out of her house immediately."

"Dio mio!" he exclaimed. "Still, it is not a bad thing, huh? You would want a home of your own as you prepare for the birth."

I hadn't really let myself think about this too much. Would I have the baby at home? In hospital? And if an adoption was to be arranged, would they take the baby from me immediately?

"Don't worry." Leo changed the umbrella to the other hand and slipped his arm around me. "I will find you a good place to live. A place where you can be happy, yes?"

"That would be wonderful," I said.

"Give me a day or two and let me see." He came to a halt outside a rather grand-looking trattoria and ushered me inside. We then had a meal of spaghetti with clam sauce, a veal cutlet and for dessert a sponge cake with a hot chocolate sauce. I ate every morsel, realizing that I had eaten almost nothing for the past twenty-four hours. It would be good to cook for myself, I thought. I could eat the food I wanted, good nourishing food like the doctor recommended.

I felt hopeful and energized as I went back to my afternoon classes.

Henry came to sit beside me. "I saw you with a man," he said. "Just a friend?"

"Just a friend," I replied. "Why, are you jealous?" I grinned, teasing him.

He flushed, and I realized that perhaps he was. That was something I hadn't anticipated. He must be several years younger than me. And I hadn't encouraged him in any way. But then saw that perhaps I had. I had sought out his company to go and eat, to spend time on free days, mainly because he was friendly and safe and I enjoyed speaking English with him.

Now I didn't know what to say. "You should find yourself a nice Italian girl your own age," I said.

"You make it sound as if you are a grandmother. There's not that much difference between us. I'm twenty-four, and you are?"

"Thirty," I said. "Practically middle-aged."

"It doesn't matter. I think you're beautiful. And kind. I like that."

Oh dear. How could I ever tell him the truth? He'd be devastated. It seemed that my whole life was a minefield of not wanting to let someone down.

December 13

Leo met me at lunchtime to tell me he had found the perfect flat for me.

"It is here, in Dorsoduro," he said. "So you will not have to cross that infernal bridge in the wind and rain. And also it is far from places where my family go. And it's very nice. You'll like it."

He led me away from the accademia to the other side of the island. As we walked, I was surprised to see straw placed outside some of the houses. Not much straw, sometimes on the doorstep and sometimes in baskets.

"Is the straw some kind of defence against the aqua alta?" I asked, making Leo laugh.

"It is for Santa Lucia's donkey," he said.

"What?" Why did everything that happened in this city surprise me?

"It is Santa Lucia's Day. A big day for us, as her bones are contained in a church here. The little children believe she brings presents, so they leave out straw for her donkey. And we have a special pasta dish, made just for today." He paused. "You see, we are very much into tradition here. We love our saints."

"And you? Do you love your saints?"

"Of course," he said. "Who else would talk to God on our behalf?"

I said nothing but realized that I would probably never understand the Venetians. A strong, cold wind greeted us as we came out to the waterfront called Zattere. How well I remembered when the bridge of boats had crossed to Giudecca. Now the wide promenade was almost deserted. We turned left and passed an impressive church.

"The Jesuits," Leo said. "They do everything splendidly. No expense spared." Finally we came close to the tip of the island, and Leo paused in front of a tall and quite imposing yellow building with blue shutters.

"Here?" I asked, looking at the three marble steps leading up to a front door with a lion's head knocker on it. "Who lives here?"

"Nobody at the moment," he said. "The building belongs to my family. The lower floors are offices but are little used at the moment as we have transferred most of our business to the shipping terminal. But come. Let me show you."

He took out a large key and opened the front door. We stepped into the gloom of a foyer, the only light coming from a skylight several floors above, giving the feeling of being in an aquarium. A marble staircase curved upward. Leo led the way. The staircase up to the next landing was less impressive, being made of simple wood.

"I'm sorry about the stairs," he said, "but you will have your privacy."

We came to a halt on a dark landing, and Leo felt around for a light switch. When he turned it on, I saw several doors, but he opened one into what looked like a broom cupboard.

"You see?" he said, going into a small anteroom stacked with odds and ends, then opening the door at the rear. "The building was designed in the old days when there was smuggling and people needed to disappear occasionally. There are several of these secret apartments in the city. Most people will think it just leads to the roof, because that's what it says on the door. Come."

And he started up the fourth staircase, this one extremely narrow. We came out into a big room, and I gasped. Windows looked out to a magnificent view—across to Giudecca, the island of San Giorgio Maggiore and even around to the St Mark's Basin.

"It's good?" Leo asked, looking pleased at my expression.

"It's magnificent."

"See, there is a bathroom, and a little kitchen, and a bedroom at the back. I'm not sure about the bed. It may not have been used for a long time. I'll have a new one delivered." He opened another door, and there was a tiny bedroom, just big enough for the bed and a chest of drawers. "And any other furniture you might need," he said, coming back into the main room. "I don't know how warm the bedroom would be. There is a stove, but it will need coal."

I noticed the furniture for the first time. A couple of brocade armchairs. A table and two chairs in ornately carved wood, and in the window a beautiful writing desk. I looked around. "How is it heated?"

"The stove in the corner," he said, indicating the same sort of porcelain stove my landlady had. My first thought was of trying to haul coal up four flights.

"There is a pulley outside," he said. "You put the coal in the bucket, and up it comes. But do not worry. You will not have to do this."

"Why not?"

"I have arranged for a woman to come in," he said. "Francesca. She is the mother of one of our employees. A local woman. Used to hard work and needs a job as her husband has just died. She has had six children. She will take good care of you. You tell her what you want done, and she will do it—the cooking, the cleaning, the shopping. Whatever you want. I think you will be happy here, yes?"

I couldn't take my eyes off the view. "Yes, I think I will," I said. Then my practical side took over. "But isn't the rent very expensive?"

He laughed. "No rent," he said. "It's yours."

"What?"

"I'm giving it to you. I've talked to our lawyer, and he is drawing up a ninety-nine-year lease for this floor. It belongs to you now. Stay as long as you want, or go, knowing you can always come back."

"Leo, I don't know what to say," I muttered, terrified I might cry.

"Cara mia, it's the least I can do," he said tenderly. "And selfish, too. I want a place where I can visit you."

This set off an alarm bell in my head. I wanted to have the chance to see him, but . . . "Leo, you should understand that I'm not going to be your mistress," I said.

"But cara . . ."

I took a step away from him. "Isn't that what rich men do? They buy a nice flat so they can visit their mistresses whenever they want? So convenient."

He touched my arm, gently. "Julietta, no. I promise you that was not my intention. I will be honest. I would like to make love to you again. But if you do not wish it—so be it. We will be close friends. The apartment is for you because you are the mother of my child. I want you to be safe and well provided for." He put a gentle hand on my arm. "Please do not be angry. My intentions were good."

I was in such a precarious position, I had to believe him and be grateful.

CHAPTER 32

Caroline, Venice, October 13, 2001

A good wall heater arrived, delivered by a couple of workmen and making the bedroom cosy. Caroline went through her aunt's clothes, putting them into piles to donate or discard. She realized now that she had some true vintage pieces amongst them: a tea dress, a long evening dress, a fringed shawl. Those she would keep, but the jumpers had long ago succumbed to moths, and she carried them down to a nearby rubbish skip along with long-expired items from the kitchen and bathroom. She kept a couple of lace-edged hankies and a bottle of eau de cologne that was miraculously unopened and still good. Then she went through the paintings and drawings once more. She'd definitely keep the sketches of Venice. Maybe the Da Rossi family would like the sketches of the baby, if it proved to be Luca's father. She put them aside, noting that they ranged from a chubby newborn to about a one-year-old. No drawings after that. So perhaps she stopped looking after the child when he was one—or, more likely, she had to flee. It would be interesting to know if there were any records of where she lived in Switzerland. The Swiss were so organized, there were bound to be! She smiled at the thought.

By the third day in the apartment, she realized there was nothing to keep her any longer, apart from meeting Luca's father if and when he arrived. The flat was immaculate. The drawers cleaned out, the old suitcase packed with the things she'd be taking with her. The weather had turned colder, and she thought of Granny's warm kitchen and hearty soups. She also thought of Teddy. How long since Josh had let her speak to him? Had he convinced Teddy that he didn't want to go back to England? She didn't know if Josh had replied to the email she had sent him because she did not have a connection and didn't know where to find one. Worrying thoughts crept into her head as she lay in that warm bedroom. What if Teddy was sick and she didn't know and Josh couldn't contact her? But she had given Granny the address, and Granny could telephone her. *Stop worrying,* she told herself. *Enjoy this moment. Enjoy the beauty. Be free. Be hopeful.*

At the end of the week, her mobile rang, and it was Luca. "My parents arrived home and are settled in. Would you like to join us for dinner tonight?" He gave her the address.

At eight o'clock, dressed as smartly as possible, she came out of her building to find it was pouring rain again. Waves slapped over the Zattere. Goodness, she was going to arrive looking like a drowned rat, she thought. Now she had two choices: she could cross Dorsoduro, being mainly sheltered in narrow streets, but then she'd have to brave the full force of the storm on the Accademia Bridge, or she could wait for a vaporetto and have to travel all the way around until finally it came back to the Grand Canal. She decided to risk the former, managed to get across Dorsoduro without getting too windblown, but then had to battle to keep hold of her umbrella over the bridge. On the St Mark's side, she was able to stay fairly sheltered under balconies while she located the building (with some difficulty in spite of the directions Luca had given her). It was an elegant white marble structure with a doorman in uniform who saluted her and pressed the button on the lift to the top floor.

Inside the lift she removed her headscarf and tried to smooth her hair into place. *I must look a fright,* she thought. As she stood at a white-painted front door, she experienced a shiver of nerves. Even at her best she would look dowdy compared to Luca's family, and she certainly was not looking at her best right now. What if it was a big dinner party? But then Luca opened the door.

"Caroline, I am so sorry. The rain did not begin here until it was too late, or I would have come for you. Here, let me take that wet coat." He helped her off with it and deposited the dripping umbrella into a stand in a square marble hall. Then he gave her an encouraging smile and led her inside. The room was spacious but not overpowering, with some good pieces of furniture but essentially liveable. A couple was sitting on either side of a fireplace. The man stood up as she entered. "So Father, this is Mrs Grant, the English lady I was telling you about. Caroline, this is my father and mother, the Count and Countess Da Rossi."

The words "Count and Countess" brought her up short. Why had he not mentioned that his family was noble? The proprietress at the pensione had called them "one of the great families," so Caroline should have been prepared. The man must have noticed her uneasiness. He came forward with his hand extended.

"Dear Mrs Grant. Welcome. I am so sorry that you got caught in the sudden rainstorm. I'm afraid this is a disadvantage of living in Venice in the winter months. Luca, pour some Prosecco for our guest."

"Come and sit beside me." The countess patted the sofa beside her. "You must warm up after your ordeal. And we can speak English."

She looked younger than her years, although her husband looked his age, with a shock of iron-grey hair. The countess's hair was still an attractive red-blonde. Whether this was natural or not, Caroline couldn't say. But she did notice that the countess was most elegant in a plain grey cashmere dress with a Hermès scarf at her neck.

"It's kind of you to have me when you must be jet-lagged," Caroline said.

"Not at all. It stopped us from falling asleep at seven o'clock and then waking in the middle of the night," the count said. "So our son tells us that you have inherited a floor of one of the Da Rossi buildings. How fascinating. And we don't know how or why this lease was granted?"

"We don't," Caroline said. "All we can think is that it was wartime and maybe they were glad to have the building occupied."

"Possible, I suppose," the count said. "So what do you plan to do with the place? Keep it as a holiday retreat?"

"I'm not sure yet," Caroline said. "It's all been a bit of a shock. We had no idea, you see. My great-aunt was a private person and never mentioned to any of us that she had lived in Venice. The first I knew was that I inherited the key to her bank vault."

Caroline looked up as there was a satisfying pop and Luca uncorked a bottle of Prosecco.

"She was a woman who liked to travel? A fashionable type?" the count asked.

Caroline smiled. "Quite the opposite when I knew her. She was quiet, reserved—the epitome of a British spinster. That's why I'm still so surprised. We were wondering . . ."—she paused, and glanced across at Luca, who was now coming towards her with a glass—"if maybe she had been employed by your family as a nursemaid, a nanny. Although she may have left Venice when you were still a baby. Do you remember your nanny?"

His face lit up, making him suddenly look much younger. "But yes. As it happens, I do remember her well," he said. "She was very nice. Warm. Unlike my mother, who rarely came to visit the nursery."

"And your nanny's name? Did you know that?"

"Let me see. Of course I always called her Nanny. Yes. It was Julie . . ."

"Juliet?"

"No, no. Giuliana. She was a big woman. Arms like tree trunks." He laughed. "She'd envelop me in her arms and make everything all right. She spoke Venetian to me."

"Ah." Caroline nodded. "So not my great-aunt then."

"But Caroline has sketches of a baby that looks a lot like you—like that old portrait of you that used to hang on the nursery wall. Whatever happened to that?" Luca asked.

"I've no idea. It disappeared years ago." He looked up. "Ah, good. Here is food at last." And a maid came in with a tray of prawns, olives, bruschetta with various toppings. Conversation waned as they ate. Then they were summoned in to dinner. Talk turned to Luca's experience in the

United States, his mother's family, the difference in lifestyle. "My cousins—they all had a car when they were sixteen. Can you imagine?" he said. "I had to wait until I was twenty."

"Where is there to drive in Venice?" his father asked, and they all laughed.

The countess asked about Caroline, and she found herself spilling out some of the story about Teddy, stuck in New York because of the attack on the World Trade Center.

"How you must miss him," the countess said. "I'm sure he'll be able to fly soon."

"I have been telling her that I think she should just go and get him," Luca said. "What child would not want to fly home with his mother?"

"I'm just praying that they haven't poisoned his mind against me," Caroline said. "My ex-husband could be very manipulative. But surely you don't want to talk about my worries. I came here to find out about my great-aunt, but I think we're never going to know any more."

"You say your aunt did sketches of Angelo when he was a baby?" the countess asked.

Angelo. She hadn't heard his first name before, and her thought went instantly to the painting that hung on her great aunt's wall at home. Angelo. The little angel. It was him. As she raised her eyes, she found the count looking directly at her. There was something in his gaze she found disquieting. In his eyes. Then she realized what it was. He was looking at her exactly as Aunt Lettie had done before her sight failed. Head slightly to one side, eyebrows slightly raised. And then she knew. Aunt Lettie wasn't his nanny. She was his mother.

CHAPTER 33

Caroline, Venice, October 2001

It was hard to get through the rest of the meal, to chatter lightly while thoughts whirled in her head. The moment she had made the connection, she could see other similarities—the shape of his upper lip, his long fingers, the hint of auburn in his grey hair. So Aunt Lettie had had a child out of wedlock, presumably with Luca's dead grandfather. But would the family have legitimized him? Would that old woman in the nursing home have accepted him as her son? She remembered Angelo saying, "Unlike my mother, who rarely visited the nursery."

Somehow she survived the rest of the evening. Coffee was served in tiny cups and limoncello in small crystal glasses. Not used to much alcohol, Caroline found she was relaxed, almost pleasantly sleepy, until she was jarred awake by the loud blaring of a siren.

"Oh no." Luca's mother got up and went over to the window. "Not aqua alta, this early in the year, surely?"

"It's been happening earlier and earlier, hasn't it?" Angelo said. "Climate change. That's what they are shouting about, isn't it?"

"What is it?" Caroline asked, nervously.

"When rain and high tide come at the same time, we have flood here," Luca's father said. "And here in St Mark's sestiere is some of the worst. Luca, you should probably take the young lady home before she has to swim, eh?" He laughed and patted Caroline's knee.

"Oh no, it's all right. Luca doesn't have to . . . ," Caroline began, glancing up at him.

But the contessa interrupted. "Of course he will take you home. He has the boat, although it may be a bumpy ride."

Luca had already risen to his feet. "Are you ready now? My parents are right. We should go if we do not want to walk through high water."

" ' Wade,' " his mother said. "That is the right word, Luca."

Luca glanced at Caroline and rolled his eyes, making her smile. "Always she corrects my English. Let us go, Cara."

Caroline reacted to this shortening of her name. Only Josh had called her that. She thanked Luca's parents and was given a warm hug by the countess.

"Lovely to meet you, my dear," she said. "We must do this again on a less wet evening if you're planning to stay awhile."

She let Luca help her on with her still-damp coat and accompanied him into the lift.

"Your parents are very nice," Caroline said as

they descended. "Not at all how I imagined a count and countess would be."

"And how should a count be?" Luca looked amused.

"Stuffy. Aristocratic."

He laughed. "I will be il Conte one day, and I don't intend to be at all stuffy. But it is my mother who has always prevented my father from being stuffy. She is a great believer in equality. If she had not married him, she would have studied law, you know. She comes from a family of prominent lawyers in New York. In fact she went home intending to go back to university there, but my father pursued her and said he couldn't live without her. So she left everything behind and married him. A passionate man, my father. But then, most Italian men are." He gave her a wicked little grin.

"What a romantic story," she said.

They came out to the street to find rain beating down and water already pooling over the cobbles.

"Oh, I am afraid we will get a little wet," Luca said. "Come under my umbrella. My boat is not too far away." He put an arm around her, as if this was a most natural thing to do, and led her through a narrow gap between buildings until he reached the launch, which was tied to a gondola post. Then he walked across the prow, balancing precariously, and hauled the boat closer in to shore for Caroline to step in.

"Sorry, we can't go fast this time," he said. "Grand Canal has a slow speed, so that the buildings are not damaged. But you will get a little shelter from the rain in the cabin."

"But you will be soaked."

He shrugged. "No matter. See, the rain is already easing. And we shall be back in Dorsoduro soon."

"I'll hold the umbrella over you," she said.

"That's not necessary. I like the rain in my face. Besides, the wind would soon blow it away."

He revved the engine and reversed the boat into the Grand Canal. There was almost no traffic. Caroline came to stand beside him, staring out as wind and rain blew into her face.

"Don't you want to sit where you can be dry?" he asked.

She shook her head, wondering how to tell him her suspicion.

"What is wrong?" Luca asked, looking at her. "I noticed this evening that you seem preoccupied and upset."

Caroline hesitated. "I don't know if I should tell you this," she said. "And we probably should never mention it to your father, but I think my great-aunt Juliet was his mother."

He gave her an astonished look, then shook his head, laughing uneasily. "But no. This cannot be. He had a mother. My grandmother. You met her."

"A mother who rarely visited his nursery. That's what your father said. A mother who reacted with such anger when she saw me. She recognized a family resemblance, Luca, as I did. Your father looked at me in exactly the same way my aunt used to. There was something about his eyes. It's uncanny. That's why there were so many sketches of him as a baby—because she was forced to give him up."

He gave an embarrassed cough. "Caroline, don't you think you are maybe going too far? Maybe you want this to be true? I know my grandmother. I remember her before she became this sad old woman. She was never warm, I agree. She never showed affection, but she was a person who liked to be adored. We had to gather around her at her birthday and give her lavish gifts. Completely self-centred, always. Can you imagine such a person welcoming another woman's child? A woman who had betrayed her with her husband?"

"I agree. It is hard to understand. But they have ways of proving it these days with DNA. They can determine who you are related to. If we could get a sample from your grandmother and your father, then we'd know for sure."

"And how would you do that without either of them finding out?" he asked. "Surely such a thing would take weeks, if not months. I don't think there are many facilities that can do such tests."

He paused, looking at her. "Besides, I don't know if I'd want to know the truth."

They headed up the Grand Canal, then turned into a side canal, passing the Pensione Accademia where she had stayed. Coming towards them was a single gondola, with a pudgy, aged and miserable-looking gondolier at the oar, the collar of his black oilskin turned up against the rain.

Not how you'd expect gondoliers to look, Caroline thought. Then suddenly it hit her. She might have proof. She would show Luca. They came out to the other side of Dorsoduro, and he brought the launch to the dock nearest her building with some difficulty as waves still splashed over the waterfront. He tied up, then took Caroline's hand to steady her as she stepped out. Just as she was stepping ashore, a wave gave the boat a big lurch and she half tumbled into Luca's arms.

"Don't worry. I've got you," he said. His breath on her cheek was warm.

"Thank you." She righted herself with an embarrassed grin. She fell into step beside him as they made for the big front door. "Luca, I think I can prove this to you. Or maybe not prove, but at least let you know I am on the right track."

"How is that?"

"If you come up to the flat, I can show you."

A flash of amusement crossed his face. She saw his eyes sparkle in the lamplight. "Isn't this like you English say, 'Come and see my etchings?' "

Caroline's face flushed with embarrassment. "Certainly not. I only wanted . . ."

He put a hand on her arm. "Don't worry. I was just teasing. I'm sure your motives are the most pure. Although . . ." He left it at that and, keeping his hand on her arm, steered her to the front door.

At this time of night it was locked. Caroline fished in her handbag while the wind snatched at her coat and skirt. Finally she retrieved the key, handing it to Luca, who fitted it and then opened the door. They stepped into complete blackness.

"Merda!" he muttered, as he tripped over the threshold. "Where is the damned light? Don't tell me they turn off the electricity."

"It's been on in my flat," she said.

He fished around but couldn't locate the switch. "Momento." He reached into his pocket and flicked on a cigarette lighter. "I still don't see it. We'd better go up. You go ahead."

He held up the lighter as Caroline went up the stairs ahead of him. As she reached the first landing, she turned to look for the second staircase, let out a scream and stepped back, bumping into Luca and almost knocking them both down the stairs. A white figure hung in the doorway to her left.

She grabbed on to Luca. "That thing. A ghost! Over there."

"It's okay. I've got you," he said, his arms

coming around her. His own voice was shaky.

Luca held up the light, then laughed. "A painter left his white coat over a ladder." Then without warning he let the lighter snap shut, wrapped her into his arms and kissed her. Caroline was so startled that she didn't know how to respond, only aware of his mouth, cold lips, pressing ravenously against hers. And to her embarrassment she found herself responding to him.

"I'm sorry," he said as they broke apart. "But when a strange woman throws herself into my arms for the second time in one night, it is a little hard to resist."

"Don't apologize," she said. "I did fling myself at you, didn't I?" She laughed, uneasily. "Besides, I rather liked it."

Luca had rekindled the lighter and found a switch on the wall. The landing was bathed in the harsh light of a bare light bulb, revealing the painter's white coat draped harmlessly over the ladder. They went up the second flight and then through the storage space, where Caroline opened the door leading up to her flat. After what had just passed between them, she wasn't quite sure how to handle Luca's presence. *This is crazy,* she thought, but she had to show him. She had to verify for herself what instinct had told her.

She let them into the flat and then took off her mac. "Take off that wet overcoat," she said.

"Should I make us a hot drink? Why don't you sit down and let me find the sketchbook I want to show you." She realized she was talking rather fast. Nervous. Now that he was here, she was feeling awkward.

"What about a glass of wine first? All those stairs have made me thirsty," he said. He was already walking through to her kitchen, where he found an open bottle and poured two glasses. "You need a refrigerator," he said. "Although this is quite cold."

He handed her a glass, and they clinked them together in a toast, his eyes challenging hers.

"I've just been thinking," he said. "If what you say is true, then we are cousins. What a pity."

"You don't want to be my cousin?"

"I'm not sure what your laws are about cousins in England, but here . . ."

She picked up his meaning and again excitement fluttered. "We'd only be second or third cousins," she replied. "Juliet Browning was my great-aunt, not my grandmother."

"Ah yes. That is good to know." He took a long drink, then made a face. "You drink cheap wine. I shall have to educate you."

"We drink what we can afford," she said. "But I could do with educating. I've only drunk what we call 'plonk' in my life."

" 'Plonk.' " He chuckled at the word. "You English have strange words."

"I suppose," Caroline began, as she crossed the room to the window, "if we are related, you and I could do the DNA test. We wouldn't need your grandmother at all."

"You may be right," he said. "But these tests take weeks, don't they? And anyway, I still can't believe what you say is true."

"Just wait until you see this." Caroline opened the desk and took out Aunt Lettie's first sketch-book. He sat in one of the armchairs, and she came to perch on the arm beside him.

"My aunt's sketchbook from her first visit in 1928," she said. "She was eighteen. It says so on the front page." She flipped through the pages and then came to the portrait of the man she had always assumed to be a gondolier. "There," she said, placing the book into his hands. "He looks very like you, doesn't he?"

She heard Luca's intake of breath. "Yes," he said at last. "It is my grandfather, I'm sure. I have seen photographs. They have always said I look like him."

"So I wasn't wrong?"

"This was when she was eighteen, you say? Nineteen twenty-eight? And my father was not born until 1940. She must have been his mistress for many years," he said slowly. "He gave her this place so they could be together."

Caroline wrestled with the Great-Aunt Lettie she knew being anyone's mistress, being kept in a love nest. "Not when she was eighteen," she said. "She only came on a brief trip."

"But they met, and he never forgot her. Perhaps they stayed in touch, and she found ways to come and visit."

"She came back in 1938 with a group of girls from the school where she taught," Caroline said. "I have her sketchbook from that time, too."

"She said she was bringing schoolgirls, but actually she came to see him," Luca said. "They were in love." He looked up, and his eyes met hers.

"So why didn't he marry her? Why did he marry your grandmother?" Caroline asked.

Luca put a hand on her arm and caressed it. She found it disquieting. "In families like mine, we marry for the right connections. My grandmother came from a powerful family. A rich family. It was a good match. I expect it was arranged when they were babies."

"So he married someone he didn't love, just for business reasons?"

"That is how it goes."

"Not any more, surely? You didn't marry for business reasons?"

"Ah, but I did. That was part of the problem," he said quietly. "I don't think I ever really loved her. Everyone said, 'She's so suitable, she's so accomplished, what a good wife she will make.' But she didn't. She drank too much, even at twenty-four. Our life was always in turmoil. And it sounds awful now, but in a way I was relieved when she died."

"I'm so sorry, Luca."

"I'm not. It took me a while, but I'm ready to move on."

"To find the next suitable bride?" she asked, teasing now.

He shook his head. "My father dared to defy family and marry my mother, although her family is not without money and connections. And we no longer have the power we used to have before the war. So I don't think it matters as much anymore."

A squall of rain peppered the window. Luca looked up. "It seems the rain has set in for the night. And the aqua alta, too. I do not think I want to go all the way across to the Lido in this weather," he said. "In fact it would be quite foolishly dangerous." His voice became softer. "You are not going to turn me out into the storm, are you?" His hand moved down her arm, his finger tracing a line over her hand. "I think I should like to make love to you. Would that be so wrong? Even if I am your cousin."

"Would that be wise?" Caroline asked, although she had to admit she felt a thrill of arousal. "After all, look what happened to my aunt Lettie."

"Will not happen to you, I promise." His eyes were challenging hers. "And you would not be cruel enough to send me out into the aqua alta, would you?" His finger was caressing the back of her hand. "But only if you want to. I think you do."

Caroline returned his smile. "Why not?" she said.

CHAPTER 34

Juliet, Venice, December 26, 1939

My first Christmas away from home. How strange and empty it seemed, and yet some good things have happened, too. I moved into my new home—a home that I own, at least for the next ninety-nine years, on December 16. I found there were new rugs on the floor, a new water heater in the bathroom (like my landlady's, but not so prone to exploding) and a new bed made up with clean sheets and a huge fluffy eiderdown. There were lined velvet drapes at the windows. The place was warm; there was coal beside the stove. It was a bright, sparkling day, and I gazed out at that view, feeling a great swelling of happiness for the first time in months. It was perfect.

Later that day, I met Francesca. Not exactly the warmest person but clearly used to hard work. She spoke with such a strong Venetian accent that I could hardly make out what she said, but at least she understood my Italian. She made me a wonderful mushroom risotto the first night—rich and creamy. I had already been shopping and went to bed with a hot chocolate and biscuits, feeling well satisfied. Over the next few days, I bought more items to make the place feel like home—pillows and a blanket, a bowl of oranges and a table lamp for my desk. I had fallen in love with that desk. It was gorgeous inlaid lemonwood from the south of Italy and still smelled of lemon after all these years. It had all sorts of little compartments and drawers, including, to my delight, a secret drawer that was only accessed when you pulled out one compartment and then opened it with a little key. Not that I had anything to hide, and Francesca could barely read Italian, let alone English, but it was nice to know it was there.

Classes ended for the holiday. Imelda went home to her parents, who had moved close to the Spanish border, just in case the Germans invaded France. I had bought gifts for my mother and Aunt Hortensia at the market: Torcello lace handkerchiefs, tiny glass ornaments for the Christmas tree and a box of nougat. I added a Christmas card, and inside I wrote a note. I had thought long and hard about what to say to them that might make sense and decided that of course it was money.

The reason I have decided to stay for now is a financial one, I wrote. *As you know, I am receiving a generous stipend that makes up for my teacher's salary this year. Should I come home, that money would cease, and as the school has surely hired a temporary art mistress for the year, I'm not sure how we would live. So*

I'm staying on for all of our sakes, but promise I will make a sensible decision when it becomes necessary to leave.

I felt a little underhanded about saying this, but I didn't want to cause grief to anyone. In return I received a package on Christmas Eve of my mother's Christmas pudding and a wedge of Christmas cake, plus a scarf she had knitted. I was touched.

I debated whether to buy a small gift for Henry and ended up getting him a Murano glass dog with a sorrowful face. It was enough to make anyone laugh when they were feeling low. And then there was Leo. What did one give a man who was exceedingly rich and could buy what he wanted? Then I decided that I was going to be bold for once. I saw a plain silver locket in the market. I bought it and cut off a small curl of my hair, tying it with a pink ribbon. At least he would have something to remember me by when I had gone.

I stocked up with panettone, the traditional Christmas cake that now appeared in all the bakeries, bought a chicken to roast with all the trimmings and decided to invite Henry to join me for the day. I was surprised to receive an invitation from the Contessa Fiorito, sent to me via my professor, to join her on Boxing Day for her annual party. As she was Jewish, I wouldn't have thought she'd celebrate Christmas at all. I debated long and hard about taking her a gift and then settled on a pot of white snowdrops from the market. Flowers are always so cheering, and they reminded me of the first signs of spring at home.

I didn't expect to see anything of Leo, knowing that Christmas is such a big family holiday, but I heard a tap on my door just as it was getting dark on Christmas Eve. Francesca had gone home hours before, having made me a traditional fish stew for my dinner. I gave her a generous Christmas tip and saw her smile for the first time. So I was surprised when I opened the door to find Leo there, gasping for breath. In his arms was a large box.

"I ran up all three flights," he said, giving me a kiss on the cheek as he came in. "I'm due at the family dinner, but I couldn't let the holiday pass without seeing you. I've brought you a present." He put the box down on the table, then watched with anticipation as I opened it.

It was a large box, and I couldn't think what it might be until—"Oh," I said, surprised and pleased. "It's a radio! How wonderful."

"I wanted you to know what was going on in the world," he said.

"I have a small gift for you, too," I said, and handed him the leather box, tied with a ribbon. He glanced up at me, questioning, then opened it. When he saw the locket, a smile spread across his face. He took it out, opened it and held it in his palm.

"Your hair?" he asked. "A lock of your hair?"

I nodded. "I wanted to give you something to remember me by when I have gone."

"As to that," he began, "I have come to make a suggestion to you."

He paced a little, then took a seat in one of the armchairs. The heavy drapes were closed, keeping in the warmth from the stove.

"Would you like a glass of wine?" I asked.

He shook his head. "I don't have time, cara. I'm sorry. But I have been thinking about the best solution for you and the baby, and I would like to present it to you. You say you want to give up your child and find a good family for him. Well, I have found one."

"You have?" I could hear my voice wobble because this sounded so final.

He nodded. "I would like to adopt him legally and raise him in my home as my son. He will inherit everything, including the title one day. He will be well looked after and loved. Does this meet with your approval?"

I was so stunned I couldn't say anything as I tried to come to terms with this. "But what about Bianca?" My voice was now shrill. The shock had been great. "Surely she will not welcome another woman's child into her home, especially if she found out the child was a result of our affair?"

He shrugged. "Bianca can't have children, so it seems. I didn't find this out until we married. Her doctor says 'can't have,' but it might be 'won't have.' Either way, I would have no heir unless our son is legally mine."

"You're very sure it's going to be a boy."

He gave a cocky smile. "The men in my family are very virile. We produce sons."

"And if it's a girl? You won't want her?"

"It won't be." He leaned forward and grasped both my hands. "So does this make sense to you? It is a good solution, is it not? For both of us?"

"How do I know Bianca will treat the baby well? She may be jealous. I wouldn't want to put my child into danger."

"Bianca could not be less interested in babies, I assure you. We will hire the best nursemaid, and he will be loved and spoiled."

"How will you explain this sudden arrival of a baby to the community? I've already been made aware of the power of gossip in this town."

"Ah, I've thought of that, too. It is a relative's child. From somewhere out in the countryside. She gave birth, bravely, but she is dying. I promised to keep the child within the family. That's what we do here."

I had been trying to digest this as he spoke. But another thought, a small sliver of hope, was creeping into my mind. "Leo, if Bianca can't have children and she deceived you on this, isn't that grounds for annulment?"

"Of course," he said, "in any other family. But this marriage is a business transaction. Mutually beneficial to two powerful companies. If the marriage were annulled, our partnership with Bianca's father would end. He is a proud and vindictive man. He'd ruin us. And not only that, but I fear his ties with the Mafia. If I let down his daughter, I suspect I would wind up floating face down in the lagoon."

"Oh gosh," I said. "How complicated."

"It is," he said. "I do not think you understand family obligations in the way that we do here. It is a sacred duty to put family first."

He glanced at his watch and stood up. "I'm so sorry. I must leave you now. Run all the way. At least there is no aqua alta to wade through to midnight Mass. God bless you, cara mia. Buon Natale." He blew me a kiss and was gone, leaving me with whirling thoughts and a knot of anguish in the pit of my stomach.

Henry came on Christmas morning, bearing a bottle of Prosecco and a beautiful leather portfolio "to carry and store your artwork." I was touched and a little embarrassed. I felt my cheeks burning.

"Henry, how very kind of you," I said. "And I have a small gift for you, too."

404

When he saw the glass dog, he laughed. "What a sad face. A real hangdog!"

"I wanted to cheer you up when you felt homesick," I said. "But I think the Christmas dinner will cheer us both up."

We had a glass of Campari with some olives, then the roast chicken with roast potatoes and Brussels sprouts and carrots, and then the Christmas pudding. Henry had not tried one before, and I'm not sure he really liked it, but he was polite and appreciative. To walk off our meal, we strolled along the Zattere. It was quite deserted, and from inside homes came the sound of music and laughter, reminding me strongly that it was a day for families. We wound up with tea and cake, again a new experience for Henry.

"Thank you for this," he said. "I was dreading the holiday alone, frankly, and now I've enjoyed myself."

I had, too. And the next day, we took the boat together over to the Lido and the Contessa Fiorito's villa. The house was decorated with greenery and glass ornaments, and chandeliers sparkled from the ceiling. Professor Corsetti and his wife were there, as was the British consul, the smiling priest and other people I had met before. No sign of Josef, however. I asked the contessa about him.

"I have found him a safe haven amongst other artists in Florence. Now I am working on bringing a young woman. One at a time, I'm afraid, and there are so many I can't help."

"Do you think the treatment of Jewish people will spread here?" I asked. "Mussolini is such an admirer of Hitler."

"I think there are people in Italy who would like to see Jews rounded up and sent to camps, but not here in Venice. Not amongst people of culture. Our Jewish community is such a part of the city and well respected. I think we are safe here."

We had been standing together, apart from the others, and I wondered if I should tell her about my pregnancy. Was it fair to withhold this information from her? I certainly didn't want her to learn it from local gossip. But now was not the right time. I'd make a point of coming over to visit her alone, some other time. I thought she would be the kind of person who would not judge, but one couldn't be sure . . . Then a devastating thought occurred to me. *Professor Corsetti! My professors at the accademia.* Was there a policy against people like me? Would I be allowed to continue my studies? When I saw him over at the table, helping himself to some pâté on a cracker, I decided that I had to know. I went over to him.

"Can I have a word with you, please?" I asked. "In private?"

He looked suspicious but came with me into the small anteroom. "Well?" he asked.

I told him I was going to have a baby, that the father couldn't marry me and that I'd like to continue my studies for as long as possible. Would that be a problem?

"Do you think you will be too weak to hold a paintbrush? To stand at an easel?" he asked. "Or do you think the size of your girth might get in the way?"

"No!" I exclaimed.

"Then what might be the problem?"

"That you don't want me in your class anymore and think I might corrupt other students."

He looked at me, then burst out laughing. "My dear girl, in my world everyone has a lover or a mistress, is homosexual or bisexual and certainly has the odd illegitimate child. Nobody will raise an eyebrow, I assure you." He hesitated. "But you. I am concerned about you. Are your studies more important to you than your safety and well-being? Would you not rather be at home for this momentous event? Amongst those who can take care of you?"

"Yes, I would," I said, "but I do not wish to cause shame and embarrassment to my mother, so I'm staying away. When the time comes, I will give up my child and go home."

"A noble sentiment. I wonder if you'll go through with it."

CHAPTER 35

Juliet, Venice, February 21, 1940

My life has settled into a comfortable routine. I go to my classes, I have lunch with Henry or occasionally with Leo, I come home to find my flat warm and spotless with a meal waiting for me, thanks to the good Francesca. The weather has been bleak and gloomy with lashings of rain and several occasions of aqua alta, but this part of Dorsoduro does not flood easily, so I've been able to get around without wet feet. Imelda did not return after the break. I was not too surprised. Travelling through France may soon become dangerous or even impossible. And I haven't seen anything of Franz either, which just leaves good old Henry and me. I have been out to see Contessa Fiorito, once to her January soirée and then once on my own to tell her my news. I felt it wasn't right to keep her in the dark any longer.

"I have to admit I suspected this," she said. "I could tell." She looked at me, her head cocked to one side in the birdlike manner of hers. "And the young man—he won't do the right thing?"

"He can't. He's married."

"A happy marriage? One he does not want to

leave for you? Divorce is becoming a little more accepted in our country, you know."

"Not a happy marriage but one he can't leave."

"I see." A long silence. "Is it possible that it is young Da Rossi?"

I flushed scarlet. "How did you know?"

"I remembered your face when I introduced you to his father. Your reaction was not that of a person being introduced to an unimportant stranger. At the time I thought that maybe you were overawed by meeting a handsome count."

"It was a shock," I said.

She toyed with her teaspoon. "Young Da Rossi. Not a happy marriage, so one understands, but not one that he can easily walk away from."

"No."

Again she stared out past me, to her lovely garden, where the palm tree was swaying in a stiff breeze. "Then you will go through this alone? And the child? You will try to raise a child alone? Your family will accept it?"

"No. I'm going to give it up. It's all arranged. It is going to a good family," I said.

"Ah. A practical young woman." She paused. "I admire you. I was not so noble in my youth. I was much younger than you when I found myself pregnant, unable to support a child, and instead had an abortion. Not a thing I would recommend. It was certainly taboo. I had it done in a back room, no sterilization. I nearly died. But in my day it was not possible to raise a child as an unmarried mother." She reached out and gripped my hand with that birdlike claw of hers. "You can always come and live with me, you know. I take in strays. I enjoy your company."

I felt tears welling up. "That's so kind of you, and I have to admit it's tempting, but I have a nice little flat of my own now in Dorsoduro. It's close to my art classes."

"Pity. I could have used your help with the planning for the Biennale. It opens in May, you know."

"It's going to go ahead, in spite of the war?"

She chuckled. "We in Venice do not let a small thing like a war get in the way of art. Of course, the number of countries will be limited: the Germans, the Russians have both already committed to their pavilions. The Americans, too. I'm afraid the art will reek heavily of propaganda this year, but it gives our Italian artists a chance to display their work—and our Jewish artists-in-exile, too."

In the new year I received a frosty letter from my mother, thanking me for the Christmas gifts and saying she was glad I enjoyed the food and the scarf. *I appreciate your concern for us,* she wrote, *and the desire to keep providing financially, but all sorts of jobs are now opening up for women in war work—factories and even the armed forces.*

I read on. *Aunt Hortensia says that if you really do not intend to return until the end of your year abroad, we should offer your room to evacuees from London. So many people are leaving the city with the threat of bombing looming in the future.*

So now it appeared that if I decided to come home, I wouldn't have a place to stay, even if I wanted one.

Carnevale was going ahead in spite of the war. It seemed the whole city dressed up and celebrated in the days leading up to Shrove Tuesday, the day before Lent started. There were masks for sale on every street corner, costumes in every shop. I didn't plan to participate, but Henry persuaded me to buy a mask and a long cape and go out amongst the crowds. It was exciting and a little alarming to see the strange figures, some with beaks, some dressed as Pierrots and Columbines, but all anonymous beneath their masks.

I was exhausted when we finally came home. Henry escorted me up the stairs, and I made us both hot chocolate. He seemed uneasy.

"I don't quite know how to say this," he blurted out, "but my father has commanded me to come home. He is sure that full-scale war could break out at any moment. German U-boats are attacking ships in the Atlantic. So I have to go."

"I'll miss you," I replied.

There was a long silence. He rose to his feet and came over to where I was sitting.

"Juliet, this may sound kooky, but I wondered if you'd like to marry me and come to America with me," he said. His face had turned bright red, and he was sweating.

I think my mouth dropped open. This was so unexpected that I was lost for words.

"Henry, it's really kind of you, but . . . ," I stammered.

"Look," he said, "I know about your baby. Imelda told me long ago. I was waiting for you to tell me yourself. I could give it a name, a home, a father. We're quite well heeled, you know. The kid would grow up with a good life."

I admit I was sorely tempted. He was a good man. Only he was so young. So naive and a little too solid.

"You are very sweet," I said, "but you go home when your father commands. What would that father think if you showed up on his doorstep with a pregnant older woman in tow?" I went over to him and put my hand on his shoulder. "Henry, I can't saddle you with me. You deserve your own good life."

"Look, Juliet," he said, "I think you're a swell girl. I'd be happy to be saddled with you. I know I'm not the smartest of guys, and I may not be sparkling and witty company, but I'd be a devoted husband, I promise."

"I'm sure you would, Henry, but the problem is I don't love you. I like you a lot. I enjoy spending time with you, but I'm not going to spoil your life. I'll miss you a lot. Who will I have coffee with and go to the festas with?"

"That man who shows up from time to time, I expect," Henry said drily. "The good-looking guy in the expensive suit. I suspect he's the baby's father. Am I right?"

"Yes, you are," I agreed. "And he can't marry me."

"But you want to stick around here to be near him, just in case?"

"No, not just in case. I know he can't leave his wife. I've accepted that."

He went to touch me, then obviously thought better of it. "Juliet, I worry about you stuck here on your own. I know there's not much sign of war at this moment, but what if it comes? What if you'd like to get home but you can't?"

I sighed. "I know, Henry. I worry about it, too. But I can't go home until the baby is born, and then I'm just praying that I can get across France."

"So come with me now. You know, if you find you don't like me that much, you can always divorce me later. They do it all the time in the US."

I took his hands and held them in mine. "You are possibly the sweetest person I have met in my whole life, and I appreciate you so much. The moment you've gone I'll be kicking myself that

I've been so stupid to let you go. But I just can't do it to you."

"Okay. If that's what you really feel." He sighed. "I'd better get going. I have a lot of packing to do. My father's booked me on a ship sailing out of Genoa in three days."

"Have a safe journey, Henry." I stood up and kissed him on the cheek. His arms came around me, and he hugged me tightly. "Take care of yourself, okay?" Then he made for the door, and I heard his feet clomping down the stairs.

CHAPTER 36

Juliet, Venice, April 9, 1940

Time just seems to have passed in a blur. There has been little mention of war on the radio. Italy is still in Abyssinia and has now annexed Albania, but Hitler has not made any move towards Western Europe. On the home front I have made progress with my painting. It seems that my pregnancy has unleashed a wave of creativity, and I want to paint all the time. Even Professor Corsetti said nice things about a nude I did in the style of Salvador Dalí. Henry's departure was followed by a spell of glorious spring weather. Flowers bloomed in window boxes and in the various gardens. The air smelled of perfume. People came out in light clothing and sat on walls enjoying the sunshine.

It seems strange to admit this, but most of the time I forgot about the baby. Apart from the increasing difficulty in negotiating the stairs, or being woken by a vigorous kick at night, it was as if it didn't exist. Easter has come and gone. Leo has been away a lot, apparently inspecting boatyards in other places for his father-in-law. So my life has been lonely but not unpleasant. Francesca and I can now understand each other. I'm pleased to think that I can now speak rudimentary Venetian in addition to my now fluent Italian. I actually dream in the language.

The impending birth was brought home to me when Francesca arrived one day with a big bag of knitting wool.

"And how is this child to be dressed?" she asked. "I see no baby clothes, and you are not knitting anything. And shawls. And blankets. And you do not even have a bassinet."

"I'm going to give my child up," I said.

She replied, "All the same, it will need to have clothing when it comes into the world. Do you know how to knit?"

"I do," I said.

"Then you'll find patterns and wool in that bag," she said. "And I'm going to ask my older daughter what things she can spare. But at least buy the poor child a new bassinet to lie in."

This awakening made me visit the doctor again. He examined me and nodded.

"All proceeding normally," he said. "It shouldn't be too long now. Here is my telephone number. You are to call me when the pains are well underway. Any time. Day or night."

Since I lived alone with no telephone, I didn't see how this could be possible. Should I stagger down the street in the middle of labour pains to find a telephone kiosk? But then Francesca announced that she had been instructed to stay with me around the time the baby was due. I was really glad. It seemed that everything was going smoothly. The child would be born. I'd recover and then go home. It's funny how easily I accepted those things at the time.

Then today, April 9, there was a news bulletin on the radio. Germany had invaded Denmark and Norway. Britain had bombed a German naval base. Suddenly it became real again, but I reassured myself that if Hitler was busy up in Norway, I'd still find a way across France.

April 25

Today was the biggest feast day in the Venetian calendar. The feast of St Mark. The square outside the basilica was jam-packed with people, and a young girl, dressed as an angel, flew over our heads on a wire to the church. I didn't get a good view as I was loath to find myself squeezed into the square, so I stood aside, under the colonnade. It was on days like this that I felt my loneliness most acutely. Festas were family celebrations. So on impulse I took the boat across to the Lido and visited Contessa Fiorito.

"What a lovely surprise," she said. "I've been thinking about you and wondering how you were faring."

"All is well," I said.

"And the baby? Who will look after you?

417

Why don't you come out here, and I'll employ a woman?"

"You are most kind," I replied, "but Francesca, who cooks and cleans for me, is going to stay overnight when the baby is due."

"And after the child is born, you'll go home?"

"That's the plan," I said.

"Then let's pray it comes to fruition," she said, eyeing me with sympathy.

April 30

I had expected the baby to have come by now, but Francesca says first babies are often late. She should know. She's had six, and now has twelve grandchildren, so I feel I'm in good hands. Leo returned home a few days ago and came to see me. He brought me a present of oranges and lemons from the south.

"Things are getting serious," he said. "I pray you can leave soon. British troops are on French soil, the French are making skirmishes over the border to Germany. It's only a matter of time before the whole thing goes up."

"I can't go anywhere until this baby decides to come." I patted my stomach.

"I don't want you to go," he said bluntly, "but I love you. I want you to be safe."

It was the first time he had ever said he loved me. My heart soared, and I fell asleep that night feeling warm and reassured. Leo would make sure everything was all right.

May 3

I woke in the middle of the night with pains that took my breath away. I called to Francesca, who was sleeping in the armchair.

"Finally, it begins," she said. She put a rubber sheet on my bed and went off to call the doctor. The pain intensified, making me cry out. Warm liquid was trickling between my legs. When Francesca returned, she took one look at me.

"Madonna," she exclaimed. "The child is almost here. Let's hope that fool of a doctor gets here in time. Otherwise." She patted my arm. "Otherwise don't worry, little one. I have assisted at births before. All will be well." She went off to boil water and came back with a damp towel to put across my forehead.

After what seemed like hours, I was pushing. I couldn't help myself. I was screaming. Crying out for Leo. Then there was a great rush of fluid, and Francesca leapt forward to grab the baby as it emerged.

"You are a lucky one," she said. "to have such an easy labour the first time. And let's take a look at what we have here."

I watched her scoop up a red bundle into a towel. At that moment I saw a little fist come out, and the child gave a great wail. Francesca nodded.

"Good lungs," she said. "A healthy boy."

Leo will be pleased, I thought. *The future Count Da Rossi.* Francesca had taken the child over to the sink and was now cleaning him off. He bawled lustily all the time. Then she brought him back to me.

"Here. Meet your son," she said and placed him in my arms. He stopped crying, and this little, perfectly formed person was staring up at me with dark, serious eyes, still trying to work out where he was.

"Put him to the breast," Francesca instructed, opening the front of my nightgown. "That will help with the delivery of the afterbirth as well as getting him sucking right away."

She held him up to me. He latched on to my breast and began sucking vigorously, all the while still staring up at me with unblinking eyes. I was unprepared for the sensations I felt, and with them came one overwhelming thought: *I can never give him up.*

CHAPTER 37

Juliet, Venice, May 3, 1940

The doctor arrived soon after, examined me and declared all was well with both of us before leaving again. Francesca made me milk with brandy. I must have fallen asleep because I opened my eyes to see Leo looking down at me with great tenderness.

"We have a fine son," he said. "What did I tell you? We Da Rossi men always produce fine sons. What shall we call him, do you think? Leonardo after me? Bruno after my grandfather?"

"Goodness no," I said. "Bruno was my landlady's cat."

He had to laugh. "After your father, then?"

"My father was Wilfred. I can't think of a more horrible name." I turned to the baby, now lying in the bassinet that Francesca's daughter had provided. He was peacefully asleep, his long eyelashes lying over his chubby cheeks. "He looks like a little angel," I said. "Like one of those cherubs in the Renaissance paintings."

"Do you want to call him Angelo, then?"

I met his gaze and nodded. "Angelo. My little angel. Perfect."

"Then I will add it to the adoption papers. They are all ready to go."

I sat up. "Leo, you can't take him now. I'm not ready to give him up."

He perched on the bed beside me. "But Cara, you should go home as soon as you feel well enough, or it may be too late. And you can't take him with you. Better to let me take him now, before you become too attached to him. I have a wet nurse lined up. A nursery. He will be in good hands."

I shook my head vehemently. "No, I'm sorry. I can't let him go. I love him already. He's my child. I just gave birth to him. I carried him around inside me. At least I want to keep him until he is weaned. Francesca says that the mother's milk protects against diseases. Give me this much."

I could see he was struggling, trying to come to terms with this. "Cara mia, you do realize that once the Germans overrun France, you could well be trapped here for a long time."

"Would that be so terrible? I could raise my son."

"I must point out that if I do not adopt him officially, he will have no papers, no legitimacy. No identity card, and those will be important. We have been instructed to carry them at all times. The government is already talking about rationing, and you would get nothing as a noncitizen. And then what? You raise him maybe two, three years. But you still can't take him home, can you? And how would you provide for him? I can give him a good life. You know that."

I did know that. "Just let's concentrate on now," I said. "Let me nurse him until he's ready to be weaned, then I'll hand him over."

"All right," he said, after a long hesitation. "If that's what you want. I owe that much to you. I will have the items from the nursery sent over here for now."

"You told Bianca, I presume? What did she say about a nursery in her house? And a strange child?"

He gave a twisted little grin. "She said, 'As long as I don't have to look after the brat, then why not? At least you'll have your precious son to inherit, and I can get on with my life.'" He paused. "Like I said, she is not maternal."

And so a crib and baby clothing arrived the next morning. Baby Angelo is now adorned in lace-trimmed robes. I had to laugh.

"These make you look like a girl," I said. He glared at my laughter. He has the most expressive little face. As I observed him, I thought: *I will take him home with me now, while I can. He's healthy. He will survive the journey. And I don't care what anyone says.*

Then I had to talk sense to myself. How could I

deny him the life that Leo would offer? The best of everything. And then he'd inherit a fortune. And I realized I couldn't be selfish. If I loved him enough, I could give him up. Just not yet.

May 12

Having sailed through a pregnancy with little inconvenience, I was rather ill during the next days. I had lost a lot of blood and got an infection. The doctor said I was anaemic and prescribed iron tonics, red wine and plenty of good meat. I still wasn't feeling up to going out and certainly not to resuming my classes when I turned on the radio to hear that the German army had circumvented the Maginot Line by crossing through the forests of Belgium and had invaded France. The British army was advancing from the Channel ports. France was at war, and I could no longer cross in safety. In a way, this calmed me. Rushing home was no longer an option. I could stay here, take care of my baby in the city I had come to love and be close to Leo. It seemed perfect at the time.

From that day on, the news only got worse. Toward the end of the month we learned that the British troops were being driven back, destroyed, overrun, and were retreating to the coast, where they were trapped on the beaches, waiting to be picked off by German bombs and guns. And then a miracle: thousands of small boats came out from England to a place called Dunkirk and brought the troops home. I wept as I read the account in the newspaper. It seemed only a matter of time before Germany invaded England, and I was glad that I had chosen to remain here, although I worried about my mother. I had not heard from them in months. I hoped that nobody would bother with two old ladies. They'd be safe enough, even if England was under German rule.

June 10

Today everything changed. Italy has announced it is joining Germany in the war against the Allies. I am now an enemy alien. I wonder what that will mean? Surely nothing much in a place like Venice. And I do have friends in high places. The irony is that our newspapers are full of news about the successful first month of the Biennale. One has to admire the Venetians to hold an international art exhibition as if nothing in the world has changed. I decided I'd visit it when I was feeling a little stronger. I needed to be reminded that somewhere in this world there was still an appreciation of beauty and the things that matter.

This afternoon I was taking an afternoon nap after Francesca had gone home when there was a tap at the door. Probably not Leo, as he usually came in without knocking. I got up, pulled on my robe and went to the door. I was surprised to find Mr Sinclair, the British consul.

"I do apologize for this visit, Miss Browning," he said. "I can see that I've come at a bad time. You are unwell?"

"No, just taking a nap," I replied, ushering him into the room. "You might have heard that I had a baby recently."

He nodded gravely. "Yes, I did hear. It must be a difficult situation for you now that Italy has entered the war. You could still go to Switzerland, I presume, or take a ship from Marseilles?"

"I'm not sure why I'd want to go home if we're about to be invaded," I said.

He frowned. "Let us hope that we British can put up a jolly good fight and make sure Hitler does not invade. Mr Churchill has taken over now, you know. He's not a namby-pamby like that lily-livered Chamberlain. If he'd been in power all along, maybe we would have stopped Hitler in his tracks before Poland. Although maybe not." He shrugged. "The little blighter has been dreaming of world domination for years. Building up a mighty army. But we English have more grit and stamina than the Germans. Hitler won't find us easy to conquer, I can assure you."

"I hope you are right," I said. "Can I make you a cup of tea?"

"Very kind of you." He took a seat in one of

my armchairs. "That's something you won't be able to find much longer," he said. "They are instituting strict rationing here, and you'll not get a ration card. Besides, Italians don't drink tea, and the British expatriates have nearly all left."

I went to put a kettle on. "And what will happen to you, now that we're at war?" I asked.

A spasm of pain crossed his face. "Ah, that's the problem. I've been recalled as of today. I'm to go across Spain to Portugal, where an aircraft will take me home." He looked at me with kindness. "I wish I could take you with me, but I can't. So I have an ulterior motive for visiting you, apart from saying goodbye. I wondered if you'd care to work for your country?"

When I looked surprised, he went on, "What I have to say from now on is all top secret, and you must sign a document to verify this." He reached into his pocket and put a sheet of paper on my table. "Are you prepared to sign?"

"Before I know what is entailed?"

"I'm afraid so. That's how it works in wartime."

I glanced across at Angelo's cot. "I have a baby," I said. "He's my first responsibility. I can't be a spy or run messages for you. I couldn't leave him or take that kind of risk."

"Of course not," he said. "You wouldn't have to leave your own home. I think you'd be quite safe. And you'd be doing a great service to your country."

I hesitated, staring at him, then walked over to the table. "I suppose there is no harm in signing. I can still say no to what you propose?"

"Oh, absolutely." He sounded far too cheerful.

"Very well, then." I scanned the document, noting that betraying the trust could result in prison or death. Hardly reassuring. But I signed. He took it back and slipped it inside his jacket.

"You have a fine view here, Miss Browning," he said.

"I know. I love it."

"And I understand you own this place."

"You seem to know a lot about me," I said.

"We do. I'm afraid we had to check into your background before making my request of you."

"And that request would be?"

In the kitchen alcove the kettle boiled, sending a loud shriek that made me rush before it woke Angelo. I poured the water into the teapot, then returned to the living room.

"You are in a prime position to watch the movement of ships. You know the Italians have navy vessels stationed here. Now they will be allowing the German navy to use this as a base from which to attack Greece, Cyprus, Malta. I'd like you to give us a daily account of shipping activity. If ships leave the harbour here, you tell us and we'll have planes ready to intercept."

"How would I tell you? Who would be left to tell?"

"Ah." He turned a little red. "Someone will be sent to install a radio. It will be hidden so that nobody else knows about it. You can't use it when that woman of yours is here. She cannot be allowed to see it. Is that clear?"

"Of course. Although she is not the brightest. She probably wouldn't know what it was."

"Nevertheless"—he held up a warning finger—"you will broadcast as soon as possible after you witness shipping activity."

"To whom do I broadcast? And what do I say?"

"Patience, dear lady. All will be made clear," he said.

I went back into the kitchen and poured two cups of tea, then carried them back on a tray to where we'd been sitting. Mr Sinclair took a sip and gave a sigh of satisfaction.

"Ah, tea that tastes like tea. One thing I shall enjoy when I get home."

I took a drink myself and waited.

He put the cup down. "Do you know Morse code?"

"I'm afraid I don't."

"I'll get a booklet over to you. Learn it as soon as possible. Along with the radio, you will receive a codebook. You will keep that hidden apart from the radio, in a place where nobody would think of looking. Your messages will be sent in code. For example, if you see two destroyers, you might say, 'Granny is not feeling well today.' "

"And if the Germans break the code?"

"The codes will be changed frequently. You will not know in advance how you'll receive a new booklet. Maybe a package from your auntie in Rome with recipes in it." He shrugged. "Our secret service is highly resourceful. The good thing is that you will never have to make personal contact with anyone, so should you be questioned, you will not have to worry about betrayal."

"That sounds so reassuring," I said drily and saw the twitch of a smile on his lips.

He took another sip, then put down his cup once more. "One more thing," he said. "You will need a code name for communication. What do you suggest?"

I stared out across the canal. A cargo ship was moving slowly past. Was I mad to agree to this? "My name is Juliet," I said, "so my code name could be Romeo."

"Romeo. I like it." He laughed. "I should take my leave now. As you can imagine, there is a lot to pack up and dispose of after ten years here. May I have my unused food sent over to you? And wine? I'm afraid you'll not have an easy time of getting food in the future."

"Thank you," I said. "I'd appreciate it."

"Anything else you might need that I'll have

to leave behind? Blankets? An electric fire?"

"That would be wonderful," I said. "Who knows if coal will be rationed?"

"I'll see what I can do, then." He held out his hand to me. "Good luck, Miss Browning. I think you'll need it."

CHAPTER 38

Juliet, Venice, June 20, 1940

This morning I went out to stock up on food before rationing begins in earnest, leaving Angelo asleep with Francesca in charge. It felt good to be out in the fresh air with the warm sun on me, and I lingered as I walked along the Zattere. A navy vessel approached from the dock area, reminding me of what I had agreed to do. Why hadn't I simply refused? Now I might have put myself and my son in danger. But I had been brought up to do the right thing, hadn't I?

I turned off the broad waterfront and was making my way down a side canal to where a vegetable barge was usually moored when two men in uniform came towards me. They were carabinieri, not normally seen in the city, where the city police operate. I went to walk past. But one grabbed my arm.

"You," he said, using the familiar form of the word. "Where is your identity card?"

"I'm sorry, I didn't bring it with me," I lied, trying to make my accent sound Venetian.

"Didn't you hear the directive that identity cards are to be carried at all times?" He was blocking my way forward.

"I'm sorry. I'll do better," I said.

"You'll come with me," he said.

"I've done nothing."

The older of the two, a big dark swarthy man, stepped up into my face. "Someone mentioned you are the Englishwoman. An enemy alien. You will be taken to a camp."

"No," I said, struggling to free myself. "Let go of me. You are making a mistake."

The two men were grinning as if they were enjoying this.

"You have the wrong person. I live here."

Suddenly there was a shout, and we looked up to see a large woman barrelling towards us, waving her hand in a threatening manner. "Let go of her at this moment, you Sicilian bullies," she shouted. "You leave her alone, do you hear?"

"Go about your business, woman," the man who held me said.

"I will not, until you let me take her home. This is the young lady who saved my life when the bridge collapsed at the Festa of the Redentore last year—but of course you wouldn't know about that, would you? Coming from so far away from our city. She held me above water, and I didn't drown. An angel. And I won't let you touch her, isn't that right, sisters?"

A crowd had gathered, many of them women.

"That's right," another said. "Leave her alone, or you'll have to deal with us."

"Don't think you can come into Venice and start throwing your weight around," a third said, stepping within inches of his face. "We are not Palermo or Messina here. We are civilized people. Go back where you came from."

"Step back or you could get in trouble," he said, but he didn't sound quite as aggressive.

"And you could get thrown into that canal."

"That's right. Throw them into the canal." Voices echoed up and down the fondamenta.

The officer looked around. A large crowd had now gathered, all shouting and gesturing.

"You can't come to our city and start arresting innocent citizens," a man's voice shouted from the back of the crowd.

"Come, my angel. Come with me." My saviour pulled me away from the carabiniere and tucked her arm through mine. "We're going home."

And I was led away. After we had turned the corner, I thanked her profusely.

"Nonsense. My pleasure," she said. "I live in that building over there. If you need help, you come to me. I'm Constanza, eh?"

"Thank you. I'm Julietta."

She gave me a kiss on the cheek, and I hurried home without my groceries. But I worried. How was I going to get around if streets were being patrolled? I told Francesca what had happened to me.

"Cursed Sicilians." She spat into the sink.

"Who wants them here? Don't worry, you are amongst friends."

I was going to write to Leo, but this afternoon he came running up the steps. "I heard that some carabinieri tried to arrest you," he said.

"They did. They wanted to take me to a camp."

He sighed. "I wish you had gone home when you could, Julietta. How can I protect you? I can let our police know that you are not to be touched, but these outsiders, the new paramilitary units, they are not controlled by our city government. Please stay home as much as possible until we sort things out for you."

"How can we sort things out?" I said, hearing my voice tremble a little. "I'm an enemy alien, aren't I? I'm supposed to be in a camp."

"Then you really must go to Switzerland right away," he said.

"I can't leave Angelo. I really can't."

"Cara." He touched me gently. "The longer you hold on to him, the harder it will be. I want your safety, and that of my son."

He went, leaving me feeling nervous and near despair. I gazed down at Angelo as I nursed him, and he sucked lustily, his chubby hand resting on my breast. *He will be all right whatever happens,* I thought. But what if I was taken to a prison camp? When would I realize I had to leave? Was it too selfish of me to hang on here as long as possible?

I didn't see Leo for two more days. I stayed home, looking anxiously out of the window. A delivery was made from the consul with boxes full of wonderful and necessary items: tins of fruit, tomato paste, sardines, bags of dried beans and pasta, coffee, tea, wine, olive oil, and several fluffy blankets plus the incredible electric fire. I nearly wept with gratitude and shared some with Francesca, who was equally grateful. Then Leo came back, looking rather pleased with himself.

"All is well," he said. "I had a little talk with my father. A useful man to know. Fortunately someone in city government owed him a favour, so here is your identity card and here is your ration card."

He placed them on the table. I picked them up and looked at them. "Giuliana Alietti?" I asked.

"Used to work for us but recently died, unfortunately. Her husband had just turned in her cards. It seemed like a pity to waste them. The photograph is not unlike you. But still, proceed with caution. I'm sure there is a rumour in this neighbourhood that you are a foreigner. And there will be the odd person who hopes to be paid for information. But as long as I am here, all you need to say is 'I am in the employ of the Count Da Rossi.' That should suffice."

"I hope so," I said.

He went over to Angelo's crib. The baby was

awake and looked up at him with unblinking eyes.

"I think he is getting your auburn hair," Leo said, glancing up at me. "And maybe your blue eyes? They don't seem to be brown."

"All babies have blue eyes, so I'm told by Francesca, who knows everything," I replied. "They change to the real eye colour at a few months."

"Good. I hope he will look like you," Leo said. "That way I will remember you all my life."

I didn't know how to answer that, but my heart ached.

July 21, 1940

Almost a month has passed. I am still a little afraid to go out. Is anyone watching where I live? I have reluctantly decided I shouldn't risk going to the Biennale, although the contessa tells me it has some interesting exhibits this year. I shall continue to see her. There is a vaporetto stop not far from my residence, although the navy has now requisitioned most of the ships and so service out to the Lido is far less frequent.

A strange Englishman came late one night, and the secret radio is now under the floorboards beneath the bedside table in my bedroom. I have to drag the table out and lift up the square of floorboard, and the radio is attached underneath.

All very neat. He showed me how to operate it, how to read the codebook. I have been trying to learn Morse code, but I don't think I'm very good at it. He also left a pair of powerful binoculars for spotting ships that sail from the mainland, in case the Germans decide to build a new harbour of their own. As of yet I have nothing to report. All is serene, and life goes on as it does every other summer.

Today was the Feast of the Redeemer. This time, on a clear sunny day, I watched the pilgrims go over the bridge of barges to the church and then return, carrying candles. It was hard to believe that a year ago my whole life was different. And yet how could I regret Angelo? I love him with all my heart. I didn't realize humans were capable of such love.

CHAPTER 39

Juliet, October 23, 1940

What a strange year this has been. In Venice nothing much has changed except food has become scarce. Produce no longer flows in so frequently from the Veneto. I think it is diverted to feed the big cities of Milan and Turin, where the factories are making war equipment. Luckily, my friend Contessa Fiorito, whom I visit regularly, has created a vegetable garden on her property and keeps me supplied with fresh produce. This will end soon, as the weather has turned cold and wet suddenly.

The contessa has stepped up her efforts to extricate Jews from Nazi Germany. It seems strange to me that the Nazis have made it so clear the Jews are not wanted and yet they forbid them to travel.

"I don't know how long I can continue this little service," she said to me last week. "Now that we are allies of the German bullies, our government is falling into line with Hitler. There is a plan to make all Jews wear the Star of David and move to selected areas."

"Will you have to do that?" I asked, my heart leaping in fear.

She smiled. "My darling, nobody knows I am Jewish. And those who do value what I offer this city and will conveniently forget. So don't worry. I am quite safe. It is you that I worry about."

"I think I'll be all right," I said. "Leo instructed me on how to say, 'Of course I have my identity card' and other useful and not so polite things in Venetian. Most of the enforcers are from the south and can't understand the language."

She reached out then and laid her slim and bony hand on my knee. "Then there is a small favour I wish to ask of you."

"Of course," I said. "You have done so much for me."

"There is a person I wish you to meet at the station. Josef is no longer with me. I have sent him on to a friend. Umberto is too old to go rushing around, and besides, he does not approve of what I do. My only other servant at the moment is the little maid, and she would be hopeless."

"What about Vittorio?" I asked. "I haven't seen him recently. Is he not here?"

"I told you once that Vittorio knows who butters his bread," she said, giving me a little smile. "He has latched himself on to Mussolini's inner circle. It seems they are interested in acquiring art, one way or another."

"Oh dear," I said, actually feeling relieved that he was not going to be hanging around her. "Very well. I'll be happy to meet this person for you."

"She is the daughter of Anton Gottfried, the former first violinist of the Vienna Staatsoper orchestra. Her father is under house arrest in Vienna and fears for his safety, but he wants to get Hanni away. And a chance has presented itself. The girl attended a Franciscan convent school until she was barred from doing so. The nuns are fond of her, it seems. Two of them are leading a pilgrimage to Rome this week and have agreed to take Hanni along. When the train stops in Milan, she will be put on a train to Venice. She arrives around noon on Friday. Can you meet her for me?"

"Of course," I said. "What does she look like?"

"I have no idea." The contessa laughed. "A Jewish girl of around twelve from Vienna. And I'm not sure if she speaks anything other than German. Do you speak any of that language?"

"I'm afraid not. But maybe she has learned English or French in school."

"Let us hope so, or we shall have a difficult few days." She smiled. "I'll try to remember my Yiddish, but I haven't spoken it since I was a young child." Then the smile faded. "Let's hope they do not choose to do identity checks on that particular train."

I was certainly nervous when I stood in the station waiting for the arrival of the train from Milan that would bring the Austrian girl. What if she wouldn't go with me? What if I couldn't communicate with her? What if the bully carabinieri were watching and saw that she was Jewish? My heart was thumping within my chest as the train puffed its way to the plat- form. Passengers emerged through the steam. Businessmen hurrying with determination, grand- mothers from the countryside, carrying bags of produce to share with city-living relatives, and then, a pale and skinny girl, her hair in tight braids, carrying a small suitcase and looking around with big frightened eyes.

I went up to her. "Hanni? Hanni Gottfried?"

"Ja." Her eyes darted nervously.

"Do you speak Italian?" I asked.

She shook her head.

"English?"

Another shake.

"Je parle un peu français," she said.

"Eh bien, moi aussi," I replied. And I told her Contessa Fiorito had sent me. I was going to take her to the contessa's villa. A relieved smile spread across that tight little worried face.

"I'm taking you to her now," I told her. "She lives on an island. It's very beautiful. You will like it."

She took my hand, and we went down to the vaporetto dock. We made the trip with no problems, and I saw her hesitate, looking worried, when she saw those impressive iron gates.

"She lives here?" she asked me in French.

I nodded. "You will have a good time here. She eats well. And she's a very kind person."

She gave me a brave little nod. *Poor little thing,* I thought. *Having to leave her family to God knows what fate and come all this way alone.* I longed to wrap my arms around her. Instead I led her up to the front door. The contessa opened it herself and took one look at the child.

"Mayn lib meydl. Du bist oyser gefar mit mir," she said in what I presumed was Yiddish. Then she threw her arms around the girl.

I had not seen such demonstrations of affection from the contessa before, but she was clearly moved. I watched her wipe her eyes as she let the girl go.

"I'm sorry," she said to me in Italian, "but she looks just like me at the same age. A refugee child just like her. Poor little thing. Who knows if she'll ever see her parents again."

I was invited to stay for lunch, but I had to rush to catch the only trip back to the mainland. My faithful Francesca had agreed to stay on until I returned, but Angelo would need a feeding and would let the world know it. Leo's company was using the ground floor mainly for storage. I was glad that the floors below me were empty, so that the cries of a baby would not easily be heard. The trip across the lagoon was rocky, and clouds over the mainland promised rain at any moment.

I thought of the little girl I had just delivered and wondered what her fate would have been if the contessa had not rescued her. But then I found myself wondering how long she could stay safe. Would Jews be rounded up here soon? And then what?

Christmas 1940

I never thought I would write again about a time of great happiness, but as the end of the year approaches, I am feeling full of love and gratitude. Of course, I worry about my mother. I haven't received a letter in several months, not since France fell to the Germans and Italy entered the war. And I can't risk sending her a parcel. The postal clerk would be interested to see an English address. All the news from England has been bad: nightly bombing raids on London, and Germany poised to invade.

On Christmas Eve, I decorated the flat. There were no Christmas trees available, but I found a pine branch blown down by the wind in the Giardini and stuck it in a pot, hanging glass ornaments from its branches. Angelo is quite fascinated. Luckily he can't crawl yet, or I fear it would be toppled in seconds. He sits up, turns over and wriggles across the floor with great agility. And he laughs—a deep belly laugh that is so satisfying to hear. And he has two teeth, which he likes to try out when he is nursing. I'm not sure how much longer I can go on, but I must. The moment I stop is when I must give him up.

Darkness had fallen when there was a tap on the door and Leo came in. He carried a stuffed horse on wheels, a bottle of Prosecco, a panettone and a bag of oranges. We sat and had a drink together while Angelo lay on the rug, staring up at his new prize.

"I have a gift for you," I said. "For the man who has everything."

"I don't have you," he said softly.

I handed him a scroll, tied with a ribbon. He opened it and found it was a watercolour of Angelo. I had tried to draw and paint him ever since his birth, and this one had just captured his look of delight and mischief as he reached for a toy.

"It's wonderful," Leo said. "I'll have it framed. You are very talented. Have you gone back to your art classes, or are you now a master?"

I laughed. "My stipend was only for one year," I said. "The year finished right after Angelo was born."

"If you want, I will gladly pay."

I shook my head. "No. This isn't the right time. I want to enjoy every minute with Angelo before . . ." And I couldn't finish the sentence.

"I have a little gift for you, too," Leo said. He

445

handed me a box. Inside was an old-fashioned ring, set with a row of diamonds. "It belonged to my grandmother," he said. "Bianca had no interest in any of the family jewellery. I want you to have it, to let you know that if I could have married you, you would have been my choice."

"Oh, Leo." I tried not to cry, but the tears came anyway, and I fell into his arms. They came tightly around me, and he was kissing me. I felt desire, but I pulled away. "Oh no," I said. "I remember what happened last time. We can't let that happen again."

"I just want to kiss and hold you," he whispered. "No more, I promise."

And so we sat together, his arms around me, while outside we heard Christmas carols being sung. It was a moment I will treasure forever.

CHAPTER 40

Juliet, Venice, spring 1941

News from the war filters through only occasionally. We hear about the bombing in England, but little of the Italian army, now being defeated in North Africa. Many prisoners taken. Local women worrying about their sons, including Constanza, the woman who saved me from the carabinieri. She hasn't heard from him in months, not knowing if he's alive or dead. I feel a pang of guilt every time she mentions it, knowing that my mother may be feeling the same. I've tried writing letters, but they don't get through, or if they do, no reply ever makes it.

In spite of the war, the days pass pleasantly enough, even though I worry about being interrogated every time I go out. Of course, I do my daily scanning of the canal. I make a note of the German and Italian navy boats going past and then feel a small sliver of pride when a particular boat does not return to port. I have become skilled in Morse code and can quickly adapt when a new codebook arrives in a basket of produce or someone slides one under my door. I have no idea who delivers them. I don't want to know. I have kept the radio hidden from Francesca. She is a good woman but rather a lazy cleaner, and I'm sure she would never think of pulling out the bedside table to dust behind it. And if she did, she would probably not be interested in that square cut in the floorboards. She is remarkably disinterested in anything outside of her own little world. Her children, her grandchildren, the neighbours—and her interest ends there. She probably doesn't even care there is a war on, except that her oldest grandson is coming up for enlistment age and she can't stand margarine.

Other than my daily report, I take care of my child, and I go for walks on fine days. The weather has been glorious lately. The swallows have returned, and I watch them wheeling and diving overhead, their high-pitched cries echoing above the buildings of the city. Most days I take Angelo in his pushchair to the nearby park to watch the pigeons or the boats passing along the Giudecca Canal. He has become too mobile and wants to run around and catch those pigeons. At least once a week, I go over to the Lido, now taking Angelo with me. Clearly the contessa adores Hanni, absolutely spoiling her, but nothing can make up for the fact that she misses her parents. She tries to be brave and grateful, but she is a sensitive child and worries a lot. Every now and then, she will ask about her family.

"Do you think my parents will ever make it to Venice now?" she asked me once, when we were in the middle of a card game. "Why don't they write?"

"I'm sure they have tried to write to you, darling," I said. "Perhaps they are not allowed to. Perhaps they do write and then the letters are taken at the border."

"They are in danger, aren't they?" she asked.

"They may be," I agreed. There was no sense in giving her false hope. "That was why they sent you away when there was a chance."

"Yes." She went back to the card game. Hanni is making great strides with her Italian, and I help her with other schoolwork, too. She is very bright, and I hate to think of what she has lost. Surely in normal times she would have been headed for a university. Following her father, she is very musical and plays the piano well. Angelo is fascinated with the piano, and I love to see them together, Angelo seated on Hanni's lap as she puts his chubby little fingers on the keyboard to play a nursery song and he looks up at her in wonder.

Such are the small memories I shall treasure forever. He will be a year old, and I know that I must hand him over soon. And then what? Then I must surely go to Switzerland and wait out the war there. It might be safe here now, but one never knows how soon things can change. As long as Leo is nearby, I don't worry too much. He comes to visit often, usually bringing a toy, a cake, a pat of butter. Butter has all but disappeared from the shops. It's only filthy-tasting margarine now. And meat is a rarity. None of this matters as my fake ration card has now expired and I rely on Francesca and the contessa to keep us in food. At least here in Venice we have our fish and our mussels and clams. I have learned to make Francesca's linguine with clam sauce. She tried to show me how to make the spaghetti with seppie—the cuttlefish ink—but my memory of the disaster at the professor's house is all too vivid.

May 3, 1941

We celebrated Angelo's first birthday. Francesca baked a cake—a miracle with eggs and butter now being unavailable. I knitted him a stuffed bear with yarn from a jumper I no longer wore. It looked rather amateurish, but he seemed to like it. Leo came over for tea and cake and brought with him a wooden train set.

"It used to be mine," he said. "He will have many toys when he comes over to our house. The time is now right, is it not?"

I looked at my son, sitting on the rug, pushing the engine around the floor and making the sort of noises that little boys make. "Can I come and visit him once he is with you?" I asked.

Leo frowned. "That would not be wise, I think. He is still young enough that he will forget. We can't keep reminding him of the world he has lost. Let him embrace the new one, come to love his nursemaid and have me to adore him."

"So I end up with nothing?" I heard my voice crack.

"I am sorry with all my heart, cara mia. But we have to do what is best for his future and his safety. What if you had to leave in a hurry in the middle of the night? What if, God forbid, the secret police came for you?" He saw the look of fear crossing my face. "While I am here I like to think you cannot be touched, but things are changing. My father has become disillusioned with Mussolini and is distancing himself, fearing that no good outcome will happen. So let us act while we can."

He looked at me. I tried to nod and agree, but I couldn't. "I love him so much, Leo."

"I know. That's why you can give him up. Because you love him."

Angelo tottered over to Leo with the train in his hand and hauled himself up against Leo's knee. "Papa," he said, holding out the train.

"I will bring the papers over for you to sign," he said. "Everything is ready for him."

"Just give me time to say goodbye. Let me paint one last picture of him."

"Of course." He stood up, sweeping the boy into his arms. "I do not wish to cause you pain, Julietta. If there were any other way, I would do it. All I want is to keep you both safe."

He handed Angelo to me, kissed the top of his head and then kissed me before he departed.

July 8, 1941

I haven't seen Leo recently. I gather he has been busy on some kind of assignment he can't tell me about. When he did drop in for a second or two, there was no mention about handing over Angelo. So far I haven't managed to finish the painting. I wonder why. Then this evening, late, Leo arrived. He looked worried.

"Cara, I have to go away, tonight," he said. "I couldn't leave without telling you."

"Where?" I asked.

"I cannot say. And I don't know how long I will be gone. Take care." He took me into his arms and kissed me with great passion. He released me, looked down into my face and then almost ran out of the door.

So now my protector is gone. The wise thing to do would be to take Angelo to the palazzo now. But frankly I no longer feel that I am in danger. I am known by my neighbours. We pause and chat around the vegetable barge. I exchange pleasantries with the old men when I take Angelo to the park, and they give him crumbs to feed the sparrows and pigeons. Even the local policeman knows me and bids me bondì.

Then as I lie in bed, with thoughts flying around my head, a brilliant idea comes to me: I don't have to give him up. I will introduce Angelo as an Italian orphan, his mother a casualty of the war. I adopted him and I'm taking him with me back to England. I could escape now, at least as far as Switzerland—if the Swiss are still taking in refugees, of course. But I can't leave without saying goodbye to Leo. I must wait for him to return first. I worry about him. Why did he have to leave in such a hurry when he had assured me he was in a protected occupation and his family was valuable to the war effort?

September 24, 1941

Today was the Regata Storica—the historical regatta that takes place at this time every year. Crews in period costume rowing enormous gondolas up the Grand Canal. Boats of all sizes. In spite of the war, it was still as well attended as ever, with people cheering for their favourites. Except the vendors were not present selling balloons and gelato. And the army and police were watching from the shadows. As the races ended and I headed for home, I was stopped at a checkpoint. "Identity card?" I was asked.

I pulled it out and showed them. I had deliberately made it rather the worse for wear, crumpling the photograph so that nobody could see it wasn't me. The officer stared at it, then up at me.

"This is you?" he demanded.

"Of course." I stared at him.

"The hair is darker."

"I dyed it once. Now it's my own colour."

"You were born in Venice?"

"I was."

He was still frowning. "There is something about you. Not right. You will present yourself at the *questura* in the morning, do you understand?"

"I have a young baby. I can't leave him."

"Bring him. We will need to see his birth certificate and identification."

He held out his hand. "Give me your identity card. You will have it returned to you in the morning if all is well."

I don't know how I made it home safely. I was shaking. They would check my identity card and find out that I was a fraud—an enemy alien in their midst. They might even search my flat and find the radio under the floorboards. They shot spies, didn't they? Until now I hadn't really felt that I could be in any danger. Now I realized the full enormity of what might happen to me. Then suddenly I stopped short in the middle of a bridge, causing a man walking behind me to bump into me and utter some not too polite words.

They didn't know where I lived! The identity

card had Giuliana's address on it. They would check that address and find that she had died, but they wouldn't know where I was or my real name. I just wouldn't go to the questura in the morning. I'd go into hiding. I hurried home, threw some random clothes and baby things into a suitcase and woke Angelo from his nap.

"Francesca, I have to go to a friend for a few days," I said, babbling the first words that came into my head. "She is not well. She has broken her ankle, and I said I'd keep her company. I'm not sure when I'll be back, but you don't need to come here until I send for you."

"Va bene," she said, nodding at the thought of time off. "I'll still get paid, sì?"

"You'll still get your normal wages." I wasn't quite sure how she was paid, but I suspected that Leo had set up an automatic payment for her, the way he had for me. Which made me decide I should take out money while I still could.

I wrote a letter to Leo, in case he returned while I was away. In the note I said I had gone to visit an old mutual friend. He would know who that was since I had spoken about her a lot. I was going to head straight for the Lido and take out money at the branch of the Banco de San Marco there—until I realized I'd have to show identity. So instead I waited impatiently until the next morning, left Angelo with Francesca and made my way across to the bank behind St Mark's

Square and my friend Signor Gilardi. I asked to withdraw all the money from the account. Signor Gilardi counted out banknotes for me and handed them over with a smile.

"A big purchase, signorina?"

"I'm going to visit a sick friend." I repeated my alibi. "I don't know how long I'll be away."

"I wish you good journey, then."

I came out and rushed back to Angelo, making sure that I avoided any streets where I might bump into a policeman. I was sweating and out of breath by the time I staggered up the stairs and downed a glass of water.

"I can make tea or coffee," Francesca said. "Sit down. Rest a while."

"No, I should be going. The only vaporetto leaves in half an hour." I bade her farewell. Then I carried Angelo downstairs and put him into his pushchair. He sat up, excited that we might be going to the park. But instead I went to the vaporetto dock and took the next boat out to the Lido. As we crossed the lagoon, we heard the loud blast of a ship's siren, and a large German gunboat sailed past us. And I wasn't there to record it, I thought. Would there be Allied deaths because of me? Was I putting my own safety first?

When we docked I pushed Angelo down the broad boulevard to the tall wrought iron gates and prayed that the contessa would be home. In the past she had visited friends all over Europe, but now I suspected she wouldn't want to travel outside the city. Sure enough, I was shown in by Umberto and heard voices coming from the back garden. I went through to a charming scene. The new gardener, whom I suspected was another of the contessa's rescued German Jews, had put up a swing on the big tree, and Hanni was swinging while the contessa watched her. Hanni spotted me and jumped off the swing with a squeal of delight.

"What a lovely surprise, my dear." The contessa held out her hand to me. "I didn't expect to see you today."

"A bit of an emergency," I said. I turned to the girl. "Hanni, would you take Angelo and play with him for a while?"

Hanni nodded and took Angelo from me. He went willingly, giving her an excited smile and babbling away.

"What's wrong?" the contessa asked. I told her.

She frowned. "That's bad," she said. "But you did know you were living on borrowed time, didn't you?"

"I think I'll be relatively safe if I stay home and I'm careful," I said, "but I can't leave the city with no identity card."

"That's true. You should stay here. The police are too lazy to come out here, unless they want to swim."

"I'd like to stay here for a couple of weeks, if you don't mind," I said.

"Stay here permanently. I have plenty of room and good food, and Hanni adores your son. You can help her with her schoolwork. I am coaching her in Italian and French, but my mathematic skills are from a different age."

"I'd be happy to," I said. And I thought, *I can stay out here. Safe. Away from the police, until Leo returns.* But then there would be no radio transmissions of ships leaving port. If British ships were sunk, it would be my fault.

CHAPTER 41

Juliet, Venice, December 1941

I don't know where the time has gone. Recently there is a spirit of optimism because the Americans have entered the war on the side of the Allies. "They'll bring it to an end quickly," the old men in the park say. The year has gone smoothly enough, although with no identity card I worry about being questioned every time I go out. I have been spending most of my time at the contessa's villa. She wanted me to stay with her all the time, but my conscience got the better of me with regard to my duty to monitor shipping, so I try to spend a couple of days a week at the flat, leaving Angelo in the safety of the Lido. Luckily German shipping has decreased recently after Hitler invaded the Soviet Union in June and turned his efforts to that direction. I hope that means that he is no longer planning to invade Britain and that the bombing has lessened. Still nothing from my mother and no way of communicating with her. Also nothing from Leo. I am very worried, but I hope he is on some kind of secret mission and will return safely.

Angelo is growing into a sturdy and active little boy. His hair is indeed taking on my auburn shade, and his eyes are a wonderful deep blue. Such a handsome little fellow! He climbs all over the furniture, runs around the contessa's garden and delights in playing with Hanni, who is now fluent in Italian and seems quite at home. We have had no word from her parents, however. That may be a precaution not to give away her whereabouts. But she seems to be accepting the fact, and I hear her singing in her sweet high voice German nursery songs to Angelo: "Hoppe hoppe Reiter. Wenn er fällt, dann schreit er . . ."

We have had several visits from Vittorio recently. He turned up out of the blue, just as charming and attentive as ever. I suspect he may have fallen out of favour with the powerful men in Rome. That man makes me nervous for some reason. Clearly he resents that the contessa is fond of me. He also resents Hanni's presence. The contessa has asked him to take some of her more valuable paintings into storage at his gallery, just in case. She seems to be quite happy that he'll look after them for her. I'm not so sure. He always strikes me as someone who will change sides whenever the wind blows.

Francesca comes once a week to clean when I am not at home but every day to cook and shop for me when I am there. With Christmas around the corner, I came back into the city to try to do some shopping at the holiday markets, which are still taking place outside the churches. I wanted to give the contessa something, and Hanni, and of course Angelo. I tried to think what the contessa might like and wondered if I dared to paint a picture for her. She who has old masters hanging from her walls. But she is a patron of the Biennale, which, I'm told, will take place as usual next year, war or no war. So I have been painting her an abstract. Professor Corsetti has been out to visit the contessa several times and has encouraged me to keep painting. I showed him the portrait I was painting of Angelo and he made good suggestions. But now it is almost finished, and I am quite proud of it.

The contessa's new gardener, Peter—or rather Pietro now—is building Angelo a wooden engine he can ride on. Angelo and I returned to the city for a few days. I felt guilty if I was not doing the job I had promised to do, and I wanted to shop for Christmas presents. So I left Angelo in Francesca's care and went to the market to see if there were any oranges or sweets, also to find something for Hanni, and found a little glass flute that actually plays. And in my favourite bookshop a couple of books in German. I don't want her to forget her native language. I couldn't think what to get for Francesca, who is so completely practical, so I decided she wouldn't be offended if I gave her some money. Living with the contessa much of the time has meant that I have not used my monthly allowance. I have offered to pay my share for food, but she has turned me down. I'm exceedingly grateful because I have no ration card. I don't quite know what I'd do without her and Francesca. And Hanni. I have become so fond of that girl. In some ways she is wise beyond her years and affectionate, too. It was as if having a baby has somehow opened my heart to the possibility of love. I love it when she sees me coming and rushes to hug me. The contessa adores her.

"If anything happens to me, Juliet," she said the other day, "I have made a provision in my will that she will be taken care of and her university will be paid for. She deserves a good life."

"Don't say that about anything happening to you," I said, giving an involuntary shudder. "You've said many times that Jewish people in Venice are safe."

She gave me a long hard stare. "One never knows what tomorrow might bring," she said.

I finished my shopping, found a little pot of cyclamens at the market and came back to the flat feeling quite pleased with myself. It was going to be a jolly Christmas with Angelo now old enough to participate. The room was unusually quiet when I entered the flat.

"Francesca?" I called. "Is Angelo sleeping?"

She came out of the kitchen, her face a stoic mask. "They came for him," she said.

"What? Who came for him?"

"They didn't say. They just took him, and when I tried to intervene, one man said, 'Stand aside, woman.'"

The world stood still. My heart was thumping so loudly that I was sure she must hear it.

"Were they police? Army?"

She shook her head. "I think they were men who work for the Da Rossi family."

"They had no right!" The words spilled out. "They can't take my son. I'm going to get him back right now."

"You can't. They are powerful people, signorina. I tried. I tried to stop them."

"I don't care if they are powerful. I'm going to get him back."

I ran all the way down the stairs, trying to control my racing thoughts. Did this mean that Leo was safely back home and had taken his son? If not, who would have ordered this outrage? Leo's father, who wanted a grandson and heir? Surely not Bianca, the unmaternal one. I was usually careful about crossing the city by the main thoroughfares during daylight because I had no identity card, but today I didn't care. Past the accademia building and over the bridge to the Da Rossi palazzo. I didn't even hesitate as I went up those austere steps, past the stone lions on either side, and hammered on that enormous front door.

A male servant opened it. "Is Signor Leonardo Da Rossi returned?"

"No, signora," he said. "He has not. It has been many months since we have seen him."

"Then I need to speak with Signora Da Rossi," I said.

"May I tell her who is calling?"

"You may. It is Angelo's mother. I have come about my son."

I waited, gasping for breath because I had run all the way, my heart still thumping in my chest.

He returned. "The signora is not available for visitors right now."

"Rubbish!" I said and pushed past him before he could grab me. I had no idea where I might find anyone in a house this size. I blundered forward through a marble foyer, hearing the footman shouting after me.

A maid came out. "Where is Signora Da Rossi?"

"In her bedroom, signora, but she doesn't . . ."

I was already running up the stairs. I opened one door, then another, and then found a bright, pretty room overlooking the Grand Canal. Bianca was sitting at her dressing table, applying her makeup. She spun around in horror as I barged in.

"What in God's name?" she shouted. "Get out immediately."

"Signora Da Rossi, I'm sorry to intrude like this, but I am—"

"I know who you are," she said, eyeing me

with cold distaste. "Believe me, I know all about you."

"I have come for my son," I said. "I won't go without him. Where is he?"

With an almost triumphant look in her eyes, she said, "Your son is not here."

"Your men took him. Francesca told me."

"I don't know what you are talking about."

The footman was now standing in the doorway. "Giovanni, have this madwoman removed. She is annoying me."

"I am not leaving without my son. Do you want me to go to the police? They will search the house and find my child."

This was an empty threat and she knew it.

"The only child in this house is the son of this family," she said. "The heir. Angelo Da Rossi. Now please go before I have you thrown out."

"Tell me one thing," I said. "Did Leo order this?"

"Of course," she said. "He left instructions before he went away. It's what he always wanted. I just couldn't be bothered to get around to it before. I have no interest in babies. But now that Leo is gone and might not come home, an heir is all-important for a family like this, is it not?"

"Might not come home? You've had news?"

"No news. That's the point. He is missing. We have to accept that your precious Leo is probably dead. Now go. Get out of my sight and do not return. If I ever see you again, I shall delight in calling the police to tell them that we have captured an enemy alien." She waved an impatient hand. "Please escort this woman to the door, Giovanni."

A strong hand gripped my forearm, and I was led away. I was trying desperately to think of something—anything—to get to my son. But I realized it was hopeless. I had no proof he was mine. I had no right to be in this city. An enemy alien. Even if I managed to creep in and steal Angelo back, they would find me and arrest me, and I'd wind up in a camp.

He'll be well looked after, I tried to tell myself. I was shaking so hard that I put my hands up to my face to stop the sobs. *He'll grow up to be Il Conte Da Rossi. What more could any boy want?*

And I knew the answer. He would never have a mother who loved him.

I opened my journal and tried to write it all down. Everything except my feelings. How can you put a broken heart on to a piece of paper? The full enormity of what had happened hadn't completely engulfed me yet, but I knew that it would, soon enough. Never to see him again. Never to hold him in my arms and have him look up at me with that sweet smile and say, "Mama." How would I bear it? And yet I had no choice.

After I have recorded this, I will close my

journal. How could I ever write in it again when there was so much that would give me pain? I opened my desk, removed the drawers, slid back the panel, took the little key and accessed the secret drawer to hide the journal away. There it will stay for now, and I won't be tempted to read of happier times.

CHAPTER 42

Caroline, Venice, October 20, 2001

She should be going home, Caroline kept telling herself. That incident with Luca had been madness, a way of wanting to get back at Josh, to remind herself that she was still desirable.

It meant nothing, she repeated to herself, but she couldn't deny her attraction to Luca. Not that she believed he was equally attracted to her, although he had somehow found time to visit every day for the past week and invited her out to his penthouse on the Lido—"where I have plenty of good wine that is not 'plonk' and a bed that is not quite as narrow and uncomfortable as this one!" And he had laughed.

"Luca," she had replied, annoyed with herself for blushing, "this is crazy. We hardly know each other. I'm not the sort of woman who jumps into bed with any man she meets."

"Of course you are not, Cara," he replied. "But we are both grown up with no ties, and I like you, and I can tell you like me. So why not? You are not even a Catholic. You won't have to go to confession like me."

"You still do that?"

"Of course. One has to. But don't w
We have a tame priest who gives really ligh
penances." He laughed. "There is a lot you will
have to learn about the Venetian way of life. And
I shall be happy to instruct you."

She told herself that she should have felt guilty
and was surprised that she didn't. *I'm a grown
woman,* she thought. *Twenty-seven years old and
unattached. What is wrong with a relationship
with a man who is also unattached?* And the
comment about instructing her on the Venetian
way of life. Didn't that imply he wanted her to
stick around—that he saw some kind of future
together?

The weather had been horrible, with several
occasions of aqua alta, so she had not yet taken
Luca up on his invitation to see his place on
the Lido. He had spent the night at the flat
several times, and she did feel guilty about not
wanting to leave. Somehow staying on and
getting involved with Luca seemed disloyal to
her grandmother and like she was abandoning
her son. But there wasn't much more she could
do for Teddy at the moment. She had found a
nearby café where she could use Wi-Fi to keep
in touch with Josh. His latest email contained a
report from the psychiatrist confirming Teddy's
anxiety and saying that he seemed to feel safe
in his current environment. *Any attempt to move
him could be detrimental to his mental health*

had been the conclusion. The email threw Caroline into turmoil.

"I don't know what to do, Luca," she said. "I don't want to do anything that might damage my son, but my heart tells me that he'd be much more secure with his mother to hug him. And to be at his great-grandmother's house with lots of room to run around."

"I say always do what your heart tells you, Cara," he replied, and the way he looked at her made her feel that he wasn't just talking about Teddy.

Was he saying she should go to New York now, do what she felt was right? But she still had not scattered Aunt Lettie's ashes, and until she did that, she couldn't leave. *Tomorrow,* she thought. *Tomorrow I will go.* The next day she was cleaning the flat prior to leaving when she had a surprise visit. The feet that came up the stairs were not heavy like Luca's but lighter. She opened the door and his mother stood there, gasping a little.

"Goodness," she said. "This is quite a climb. May I come in?"

"What a surprise, contessa." Caroline ushered her in. "Please, sit down. Would you like a glass of water or a cup of tea?"

"Just water, thank you, honey," Luca's mother said. "I hope you don't mind my barging in like this, but I've been thinking about your

He came, an hour later.

"You've been crying." He reached out to brush a tear from her cheek.

Caroline nodded. "It's so sad, and the worst thing is that we don't know what happened."

"What do you mean?"

"The diary leaves off after Angelo is taken."

"Taken?"

"By your family. Adopted, presumably. We know she wound up in Switzerland. But it doesn't say when she went, whether she saw your grandfather again or whether he was dead by that time. You said he was killed in the war?" She poured him a glass of wine. "Don't look like that. It's the bottle you bought," she said, "not the plonk."

He sat in one of the armchairs and started to read. She perched on the arm beside him, no longer self-conscious of brushing against him, having to interpret when he couldn't read a particular word or didn't know what it meant. Occasionally he looked up, nodding. "Ah, she went to the accademia. Of course."

Then came the mention of the Contessa Fiorito. "I know her villa," he said. "It is now a museum of modern art. She left it to the city in her will."

He read on. Caroline sat still and said nothing. When he came to a piece of special significance, he looked up at her. "So she wasn't ever really his mistress. I mean, only that once. But he loved her, didn't he?"

Caroline nodded. "Yes, he did."

He read on. "And my father . . . ," he said, pointing at the page, his voice cracking with emotion. "It's all here."

"Yes."

When he came to the end, he closed the book and put a hand on her knee. "So that is all. We will never really know what happened. There are no more diaries?"

"Not that I have found. All we know is that she made it to Switzerland and he died."

"I believe I was told that he was shot, trying to escape from a prison camp."

Caroline looked up in horror. "An Allied prison camp?"

"No, a German one. It was after Italy changed sides. He was aiding the Allies."

"Oh. How sad. I wonder if . . ." She turned away. "Never mind."

"And all these years she never spoke about it," Luca said.

"Not a word to anyone. We all believed she was the typical British spinster lady, refined, remote, who had never had a life of her own, outside her family." She reached out a hand and laid it on his. "Will you come with me when I scatter her ashes?"

His fingers intertwined with hers. "Where will you do this?"

"I want to find their special tree. I thought I'd scatter the ashes around it."

"All right." He hesitated, then said, "Cara, I did something a little illegal."

"Yes?" she asked nervously.

He grinned. "I bribed someone to get me my grandmother's medical records."

"How did you do that?"

"You don't need to know. But I can tell you this. There is no mention of her giving birth to a child in 1940. Or at any other point."

"I see." She was silent for a while, and then she said, "So that proves it. It's all true. My great-aunt was your grandmother."

"It would appear that way."

She gave a nervous little laugh. "We really are related."

"How about that?" He chuckled. "But luckily not closely enough to cause a problem." Then his face became sombre again. "My father should never know, don't you think?"

"Definitely. Neither should my grandmother. It will remain our secret." She paused, then said, "When would you like to go to scatter your grandmother's ashes?"

They waited for the first fine afternoon. His boat sped them to the Giardini. They walked together amid the swirls of dying leaves until they stopped and both said, "Oh" at the same time. There was the sad statue, now missing more fingers, its legs weathered from the salty wind, almost swallowed behind large bushes and a towering tree. Caroline opened the little urn and tipped out some of the contents, slowly, reverently. "Goodbye, dear Aunt Lettie," she whispered. Then she handed the urn to Luca, who walked around the tree, gently sprinkling ashes.

"Goodbye, dear Grandmother," he added. "I wish I could have met you."

As if in answer, a breeze sprang up, catching leaves, mingled with ashes, swirling them overhead, then carrying them out into the lagoon.

On the way back they stood together at the helm in silence until Luca said, "I spoke with my mother. She told me she came to see you. She also told me . . ." He broke off. "Never mind that now. We both think you should just fly to New York and bring your son home." He paused. "I have to go on business anyway soon. Would you like me to come with you?"

Caroline stared out, not daring to look at him. "If you want to."

"I do," he said.

CHAPTER 43

Juliet, Venice, July 1942

I have not written a diary for such a long time. It has been too painful, but I must put some of the events of the past months down on paper or they will stay forever as a burden in my heart.

After Angelo was taken from me, life essentially had no meaning. Frankly I didn't care if I lived or I died. There were times when I stood on the Accademia Bridge and wondered if I should just jump off. But I have kept on existing. I have divided my time between the contessa's villa and my top-floor flat. I have found my spying activities to be a chore, something I am unwilling to do in my bitterness and grief. Why should I save lives when mine has been brutally snatched from me? And yet my British sense of duty won't leave me. And so I have spent at least two or three days a week sitting in my window. Francesca comes occasionally, bringing me food, but I have lost interest in eating. I have taken my binoculars to the canal, where I can spy on the Da Rossi palace, hoping to catch a glimpse of Angelo. But then I was accosted by a strange man.

"What are you doing?" he demanded.

"Bird-watching," I said quickly. "There is a

seagull's nest on the roof over there. New chicks in it."

He accepted this, but I realized the danger I was putting myself in. Part of me still wanted to escape to Switzerland and safety, but how could I travel with no identity card? Even if I didn't take the train but used local buses on my journey north, I would be a target of suspicion. Someone would report me along the way. There would be checkpoints. And I would need to eat. To buy food. And I have no ration card. So I am stuck, whether I want it or not. And I keep telling myself that Leo will come home. He'll come back to me, and everything will be all right. Although now I have to accept that he will not give me back my son. A nagging sliver of doubt always lurked that Leo had indeed orchestrated the raid. Had he instructed his men, "If I am not back by this time, go and bring the child to the palazzo"?

I couldn't believe he could be so cruel to take Angelo without allowing me to say goodbye, but perhaps he thought it was for the best, knowing how hard I'd find it to let go.

I try to find solace in the time I spend with the contessa and with Hanni. I helped do some of the cataloguing for the Biennale, which amazingly has taken place as if there was no war. Vittorio was very much in evidence, strutting around with a great air of importance, giving orders to those building the displays in the pavilions, and also persuading the contessa to buy certain pieces. I was rather gratified that he spotted the picture I had painted for her on her library wall.

"Where did you get this one?" he asked. "I hope you didn't pay too much for it."

"Do you like it?"

He frowned. "It has a certain appeal," he admitted. "A pleasing use of colour. Another of your Jewish refugees?"

"No, my darling house guest." She took my hand. "She has talent, don't you think?"

It was one small moment of satisfaction in a long line of darkness.

Leo has not returned. I have to accept what Bianca thought: that he is missing, either dead or captured. I pray the latter. If he is in British hands, he would be treated fairly. But then why hasn't he been able to write a letter home?

September 1942

The Biennale came and went, mostly populated by Mussolini's henchmen or German officers, strutting around. This year, of course, there were no Russians since Hitler had turned on his former best friend, Stalin. And the occasional snippet of good news has been that the Allies were making progress since the Americans came into the war. Battles were being won in North Africa. England was no longer subject to daily bombing. I found myself wondering and worrying more and more about my mother. Since I had become a mother myself, I realized what a wrench it must have been to let her children go so far away. She must be worrying about me every day, and I could do nothing to alleviate that worry.

The contessa's steady stream of Jewish refugees has ceased. We hear dire news from Germany. Jews have been rounded up and shipped off to work camps in Eastern Europe. There are now no Jews left in Germany's cities, or in Austria either. We fear the worst for Hanni's parents but wisely keep our worries to ourselves. And she no longer asks us about them. Let her be happy and enjoy childhood while she can. I have made sure she kept up with her schooling. She practices her piano and loves to go to the beach with me during the hot weather. We swim together in the warm Adriatic, floating on the calm surface as if we hadn't a care in the world for those few moments. Then she splashes me, I chase her and she screams in delight like any normal girl. I'm afraid I am coming to love her, and it will break my heart for a second time when I have to go.

Things in Italy also seem to be getting worse for the Jews. They are now instructed to wear the yellow star and not to leave the Cannaregio district of the city. The contessa laughed when I asked her whether she was going to wear a star, or make Hanni wear one.

"Dear child, don't worry so. Everybody knows me. I am the wife of an Italian count," she said. "We are quite safe."

But still I began to worry. Maybe she did, too, because the other day she took me into her library and sat me down. "If anything should happen to me, I want you to take the folder in this drawer for safekeeping," she said. "Even Vittorio does not know about it." She opened the drawer and untied a plain cardboard folder. "Most of the sketches it contains are not worth a second look, but in the middle I have placed some important works: an early Picasso, a Miró and a couple of others. I would not want them to fall into the wrong hands. You will keep them safe for me, yes?"

"Of course I will," I said, "but you yourself have told me that nothing will happen to you."

"One never knows anything in this life, but I shall sleep more soundly knowing that the wrong people will not get their hands on my treasures." She paused, then looked up. "And if something does happen to me and I don't return, I have left them to you in my will."

November 1942

I have kept up my observations and radio communication. It took me a while to realize I had received no updated codebook for too long.

Have they decided they no longer need to update codes, or has my radio receiver been discovered and now there is an enemy chuckling at my daily briefs? I fear it is the latter. Will it only be a matter of time before the enemy traces the source to me? I hesitate between ceasing all messages or keeping on, knowing they might soon discover me. *What does it matter either way?* I thought. I have no Leo, no Angelo. My life has ceased already. Francesca comes to clean occasionally or to bring me produce she has managed to find at the market. Since I eat well at the contessa's, I don't need much.

September 1943

A whole year has passed as if in a cloudy dream. In Venice there is finally optimism. Earlier this year the Allies invaded Sicily. And then the south of Italy. More German ships arrived in the lagoon. I kept sending my messages, hoping they were received. Then on September 8 we got the news we had been waiting for. The Italian government surrendered to the Allies. We were no longer enemies! There was celebration in the streets. "Our boys will soon be home" was the word on every street corner. The joy was short-lived, however, as the Germans were swift in their retaliation.

The German army has invaded. We have troops

marching through the city. They have taken over several palazzos, including the Palazzo Rossi. I worried about Angelo but heard the family had moved out to the villa in the Veneto. "Please keep him safe," I pray every night.

Yesterday I overheard two women talking, saying that the Germans were building a holding camp on the Lido for all the Jews. "And good riddance," one of them said. "Never wanted them in my city in the first place, filthy foreigners."

I rushed over to the Lido and found the contessa and Hanni sitting in the conservatory. Hanni was reading in Italian to the contessa. I imparted the awful news.

"Yes, my dear, I have heard. I feel so badly that there is nothing I can do. I can't reason with these men. The only thing is to lie low and wait for your countrymen to come swiftly up through Italy. It can't be long now, surely. The Germans have built a line of defence just north of Tuscany, but I don't think they will guard the eastern shore so fiercely. I expect the Allies here very soon, then all will be well."

"But you are living so close to the camp they are building. Why don't you come and stay with me for a while in Dorsoduro?" I asked.

"But I like my home." She waved an elegant hand around the room. "And I have my dear Umberto and my darling little Hanni."

"You don't think Hanni is in danger?"

She shrugged. "She is not on any list. She doesn't exist. If she stays at the villa, I can see no danger."

I prayed she was right. I observed boatloads of Jews being taken out to the Lido. The Germans have commandeered nearly all the vaporetti, so it has become almost impossible to get around. After a few days I realized I had to get out to the Lido and check on my friends to make sure they were still safe. When a fishing boat docked on the Zattere, I was bold enough to ask the fisherman if he was going back to one of the islands after he had sold his catch. The fishermen all lived out on the barrier islands. I had sketched them and their boats several times. When he told me that was his intention, I asked if he could drop me off at the Lido.

"You want a swim when the place is crawling with Germans?"

"No. I have a dear elderly friend, and I have to make sure she is all right."

"Va bene," he said. "Hop on board."

And so an hour later we were crossing the lagoon. A German patrol boat pulled up beside us.

"You! Where are you going?" a German voice shouted.

"Home. I'm a fisherman. I've just sold my catch."

"Do you have a permit?"

"Of course. What do you take me for?"

"And the woman. Who is she?"

I felt my heart skip. I had no identity card.

"My wife. Who else? She helps me take the money. Makes sure I don't slip any into my pocket to buy wine."

"On your way, then." The German waved us on.

I let out a huge sigh of relief. "Thank you. That was quick of you."

"I don't want any German to get his hands on a nice Venetian girl," he said.

I felt a surge of pride. My accent was now flawless. I could pass as a Venetian.

I was dropped off at a small, out of the way jetty. "Not near their filthy camp," he said, "and you take care of yourself."

I hurried to the villa. I knocked, but nobody came to the door. I went around to the garden at the back, rapping on the glass of the conservatory. A growing dread gripped me. What if the place had been taken over by Germans? Where was the contessa? And Hanni?

"Umberto!" I called through the door. "*Sono io*! It is I. Julietta. Let me in."

I waited. Nobody came. I tried all the doors and at last I found a window half open. I crawled into the house.

"Contessa?" I called. "Umberto?"

I went from room to room. Everything was in

485

its usual place—a newspaper on the table, a glass of lemonade half drunk. I checked the kitchen, the servant's quarters. No sign of life. Then slowly I went up the stairs.

It's all right, I told myself. *She had to leave in a hurry. She's gone away. Somewhere safe. Taken Hanni with her. No time to let me know.*

I pushed open one bedroom door after another. There was no sign of clothing having been packed. A robe still lay across a silk counterpane. Then I opened another door to a smaller bedroom. I was about to leave when something moved. I jumped, terrified.

"Who's there?" I demanded.

"Julietta?" whispered a small voice.

"Hanni?"

She crawled out from under a bed, her eyes wide with fear. "Oh, Julietta. You've come."

And she flung herself into my arms.

"My darling. What happened? Where is the contessa?"

"They came," she said. "Nazi soldiers. They took her away. She saw them outside and told me to go and hide. I didn't know what to do or where to go."

"What happened to Umberto?"

"I don't know. He went. When I came downstairs, there was nobody." She was crying now. "They took her. Where did they take her?"

"It must have been to one of those camps for Jewish people they've built on the Lido." I put

486

an arm around her. "Don't worry. The contessa is a powerful woman. She's well respected in this city. They will let her go quickly. And until then, I'll take care of you, Hanni. I won't let anything happen to you. I'll take you back with me. You can hide out in my flat until the Allies get here and the horrible Nazis are driven out."

She took my hand and gazed up at me with such gratitude in her eyes that I felt myself tearing up and a great welling of tenderness.

"I'm so glad you are here, Julietta."

I wrapped her into my arms. "Don't worry, my darling. I won't let anything happen to you, I promise."

We were just coming down the stairs when we heard the sound of the front door opening. I motioned to Hanni. "Run and hide again and don't come down until I tell you," I whispered.

I took a deep breath and strode confidently down the stairs, only to see Vittorio coming in through the front door.

He stopped, surprised to see me. "Julietta. What are you doing here?"

"Oh hello, Vittorio," I said in my breeziest voice. "I came to call on the contessa, but I see she's not here. Nobody's home. I suppose they must have gone out to the country."

"Yes," he said. "That must be right. I was wondering about the child—the Austrian Jew. Did she take her, do you know?"

"Obviously," I said. "She wouldn't go away and leave a little girl alone, would she? She adores that child."

"You're sure the girl is not still here?" He was looking around.

"Quite sure," I said. "I've been all over the house. And as I just said, I'm sure the contessa wouldn't just leave her behind."

I moved so I was standing at the bottom of the staircase in case he decided to go and look for himself, although why there was this interest in Hanni I could not imagine. I tried to keep my voice calm and pleasant. "Do you happen to know the address of these friends in the country that she talked about? The Salvis? Over in Tuscany, wasn't it? Cortona?"

"Yes," he said, "I think that was it." His eyes were scanning the place as he talked.

"But you don't know the address?"

"It might be in her desk, unless she has taken her address book," he said. "Do you want me to look for you?"

"I can look," I said. "I don't want to hold you up. I suppose I'll just have to go back to the city and wait until she comes back. I'll miss her and my weekly visits."

He nodded. I wasn't going to leave, and neither was he.

"Was there something you wanted?" I asked. "Something I can help you with?"

He frowned. "She asked me to take some of her more valuable artwork for safekeeping to my gallery. I thought this might be a good time."

"Good idea," I said. "I've heard what these Nazis are like—looting treasures wherever they go."

He was still frowning. "Are you going back to the city now?"

"I'm worried about old Umberto," I said. "Where do you think he has gone? Would the contessa have taken him, too?"

"Hardly likely," he said. "I expect the old man has returned to his family. He has a daughter living nearby, you know. On the island of Vignole."

We stood looking at each other.

"Well, I expect you want to get on with selecting paintings for safekeeping," I said. "Would you like me to stay and help you?"

"That's not necessary," he said. "I need to take measurements. Have crates built."

"I think you should not waste any time. The place is crawling with Germans. If I were you, I'd remove the most valuable pieces and store them where they can't readily be found. Maybe in the gardener's quarters? Or Umberto's old room?"

"That's not a bad idea," he said. "I wonder if they are open or if I can find the keys?"

"I believe they kept the spare keys by the

kitchen door," I said. I had no idea if this was true, but he nodded and to my relief headed down the hall towards the kitchen and servants' quarters. I sprinted up the stairs, keeping as quiet as possible.

"Hanni, come with me now," I said. I put my fingers to my lips and tiptoed her down the stairs. "Go out into the garden and hide amongst those big bushes by the gate," I said. "I'll come in a minute."

"What about my things?"

"I'm afraid we have to leave everything. I expect I can come back for them later, but now it's too dangerous. Just go."

She darted out of the front door, and I watched her until she disappeared amongst the shrubbery. I didn't waste another minute but went through to the library. I took the cardboard folder from the drawer, removed the drawings from it and stashed them under my coat. Then I went back towards the kitchen, to find Vittorio coming towards me.

"You were right. There is a bunch of keys. I will try one for the garden storage place."

"I couldn't find her address book, unfortunately," I said. "So I must head home. There are so few vaporetti these days."

"It was a pleasure to see you again, Miss Browning," he said, giving me a little bow.

"The feeling is mutual, Signor Scarpa."

I walked out of the door and down the front

path, feeling his eyes still upon me. I heard the door closing and breathed a sigh of relief. When I was close to the front gate, I paused, checking my surroundings, until I was sure that nobody was in sight. Then I whispered for Hanni. She came out. I took her hand, and we walked briskly down the boulevard.

"Listen," I said. "If anyone asks you, you are my little sister, Elena Alioto. Capisce?"

She nodded, her eyes still wide with fear.

"They will take me, too, when they find out I am Jewish?"

"Don't worry, my darling. I will protect you," I said. "This will all be over soon, I promise. Until then, you must be brave."

There was a crowd waiting at the vaporetto dock, which was good news. It meant a boat might be coming soon. And sure enough, it arrived. It was horribly overcrowded, but they let us all squeeze aboard. I found a corner and pushed Hanni into it, hidden behind me, until we reached the San Marco stop. Then we went home without incident.

CHAPTER 44

Juliet, Venice, September 1943

That evening I tucked Hanni into my bed. I sat beside her, stroking her hair as her eyes closed, trying not to think about how close she had come to being taken to that awful camp. And what about my dear contessa? Surely she could pull strings in the right places to be released. She was, after all, a rich and powerful woman, a benefactor of the city.

It was as if Hanni could read my thoughts. Her eyes opened and she looked up at me. "She will be all right, won't she? They'll let her go?"

"I'm sure she will, darling. Don't worry. Get some sleep."

She drifted off, but I sat up, staring out of the windows at the moon over the Giudecca Canal. Such a beautiful, peaceful scene, until I spotted a German gunboat. I couldn't use the radio. Hanni would see, and I couldn't risk her being questioned. So I watched until it disappeared into the darkness. I found it hard to believe that the contessa was gone. She had felt herself to be so safe, and yet they had come for her, just like all the other Jews. It hadn't mattered that she was the wife of an Italian count or that she was very rich. She was Jewish. That was all that mattered.

And then suddenly I thought, *Someone must have betrayed her.* And I knew instantly who it was. I had seen the gleam of greed and acquisition in his eyes. He had betrayed her and would now help himself to her art. I realized now why I had never liked him, never trusted him. I also realized what a narrow escape Hanni had had. He wanted all Jews locked up. He had come back for her!

I had looked around cautiously when I returned home, making Hanni wait in the shadows across the street until I was sure nobody was watching. Then I whisked her inside and hurried her up the stairs. While she admired the view from my windows, I took out the drawings I had smuggled out of the contessa's villa. Even my amateurish eye saw that one or two were indeed priceless. I slipped them amongst my own sketches, putting them into the secret drawer in my desk, just in case.

I have kept Hanni hidden up in the flat. In truth I hardly go outside myself. I told Francesca that she was the granddaughter of a fisherman I had met and he wanted her safe in the city away from the Nazis. Francesca, not being overly endowed with curiosity, seemed to accept this with no problem. I told Hanni to talk as little as possible so that Francesca did not hear the difference in accent. I didn't think she would notice, but one couldn't be too careful.

October 18

Life is becoming increasingly difficult. Germans patrol the streets. There are no more deliveries of coal. I thank God and the consul for my little electric fire, which keeps the bedroom warm. Also that the electricity remains on at least part of every day. When it is on, I heat hot water bottles and put them into my bed for the night. Food has also started to become a problem. Without the contessa's produce, we are using the last of my backup supplies—pasta and beans like the rest of the city.

After Hanni had been with me for two weeks, I dared to make a trip to the contessa's villa. The fact that she hadn't returned convinced me that she was now in a camp. The walls had been stripped of paintings, but the larder had not been raided. I went around the garden and picked some late greens and early lemons. I came back with as many supplies as I could carry. That night Hanni and I had a feast of ham and spinach and chocolate biscuits. I opened our last bottle of wine. I remember it clearly, every minute of it. I think it was the last time I experienced happiness.

October 19

The next day a note arrived for me, pushed under my door. I had no idea who delivered it. It said, *MEET ME. MY TREE. 8 PM. TUES.*

That was all. Unsigned. Printed. But it had to be Leo. Who else could it be? Unless it was a trap. How could he be here, after all this time? And yet who else would mention a special tree, a hiding place? And so at seven thirty I set out, walking over the Accademia Bridge, behind St Mark's to the Giardini. I passed very few people along the way. Now that the city was patrolled by Germans, it was not wise to be caught out in the streets. But I knew the city well enough to avoid the bigger streets that soldiers might frequent. It was a long walk, and I was breathless by the time I entered the darkness of the gardens. Trees and bushes loomed, looking menacing in the occasional lamplight. There were piles of damp leaves underfoot. At least it wasn't raining. That was one blessing.

I found the tree with no hesitation. The bushes around it had not been trimmed for some years, partly hiding the statue. I had walked past it several times, pausing to look at the sad face of the Greek god as the sea ate away more of his body, and I had remembered every detail of that magical night with Leo when I was eighteen and the world was full of romance and possibility. I walked warily past the statue, still not daring to hope it was Leo, still half expecting a trap. If I was taken, what would happen to Hanni? Surely Francesca would look after her?

Then I heard the whisper, only just discernible over the night breeze from the lagoon.

"Julietta?"

I squeezed past the bushes that were now invading the hiding space between the statue and the big tree, and he was there. I sensed, rather than saw him. "Leo!"

We fell into each other's arms, kissing with hunger and urgency.

"Where have you been? I thought you were dead."

"Listen," he said. "I have no time. I am a wanted man. A boat comes for me in a few minutes, but I wanted to do this one thing for you: to give you a way to safety. Here." He thrust an envelope into my hands. "This is how you get to Switzerland. Go now. Do not wait another second. As the Germans continue to become more desperate, they are also becoming more ruthless. If one of their number is killed, they will round up whole towns and machine gun the entire population. And you will be shot as an enemy spy. You must go. Do you understand?"

"Yes, but you? Why are you wanted?"

"I have been working for the Allies for a long time," he said. "You know my feelings about

Mussolini and how wrong it was for us to be involved in this senseless war. I wanted to do something about it. Now I have been betrayed. It is only a matter of time before they find me."

"Then come with me to Switzerland, now."

"I wish I could, but I cannot. I must make my way back to the Allies in Umbria. But for you—I have a letter from your family in Stresa, a travel pass to visit your dying grandmother. You remember I told you of Stresa? It is on Lake Maggiore. At the other end of the lake is Locarno. Switzerland. Safety. You go to Stresa and you pay a boatman to take you. You still have money?"

"Yes, I have taken money from my account to keep for emergencies."

"I have put more into that envelope. Take it and go—now."

"Angelo," I began. "Have you seen him?"

"No, but I'm told he is safe at our villa. You gave him up, then. You did the right thing. I am more proud of you than you can ever know. At least our son is safe, whatever happens."

How could I tell him that his family snatched Angelo from me? But at least I knew he had not ordered it. It was one small comfort.

"Leo"—I took his face into my hands—"I love you. Please take care. Come and join me."

"I will. I promise. As soon as I can. Go to Locarno and wait for me. I'll find you there."

"Yes." I felt an absurd swell of happiness.

"Go now. I won't leave this place until you are safely far away. And take care on the way home."

"I will, *amore mio*."

He kissed me again. Twigs scratched me as I scrambled out of the bushes. I felt my cheek bleeding, or was it a tear trickling down? I don't know.

I made my way back to my flat. On the way I heard Germans singing in a bar—a coarse drinking song and lots of laughter. More than once I had to slip into a doorway and once into an open church until a patrol had passed. The Accademia Bridge was the worst because it was so exposed. But I walked across as if I belonged there, and nobody stopped me. Hanni was already sleeping peacefully when I arrived home, breathless and with heart beating rapidly. How I envied the young and their ability to adapt. I hurriedly packed a few things into a rucksack. I couldn't risk taking a suitcase with me. Too obvious. Besides, there was not much that was precious to me. Leo's ring was on my finger. I took out my British passport, money, the keys to my bank vault and my flat and the secret drawer in my desk. The drawings should stay safely hidden, along with the diary I had kept for so long, until I could return for them, after this nonsense had ended. But I did take the one painting of Angelo I had finished. It was a small oil painting in the Renaissance style of Angelo as a cherub. I removed the canvas from its frame and wrapped it around my toothbrush holder, tying it with a ribbon.

Then I ate a good meal, packed some bread, cheese and fruit for our journey and climbed into bed beside Hanni. Of course sleep wouldn't come. I kept thinking about Leo. Would he get away safely? Could he make it back to the Allies? Would I ever see him again?

October 20

At first light I woke Hanni and told her of our plan. I left a note for Francesca, along with some money, telling her to help herself to our supplies and that I hoped to be back someday. We ate our last eggs for breakfast, and then we set off. As we walked I instructed Hanni to remember at all times that she was my little sister and we were going to see our grandmother in Stresa. Lake Maggiore. Mountains.

"You know all about lakes and mountains, don't you?" I asked.

She nodded, her face lighting up in a smile. "Every winter we went skiing at Kitzbühel. And in the summer we went up to our little house in the Vienna Woods. It was so beautiful."

"It will be beautiful where we are going, too," I said. "You'll love it. Good mountain air."

We reached the station. A train for Milan was

leaving in an hour. From there it would be a short journey on a local train to Stresa. The train arrived. We boarded. Nobody questioned us. In the carriage was an older couple and a priest. We chatted. I told them about my grandmother.

"Your little sister is very shy," the man said when Hanni only answered in monosyllables.

"I'm afraid this German invasion has terrified her," I said.

"I don't blame her. I can't wait to get away," the wife said. "Our cousin lives on a farm in Lombardy. We wanted to be out of the city."

The priest said nothing.

We pulled into Milan with no incidents. The beautiful big station with its gleaming marble floors and new murals was a treat to the eye, and almost empty, apart from German soldiers lounging in corners, guarding exits. I checked the board. A local train that would call at Stresa was leaving in twenty minutes. I couldn't believe our luck. We headed for the platform. The train was there. A few people were already boarding.

"Just a minute, Fräulein," a voice behind me said. I turned to see two German soldiers behind me. "Your pass, please?" he asked in Italian.

"I have a letter," I said. "It is stamped by the authorities, and I am told it is all I need. I go to visit my grandmother in my hometown. She is not expected to live."

He scanned the letter. "And this child?"

"Is my little sister."

"The letter does not mention her."

"That is because originally she was going to stay with my aunt. But then she changed her mind. She does not want to leave my side."

"You will come with me, please," he said.

"But my train leaves in a few minutes. Who knows when there might be another one?"

"You will come with me."

I had no choice. We were marched to an office behind the platforms. A man was sitting at a desk, not a soldier but in a black uniform.

"And what do we have here?" he asked.

I handed him my letter and told him about my grandmother and my sister.

"Take the child away," he said brusquely. I didn't understand German, but I got the gist, especially from Hanni's horrified intake of breath. Hands snatched her from me.

"No, please," I begged. "She is so afraid without me."

"No, Julietta!" she begged as she was taken from the room.

"You must think me very stupid, Fräulein," he said. "I can smell a Jew a mile away. And you, I am sure, are not Jewish. Lucky for you. But my Italian is not so good. Shall we revert to a more familiar language? I happen to speak English quite well."

I suppose my face must have registered my

shock because he laughed. "Oh yes. We know all about you, dear English lady. Your housekeeper told us you had left. We searched your dwelling, and we found the radio. A rather primitive device no longer of any use, of course, but a valiant attempt. So please take a seat. We have a few questions we want to ask you."

I was glad he said that because my legs wouldn't have held me up much longer.

"So you can make it easy for yourself or very hard. Who gave you the radio?"

That was easy. He was long gone. "When the English had to leave Venice, the former consul came and asked me if I would monitor the shipping for them. In those days it was Italian vessels. I agreed. A man came and installed the radio. He gave me instructions on how to send messages and how to read codes. I never knew his name. I never saw anyone after that. Codebooks were dropped off at my door. But none for a long while now. I presume this small outpost is of no use to anyone."

"Or your contact has been captured by us and the chain of communication has been broken."

I decided to appeal to him as a human being. "You speak very good English," I said.

"Yes, I studied for one year at Cambridge, before the war," he said.

"What did you study?"

"Philosophy." He laughed. "The fools never realized I was sent by the German government. You British were so hopelessly unprepared."

"Nevertheless we seem to be winning at last," I couldn't help but saying.

His expression changed. "You realize I could have you shot right now as a spy." He paused, savouring those words. "But as it happens, the spying is a noble cause, not your most serious offence. You were aiding a Jew to escape, were you not? Your housekeeper alerted us to the fact that you had a Jew in the house. Like most good Christians, she has a profound distrust of Jews."

"What will happen to her?" I cried. "She's only a child. An innocent child."

He gave me a look of utter scorn. "A Jewish child. I begrudge the amount of air she breathes. She will be sent to a camp like all Jews." He paused. "As will you. I don't have the time or the men to deal with you here. There is a camp for non-Jewish political prisoners north of Milan. That is where you will go."

"And Hanni?"

"The girl will go with other Jews to a camp somewhere in Eastern Europe. Poland, I believe."

"Can I not say goodbye to her?"

Again that withering smile. "Your devotion to a Jew is quite touching, Fräulein. Are you sure you have no Jewish ancestry yourself?"

"As you can see from my red hair, I am entirely

Celt," I said. "But I would stand up for the ill treatment of any human being."

He said something rapidly in German. I was grabbed by the arm and dragged out of the room. I tried to get a glimpse of Hanni as I was hurried across the station, but then I was shoved into the back of a lorry. The door was slammed on me, and I was driven away in darkness.

CHAPTER 45

Juliet, a camp in the north of Italy,
November 1943

Of the next weeks I will say little. I was housed
in a barrack with around thirty other women.
Some had been working with the partisans. Some
had written or spoken against Mussolini. Others
had helped Jews. Most of them were young.
Some had already been raped by the Germans
before they came to the camp. I think all of us
were traumatized to a certain extent. We didn't
talk much, as if we didn't want to risk making
friends, and I was suspicious to them, as I was
English and not one of them. That was fine with
me. I had no words left to speak. No tears either.

We slept on wooden bunks, stacked three
high. Our mattresses were stuffed with straw
and crawling with fleas. After a few days I was
covered in bites. It had also become bitterly
cold, and the huts were not heated. Our clothes
and belongings had been taken. We were made
to wear a prison uniform of coarse cotton that
did nothing to keep out the wind when we had
to stand for morning roll call. We shared a
blanket at night, huddling against each other

for warmth. We were fed a meal of soup each day—sometimes with pasta, sometimes beans, sometimes just hot water with bits of greens. And a piece of stale bread. While I was there, one of the women became really sick and was carried off. I never saw her again, so I don't know if she died or recovered in hospital.

The only saving grace was that the camp was still run by Italians and not Germans. That meant that standards were not as rigid or brutal as they might have been. If we had a decent guard on duty, he wouldn't keep us standing outside in the cold for roll call. He'd send us back inside and take roll while he smoked a cigarette. On particularly good days, he handed it, half smoked, to one of us and it was passed around—one puff per woman. Luckily I didn't smoke. I would give my puff to someone else and get an extra piece of bread in exchange.

Every now and then, a German armoured car would drive up. Someone would be hauled off for questioning and either return with marks of brutality upon her or not return at all. Every time we saw the gate opening and a motor car driving through, we held our breath, or even clutched at each other. I knew it would be my turn one day. Would they believe that I had nothing to tell? How would I hold up under torture?

There were good days amongst the bad. When the weather was clement, we were allowed to walk around outside. Our camp was divided from the men's section by a high barbed wire fence. On fine days we watched the men playing football. They waved and called out to us, unless a strict guard was on duty who would prod them to silence with his rifle butt. Then one day, after I had been there for what seemed like an eternity, we were sent outside while those women on clean-up duty replaced the straw in the bedding. The men were playing football while others cheered them on. We went to the fence to watch, and I found myself staring directly at Leo.

He rushed over to the barbed wire. He looked thinner than I remembered, his face gaunt and bony. "Julietta, what are you doing here?"

"I was betrayed," I said. "Someone told the Germans that I was not who I claimed to be and that I was escorting a Jewish child."

I didn't want to say that the someone was Francesca. I had always treated her with great kindness and assumed she was fond of me. Perhaps she had been paid for information. Perhaps her dislike of the Jews had pushed her over the edge, or the fact that I was leaving, which meant she would no longer be paid. I don't know what makes people act badly in time of war.

"This is terrible. We must get you out," he said.

I had to laugh. "You're in a fine position to talk. Were you caught going back to the Allies?"

"I, too, was betrayed," he said. "But I am hopeful that I shall be released when my family learns of my plight. My father is unfortunately no longer in favour, but my father-in-law has prospered and has learned to work with the Germans. We'll just have to see how fond he is of his only son-in-law."

"No talking!" A guard was striding in our direction, waving a gun in menacing fashion. "Move away from the fence, both of you." He reached Leo. "This is no time to flirt with young women."

"I am not flirting," Leo said. "This woman is the love of my life, the mother of my child. Do you begrudge us a few minutes together when we are doing no harm?"

There is one thing that Italians prize, and that is family. I saw his expression soften.

"You have a bambino?" he asked me.

I nodded. "His name is Angelo. He's almost four."

"Very well," the guard said. "When I am on duty, you can meet behind that guard tower in the corner. But only when I am on duty, understand?"

"Thank you," I said.

"You're a good fellow," Leo added. "Too good for a position like this."

"I had to feed the family. They were starving," he said. "We have a farm. The Germans took away all our livestock and our olive oil. Cursed

Germans." And he spat. Then he looked around. "Only don't tell anyone I said that."

We had an ally. We met several more times, then Leo came to the fence with an excited smile on his face. "Here, take this," he said. He handed me an envelope.

"What is it? A love letter?"

"No. It's your ticket to freedom. My father-in-law has come through. It is a pass ordering my release. I'm giving it to you."

"Don't be silly," I said. "I can't take your pass, even if I could. Presumably it's in your name."

"No. It says *the bearer*. You are now the bearer. Show it to the camp commander, and you'll be out of here."

"But what about you? I'm not leaving you behind."

"You won't. I've already written to my father-in-law saying that a spiteful guard ripped up the first pass, so could he send another in a hurry. I should be out by the end of the week."

I stared down at the envelope in my hand.

"Go on," he said. "Go now. You'll have time to make it to Stresa by nightfall, and then you'll negotiate for a boat—if they give you your possessions back, which they are supposed to do. My father-in-law's name is Antongiovani, in case you need to use it. A good friend of German high command in Italy."

"Leo." Still I hesitated. "I can't leave you."

"I'm not using the pass while you are still here," he said. "Do you want us both to die of cold and disease because of your stubbornness?" His voice softened. "Please go. I've given you enough pain in life. Let me at least do this for you."

"You have not given me pain. You have given me more happiness than you can ever know. Angelo was the best thing that ever happened to me. And you—I can't tell you how much having you in my life has meant to me."

He reached a hand through the barbed wire. "You are the love of my life. I will find you, I promise, wherever you are. And after the war we will go somewhere together—Australia, America—and make a new and happy life."

I reached my own hand through and our fingertips just touched.

"And Angelo?"

"I'm afraid we must leave him where he is. He is, after all, the heir. There must always be an heir, and if I desert my post, it is up to my son. But you and I, we will have more children, won't we?"

"Oh yes," I said.

"I won't say goodbye, amore mio. I will say arrivederci, au revoir, auf Wiedersehen . . . until we meet again. Stay strong. My love goes with you."

He mouthed a kiss. I mouthed one back. His

fingertips brushed mine one last time. Then I turned and walked away.

Switzerland, November 21

I made it to Stresa with no problem, but I couldn't find a boatman willing to risk his life for me. I had decided I would have to make my way to Switzerland through the mountains on foot. A daunting prospect. But then there was a rainstorm. Everyone was sheltering behind closed shutters. I dared to steal a rowboat and set off as the rain pounded down on me. I rowed all night, until my hands were blistered, and at first light I sheltered under a willow tree. Luck was with me. It kept raining, so there was very little traffic on the lake. I kept baling out the boat and rowing, and on the third morning I saw the sun gleaming on snowy peaks ahead of me. I had reached the head of Lake Maggiore. I was in Switzerland.

CHAPTER 46

Juliet, December 1945

I am writing this on a train bound for the French coast and then a boat to England. I waited for Leo. He never came. I wondered if he was still in prison, or if he had gone home to his family after all. I spent two weeks recovering in a Swiss hospital and then was found a job at a girls' convent school in Lausanne. It was peaceful and quiet amongst the nuns, but nothing could heal the ache in my heart. I dreamed about Leo. I dreamed about Hanni. I dreamed about Angelo. When the Allies finally liberated Italy, I wrote to Leo's father and received a short reply: *Leonardo Da Rossi was shot, trying to escape from a prison camp, November 1943.*

As soon as the war ended, I tried to search for Hanni. I joined an organization helping refugee children, but there were almost no Jews amongst them. It seemed that every Jew had vanished from the face of the Earth. It took a while before we learned names like Auschwitz, Treblinka, Bergen-Belsen. And then we knew. And there were no tears left to cry.

I didn't go home as soon as the war ended. At first I wanted to find Hanni, and then, when I learned the awful truth, I wanted to do something useful—something to somehow make up for the fact that I had promised to keep her safe and I had failed. But I did write letters home. My mother was delighted to hear from me and glad that I had been working with refugees in Switzerland. She got it into her head that I had been doing this throughout the war and wrote long letters telling me how much they had suffered in England while I had been living on good Swiss milk and cream. I am not going to disillusion her. I have also decided that I am not going back to teaching again. Every time I looked at one of the young girls, I would see Hanni and know that I hadn't been able to save her. I pray that Angelo is thriving. I will not be going back to Venice to see for myself. I will never go back again. Too many painful memories. I will start a new chapter in my life, reinvent myself as a new person—an automaton with a padlock around my heart. And I find that I have no desire to paint again.

I was going to keep these recollections, but now I realize that I don't want anyone to know. And I certainly won't want to read them again. The only stories worth reading have happy endings. And so I have decided, as we cross the Channel, I shall tear them up and throw them into the sea, as if this chapter of my life never existed.

CHAPTER 47

Postscript: Caroline, October 28, 2001

The plane gathered speed, lifted into the air and then wheeled to the right. Below her Caroline saw the whole of Venice spread out like a map, the tower of the campanile rising above the domes of St Mark's, the canals sparkling as they divided the city into little islands within the island. There was the Zattere and the building with her flat, awaiting her return. Caroline allowed herself a small glow of happiness. Luca was right. It was a time for new beginnings. And just one of them, she suspected, might include him. She was flying home to England now, but he was to join her. He had already bought them tickets to New York and reserved a suite at the Plaza. When Caroline had offered to pay, he had laughed it off and said, "Business expense."

What had made this even sweeter was that she'd had several emails from Josh in the last few days.

Cara, I've been trying to reach you, one of them said. *Your grandmother said your phone isn't working in Italy. Is that true, or are you just avoiding me? Answer, please.*

And then, *Cara, we need to talk. I'm not sure*

how things are working out here. I don't seem to be getting any more commissions, and I can't go on living off Desiree forever. Frankly, I'm not so sure I want to stay on indefinitely. This life is so incredibly phony. It's all about show. Call me as soon as you get back to England. You are coming home soon, aren't you?

The plane levelled out and the seat belt sign was turned off. As she stared out, watching white puffball clouds drifting below the wing, she realized, with stunning clarity, that she didn't want Josh back. He had said that he only married her to do the right thing. Well, maybe the same had been true for her. She had thought she was in love, but she had been twenty. What did she know about love at that age? Or about life? Girls' boarding school to college, sheltered all the time. She simply hadn't been ready for marriage or a long-term relationship. The one thing that held them together had been Teddy. And now they had both matured, gone their own ways, and she was ready to move on.

And if that moving on included Luca? Included a life that was at least partly in Italy? She realized it was far too soon to make such momentous decisions, but it was good to be able to look forward again. Maybe she would go back to fashion design, or maybe pursue some other kind of art, maybe just rent out her flat in Venice for most of the year and enjoy life. And she found herself wondering if this was what Aunt Lettie wanted when she left her that cardboard box.

"My Angelo," she had said. Not "Michelangelo," but "my Angelo." Had her real wish been to have Caroline complete the life that had been denied to her? Find Angelo? Find happiness? Had she maybe known about Luca and hoped . . . Caroline smiled to herself.

"I did it, Aunt Lettie. It's all working out as you wanted," she whispered.

She reached under her seat for her backpack and brought out the folder containing Great-Aunt Lettie's drawings. She was still curious why these particular sketches had been precious enough to hide them away, when others, equally good, had been left in plain sight. She turned them over, one by one, until she stopped, staring, frowning. This was not Great-Aunt Lettie's work. Even though it was a rough sketch, it had been done by a much more skilled hand. Was it a copy? A print?

But no, she could see the impressions of the ink and where it had dried on old paper. And it was signed in the bottom corner. *Picasso.*

"The sketches," she whispered to herself. Aunt Lettie had sent her here to find the sketches. She had no idea how her aunt might have acquired such things, but she realized the implication. If they truly belonged to her great-aunt, Caroline might now be exceedingly rich. And then she remembered that brief mention in the diary:

Contessa Fiorito saying that in her youth she had modelled for some of the great artists and they had given her sketches as a thank-you gift. Was this one of the same sketches? Had the contessa given them to Great-Aunt Lettie? Hadn't she mentioned leaving them to Juliet in her will if anything happened to her? There would be some digging to do, but Luca could help with that.

She couldn't wait to show them to Luca. She couldn't wait to see Luca again. And she pictured Josh's face when she arrived in New York with Luca at her side, to bring Teddy home.

ACKNOWLEDGMENTS

My thanks, as always, to Danielle and my brilliant team at Lake Union, and to Meg, Christina and the equally brilliant team at Jane Rotrosen Agency. Also heartfelt thanks to Clare, Jane and John, who always provide such thoughtful insights and suggestions.

Thanks to the librarians at the Correr Museum Library in St Mark's Square, who enthusiastically provided me with more research materials than I could ever tackle.

Venice has always held a special place in my heart, ever since my parents used to rent a little villa in Treviso, half an hour outside the city, when I was a teenager. They'd drive across the causeway, park and give my brother and me some money. "See you at five o'clock," they'd say, and we were free to wander, explore, buy gelato. I've been back many times since, including reading through lots of history books in the library of the Correr Museum last summer. And every time, I find the city takes my breath away. It is indeed La Serenissima.

ABOUT THE AUTHOR

Rhys Bowen is the *New York Times* bestselling author of more than forty novels, including *Above the Bay of Angels*, *The Victory Garden*, *The Tuscan Child*, and the World War II–based *In Farleigh Field*, the winner of the Macavity and Left Coast Crime Awards for Best Historical Mystery Novel and the Agatha Award for Best Historical Mystery. Bowen's work has won twenty honors to date, including multiple Agatha, Anthony, and Macavity Awards. Her books have been translated into many languages, and she has fans around the world. A transplanted Brit, Bowen divides her time between California and Arizona. To learn more about the author, visit www.rhysbowen.com.

Books are produced in the United States using U.S.-based materials

Books are printed using a revolutionary new process called THINKtech™ that lowers energy usage by 70% and increases overall quality

Books are durable and flexible because of Smyth-sewing

Paper is sourced using environmentally responsible foresting methods and the paper is acid-free

Center Point Large Print
600 Brooks Road / PO Box 1
Thorndike, ME 04986-0001 USA

(207) 568-3717

US & Canada:
1 800 929-9108
www.centerpointlargeprint.com